THE ROYAL RANGER

www.**rangersapprentice**.co.uk

CHARACTER PROFILES

WILL has been a Ranger for many years, having trained with the legendary Ranger Halt. Delivered to Castle Redmont as an orphan, he does not know the true story of his parents. When he was younger he dreamed of becoming a Knight, but he found his true path as a Ranger. Will is known for his loyalty and bravery, and has proven himself in countless battles. Now a grown man, he has recently been struck with personal tragedy, and the once mischievous and spirited young man has grown grim and humourless, and is now driven by a black passion for revenge.

MADDIE — or, to give her formal title, Princess Madelyn of Araluen — is the 15-year-old daughter of Princess Regent Cassandra and Sir Horace. Bright and cheerful, she frequently defies the wishes of her parents to spend her time hunting game in the forests around Castle Araluen. Though she is heir to the throne, she does not wish to spend her life in a protective cocoon, and longs for a chance to learn the skills necessary for leading men into battle.

HALT is a renowned member of the Ranger Corps, known for his mysterious ways and his unstoppable nature. Halt is a superb archer and uses a massive longbow. Like all Rangers his skill with the bow is uncanny, deadly accurate, and devastatingly swift. Although he rarely shows emotions, he thinks of Will as his son. He is now officially retired, but still occasionally carries out missions at the request of the Corps Commandant.

HORACE is the premier Knight of the Kingdom. Like Will he was an orphan, and grew up as a ward of Castle Redmont. As a younger boy he used to bully Will, but now they are firm friends, having helped each other out on countless missions. He later married Princess Cassandra, the heir to the throne of Araluen, and his daughter will one day rule as Queen. He is dependable, loyal to the knightly code of conduct, and known for his hearty appetite.

GILAN was once Halt's apprentice and is the only Ranger who carries a sword. He is tall and humorous, in sharp contrast to his former master. He is generally considered the best in the Corps at unseen movement. For all his jokes and light-hearted manner, Gilan is serious about being a Ranger, and his skills have seen him promoted quickly to the upper ranks of the Corps.

JORY RUHL is a former mercenary who now leads a gang of criminals who have been preying on villages in Anselm and its neighbouring fiefs, capturing children and demanding ransoms from their parents. Having shown he is prepared to murder innocents to preserve his freedom, Will is determined to stop him and his gang at any cost.

HAVE YOU GOT WHAT IT TAKES TO BE A RANGER?

The Rangers are an elite Special Forces Corps in the medieval Kingdom of Araluen. They are the eyes and ears of the Kingdom, the intelligence gatherers, the scouts and the troubleshooters.

Rangers are expert archers and carry two knives — one for throwing, and one for hunting. They are also highly skilled at tracking, concealment and unseen movement. Their ability to become virtually invisible has led common folk to view them with fear, thinking the Rangers must use black magic.

Occasionally, a young man who is judged to have the qualities of honesty, courage, agility and intelligence will be invited to undertake a five-year apprenticeship — to develop his natural abilities and instruct him in the almost supernatural skills of a Ranger.

If he passes his first year, he is given a bronze medallion in the shape of an oakleaf.

If he graduates, the bronze will be exchanged for the silver oakleaf of an Oakleaf Bearer — a Ranger of the Kingdom of Araluen.

HAVE YOU READ THEM ALL?

THE RUINS OF GORLAN (BOOK 1)

Will's training as an apprentice is gruelling, but his skills will be
needed if he is to prevent the King's assassination.

THE BURNING BRIDGE (BOOK 2)

Will faces his most dangerous mission yet: the King's army has
been deceived, and are headed for a brutal ambush.

THE ICEBOUND LAND (BOOK 3)

Will is trapped on a ship headed to the icebound land of Skandia.
If he cannot escape, he faces a life of backbreaking slavery.

OAKLEAF BEARERS (BOOK 4)

Evanlyn has been taken captive by a mysterious horseman,
and Will's attempts to rescue her lead him to the territory
of a fearsome new enemy.

THE SORCERER IN THE NORTH (BOOK 5)

Will is a Ranger at last, but his new land is under threat
from the terrifying figure of the Night Warrior.

THE SIEGE OF MACINDAW (BOOK 6)

A renegade knight has captured Castle Macindaw,
and someone Will loves is being held hostage.

ERAK'S RANSOM (BOOK 7)

The Skandian leader has been taken by a dangerous desert tribe.
To save him, Will must face violent sandstorms, warring
tribes and hidden danger.

THE KINGS OF CLONMEL (BOOK 8)

The surrounding kingdoms are falling prey to a religious cult. Only Clonmel is uncorrupted, but it too will fall without the Rangers' help.

HALT'S PERIL (BOOK 9)

Will and Halt are determined to stop a renegade outlaw group, but their battle is deadly and Will faces the prospect of returning home alone.

THE EMPEROR OF NIHON-JA (BOOK 10)

Will must restore order to Nihon-Ja by facing the highly-trained Senshi warriors, who intend to overthrow the Emperor.

THE LOST STORIES (BOOK 11)

A collection of tales that reveal the unheard legends of the Rangers of Araluen.

THE ROYAL RANGER (BOOK 12)

Will is given an apprentice of his own, but can he turn his back on the dark path of revenge he is set upon?

THE ROYAL RANGER

BOOK 12

CORGI YEARLING

RANGER'S APPRENTICE: THE ROYAL RANGER
A CORGI YEARLING BOOK 978 0 440 86994 8

Published in Great Britain by Corgi Yearling,
an imprint of Random House Children's Publishers UK
A Random House Group Company

Originally published in Australia in 2013 by Random House Australia (Pty) Ltd

This edition published 2013

3 5 7 9 10 8 6 4 2

Copyright © John Flanagan, 2013
Cover design copyright © www.blacksheep-uk.com, 2013
Cover illustration copyright © Jeremy Reston, 2013

The right of John Flanagan to be identified as the author of this work has been asserted
in accordance with the Copyright, Designs and Patents Act 1988.

All rights reserved. No part of this publication may be reproduced, stored in a
retrieval system, or transmitted in any form or by any means, electronic, mechanical,
photocopying, recording or otherwise, without the prior permission of the publishers.

The Random House Group Limited supports the Forest Stewardship Council® (FSC®),
the leading international forest-certification organisation. Our books carrying the FSC
label are printed on FSC®-certified paper. FSC is the only forest-certification scheme
supported by the leading environmental organisations, including Greenpeace. Our paper
procurement policy can be found at www.randomhouse.co.uk/environment

MIX
Paper from
responsible sources
FSC® C016897

Corgi Yearling Books are published by Random House Children's Publishers,
61–63 Uxbridge Road, London W5 5SA

www.**randomhousechildrens**.co.uk
www.**randomhouse**.co.uk

Addresses for companies within The Random House Group Limited can be found at:
www.**randomhouse**.co.uk/offices.htm

THE RANDOM HOUSE GROUP Limited Reg. No. 954009

A CIP catalogue record for this book is available from the British Library.

Printed and bound in Great Britain by CPI Group (UK) Ltd, Croydon CR0 4YY

For my family

One

It had been a poor harvest in Scanlon Estate. The wheat crop had been meagre at best, and the apple orchards had been savaged by a blight that left three-quarters of the fruit blemished and rotting on the trees.

As a result, the share farmers, farm labourers, orchardists and fruit pickers were facing hard times, with three months to go before the next harvest, during which time they would have nowhere near enough to eat.

Squire Dennis of Scanlon Manor was a kind-hearted man. He was also a practical one and, while his kind-hearted nature urged him to help his needy tenants, his practical side recognised such an action as good business. If his farmers and labourers went hungry, chances were they would move away, in search of work in a less stricken region. Then, when good times returned to Scanlon Estate, there would be insufficient workers available to reap the harvest.

Dennis had acquired considerable wealth over the years and could ride out the hard times ahead. But he knew that such an option wasn't available to his workers. Accordingly, he decided to invest some of his accumulated wealth in them. He set up a workers' kitchen, which he paid for himself, and opened it to the needy who lived on his estate. In that way, he ensured that his people received at least one good meal a day. It was nothing fancy — usually a soup, or a porridge made from oats. But it was hot and nourishing and filling and he was confident that the cost would be more than repaid by the continuing loyalty of his tenants and labourers.

The kitchen was in the parkland in front of the manor house. It consisted of rows of trestle tables and benches, and a large serving table. These were sheltered from the worst of the weather by canvas awnings stretched over poles above them, creating a large marquee. The sides were left open. In bad weather, this often meant that the wind and rain blew around the tables. But farm folk are of hardy stock and the arrangement was far better than eating in the open.

In fact, kitchen was a misnomer. All the cooking was done in the vast kitchen inside the manor house, and the food was carried out to be served to the hungry tenants and their families. The estate workers understood that the food was provided free of charge. But it was a matter of principle that any who could afford a small payment would do so. Most often, this was in the form of a few copper coins, or of produce — a brace of rabbits or a wild duck taken at the pond.

The kitchen operated for the two hours leading up to dusk, ensuring that the workers could enjoy a night's sleep without the gnawing pains of hunger in their bellies.

It was almost dusk when the stranger pushed his way through to the serving table.

He was a big man with shoulder-length dirty blond hair. He was wearing a wagoner's leather vest, and a pair of thick gauntlets were tucked into his belt, alongside the scabbard that held a heavy-bladed dagger. His eyes darted continually from side to side, never remaining long in one spot, giving him a hunted look.

Squire Dennis's chief steward, who was in charge of the serving table, looked at him suspiciously. The workers' kitchen was intended for locals, not for travellers, and he'd never seen this man before.

'What do you want?' he asked, his tone less than friendly.

The wagoner stopped his darting side-to-side looks for a few seconds and focused on the man facing him. He was about to bluster and threaten but the steward was a heavily built man, and there were two powerful-looking servants behind him, obviously tasked with keeping order. He nodded at the cauldron of thick soup hanging over the fire behind the serving table.

'I want food,' he said roughly. 'Haven't eaten all day.'

The steward frowned. 'You're welcome to soup, but you'll have to pay,' he said. 'Free food is for estate tenants and workers only.'

The wagoner scowled at him, but he reached into a grubby purse hanging from his belt and rummaged around. The steward heard the jingle of coins as he sorted through the contents, letting some drop back into the purse. He deposited three pennigs on the table.

'That do?' he challenged. 'That's all I've got.'

The steward raised a disbelieving eyebrow. He'd heard the jingle of coins dropping back into the purse. But it had been a long day and he couldn't be bothered with a confrontation. Best to give the man some food and get rid of him as soon as possible. He gestured to the serving girl by the soup vat.

'Give him a bowl,' he said.

She dumped a healthy portion into a wooden bowl and set it before him, adding a hunk of crusty bread.

The wagoner looked at the tables around him. Many of those seated were drinking noggins of ale as well. There was nothing unusual in that. Ale was relatively cheap and the squire had decided that his people shouldn't have a dry meal. There was a cask behind the serving table, with ale dripping slowly from its spigot. The wagoner nodded towards it.

'What about ale?' he demanded.

The steward drew himself up a little straighter. He didn't like the man's manner. He might be paying for his meal, but it was a paltry amount and he was getting good value for his money.

'That'll cost extra,' he said. 'Two pennigs more.'

Grumbling, the wagoner rummaged in his purse again. He showed no sign of embarrassment at producing more coins after claiming that he had none. He tossed them on the table and the steward nodded to one of his men.

'Give him a noggin,' he said.

The wagoner took his soup, bread and ale and turned away without another word.

'And thank you,' the steward said sarcastically, but the blond man ignored him. He threaded his way through the tables, studying the faces of those sitting there. The steward watched him go. The wagoner was obviously looking for someone and, equally obviously, hoping not to see him.

The servant who had drawn the ale stepped close to him and said in a lowered voice, 'He looks like trouble waiting to happen.'

The steward nodded. 'Best let him eat and be on his way. Don't give him any extra, even if he offers to pay.'

The serving man grunted assent, then turned as a farmer and his family approached the table, hopefully looking at the soup cauldron.

'Step up, Jem. Let's give you and your family something to stick your ribs together, eh?'

Holding his soup bowl and ale high to avoid bumping them against the people seated at the tables, the wagoner made his way to the very rear of the marquee, close by the sandstone walls of the great manor house. He sat at the last table, on his own, facing the front, where he could see new arrivals as they entered the big open tent. He began to eat, but with his eyes constantly flicking up to watch the front of the tent, he managed to spill and dribble a good amount of the soup down his beard and the front of his clothes.

He took a deep draught of his ale, still with his eyes searching above the rim of the wooden noggin. There was only a centimetre left when he set it down again. A serving girl, moving through the tables and collecting empty plates, paused to look into the noggin. Seeing it virtually empty, she reached for it. But the wagoner stopped her, grasping her wrist with unnecessary force so that she gasped.

'Leave it,' he ordered. 'Haven't finished.'

She snatched her wrist away from his grip and curled her lip at him.

'Big man,' she sneered. 'Finish off your last few drops of ale then.'

She stalked away angrily, turning once to glare back at him. As she did, a frown came over her face. There was a cloaked and cowled figure standing directly behind the wagoner's chair. She hadn't seen him arrive. One moment, there was nobody near the wagoner. Then the cloaked man appeared, seemingly having risen out of the earth. She shook her head. That was fanciful, she thought. Then she reconsidered, noting the mottled green and grey cloak the man wore. It was a Ranger's cloak, and folk said that Rangers could do all manner of unnatural things — like appearing and disappearing at will.

The Ranger stood directly behind the wagoner's chair. So far, the ill-tempered man had no idea that he was there.

The shadow of the cowl hid the newcomer's features. All that was visible was a steel-grey beard. Then he slipped back the cowl to reveal a grim face, with dark eyes and grey, roughly trimmed hair to match the beard.

At the same time, he drew a heavy saxe knife from beneath the cloak and tapped its flat side gently on the wagoner's shoulder, leaving it resting there so the wagoner could see it with his peripheral vision.

'Don't turn around.'

The wagoner stiffened, sitting bolt upright on his bench. Instinctively, he began to turn to view the man behind him. The saxe rapped on his shoulder, harder this time.

'I said don't.'

The command was uttered in a more peremptory tone, and some of those nearby became aware of the scene playing out at the table. The low murmur of voices died away to silence as more people noticed. All eyes turned towards the rear table, where the wagoner sat, seemingly transfixed.

Somewhere, someone recognised the significance of the grey mottled cloak and the heavy saxe knife.

'It's a Ranger.'

The wagoner slumped as he heard the words, and a haunted look came over his face.

'You're Henry Wheeler,' the Ranger said.

Now the haunted look changed to one of abject fear. The big man shook his head rapidly, spittle flying from his lips as he denied the name.

'No! I'm Henry Carrier! You've got the wrong man! I swear.'

The Ranger's lips twisted in what might have been a smile. 'Wheeler . . . Carrier. Not a very imaginative stretch if you're planning to change your name. And you should have got rid of the Henry.'

'I don't know what you're talking about!' the wagoner babbled. He began to turn to face his accuser. Again, the saxe rapped him sharply on the shoulder.

'I told you. Don't turn around.'

'What do you want from me?' The wagoner's voice was rising in pitch. Those watching were convinced that he knew why the grim-faced Ranger had singled him out.

'Perhaps you could tell me.'

'I haven't done anything! Whoever this Wheeler person is, it's not me! I tell you, you've got the wrong man! Leave me be, I say.'

He tried to put a sense of command into the last few words and failed miserably. They came out more as a guilt-laden plea for mercy than the indignation of an innocent man. The Ranger said nothing for a few seconds. Then he said three words.

'The Wyvern Inn.'

Now the guilt and fear were all too evident on the wagoner's face.

'Remember it, Henry? The Wyvern Inn in Anselm Fief. Eighteen months ago. You were there.'

'No!'

'What about the name Jory Ruhl, Henry? Remember him? He was the leader of your gang, wasn't he?'

'I never heard of no Jory Ruhl!'

'Oh, I think you have.'

'I never have! I was never at any Wyvern Inn and I had nothing to do with the . . .'

The big man stopped, realising he was about to convict himself with his words.

'So you weren't there, and you had nothing to do with . . . what exactly, Henry?'

'Nothing! I never did nothing. You're twisting my words! I wasn't there! I don't know anything about what happened!'

'Are you referring to the fire that you and Ruhl set in that inn, by any chance? There was a woman killed in that fire, remember? A Courier. She got out of the building. But there was a child trapped inside. Nobody important, just a peasant girl — the sort of person you would consider beneath your notice.'

'No! You're making this up!' Wheeler cried.

The Ranger was unrelenting. 'But the Courier didn't think she was unimportant, did she? She went back into the burning building to save her. She shoved the girl out through an upper-floor window, then the roof collapsed and she was killed. Surely you remember now?'

'I don't know any Wyvern Inn! I've never been in Anselm Fief. You've got the wrong —'

Suddenly, with a speed that belied his bulk, the wagoner was on his feet and whirling to his right to face the Ranger. As he began the movement, his right hand snatched the dagger from his belt and he swung it in a backhanded strike.

But, fast as he was, the Ranger was even faster. He had been expecting some sudden, defiant movement like this as the desperation had been mounting in Wheeler's voice. He took a swift half step backwards and the saxe came up to block the wagoner's dagger. The blades rang together with a rasping clang, then the Ranger countered the wagoner's move with his own. Pivoting on his right heel, he deflected the dagger even further with his saxe and followed the movement with an open-palmed strike with his left hand, hitting Wheeler on the ridge of his jawline.

The wagoner grunted in shock and staggered back. His feet tangled in the bench he'd been sitting on and he stumbled, crashing over to hit the edge of the table, then falling with a thud to the ground.

The wagoner lay there, unmoving. An ominous dark stain began to spread across the turf.

'What's going on here?' The steward moved from behind the serving table, with his two assistants in tow. He looked at the Ranger, who met his gaze steadily. Then the Ranger shrugged, gesturing towards the still figure on the ground. The steward tore his gaze away, knelt and reached to turn the heavy figure over.

The wagoner's eyes were wide open. The shock of what had happened was frozen on his face. His own dagger was buried deep in his chest.

'He fell on his knife. He's dead,' the steward said. He looked up at the Ranger, but saw neither guilt nor regret in his dark eyes.

'What a shame,' said Will Treaty. Then, gathering his cloak around him, he turned and strode from the tent.

Two

The first streaks of light were staining the eastern sky. In the parkland surrounding Castle Araluen, birds began singing to herald the coming day — at first in ones or twos, but gradually swelling into a general, joyous chorus. Occasionally, one could be seen flitting between the well-spaced trees, in search of food.

The large castle drawbridge was currently raised. That was a matter of course. It was raised every night at nine o'clock, even though Araluen had been at peace for some years now. Those in command of the castle knew that the peace could be shattered without warning. As King Duncan had said some years previously, 'No one ever died from being too careful.'

There was a small wooden footbridge in place across the moat — little more than a pair of planks with rope hand rails. It could be quickly withdrawn in the event of an attack. At its outer end, a pair of sentries stood watch. There were more lookouts on the castle walls, of course.

Multiple pairs of eyes scanned the well-tended parkland that stretched for several hundred metres on all sides of the castle, and the thickly wooded forest beyond.

As the two sentries watched, one of them nudged his companion.

'Here she comes,' he said.

A slim figure had emerged from the trees and was striding up the gently sloping grassed field to the castle. The newcomer was dressed in a thigh-length leather hunting vest, belted at the waist and worn over a long-sleeved, thick woollen shirt and wool breeches. The breeches were tucked into knee-high boots of soft, untanned leather.

There was nothing about the figure to indicate that it was a girl. The sentry's knowledge arose from the fact that this was a regular occurrence. The fifteen-year-old girl often sneaked away from the castle to hunt in the forest, much to the fury of her parents. The castle sentries found this amusing. She was a popular figure among them, bright and cheerful and always ready to share the proceeds of a successful hunt. As a result, they turned a blind eye to her comings and goings, although they didn't advertise the fact. Her mother, after all, was the Princess Regent Cassandra, and no low-ranking soldier would risk her ill favour, or that of her husband, Sir Horace, the premier knight of the Kingdom.

As Maddie — or, to give her her formal title, Princess Madelyn of Araluen — came closer, she recognised the men on post. They were two of her favourites and her face lit up with a smile.

'Morning, Len. Morning, Gordon. I see you've had a quiet night.'

The sentry called Gordon smiled back at her. 'That was until a fierce warrior maiden burst out of the forest just now and threatened the castle, your highness,' he said.

She frowned at him. 'What have we said about this *your highness* business? It's all a bit too formal for five o'clock in the morning.'

The sentry nodded and corrected himself. 'Sorry, Princess.'

He glanced back up at the walls of the castle. One of the sentries there waved in acknowledgement of the fact that they had recognised the princess as well. 'I assume your parents don't know you've been out hunting?'

Maddie wrinkled her nose. 'I didn't want to bother them,' she said innocently. Gordon raised an eyebrow and grinned conspiratorially. 'I'm perfectly safe, as you can see.'

The sentry called Len shrugged uncertainly. 'The forest can be dangerous, Princess. You never know.'

Her grin widened. 'Not too dangerous for a fierce warrior maiden, surely? And I'm not defenceless, you know. I've got my saxe and my sling.'

She touched the long double leather thong that was hanging loosely around her neck. Then, as mention of the sling reminded her of something, she delved into the laden game bag slung over her shoulder.

'By the way, I got a hare and a couple of wood pigeons. Can you use them?'

The sentries exchanged a quick glance. They knew that if Maddie suddenly produced fresh-killed game in the castle, questions would be asked as to how she had obtained it. On the other hand, the addition of some fresh meat would be a welcome change to the soldiers' table.

Gordon hesitated. 'The pigeons are all right, Princess. But the hare? If my wife's found cooking that up, folks might think I'd been poaching.'

Only the King, his family, or senior officials and warriors had the right to take game such as hares in the environs of the castle. Rangers, of course, hunted wherever they chose, with a fine disregard for such matters. Ordinary people were allowed to hunt smaller animals such as rabbits, pigeons and duck. But a hare was a different matter. A peasant or soldier could be fined for taking one.

Maddie made a dismissive gesture. 'If anyone asks, say I gave it to you. I'll back you up.'

'I wouldn't want to get you into trouble.' Gordon hesitated still, his hand halfway out for the hare.

Maddie laughed carelessly. 'Wouldn't be the first time. Probably wouldn't be the last. Take it. And you take the pigeons, Len.'

The sentries finally gave in, taking the game and chorusing their thanks. Maddie brushed their gratitude aside.

'Think nothing of it. I don't want to throw them away and see good food go to waste. And you're saving me a lot of explanations.'

The guards stowed the animals in the small sentry box that gave them shelter in bad weather. Maddie waved to them and stepped lightly across the footbridge, letting herself into the small wicket beside the main castle gate. The two sentries smiled at each other. This was one of the perks of being assigned to the outside sentry post.

'She's a nice kid,' Len said.

Gordon, who was the older of the two by some years, agreed. 'Like her mother,' he said. Then he added thoughtfully, 'Mind you, Princess Cassandra used to stalk *us* when she sneaked out of the castle as a girl.'

Len raised his eyebrows. 'Really? I hadn't heard that.'

'Oh yes.' Gordon nodded, remembering. 'She practised her stalking skills on the sentries. Then she'd let fly with *her* sling and hit the heads of our spears. A right terror, she was, until we got used to her tricks.'

Len was trying to equate the current Princess Cassandra — the caretaker ruler of the Kingdom — with the picture his companion had drawn of a wild, adventurous tomboy terrorising the castle guards.

'You'd never pick it now. She's so calm and dignified, isn't she?'

Three

'WHERE THE BLIND, BLUE, BLITHERING BLAZES HAVE YOU BEEN?' the calm and dignified Princess Cassandra demanded.

Maddie froze in shock as her mother's words echoed round the living room of the royal apartment.

She had tiptoed up the tower stairs and crept silently into the room, unlatching the door carefully, then opening it quickly to prevent any long, lingering squeaks from the hinges. The interior was in darkness, with heavy drapes across the window and only a few glowing embers in the fire grate.

She had paused just inside the door, senses alert for any sound or any hint of another's presence in the room. She had taken off her boots before climbing the stairs and now held them in her left hand. Satisfied that her parents were still asleep in their chamber, she had begun stepping carefully across the thick carpet towards her own suite of rooms.

Then her mother — as skilled in the art of ambush as most mothers are — had startled her with her furious, echoing roar.

Maddie froze in mid-stride, one foot poised above the carpet. She looked frantically around the room. She had been convinced that it was empty. Now she made out the dim form of her mother seated in a large, high-backed armchair.

'Mum!' she said, recovering quickly. 'You startled me!'

'I startled you?' Cassandra rose from the chair and crossed the room to face her daughter. She was in her nightgown, with a heavy robe over it to protect her from the chill. An observer would have remarked on the similarity between the two women. Both were small in stature, slender and graceful in their movements. Both had green eyes and attractive features. And both had the same determined tilt to their chins. In times past, people had mistaken them for sisters and it was no surprise that they had. They shared the same mass of blonde hair, although there were occasional grey streaks in Cassandra's now — testament to the strain that she had been under, managing the Kingdom for her invalid father these past three years.

'I startled *you?*' she repeated from closer range, her voice rising a few tones with incredulity.

'I thought you were asleep,' Maddie said, trying an innocent smile. In fact, she was sure her mother had been asleep when she had left the apartment, several hours before. She had peered into the royal bedchamber to make sure of it.

'I thought *you* were asleep,' her mother replied. 'I seem to recall that at the ninth hour you made a big fuss about how tired you were.'

She feigned an enormous yawn. Maddie was uncomfortably aware that it was an excellent impersonation of her own performance the previous evening.

'Oh, I'm *soooo* tired!' Cassandra said, still mimicking her in an exaggerated little girly voice. 'I'm afraid I'm off to bed right away.'

'Ah . . . yes,' Maddie said. 'Well, I woke up. I was starving, so I went down to the kitchens to get something to eat.'

'Carrying your boots,' Cassandra observed. Maddie looked down at them, as if seeing them for the first time.

'Um . . . I didn't want to get mud all over the carpet,' she said quickly. Too quickly. Speaking quickly often results in a mistake.

'That would be mud from the kitchen,' Cassandra said evenly.

Maddie opened her mouth to reply, but could think of nothing to say. She shut it again.

'Madelyn, are you crazy?' Cassandra said, her anger finally bursting like water gushing through a fractured dam. 'You're a princess, the heir to the throne after me. You can't go gallivanting off in the forest in the dead of night. It's just too dangerous!'

'Mum, it's just a forest. It's not dangerous. I know what I'm doing. I saw a badger,' she added, as if that would excuse what she'd been doing.

'Oh well, if you saw a badger, that makes it all right!' Cassandra's sarcasm cut like a whip. 'Why didn't you mention the badger immediately? Now I can go back to bed and sleep peacefully because I know you weren't in any danger. How could you be if you saw a blasted badger?'

'Mother . . .' Maddie began in a tone that implied her mother was being unreasonable. Maddie only called Cassandra 'mother' when she was exasperated by what she saw as obsessive, over-controlling behaviour.

Cassandra was all too well aware of that fact and her eyes flashed with anger.

'Don't you *Mother* me, Madelyn!' she snapped.

Madelyn's shoulders straightened and she stood a little taller. She was two centimetres shorter than her mother and, at times like this, she felt that deficiency put her at a disadvantage.

'Then don't you *Madelyn* me!' she retorted crisply. Cassandra only called her by her full, formal name when she felt she was being irresponsible, immature and infuriating.

'I'll *Madelyn* you any time I please, young lady!'

Maddie rolled her eyes. 'Oh, we're on to *young lady* now, are we?' she said wearily. She made a beckoning gesture with her hands. 'Let it all out. Let's hear the litany of my sins. I'm a terrible girl. I'm irresponsible. I'm a disgrace to the royal house of Araluen.'

She stood facing her mother, one hand on her hip in a petulant pose, as totally infuriating as only a teenage girl can be when she knows she's in the wrong but refuses to admit it.

Cassandra's hand twitched and she felt an overwhelming urge to slap her daughter. She shoved her hands into the pockets of the gown to prevent any such action. She took a deep breath and lowered her voice.

'There are bears in that forest, Madelyn. What would you do if you ran into one?'

'Dondy says that if you meet a bear, you crouch down, stay still and don't make eye contact.' Dondy was the royal forester and hunt master.

'He also says that's a last resort and it's only successful half the time.'

'Then I'd run the other way. Or climb a tree. A small, thin tree so he couldn't climb after me.' She added the last quickly, before Cassandra could point out that bears were able to climb trees.

It was obvious that she wasn't going to surrender this point. Cassandra changed tack. 'There are criminals too. Brigands and bandits and outlaws. They hide out in the forest.'

'They're pretty few and far between these days. Dad has seen to that,' Maddie replied. Horace had recently conducted a series of armed sweeps to drive the outlaws from their lairs in the forest.

'It'd only take one. You're well known. You could be kidnapped and held to ransom.'

'He'd have to catch me first,' Maddie said stubbornly.

Cassandra turned away, throwing her hands in the air in resignation. 'Mind you, we'd have to be willing to pay to get you back,' she muttered. Her tone indicated that this would be no certainty.

The door to the bedroom opened, emitting a shaft of light into the dark room. Horace entered. His hair was tousled and his nightshirt was tucked into his trousers. His feet were bare. So was the blade of the sword in his right hand. It glinted in the light of the lantern he held in his left hand, sending random reflections darting around the walls.

'What's going on?' he said. Seeing only his wife and

daughter in the room, he set the sword to one side, leaning it against the wall. He held the lantern higher, studying his daughter in its light.

'You've been hunting again,' he said. His tone was a mix of anger and resignation.

'Dad, I've just been out for an hour . . .' Maddie began, sensing that her father might be more reasonable than Cassandra. She knew she could usually bring him round to her way of thinking.

'I've been waiting over two hours,' Cassandra snapped. 'I found your bed empty and I've been sitting here ever since.'

Horace shook his head. Any hopes that he would be more forgiving than her mother were dashed by his next words.

'Are you stupid, Maddie? Or are you just determined to defy your mother and me? It's got to be one or the other, so tell me. Which is it?'

It wasn't fair, Maddie thought, the way adults gave you two equally damning alternatives and insisted you pick one. She folded her arms and dropped her eyes from her father's angry gaze.

'I'm waiting,' Horace said.

Maddie set her jaw. She glared at her angry parents and they glared back. At last, Cassandra couldn't endure the silence.

'Maddie, you're the heir to the throne. You'll rule Araluen one day —' she began, and Maddie seized on the opening she'd created.

'And how can I do that if you keep me locked up in a

protective cocoon? If I know nothing about facing danger and making decisions and thinking quickly?'

'What?' her mother said, frowning. But Maddie kept going.

'If I were a boy, Dad would be teaching me how to fight and ride and lead men in battle . . .'

'I taught you to ride,' Horace said, but she shook her head impatiently.

'If I do become queen, how can I order men to go out and fight for me if I don't know the first thing about it myself?'

'You'll have advisers,' Cassandra said. 'People who do know these things.'

'Not the same! I'll be expected to make decisions.' She pointed a finger at her mother. 'Of all people, you should understand that! When you were my age, you fought the Wargals, were abducted by Skandians and commanded archers against the Temujai. You fought alongside Dad!'

'That was by accident. I didn't set out to do those things!'

'But you *did* choose to go to Arrida and fight the Tualaghi. And you chose to go to Nihon-Ja and rescue Dad. You killed the snow tiger —'

'Alyss killed it,' Cassandra put in but Maddie ignored the interruption.

'And you used to sneak out into the forest and practise with your sling . . .'

Cassandra's head snapped up. 'Who told you that?'

'Grandpa. He said he used to be worried sick about you.'

'Your grandfather talks too much,' Cassandra said,

thin-lipped. 'In any event, even if I did do those things, that doesn't say you should do them too.'

'But people respect you! They know you've faced danger! That's all I'm asking: some of that same respect! And I'm bored! I want some excitement in my life!'

'Well, this is not the way to get it!' Cassandra said.

'Then how? Tell me that? I don't want to spend my days learning needlework and geography and Gallican grammar and irregular verbs! I want to learn more important things.'

'Maybe we can work something out . . .' Horace said doubtfully. He could see a grain of sense in what his daughter was saying.

But she rounded on him immediately. 'Like what? What can we work out?'

He made a helpless gesture in the air. 'I don't know . . . something . . . we'll see.'

Maddie finally erupted in anger. 'Oh, great! *We'll see.* The great parental excuse for doing nothing! That's terrific, Dad! *We'll see.*'

'Don't talk to me like that,' Horace told her, although he was conscious of the fact that the phrase *we'll see* was a tried and true parental tactic for postponing difficult decisions.

'Why not? Will *we see* what happens to me if I do? What will *we see*?' She leaned towards him, challenging him, her hands on her hips. Her entire body seemed to quiver with indignation and frustration.

'All right. That's it,' Horace snapped. 'You're confined to your rooms for a week! I'll put a sentry on the door and you will not leave!'

Maddie's cheeks were flaming with self-righteous anger

now. 'That is so stupid and petty! I suppose *we'll see* how it works out!' she yelled.

'Make it two weeks,' Horace said, every bit as angry as she was. She took a breath to reply and he tilted his head to one side. 'Planning on trying for three weeks?'

She hesitated, then saw the look in his eyes. She turned away and stamped angrily to the door to her own rooms.

'This is so unfair!' she shouted, and slammed the door behind her.

Horace and Cassandra exchanged a long look. Horace shook his head, defeated, and put his arm around his wife's shoulders.

'That went well,' he said.

Four

Halt and Pauline eased their horses to a stop as the road emerged from the trees below Castle Araluen.

Neither had suggested it, nor had they exchanged a glance. It was simply a natural response to the sudden sight of the castle, with its soaring spires and turrets, and banners streaming bravely in the wind from a dozen different vantage points around the walls.

'Impressive, isn't it?' Pauline said softly.

Halt glanced sidelong at her, a half smile on his face. 'Always has been,' he agreed. 'Still, I wouldn't trade it for Redmont.'

By comparison, Castle Redmont was solid and functional, with none of the grace and beauty that Araluen offered. But it was home. It was where Halt and Pauline had spent the greater part of their lives and where they had finally revealed their life-long love for each other.

Life at Redmont was also far less formal, which was more in line with Halt's idea of how things should be.

He had little time for the strictly ordered routines and occasions of the royal palace, with its rigid adherence to protocol and rank. He thought of such behaviour as useless tomfoolery and scowled whenever he was forced to attend any sort of formal event. Thankfully, the message he had received from Gilan indicated that there would be no formality attached to this visit.

They urged their horses forward in a slow trot, their hooves raising small puffs of dust that hung in the warm air. They were travelling alone, with just a single packhorse and without any escort. Not that they needed any. Even though Halt was now retired, and his hair had turned from pepper-and-salt grey to silver, he was still the most famous Ranger in the Kingdom, and a formidable opponent for any potential highwayman. The massive longbow he carried across his saddle was evidence of the fact.

'Do you find it odd,' Pauline asked, 'to be summoned by your former apprentice?'

Halt pursed his lips. 'It wasn't so much a summons,' he corrected her. 'More a request.'

It was three years since Crowley had passed away. The Ranger Commandant had died peacefully in his sleep. It was an ironic end for his oldest friend. After a lifetime of battles and intrigue and danger, he had simply stopped breathing one night. He was found with his eyes open and a quizzical smile on his face. At least that was fitting, Halt thought. Crowley had been renowned for his impish sense of humour. He had obviously died thinking of something that amused him and Halt drew comfort from that fact.

With Crowley's death, most people assumed that Halt

would take on the mantle of Corps Commandant. But he had reacted with horror at the suggestion.

'Paperwork, reports, organisation, sitting behind a desk listening to everyone's complaints and problems. Can you see me doing that?' he had said to Pauline at the time.

His wife had smiled, looking at his severe expression. 'I don't believe I can,' she had agreed.

So the position was offered to Gilan, much to his surprise. He believed he was far too young for the job. But the appointment had been greeted with unanimous approval by his peers. Gilan was, along with Will Treaty, one of the most highly regarded of the younger men in the Corps – and one of the most widely experienced, particularly in terms of international affairs. Gilan had travelled more widely, and seen more action, than most Rangers.

And he was used to being close to the corridors of power. His father was the Kingdom's Battlemaster and Gilan had a close personal relationship with Princess Cassandra and Sir Horace, the foremost knight of the Kingdom. Even more in his favour, in the eyes of the other Rangers, he had been mentored in his early days by Halt himself.

Will might have been considered for the job, although he was younger than Gilan. But while he and Halt were highly respected, even revered, as individuals, it was widely recognised that they preferred to act independently and had a penchant for bending the rules when they saw fit. Gilan, on the other hand, was more disciplined and organised, and more suited to the task of commanding and controlling an elite and disparate group like the fifty Rangers of Araluen.

'Do you suppose he's going to ask you to go on another mission?' Pauline asked, after they had ridden for a few minutes in silence. From time to time, even though he was retired, Halt agreed to undertake missions for Gilan.

Halt considered the question now, but shook his head.

'He would have said so in his letter,' he replied. 'He wouldn't ask me to come all this way if there was a chance that I'd say no. Besides, if he wanted me to go on a mission, why would he ask you to come to Castle Araluen? I get the feeling it's something personal.'

'You don't suppose Jenny's finally agreed to marry him?' Pauline said with a smile. It had been another surprise in the past few years when Jenny had decided that she had no wish to uproot herself and her thriving restaurant business from Redmont and follow Gilan to Castle Araluen. She loved him, they all knew. But she wanted to retain her individuality and her career.

'We'll do it one day,' Jenny had told Gilan. 'But at the moment you're either completely tied up with Ranger business or away on a mission somewhere. I've no wish to be the Commandant's wife.'

Gilan had been a little stung by her frank words. 'What if I meet someone else?' he had said, somewhat archly.

Jenny had shrugged. 'Then you're free to do as you please. But you won't meet anyone as good as me.'

She had been right. So they maintained their long-distance relationship, with Gilan taking any opportunity he could find to visit Redmont Fief and spend time with her. Each time they saw each other, he renewed his offer of marriage. And she renewed her postponement.

'I don't think so,' Halt replied now to Pauline's question. 'You know Jenny. If she'd decided to marry him, she would have been bubbling over with excitement.'

'True,' Pauline agreed. She sighed quietly. 'D'you think we set them all a bad example, waiting as long as we did?'

'I don't think it was a bad example,' Halt told her. 'Besides, the waiting kept you keen.'

She twisted in her saddle to look at him. It was a long, hard look, and Halt realised that he would pay for that sally. Perhaps not today, or tomorrow. But one day – probably when he least expected it. Still, it would be worth it. He rarely scored a point in verbal battles with his wife. She had a lifetime of practice in the Diplomatic Service.

They were close to the drawbridge now. It was lowered, as was the custom during daylight hours. Two sentries stood guard at the outer end. They came to attention and saluted the pair of riders. There was no need for Halt and Pauline to identify themselves. Their arrival was expected and they were widely recognised throughout the Kingdom, and particularly here in the capital.

'Ranger Halt, Lady Pauline,' said the more senior of the two. 'Welcome to Castle Araluen.'

He gestured to them to ride past, stepping aside to accentuate the invitation.

Halt nodded to the two men.

Pauline favoured the senior sentry with a beaming smile.

'Thank you, Corporal.' She leaned forward, looking more closely at the other man. 'And is that you, Malcolm Landers? I recall you helped me with my horse last time I visited Araluen.'

The man's homely face broke into a delighted smile. 'True enough, my lady. He cast a shoe, as I remember.'

Halt shook his head slightly. His wife's ability to remember names and faces, even those of ordinary soldiers and men at arms, was a source of wonder to him. More of that diplomat training, he thought. Then he corrected himself. No, Pauline was genuinely interested in people. She liked people and she never forgot those who did her a good turn. He realised that her simple act of recognition and remembrance had won her a devoted follower. Malcolm Landers would now do anything for her.

Of course, he said silently to his horse, *being a stunning beauty helps in these matters as well.*

Not something that you'll ever be accused of, Abelard replied.

'Stop talking to your horse, dear,' Pauline said as they clopped their way across the drawbridge and under the raised portcullis.

He wondered how she knew that's what he'd been doing.

'I always know,' she said, and he wondered how she knew what he'd been wondering.

They were met in the courtyard by a young apprentice Ranger. Gilan had instituted a system whereby he 'borrowed' apprentices from their masters for two to three months, so they could assist him in his work as Commandant.

'It makes sense to give them a grounding in how the Corps is administered,' he had said to Halt. 'Who knows? Some day one of these boys may end up as Commandant.'

Halt had rolled his eyes at the thought. 'God help us,' he had said quietly.

'Good morning, Ranger Halt. Good morning, Lady Pauline,' the current Commandant-in-training greeted them. 'My name is Kane and I'm assisting the Commandant. The Commandant sends his apologies. He's addressing the final-year apprentice warriors at the Battleschool.' He looked nervously at the two visitors. 'He suggested that I show you to your rooms and he'll join you as soon as he's free. He didn't know exactly when you were due to arrive,' he added apologetically.

Pauline favoured him with a smile. 'We understand. Gilan is a busy man, after all.'

Kane gestured to a stable hand who was standing ready nearby, shifting from one foot to another as he waited. 'Can I have Murray take care of your horses?' he suggested.

Halt hesitated. Pauline knew he preferred to look after Abelard himself. But she also knew that the young stable hand would boast for years to come about the fact that he had tended to Halt's horse.

'Let Murray do it, dear,' she said quietly.

Abelard tossed his head. *I agree. He'll do a better job than you. He'll show me extra respect.*

He'll show you extra apples is what you mean.

'Don't talk to your horse, dear. People are watching,' Pauline said quietly.

Halt turned a perplexed look towards her. 'How do you know when I'm doing that?'

She smiled at him. 'Your nose twitches,' she said.

A little bewildered, Halt allowed the stable boy to take Abelard's bridle in one hand. He led Pauline's horse with the other and headed for the stables. Halt and Pauline followed Kane to an upper floor of the keep tower, where a comfortable suite of rooms had been prepared for them. On the way, Kane kept glancing surreptitiously at the famous Ranger, fascinated by the fact that he kept staring down his nose and tweaking its tip between his forefinger and thumb.

Once they reached the suite of rooms set aside for them, Pauline declared that she would take a bath, and sent servants to fetch hot water.

'I'll pay my respects to King Duncan while you're bathing,' Halt said. Pauline nodded as she unpacked several gowns and hung them in the wardrobe.

'I'll see him later, when he's had time to prepare.'

Duncan had been bedridden now for many months, following a leg injury that wouldn't heal. Formerly powerfully built and full of energy, he was a shadow of his former self. He had lost weight and muscle tone, and Pauline, conscious of the King's sense of dignity, felt that he would want time to prepare himself to look his best before greeting a female visitor. Halt nodded sombrely.

'Good idea,' he said. 'I'll give him your regards.'

Prepared as he was, it was still something of a shock when Halt was ushered into the King's bedroom. It had been some months since he had last visited the King and he was depressed to see how far Duncan had degenerated. His cheeks were hollow and waxy, his eyes overbright and feverish. And his body was gaunt, the skin seeming to hang off it. The injured leg was propped out before him, under a mound of blankets.

They chatted about inconsequential matters for a few minutes. Halt realised that, although Duncan was delighted to see him — one of his oldest friends and staunchest supporters — the King was weak and tired quickly as they talked. Halt cut short his visit and made his farewells, but Duncan beckoned him closer to the bed. The King seized Halt's wrist in a claw-like hand and leaned forward.

'Halt, keep watch over Cassandra. It's not easy for her — running the Kingdom with me laid up in bed.'

Halt forced a laugh. 'I will, my lord, but you'll be up and about before too long and you can take charge again.'

Before he had finished, Duncan was shaking his head. 'Let's not fool ourselves, Halt. I don't have long. And when I'm gone, she'll need friends.' He paused, breathing with difficulty, his eyes closed for a few seconds. Then he opened them again. 'Thank god for Horace. She couldn't have chosen a better husband.'

The old Ranger smiled fondly at the thought of the honest young knight who was so utterly devoted to the princess. 'You couldn't say a truer word,' he replied. Ironic, he thought. Horace had been an orphan, born of unremarkable peasant stock. Soon he would become the most powerful and influential man in the Kingdom, sitting at Cassandra's right hand as she ruled.

'She'll need him,' the King said. 'It's not easy for a woman to rule. There'll be those who resent her and try to test her. She'll need all the help she can get. From Horace. From you. And from Will.'

Halt nodded assurance at the King. 'We'll give it to her,' he said. Then he couldn't help smiling. 'But don't underestimate your daughter, my lord. She knows what she wants and she knows how to get it.'

A tired smile crossed Duncan's face. 'And from what I hear, her daughter is taking after her,' he said. He released his grip on Halt's wrist and, as if the effort had been too much for him, slumped back in the pillows, waving a weak hand in dismissal.

Halt crossed quietly to the door, deep in thought. As he laid his hand on the latch, he turned back to look at the King he had served for so many years. Duncan was already asleep, his chest rising and falling fitfully under the covers.

Sadly, Halt let himself out.

'None of us are getting younger,' he said, to no one in particular. Then he smiled. Abelard would have had a tart rejoinder to that, he thought.

Five

It was less than ten minutes after Halt returned to their guest rooms when Kane knocked at the door.

'The Commandant is free now,' he said. 'He asks if you'll join him in his office.'

Halt and Pauline followed the young Ranger as he led them down several levels to the administration section of the keep tower. The higher levels were given over to accommodation and suites.

Gilan's office in the keep tower was light and breezy, with the shutters thrown wide open to admit the fresh air. Rangers hated to be cooped up, Pauline knew. Although sometimes their love of fresh air could be a little extreme. Fresh air was all very well. Fresh, cold air was something else. But she was aware of this trait and so she had worn a warm stole over her gown.

Gilan greeted Halt and Pauline happily, embracing them both and accepting a kiss on the cheek from Pauline. She regarded him fondly. She couldn't help thinking of

Halt's two former apprentices as surrogate sons. She noted that his normally cheerful face carried a few more lines than it had when she had last seen him. The burden of responsibility, she thought.

Unlike Halt and Will, Gilan had remained clean-shaven. It gave him a youthful look that was at odds with his senior position in the Kingdom.

'Gilan,' she said, 'you're looking well.' And apart from those wrinkles, he was.

He smiled at her. 'And you grow more beautiful every day, Pauline,' he replied.

'What about me?' Halt said, with mock severity. 'Do I grow more handsome every day? More impressive, perhaps?'

Gilan eyed him critically, his head to one side. Then he announced his verdict.

'Scruffier,' he said.

Halt raised his eyebrows. 'Scruffier?' he demanded.

Gilan nodded. 'I'm not sure if you're aware of recent advances in technology, Halt,' he said. 'But there's a wonderful new invention called *scissors*. People use them for trimming beards and hair.'

'Why?'

Gilan appealed to Pauline. 'Still using his saxe knife to do his barbering, is he?'

Pauline nodded, slipping her hand inside her husband's arm. 'Unless I can catch him at it,' she admitted. Halt regarded them both with a withering look. They both refused to wither, so he abandoned the expression.

'You show a fine lack of respect for your former mentor,' he told Gilan.

The younger man shrugged. 'It goes with my exalted position as your commander.'

'Not mine,' Halt said. 'I've retired.'

'So I can expect little in the way of deference from you?' Gilan grinned.

'No. I'll show proper deference . . . the day you train your horse to fly backwards around the castle's turrets.'

Pauline knew that these good-natured insults could continue for some time. She decided to interrupt the flow.

'What did you want to see us about, Gil? Are you planning to steal my husband away?' she asked.

Gilan had been on the point of delivering another carefully composed insult to his former teacher. Her direct question caught him off balance.

'What? Oh . . . no. Far from it. I wanted to talk to you. Both of you.'

Pauline indicated a low table, with four comfortable chairs set around it, arranged by the fireplace. 'Then shall we sit and talk?' she suggested.

But Gilan demurred. 'Not here. I want to talk to you two, and to Cassandra and Horace. They're expecting us in the royal apartments.'

As Commandant of the Rangers, Gilan could summon Halt and Pauline to Araluen. But he could hardly do the same to the Princess Regent and her consort, old friends or not. He led the way to the door, held it open for Halt and Pauline, then led the way to the stairs.

'Upstairs . . . downstairs . . . upstairs again. Do you have any pity for my creaking old bones?' Halt complained.

Gilan was walking briskly towards one of the spiralling staircases that led to the upper levels. 'Not a bit,' he tossed cheerfully over his shoulder.

Horace and Cassandra were waiting in the living room of the royal suite. Gilan tapped at the door and, when he heard Cassandra's response, he opened the door and ushered his two companions inside.

As they entered, Cassandra rose from her seat and moved to embrace them both.

'It's so good to see you!' she exclaimed. She could not have meant it more. The responsibility of running the Kingdom was a heavy burden and Halt and Pauline were more than friends. They were lifelong supporters. Halt, in particular, had spent many years as her adviser and protector in dangerous situations, from Skandia to the mountains of Nihon-Ja.

Horace waited until his wife had welcomed them, then he embraced them both in his turn. Halt studied him carefully.

'How's life in Castle Araluen?' he asked. Horace's honest face looked a little rueful.

'It's fine,' he said. 'But I miss the old days.'

'You mean the old days when you could skive off with this rascal to all corners of the earth and avoid responsibility?' his wife put in.

'Exactly,' Horace said in a tone so heartfelt that they all laughed.

Halt turned his gaze on the princess. 'I seem to remember you doing a certain amount of skiving off yourself.'

She waved a hand in a negative gesture. 'Let's not discuss that now,' she said.

There was a light tap on the door that led to Madelyn's rooms.

'Come in,' Cassandra called, and the door opened to admit the young princess.

'Halt. Lady Pauline. How wonderful to see you.'

Madelyn hesitated for a second, then, seeming to come to a decision, crossed the room and embraced them both. While she was hugging Pauline, Halt happened to glance at her parents. As he did, he sensed the unmistakable tension in the room. Cassandra, who had never been able to hide her feelings from Halt, had a slight frown, and Horace was looking decidedly uncomfortable. Madelyn stepped back from hugging Pauline and nodded a greeting to Gilan.

Horace cleared his throat awkwardly. 'Very well, Madelyn,' he said. 'You've said your hellos. Now off you go.' He gestured towards the door leading to her apartment. Maddie smiled at the new arrivals, and retraced her steps.

'We'll talk later,' Halt called after her. He had an easy relationship with Maddie and had served as her confidant many times in the past.

She gave him a sad little smile. 'Of course,' she said, and closed the door.

Halt looked curiously at his two old friends. 'Trouble in paradise?' he said gently.

Cassandra gave an annoyed shrug. 'Oh, she's just so exasperating, Halt!' she said. 'She's headstrong and irresponsible, and so infuriating. And if you try to speak to her about it, she huffs and sighs and rolls her eyes so that you simply want to strangle her!'

Halt rubbed his beard thoughtfully. 'Sounds serious,'

he said. 'Huffing and sighing and eye rolling, you say? I've never heard of a teenage girl behaving like that.'

'You can joke about it, Halt,' Horace put in. 'You don't have to put up with it. She's had Cassandra worried sick. She sneaks off into the forest at the dead of night, alone. We've restricted her to her quarters for two weeks. Maybe that will teach her a lesson.'

Halt's expression told his old friend that he doubted it. A headstrong girl like Maddie would only become more stubborn with that sort of restriction.

Horace saw the sceptical expression and felt he had to add more. 'She's taking risks and she just assumes she can take care of herself. That forest can be dangerous!'

'But basically, she's a sensible girl, isn't she?' Halt asked. 'And I imagine she could look after herself. She's good with a saxe. I taught her, after all. And I hear she's pretty good with that sling of hers.'

'Who told you that?' Cassandra said sharply. Halt spread his hands in a defensive gesture.

'Your father might have mentioned it. I was chatting with him an hour ago.'

'Father talks too much,' Cassandra said, a scowl crossing her face.

Halt smiled tolerantly at her. Over the years, he'd learned that parents tended to be the toughest critics of their own children. Grandparents and uncles — and he classed himself as an honorary uncle to Maddie — tended to see the fuller picture, and be able to discount any minor aberrations in behaviour, gauging them against the child's overall reasonable nature.

Pauline knew it too. But she also knew that nothing

could be more annoying to parents than an outsider telling them that an errant child wasn't anywhere near as bad as they were making out.

'Perhaps it's none of our business, Halt . . .' she began.

'No. It's all right,' Cassandra said.

'What does she do in the forest?' Halt asked her.

'She tracks animals. And she hunts.'

'Is she any good?'

Cassandra shrugged uncertainly. Horace answered before he could stop to think.

'Apparently yes. She never comes back empty-handed. But she gives the game to the castle guards.'

Cassandra looked at him. 'How do you know that?' she demanded.

Horace looked confused. He dropped his gaze from hers. 'I . . . err . . . I may have heard some of the guards discussing it.'

'And you didn't choose to share this with me?'

'I didn't think there was any point. I knew you'd just get angry about it.'

'And you were right! If you'd seen your way to —'

Pauline clapped her hands sharply. It was a measure of her personality and self-confidence that she would call the Princess Regent to order in such a peremptory fashion. And a measure of Cassandra's regard for the tall, blonde Courier that she would accept such brusqueness.

'Horace! Cassandra! That's enough!' They both stopped and looked at Pauline and she continued in a milder tone. 'You're not the first parents to be driven crazy by a teenage daughter. And you won't be the last. It's difficult, I know. But don't let it become too big a thing. Keep it in perspective. You need to maintain a united front, not bicker among yourselves.'

The two looked meekly down at their shoes. Halt smiled to himself again. They looked like naughty children rebuked by a stern parent.

'And it seems to me,' he said, 'she's not the first princess to go off in the woods at night looking for adventure.'

Cassandra screwed up her lip. 'Oh, don't you start.'

'Basically Maddie's a good kid,' he continued. 'She's smart and brave and resourceful. Because that's the way you've raised her.'

'Well,' said Gilan, a little impatiently, 'if that's settled for the moment, perhaps we could discuss the reason I asked to see you all.'

They turned to face him, wondering what he was going to say. They didn't have long to wait.

'It's Will,' he said. 'I'm very worried about him.'

Six

'It's been eighteen months since Alyss's death,' Gilan said. 'In that time, can any of you remember seeing Will laugh, or even smile?'

Sadly the others shook their heads. They exchanged uncomfortable looks. Then Pauline spoke.

'It's heart-breaking. He was always such a cheerful, happy person. Always grinning, always joking. These days, it's as if a light has been extinguished inside him.'

'Of course, we can't expect him to just shake off the effects of losing Alyss in a few months,' Halt put in. 'She was his soul mate, after all, and losing her was a terrible shock to him.'

Alyss's death had been the result of a terrible, tragic mischance. She had been returning, with a small escort, from the Celtic court, where she had been overseeing the renewal of the defence agreement between Araluen and

Celtica. It was a routine trip and a routine mission. But on the way home, she had chanced upon a situation in Anselm, one of the southern fiefs.

For some months, a gang of criminals, led by a former mercenary named Jory Ruhl, had been preying on villages in Anselm and its neighbouring fiefs. They would capture children then demand ransom payments from their parents. Since villagers weren't usually wealthy people, often the entire village would be forced to contribute to the ransom.

A local constable had received word that Ruhl and his gang were meeting one night at an inn called the Wyvern. Coincidentally, this was where Alyss had chosen to stay. The constable had organised a posse of volunteers and marched on the Wyvern with them.

Unfortunately, the attempted arrest was badly bungled. Ruhl received warning of the approaching posse and he and his men were making their escape when the constable and his force arrived on the scene. A fight broke out and one of the posse was killed. Seeking to create a diversion while they escaped, Ruhl and one of his men set fire to the inn. The dry thatching of the roof was soon ablaze and smoke filled the small saddling yard. Guests in the inn began streaming out, seeking safety, and soon, in the swirling smoke and the mass of shouting, frightened people, the constable had no way of knowing who was who. In the confusion, Ruhl and his four henchmen escaped into the forest.

Alyss and her three armed guards were among the guests who had escaped from the burning building. But as she stood in the saddling yard outside, the blonde Courier had looked up and saw a face at an upper window.

It was a five-year-old girl, struggling desperately to un-fasten the latch on the window, which was jammed. As her panic grew, smoke filled the room and she began to cough, her eyes streaming. Blinded by the smoke and disoriented, she staggered away from the window and was lost to sight.

Without hesitation, Alyss plunged back into the burning inn, ignoring the warning cries from her guards. She fought her way up the staircase, which was already aflame, and headed for the front of the inn, her eyes closed and her face shielded from the raging heat by her forearm. She moved instinctively, feeling her way along the wall with her other hand.

She found the door latch and forced it open, lurching into the room where the girl had been. She dropped to her hands and knees, where there was a small pocket of clearer air, and crawled towards the window. It was visible only as a vague square of light against the black, roiling smoke.

On the floor below the window, she could just make out the crumpled form of the young girl. Alyss crawled rapidly towards her and rolled her over, seeing with relief that her chest was still rising and falling as she breathed, striving hopelessly for a lungful of clean air. Alyss stood and drew her heavy dagger. She jammed it into the narrow gap between the window and its frame and jerked on it with all her strength. With a splintering crack, the window flew open, banging back against the outside wall. Alyss stooped and gathered the girl in her arms, heaving her up onto the sill. In the yard below, her guards were watching, horror written on their faces. They could see how badly the inn was aflame. The section where Alyss now stood was one of the few places untouched so far.

'Catch her!' Alyss yelled, and shoved the unconscious girl out the window, sending her sliding down the slope of the thatch. As the girl tumbled over the edge, the three guards moved forward to catch her. The weight of the falling body sent one of them sprawling in the dust and the other two staggered. But they managed to break the girl's fall successfully. Then they looked back up to the window, where Alyss was beginning to clamber out.

A wall of flame shot up out of the thatch, between Alyss and the edge of the roof. The timbers and rafters below that point of the roof had been burning, unseen, for some minutes, and the fire suddenly broke through. Alyss was lost to sight. Then, with a terrible rumbling crash, the entire section of roof above and around where she was standing gave way and collapsed in a mass of flames and sparks. In a fraction of a second, there was nothing left but a gaping, smoking hole in the front of the inn. Then more timbers burned through and the entire front wall of the inn collapsed in on itself.

Alyss never had a chance.

'I know,' Gilan said now, breaking the long silence that had followed Halt's statement. 'It's not an easy thing to get over.'

They had all cast their minds back to the terrible day when they had heard about Alyss's death, seeing it in their minds as it had been described by Alyss's distraught guards.

'It was so typical of Alyss,' Cassandra said quietly, 'to give up her own life like that. Her guards said she never hesitated — just ran into the fire to save that girl.'

'Maybe it wouldn't have been so hard on Will if we'd been able to bury her,' Pauline said. The fire had been so intense that Alyss's body had never been recovered. 'Funerals may be terribly sad affairs, but at least they give some sense of finality to the people left behind. I know I feel as if there's a gap that hasn't been filled. It must be so much worse for Will.'

Gilan waited a few seconds before he spoke again. 'I can understand his grief and his sense of loss over this whole matter,' he said. 'That's something he'll have to come to terms with eventually. And I'm sure he will. But there's something else.'

The others all looked at him curiously. But Halt sensed he knew what the young Commandant was talking about.

'Jory Ruhl and his gang,' Halt said quietly.

Gilan nodded. 'He's become embittered about the fact that they escaped. He's set himself the task of catching them. He's on a personal quest for revenge and the obsession is feeding the blackness in his mind and soul until he thinks about nothing else.'

Cassandra gave a sad little cry and put her hand to her throat. The thought of Will, her long-time companion — almost a surrogate brother — being driven and dominated by such a black passion brought tears to her eyes. She remembered their days together on the island of Skorghijl long ago, when he had protected her and cared for her and kept her spirits up through the darkest of times. Remembered him in Arrida, coming to their rescue at the last moment, just as Halt had known he would.

You couldn't think of Will without seeing his unruly mop of brown hair and that cheerful grin on his face. Will had always been filled with an inner energy. He was enthusiastic and inquisitive, forever seeking something new and interesting in life. It was this trait that had led the Nihon-Jan people to christen him *chocho,* or butterfly. He seemed to flit cheerfully from one idea to another, from one event to the next.

Cassandra had seen Will several times since Alyss's death, although he tended to avoid his old friends. He was a grim-faced, grey-bearded figure these days. There was no sign of the old Will. Pauline was right. It was as if a light inside him had been extinguished.

'He needs something to take his mind off this idea of revenge,' Halt said. 'Can't you assign him to a mission — give him something to occupy his thoughts?'

'I've tried that,' Gilan said with a frown. He paused before continuing. 'He's refused on two occasions.'

Halt was shocked by the words. 'Refused? He can't do that!'

Gilan made a helpless gesture. 'I know, Halt. And so does Will. If it happens again, I'll have to suspend him from the Corps.'

'That would kill him,' Horace said.

Gilan looked at him. 'And he's well aware of it. But he doesn't care. And that means I can't afford to assign him another task. He'll refuse and I'll have to take action. At the same time, I can't afford to have my most effective Ranger sitting on his hands brooding about Jory Ruhl and his gang and planning how to catch them. All that aside, he's my friend and I hate seeing him this way.'

'I thought he'd already caught some of them?' Horace asked.

'Three of the five. He caught one only two weeks ago. Henry Wheeler was his name. Will confronted him and Wheeler tried to escape.'

'What happened?' Halt asked, although he dreaded to hear the answer. People didn't just 'escape' from someone as skilled and deadly as his old apprentice, and he didn't want to hear that Will had blood on his hands.

Gilan seemed to sense his thoughts. He shook his head abruptly.

'Wheeler is dead. But it wasn't Will's doing. He tried to attack Will and fell on his own knife.'

Halt heaved a silent sigh of relief. 'And the other two?' he asked.

'He captured them both and brought them in for trial and sentencing. Although he said to me that he was hoping they'd try to escape. I got the feeling that he even gave them several opportunities to do so. But they weren't stupid enough to take them.'

There was a brief silence as they thought about their old friend.

'What about Ruhl?' Horace asked.

'Will nearly caught him on one occasion,' Gilan replied.

Halt looked up quickly. 'I didn't know that.'

Gilan nodded. 'It wasn't long after he started hunting them down. He got within five metres of him. Ruhl was on a punt, crossing a river. Will arrived just too late, after the punt had left the bank. They were face to face for a few seconds. But by the time Will had unslung his bow, Ruhl had taken cover behind some wool bales. Will tried to follow by climbing along the overhead cable that held the punt against the current. But when Ruhl reached the far bank, he cut through the cable and dropped Will in the river. He came close to drowning.'

'So close,' Halt muttered. 'I imagine that makes it even worse for him.'

Gilan nodded agreement.

'So, Gil,' Pauline said, ever the one for practical action, 'what do you suggest we do — other than simply talking about it and wringing our hands?'

Gilan hesitated. He was moving onto uncertain ground here, but his instinct told him the key to Will's salvation lay with the people in this room — the ones closest to him.

'Look,' he said slowly, 'we're the ones he loves above all others. And the ones who love him. Maybe if we all talked to him together. If we got him into a room and told him how we're worried for him, how we can see the harm this quest for revenge is doing to him, well, maybe the fact that we're all saying it will get through to him. Maybe he'll . . . I don't know . . . snap out of it?'

He finished the rambling sentence on a questioning note, as if looking for one of the others to supply the answer. To tell the truth, he wasn't sure what they could achieve. But he sensed that this group of people were the key to solving Will's problem. Perhaps the combined force of their love for him could break through the dark fog that was swirling in his mind, pull aside the black curtain that had separated him from all but one thought — revenge for Alyss's death.

'I don't think just talking will do it —' Horace said thoughtfully.

Cassandra interrupted. 'But surely if we all talked to him, all of us at once, we could get through to him?'

Horace pursed his lips. 'I don't know. You know how Will is. He's stubborn. Always has been.' He glanced to Halt for confirmation, and the old Ranger nodded.

'Odds are,' Horace continued, 'if we just talk at him, he'll nod his head and pretend to agree with us. Then, when we're done, he'll simply continue on as he has been.'

He paused, his face set in a thoughtful frown. He sensed he was close to an idea but couldn't quite grasp it.

'We need a new focus for him. Something that will break his obsession with Jory Ruhl and his surviving accomplice. Something that will occupy his mind so fully that it will leave no room for thoughts of revenge.'

Gilan spread his hands in a defeated gesture. 'Well, as I said, I tried to send him on two missions and he —'

'It needs to be something more compelling, more personally involving than just a mission,' Pauline said, grasping what Horace was getting at. Like him, she felt there was an idea floating just out of reach. It was Halt who stated it.

'He needs to take on an apprentice,' he said.

They all turned to look at him. The idea, once stated, seemed so obvious. Both Horace and Pauline nodded. This was what they had been getting at, without realising it.

Gilan looked hopeful for a few seconds, then he shook his head in frustration.

'Problem is,' he said, 'we have no suitable candidates at the moment. And we can't offer him someone substandard. He'll simply refuse to take on someone who's not up to scratch, and he'll be right. I won't be able to blame him for that.'

'I wasn't thinking just any apprentice,' Halt said. 'It needs to be someone he already has a personal connection with. Someone he cares about, so that he can't refuse. It needs to be a person who will involve him emotionally — as well as physically and intellectually.' He looked at his wife. 'Remember years ago, when I sent Will off to Celtica with Gilan and I started behaving a little . . . erratically?'

'You started throwing noblemen out castle windows, as I recall,' she said, her lips twisting to contain a smile. Halt made a gesture that indicated he didn't want to get into detail about that time in his life.

'Whatever. You sensed that I needed a new influence in my life to take my mind off the things that were troubling me.'

'As I recall, you were assigned to accompany Alyss on a mission,' she said.

'And it did the trick. Her youth and cheerfulness snapped me right out of my brown mood.'

Lady Pauline arched an eyebrow. 'It didn't stop you throwing people into moats.'

'Maybe not. But he deserved it,' Halt said, showing a rare grin. Then he became serious again. 'Anyway, what I'm thinking is, if we put Will in charge of someone like I described, it might get his mind off this quest for revenge. And if we can do that, we'll be well on the way to helping him accept and live with Alyss's loss.'

'Of course, you never get over the loss of a loved one,' Cassandra mused.

Halt nodded to her. 'No. But you can learn to live with it and accept it. And gradually, the hurt becomes more bearable. It doesn't go away, but it becomes bearable.'

Gilan had been watching his former mentor carefully while he put his case. The young Commandant knew Halt, probably better than anyone else in the room.

'I take it you have someone specific in mind to be Will's apprentice?' he asked.

Halt looked at him. 'I was thinking Madelyn.'

Seven

Suddenly, everyone was talking at once.

'Madelyn? You mean *my* Madelyn?' Cassandra cried, coming half to her feet.

'You must be joking, Halt!' said Horace.

'But she's a girl!' That was Gilan.

Halt waited until they all fell silent. Then he answered them calmly.

'Yes, Cassandra. I do mean your Madelyn. And no, I'm not joking, Horace. And yes, Gilan, I am aware that Madelyn is a girl.'

He noticed that, alone among those in the room, his wife had said nothing. He glanced sideways at her and was not surprised to see that she was nodding her head thoughtfully. He gave her a brief smile. The others were all still totally nonplussed by his suggestion. Cassandra had fallen back into her chair as she realised he was serious. He spoke to her now.

'Evanlyn,' he said. Like Will, Halt usually used that

name for her in private. It was a mark of affection between them. 'Let's just think about something. If you had a son instead of a daughter, what would he be doing now?'

'I didn't have a son —' she began, but he held up his hands to still her protest.

'Just humour me. Let's say, hypothetically, you have a son. How would you be preparing him for his future as the ruler of Araluen?'

Cassandra bit her lip. She could see what he was angling at and she refused to give his suggestion any support.

Horace answered for her. 'He'd be in the army,' he said in a flat tone.

Cassandra whipped round to glare at him. 'Horace!' she cried accusingly, but Horace, tall and practical and honest, shrugged at her. There was no avoiding the answer.

Halt nodded gently, his eyes still fixed on Cassandra as she turned back to him. She flushed. He could see that she regretted the sudden surge of anger she had directed at her husband.

'That's right,' he said. 'Probably in a cavalry regiment. You would have trained him with the sword and the lance for the past few years, I would think, Horace?'

Horace nodded, a little regretfully. During the time of Cassandra's pregnancy, he had nursed visions of training a son to ride and wield a sword and a lance like his father. When Cassandra had delivered a daughter, he had felt a moment of shocked surprise. He had simply never considered that possibility. It has to be said that this was quickly overcome by a deep-seated, lasting pleasure at the prospect of raising a daughter. But he remembered those long-ago dreams now.

Halt continued. 'Probably be a junior officer, commanding a squad, learning how to lead men in combat, how to make life-or-death decisions.

'And I would guess that you wouldn't insist that he be kept away from combat. You'd recognise that he would have to be seen as a leader who shared danger with the men he commanded. Maybe he'd be assigned to a term of picket duty in the north, protecting against Scotti raiders. Or he'd be patrolling the south-west coast, fighting smugglers and Moondarkers.'

He paused, looking at the two of them. Horace was looking resigned, as if he agreed that this was what a son of his would be expected to do. Cassandra's lips were pressed together in a thin, stubborn line.

'What he wouldn't be doing would be sitting in a big, comfortable castle, surrounded by hundreds of men at arms and never knowing what it was like to face danger, to pit himself against an enemy and come out on top.'

Gilan opened his mouth to say something, but Halt held up a hand to stop him. He knew what Gilan's objection was but he'd deal with that in a minute or two.

'So why should your daughter be any different?' he asked. Cassandra's eyes flashed up to meet his.

'Because she *is* my daughter!' she snapped. 'Do you expect her to go into the army and lead a platoon of cavalry?'

'No,' Halt said in a reasonable tone. 'But I think joining the Rangers would be a logical alternative. She'd learn to command, to make decisions, to judge a situation and come up with the right answer at the right time. As for the more physical side of battle, well, we Rangers have always tended to step back and leave that to the bash and whack-ers like Horace. No offence,' he added with a small smile.

Horace shrugged. 'I recall you taking your place in the battle line more than once, Halt.'

Halt nodded. 'I have. But it's not absolutely necessary for a Ranger to do it. That was usually just vanity on my part.'

'But even so, you admit that there would be danger?' Cassandra said.

Halt turned to her. 'Of course. We live in a dangerous world. When you're dead and gone and Maddelyn inherits the throne, there will be people who won't want her there. They'll have their own agendas and their own candidates for ruler. If they think they're dealing with a helpless girl, they'll try to take advantage of the fact. They might be a little more reluctant if they knew she was a trained Ranger — and had the backing of the entire Corps. We tend to look after one another, you know.'

Cassandra considered his words. Araluen was at peace, but she was aware that there were still elements in the Kingdom who would be ready to rebel at the slightest sense of weakness from their ruler. And any change of ruler could always precipitate a power struggle among ambitious people. Cassandra's own reputation, and Horace's skill as a warrior, were enough to keep such elements at bay. The people of Araluen were aware that their future queen was not one to be browbeaten or suborned in any way. Any rebellion against her would be quickly snuffed out.

But Maddie? What would she bring to the throne? What would her reputation be? She saw now that Halt's description of her as a helpless girl was all too accurate.

Of course, she would have advisers and supporters. But Cassandra knew that the true strength of the throne came from the ruler herself. From her ability, her confidence, her skill and experience in dealing with tough and frightening situations. But still . . .

'But the danger, Halt? How can I place my little girl in danger? What if she's injured?' she said, her voice miserable.

'What if she's hurrying to a needlepoint class, trips on the hem of her long, girly skirt, falls down the stairs and breaks her neck?' Halt asked. 'You can't mollycoddle her.'

He paused, remembering his conversation with Duncan. 'Your father said that things are going to be tough for you when you inherit the throne,' he said. 'They're going to be even tougher for Maddie. She may not find someone like Horace to support her.'

Halt leaned forward and took Cassandra's hands.

'You'd be placing her in the care of the greatest, most capable Ranger Araluen has ever known,' he said quietly. He sensed the surprise among the others and looked up at them.

'Oh, Will's better than I ever was,' he said, smiling. Once, his vanity might not have allowed him to say that, but now the words came easily.

'Maybe not *better*. But certainly as good,' Gilan admitted reluctantly.

'And he's younger.' Pauline smiled.

'Thank you for that reminder,' Halt told her. Then he turned back to Horace and Cassandra. 'Think about it. Could Maddie be in safer hands? Will loves her. He's her godfather. He looks upon her as his niece, if not his surrogate daughter. You'd be entrusting her to his care and you know he would die before he let any harm come to her.'

'And Will doesn't die easily,' Horace observed. He was beginning to see the logic in Halt's idea. When he thought about it, he knew Maddie would be in safe hands with Will watching over her.

Halt sensed the change in Horace's attitude. He pressed his advantage.

'On top of that, you've said yourself that she's rebellious and difficult. Maybe she needs the discipline that life as an apprentice would bring. I'm not saying she should do the full five-year apprenticeship. A year should be enough — just so she wins her bronze oakleaf. The experience will do her a lot of good.'

Cassandra had drawn breath to reply, but now she stopped, and a thoughtful look came over her face.

'That's true,' she said softly. She had a mental picture of Maddie back-chatting Will, and finding out how such behaviour could rebound on her. Will would take no nonsense from an apprentice, even one he loved.

'Cassandra,' Pauline said and the princess looked at the graceful blonde, for a moment seeing her old friend Alyss. 'I'm reminded of a conversation I had with your father when you wanted to go to Arrida to ransom Erak. I told him, and I'll tell you now, that a queen-to-be has to do these things — has to take chances. Has to get out in the world. You can't rule properly from an ivory tower. This is a good idea all round.'

Cassandra found herself nodding. She came to a decision, looked at Horace and saw the agreement in his eyes. As always, he knew what she was thinking.

'Yes,' she said briefly.

'There is one small problem you're all ignoring,' Gilan said. 'She's a girl. We've never had a girl in the Rangers.'

'Maybe it's time we did have one,' Halt said. Pauline looked at him with absolute approval. How far her crusty, grim-faced, traditionally minded husband had come, she thought.

'But . . .' Gilan began. He was lost for words until he thought of an objection. 'She's small. How would she ever draw an eighty-pound bow? And that's our principal weapon.'

'I'm small,' Halt said. 'So's Will.'

'But girls have a different muscle structure to boys,' Gilan said. He looked apologetically at Cassandra and Pauline. 'I'm not being biased against girls here. It's just a physical fact. In general, we're more heavily muscled than you. And Maddie is a slightly built girl. She'd never build up the muscle mass that you need to shoot a longbow.'

'Well, we'll just have to find a way around that,' Halt replied. 'Maybe change our thinking a little. On the other hand, girls are lighter on their feet than boys. She'd be excellent at silent movement and camouflage. She's agile. She's nimble. And those are all qualities that a Ranger needs.'

He could see Gilan was struggling with the concept. He smiled to himself. It was actually an idea that he'd been nursing for some months. Not specifically concerning Maddie, but as a general concept. He had been aware that there was a current shortage of suitable apprentice candidates, as Gilan had mentioned. And he'd begun to think that the Corps was ignoring a potential source of such people. Half the fifteen-year-olds in the Kingdom were girls. Some of them had to be suitable candidates. There were no female Rangers simply because there never had been. That, in itself, was not a good reason. It might well be time to blow away the cobwebs and let in some new thinking.

And who better to sponsor such a new idea than Halt himself? After all, along with Crowley, he had reformed the Corps many years ago. Maybe it was time for a little more reforming.

As to Gilan's main objection — the difficulty of finding a girl strong enough to pull a longbow — Maddie was ideally suited to demonstrate an alternative solution.

'I wonder could you release your daughter from her quarters for an hour or so?' he asked Cassandra and Horace. 'I want her to show Gilan something.'

Eight

Halt, Gilan and Maddie stood in the weapons practice yard of the Araluen Battleschool. For the purposes of this demonstration, Halt had requested that Horace and Cassandra stay away. He knew there was friction between the girl and her parents and he didn't want that to interfere with her concentration.

Maddie looked curiously at Halt. She wasn't sure what was going on but she'd watched him set two old jousting helmets on posts about seventy metres from where they stood. He smiled at her.

'Gilan is interested in a potential new weapon for the Corps,' he told her. 'I thought you might be the best person to demonstrate it.'

'You mean the sling?' she said, glancing down at the double leather thongs in her right hand. When he had arranged her temporary release from detention, Halt had asked her to bring her sling and a supply of the ammunition she used.

'Exactly. Now, Gilan, would you agree that this would seem to be the optimum range for shooting at an armoured man?'

Gilan nodded. The longbow could shoot much further than seventy metres, of course. But at this range, it would still have the power and hitting force to send an arrow smashing through an enemy's steel helmet. And if the shooter missed, there would still be time for another shot.

Not that Rangers often missed — if ever.

'Then let's see *you* do it,' Halt said to Gilan.

Gilan raised his bow and, with a smooth, automatic action that came from years of practice, brought an arrow from the quiver over his shoulder and laid it on the string. Without seeming to take aim, he drew back and shot.

They heard the resounding clang as the arrow hit the left-hand helmet, punching through the steel at what would be forehead level. The helmet leapt and spun off the post, transfixed by the arrow, and rolled in the dust of the practice yard.

'Slow,' said Halt.

Gilan turned a pained eye on him. 'I'd like to see you do better,' he challenged.

Halt allowed himself a faint smile. 'Unfortunately, I've left my bow in our apartment,' he said, and Gilan sniffed. Halt glanced at Maddie. 'So we'll leave the second target to you, young lady.'

Maddie slipped the loop at one end of the sling around the middle finger of her right hand, then gripped the plaited end of the other thong between her thumb and forefinger. As she did this, she took a lead shot from the pouch at her belt and fitted it into the leather patch in the middle of the sling. Halt noted with approval that she did so without looking. Her eyes, slightly narrowed, were focused on the helmet at the far end of the practice yard.

She turned side on, advancing her left leg towards the target, and let the shot dangle behind her body, at the end of the two thongs. She swung the sling in a slow pendulum motion several times, making sure the shot was firmly settled in its pouch. She pointed her left arm and hand towards the target, then whipped her right arm up in an overhand throwing action, her arm moving in a rapid arc about twenty degrees from the vertical and her body following through on the cast. As she reached the point of release, she let go the knotted end from between her thumb and forefinger. The shot flew out of the sling, the power of her throw magnified several times by the extra length and leverage that it added to the action.

CLANG!

The second helmet spun crazily on the pole, then came to rest on a drunken angle.

Gilan nodded, impressed. 'Not bad.'

He led the way down the practice yard to examine the result of her throw. There was an enormous dent in the helmet, also at forehead height. Some traces of bright silver metal were sprayed across the steel.

'Didn't penetrate,' he said, chewing his lip thoughtfully.

Halt touched the massive dent in the helmet. 'No. But would you care to have your head inside that helmet when this happened?'

'It definitely wouldn't do the wearer a lot of good,' Gilan conceded. He rubbed his finger on the splash of silver metal. 'What are you using as ammunition?' he asked. Maddie took another projectile from the pouch at her belt and handed it to him. Gilan was momentarily surprised at the weight.

'Lead shot,' she said.

'That seems to do the trick.' He held out his hand and she passed him the sling. He examined it.

'So simple,' he said. 'And so deadly.' He handed it back. 'You use a different technique to your mother. I seem to recall that she spun it round and round, horizontally?' He demonstrated, waving his right hand above his head in a flat circle.

Maddie shrugged disparagingly. 'Not a good technique,' she said. 'I don't know how she ever hit anything. It's so hard to judge when you're spinning it horizontally.'

'Oh, she hit plenty of things,' Halt told her. 'But she had to practise for hours to get any sort of accuracy.'

'This is more efficient,' Maddie said. 'And besides, if you stand up whirling the sling around your head two or three times, you're making a target of yourself.'

'Good point,' Halt conceded. 'How many shots can you get away in a minute?'

Maddie pushed out her bottom lip uncertainly. 'I have no idea,' she said. 'I've never timed myself.'

'Then let's see, shall we?' Halt told her. He stopped and picked up the helmet Gilan had shot, pulling the arrow loose and returning it to the Ranger Commandant. Then he replaced the helmet on its post and gestured for Maddie to return to the shooting line.

'All right. Alternate between the two and we'll see how fast you are,' he told her. 'But remember, fast is no good if you aren't accurate. If you've got a big, nasty Iberian pirate coming at you with a cutlass, it's no good missing him five times in rapid succession. Better to hit him once, slowly.'

She smiled at him. 'Point taken.' She set her feet, reached into the ammunition pouch and loaded a shot into the sling. Once again, she let it swing slowly back and forth for a few seconds.

'Begin!' Halt called. Gilan's lips moved as he began silently counting off the seconds.

She let fly with the shot and, before it struck the target, she was loading another into the sling. This time, she didn't bother with those short preliminary swings but brought her arm up and over almost immediately. As she released, they heard the *CLANG* of her first shot hitting home. Then she was reloading and snapping her arm up and over once more, aiming at the first target again.

CLANG! CLANG! . . . CLANG! CLANG!

'Stop shooting!' Halt called as Gilan threw up his hand. She had managed to get six shots away in the minute he had counted to himself, although the fourth projectile had missed its target.

'Five out of six,' he commented thoughtfully. 'Not bad at all.'

Maddie turned and confronted the two Rangers, her feet set apart, her hands on her hips.

'Care to tell me what this is all about?' she challenged, looking from one to the other. As Halt opened his mouth to reply, she waved a hand to stop him.

'And don't tell me some fairy story about Gilan assessing the sling as a new weapon. If you were merely interested in the sling, why would you care how fast I can shoot?'

Gilan and Halt exchanged a quick look. It wasn't wasted on Maddie. But neither said anything.

'It's pretty obvious that you're testing me, not the weapon. The question is, why?'

'Maybe that's something your parents should discuss with you,' Halt said finally.

Maddie sighed deeply. 'Mum and Dad? All they're interested in is keeping me cooped up. You know I'm confined to quarters for another week, don't you?'

A smile touched the corners of Halt's mouth. 'I'd heard some rumour to that effect. And of course, there's no good reason why they've done that, is there?'

Maddie rolled her eyes and sighed resignedly. 'Oh, all right. Maybe I did sneak out and go hunting once or twice . . .'

Halt raised an eyebrow and she amended the statement.

'Five or six times then. And maybe I was just a little cheeky when they talked to me about it.'

The eyebrow, which had just returned to its normal position, went up again.

'All right, maybe I was a little more than that,' she admitted.

'They're only doing what they think is best for you, Maddie,' Halt told her gently. She dropped her eyes and scuffed her boot in the sand of the practice yard.

'I kno-ow,' she said unhappily. 'But do they have to treat me like a precious princess all the time?'

'Well, you are a princess — and you are precious to them,' Halt said. 'And to all of us, as a matter of fact.'

He liked Maddie. Over the years, they had formed a close bond. Gilan was aware of this. That's why he had decided to stay out of this discussion and leave it to Halt.

In spite of herself, Maddie smiled faintly. 'You always manage to tie me up in knots.'

Halt took her hand. 'All I'm saying is that they care about you. They don't mean to be so over-protective, but it's hard for them to let go of the reins. They know it too. But believe me, they are trying, and they've had an idea.'

'Which you won't tell me about?'

'No. It's not up to me to do that. You should hear it from them.'

Maddie took a deep breath. 'Then let's go back to the keep and they can tell me,' she said. 'Assuming I passed whatever test you just set me?'

Halt looked at Gilan. 'I think she passed, don't you?'

Gilan smiled at the young princess. 'Oh yes. I think so.'

Nine

$\mathfrak{M}$addie stood, nervously facing Cassandra and Horace. Halt and Gilan had left her when they reached the door to the royal apartment.

'This is between you and your parents,' Halt told her. 'We'll talk to you afterwards.'

Now she stood in silence, waiting for them to say something. Usually, she reflected gloomily, they were all too ready to talk — listing her long array of crimes. But now they seemed reluctant to begin. An uncertain look passed between them, as if each one was waiting for the other to start. The tension was getting too much for her to bear. She decided to take the bull by the horns. If it was going to be bad news — and she assumed it was — best to get it over with as quickly as possible.

'Halt said you had something to tell me,' she said.

There was another of those quick glances between them, then her father cleared his throat.

'Ah . . . ah-hum . . . well, your mother and I want to talk to you. About your future.'

Maddie's heart sank into her boots. If it was going to be an official talk about her future, she knew what it would entail. More restrictions. More rules. Less freedom. There would be long dissertations about her duty as the second in line to the throne after her mother. There would be instructions as to what she could and couldn't do. And there would be more of the latter than the former — by far. Her future was not a subject she wanted to discuss with her parents. But it was obvious she had no choice. She waited and now Cassandra spoke.

'Maddie, we can't have you running wild, doing as you choose and taking risks the way you have been doing.'

Maddie's mouth set in a thin line. She realised that she'd finally pushed her parents too far and now they wouldn't back off. It was too late to make the sort of abject — and totally false — apology that had got her out of trouble in the past. She'd gone to that well too often, and now their patience was at an end.

'You need order and discipline in your life. You need a sense of purpose.' That was her father.

Her shoulders dropped in despair. Order, discipline and purpose, she thought. Could it get any worse than this?

She thought frantically. Was there nothing she could do to stave this off? Was there no subterfuge she could attempt? She had to try.

'Mum, Dad, I know I've been behaving terribly and I can see how I've upset you. But I —'

Her mother stopped her with an impatient gesture.

'It's too late for that, Maddie. We've given you one chance after another and you've continued to do as you please and flout our authority. Well, our patience is finally at an end. Our minds are made up.'

And that was that, Maddie thought. She knew her mother well enough to know that Cassandra had a will of iron and would not be deterred from a path once she had chosen it. Maddie took a deep breath and waited for the worst.

'We've decided,' Horace said, 'to send you to Will as an apprentice.'

Maddie's heart leapt. She kept her eyes cast down, not wanting them to see the sudden light of pleasure that she knew would be all too obvious. Waiting a few seconds until she had herself under control, she looked up at them, suddenly fearful that she had mistaken what Horace had said.

'Will?' she said tentatively. 'You mean Uncle Will?'

Will was her godfather. He'd been her sponsor at her naming day and had sworn to act in place of her parents if ever that became necessary. She loved Will. When she was a child, she had often visited him at Redmont Fief, staying in his warm little cabin and going on hunting and camping trips into the forest with him. Will was fun. Will had a mischievous sense of humour that matched her own.

Of course, she thought, he'd been fairly serious since Alyss's death. She had seen him once or twice since then and he'd been grim and humourless. But that was only to be expected. He'd get over that soon enough. She realised her mother was replying to the question she had asked.

'Yes. Will. Your godfather. We're going to ask him to take you on as an apprentice and train you as a Ranger.'

'But . . . I'm a girl,' Maddie said uncertainly.

Her mother regarded her dryly. 'Sometimes I've wondered if you were aware of that,' she said.

Maddie waved the sarcasm aside. 'I mean . . . there are no girl Rangers. There never have been . . . have there?' She frowned, trying to think if she'd ever heard of such a thing. Then she shook her head. She was sure there never had been a girl Ranger before.

'You'll be the first,' her father confirmed.

'And I'll be living with Uncle Will? At Redmont?' she said. They both nodded, and she couldn't help the huge smile spreading across her face.

Castle Redmont was far less stuffy and formal than Araluen. Baron Arald and his wife, Sandra, were genial hosts and they'd always treated her with affection. Not only that, she thought, she would outrank everyone at Redmont — even Baron Arald. There would be nobody there who could tell her how to behave or what to do. This was wonderful news!

'I'd go easy on the *Uncle Will* if I were you,' Horace said in a warning tone. 'You'll be his apprentice, you know.'

'Yes. Yes,' she said excitedly, her mind racing. She could see a future of hunting parties and dances and picnics at Castle Redmont, with her at the centre of things, ordering people to do her wishes, rather than being ordered about by her parents.

Of course, she'd have to be careful that she didn't overdo it. If word got back to them that she was enjoying herself too much, they were liable to cancel the whole idea.

'Life as an apprentice won't be easy,' her mother said, eyeing her carefully.

Maddie rapidly composed her features so that she looked suitably chastened. 'I know. But I'll do my best.'

Inwardly, she was exultant. Will loved her. He doted on her. She could twist him around her little finger. She had always been able to. Why should things be different now?

'So . . . you're willing to take this on?' Cassandra said, and Maddie lowered her gaze, nodding submissively.

'I'll do my best,' she said. 'I want you to be proud of me.'

Gilan and Halt rode up to the little cabin in the trees below Castle Redmont. As they approached the cabin, they could see a curl of wood smoke from the chimney. Tug, in his stable behind the cabin, neighed a greeting to Blaze and Abelard. They responded.

'Well, at least he's home,' Gilan said.

As he spoke, the door to the cabin opened and Will stepped out onto the small verandah. He nodded to his two old friends.

'Halt. Gilan,' he said.

Halt's heart sank a little at Will's unemotional tone. Previously, their arrival at the cabin would have been an occasion for happy greetings, jokes and cheerful insults. Now Will simply leaned against a verandah post and watched them as they dismounted.

Halt stepped towards the two steps leading up to the verandah, then paused.

'May we come in?' he said pointedly. Will's offhanded manner deserved some form of reproach.

'Of course.' Will stood aside and motioned for them to enter the cabin.

Halt took off his cloak and looked around the familiar space. He frowned slightly. There were unwashed dishes on the kitchen bench and two of the chairs were pulled out from the plain pine table, sitting at random angles. The fireplace was full of dead ashes and needed a good clean-out. Will's cloak was tossed carelessly over the back of one of the armchairs that flanked the fireplace. Looking through the open door into Will's bedroom, formerly his own, Halt could see that the bed was unmade.

Will noticed the direction of his gaze and moved to close the bedroom door.

'Haven't got round to cleaning up today,' he mumbled.

Halt raised an eyebrow. 'Or yesterday, apparently.' At least, he thought, his former apprentice had the grace to look a little embarrassed.

'Sit down,' Will said, turning towards the small kitchen alcove. 'I'll make some coffee.'

Halt and Gilan exchanged a glance as they sat in the armchairs by the fire. Gilan shook his head sadly. Obviously, Halt thought, their minds were running along similar lines.

Will adjusted the draught on the pot belly stove in the kitchen then opened the firebox door and tossed in a few small sticks to get the flames going properly. He shook the kettle. There was a vague splashing sound.

'I'll get some water,' he said and headed for the door. The pump was in the yard outside. Again his friends exchanged a look. Normal routine would be to fetch fresh water first thing in the morning.

'He just doesn't seem to care about anything,' Gilan said once Will was outside.

Halt nodded, his brows coming together in a frown. 'Then it's up to us to shake him out of it.'

The door opened and Will returned with the full kettle. He set it on the hotplate, then busied himself getting cups, coffee and the coffee pot ready.

'I know why you're here,' he said.

Halt shrugged. 'Maybe you don't,' he replied.

'You're going to tell me to snap out of it and pull myself together,' Will said. 'Well, I'm sorry the place is a mess. I'm sorry I'm a mess.' Now that he mentioned the fact, Halt noticed that his clothes were crumpled and stained and his hair and beard were long and uncut. 'But I don't care about all that. All I care about is seeing Jory Ruhl on the end of a noose.'

'I can understand that,' Gilan said. 'But the Corps needs you.'

'The Corps may just have to do without me until I'm ready,' Will said petulantly. 'I have more important matters to attend to.'

Ten

There was a moment of silence in the cabin, then Halt rose slowly to his feet, his eyes blazing with anger. He pointed a finger at his former apprentice. When he spoke, his voice was barely above a whisper. But it was no less intense for all that.

'How *dare* you say that!' he spat. 'How dare you turn your back on the Corps the moment you have some personal grief in your life? I didn't spend years training you and caring about you, and watching you grow into a man I was proud of, to see you crumble like this! You took an oath when you joined the Corps. I know it meant something to you then. Does it mean nothing to you now?'

Will made an awkward gesture. 'No. I . . . I just . . .'

'Will, I'm sorry Alyss is gone. I really am. I loved her, you know. We all did.'

'Not as much as I did,' Will said bitterly.

Halt nodded. 'No. The hurt is deeper for you. And it will be harder to bear. But you can bear it. You must bear it. You have to move on.'

Will faced him angrily. 'D'you expect me to just forget about her?'

'No! I expect you to remember her always. And to cherish and honour that memory. But honouring her memory doesn't mean eating yourself up with this obsession for revenge until there's no room for anything else in your life. It's destroying you, Will.'

'Just let me find Ruhl,' Will said, a pleading note in his voice. 'Let me find him and bring him to trial and then I'll be glad to get back to being a Ranger again.'

'It doesn't work that way,' Gilan said angrily. 'You're a Ranger and you have your duties to attend to as a Ranger. We all do. You can't put them aside to suit yourself, then take them up again when you feel like it.

'You are one of the rare people who can make a difference to this world. You're a leader. You're a hero to thousands of ordinary people. They look up to you and respect you. You give them hope and something to believe in. How dare you reject that responsibility? How dare you throw their respect for you back in their faces?'

'Maybe I don't care about them,' Will said, his voice low.

'Then you're not the person I taught about honour and duty,' Halt threw at him and Will flushed.

'You're needed, Will,' Gilan said softly, the anger dissipated now. 'The Corps needs you and your friends need you.'

'What friends?' Will asked.

'Horace and Evanlyn,' Halt told him. 'Your oldest friends in the world. The man you've fought beside countless times. And the girl who faced danger with you — who refused to abandon you when the Skandians captured you at the Rift, and when the Temujai overran your position in Skandia. They're asking for your help. Are you going to refuse them — while you skulk in a corner feeling sorry for yourself?'

'They need me?' Will said uncertainly. 'What's wrong?'

'It's Maddie. Your goddaughter. She's constantly getting into trouble. She's running wild and driving them crazy. They're worried about her and they can't find a way to bring her into control. They think you might be able to.'

Will frowned. 'Me? What can I do? If they can't handle her, how do they expect me to do it?'

'They want you to train her as an apprentice,' Gilan said.

Will actually recoiled in shock at those words. 'Maddie? A girl?'

'Maddie. A girl,' Halt repeated. He reached inside his jerkin and produced a linen envelope, holding it out to Will. 'They've written to you, asking for your help.'

Will took the envelope distractedly. His mind was whirling at high speed. A girl apprentice? There had never been such a thing, he thought. Then he wondered, why not? All his life he had been open to new ideas, new thinking. Why not this? Evanlyn would have made a superb Ranger, he thought. She was brave and quick-witted and intelligent. And her daughter was the same. He glanced down at the envelope again, seeing Evanlyn's seal in the red wax that fastened it.

'I'll give you my answer tomorrow,' he said.

Later that night, Will slit open the envelope that held the letter from Horace and Cassandra.

There was a separate inclusion in the letter, but it was marked to be read second. As he studied the words before him, his heart went out to his friends. It was a short letter, but none the less poignant for its brevity.

Will,
Horace and I are in desperate need of your help. Madelyn has become almost uncontrollable and wilful — and, in spite of all our best efforts, we are at our wits' end as to what to do about her.

Madelyn, as you know, will inherit the throne one day and she needs to begin learning the discipline and responsibilities that will go with that role. But she refuses to listen to either Horace or myself. She suits herself, running off into the forest at night, putting herself at risk while she does so.

In addition, of course, she puts the Kingdom at risk. If she were to be captured or kidnapped, Horace and I would be placed in an untenable position. If she were taken by enemies of the state, we would have to choose between the welfare of our daughter and our country. We have tried to explain this but she shrugs off the possibility, laughing at what she sees to be our excessive caution.

I've tried everything to discipline her and bring her under control, but my efforts have been in vain. She insists on defying me and Horace and, living here in Castle Araluen, she's surrounded by people whom she can all too easily bend to her will. Some of these subordinates are in honest awe of her position.

Others, we fear, could be sowing the seeds for favourable consideration in the future.

Whichever reason is the case, we're watching our daughter turn into an undisciplined, self-indulgent rebel. She must learn that her privileged life also brings with it responsibilities and duties.

As we've discussed this problem, we have come to the conclusion that drastic measures are required. Maddie needs to be removed from the privileged atmosphere of life at court and made to understand the realities of this world. At the same time, she must learn the skills and self-discipline that she will need as a future ruler.

Talking about this, Horace and I have agreed that you may well be the best person to help her — and us. You love Maddie, and so do we. Just as important, she loves you and respects you. You have a special relationship with her that may well snap her out of this behaviour. People tell us it's a phase and most teenagers go through this state of rebellion against their parents. In time, she may come through it herself. But we live in uncertain times. My father is ill, as you know, and I have taken over the responsibility of running the Kingdom in his place. If anything were to happen to me, she would have to take over and, frankly, I worry that she wouldn't be up to the challenge.

Teach her, Will. Take her under your wing and teach her how to be strong and responsible and brave. She has the potential to be all these things but she needs guidance. For the sake of our long friendship, I ask you to provide it.

Evanlyn (Cassandra)

Beneath the words penned by Cassandra, Horace had added a brief note of his own.

> *Will,*
> *Please agree to our request. Cassandra won't admit it,*
> *but the strain of ruling the Kingdom is too heavy. She*
> *can't cope with the extra tension of Maddie's behaviour*
> *at the same time. I worry for her health and wellbeing,*
> *as well as that of our daughter.*
> *I would do this if I could. But I've tried and*
> *failed. Perhaps when Maddie was younger, we made*
> *the mistake of overindulging her. It's an easy trap*
> *to fall into with an only child. Now she needs an*
> *outside hand — from a person she trusts and respects.*
> *I can think of no person more suited to that task*
> *than you.*
> *If you read the extra document we've included, you*
> *will realise how seriously we view this whole affair.*
> *Use it if you must. I fear you may well have to.*
> *Over the years, you've stood by me more times than*
> *I can count. I beg you to do so one more time.*
> *Horace*

Will folded the letter and tapped it thoughtfully against his palm. Then he opened the second document. It was short and to the point — only a few paragraphs in length. But his eyes widened in surprise. Then he re-folded it and leaned back in his chair, thinking.

Gilan had tried to stir him from his obsession with revenge against Jory Ruhl and his gang. He had used words like 'duty' and 'obligation'. They were abstract terms and they paled into insignificance in the light of the heart-wrenching hurt of Alyss's death.

But this was something far more tangible and immediate. A plea for help from the two people whom he now loved most in the world — whom he had loved for years. He wavered, then asked himself the pivotal question.

'What would Alyss want me to do?'

He said the words aloud and, as ever, his dog Sable's head rose and her tail thumped once. He ignored her. He knew what Alyss would say if she were here.

She might consider the fact that, by agreeing to train Madelyn, he would be serving the Kingdom and helping secure its future. But even more important would be one overlying fact. He could almost hear her voice saying two words.

'They're friends.'

Old friends. Best friends. Friendships that had been tested in the fires of a dozen challenges. Two people who had stood by him and saved his life more times than he could count.

There was no question as to what his answer was going to be. This was a request he simply could not refuse.

Eleven

On the appointed day, Maddie arrived at Will's little cottage below Castle Redmont to begin her training.

She arrived on the correct day, but not at the correct hour. Will had expected her at the ninth hour of the morning. It was well after midday when she rode into the small clearing. By that stage, Will had given up waiting for her. For the first two hours, he sat expectantly on the verandah of the little cabin, staring down the narrow track among the trees where he knew she would appear.

Finally, with a muttered expression of disgust, he went back inside to read the latest sheaf of reports that had arrived that morning from Gilan. It was normal routine for all Rangers to study reports from other fiefs. But Will had an extra interest. He scanned the reports — gathered from Rangers all over the country and detailing local crimes and out-of-the-ordinary events — looking for any hint of activity that might indicate where Jory Ruhl had gone to ground.

He was engrossed in an account from Cordom Fief of a criminal ferry master who took on passengers to cross the Gadmun River, then robbed them, stripped them and forced them overboard to take their chances with the swift-running current. He set the report to one side, placing it in a leather folder that contained a thin sheaf of other reports that might relate to Jory Ruhl.

'Could be him,' he said to himself. 'Sort of thing he'd do.'

Sable, lying on the floor beside him, chin on her paws, opened her eyes and looked up at him expectantly, her tail swishing heavily. He shook his head. 'Just talking to myself,' he told her. 'Go back to sleep.'

Which she did, with remarkable speed.

A few minutes later, her eyes opened again and she turned her head towards the door. Shortly after she did so, Will heard Tug's quick neigh of warning from the stable. It was pitched low — a warning to Will, not the loud greeting Tug had issued to Abelard and Blaze when Halt and Gilan had come to visit. Tug's signal held no overtones of danger. He was merely reporting the presence of people approaching the cabin. Whether friend or foe, he had no idea.

Sable rose with a grunt, shook herself and headed for the door, head down, nose sniffing the ground before her. Will laid down the report, pushed back his chair and rose as well. He allowed Sable to slip through the door the moment the gap was wide enough. Then he stepped out onto the verandah, moving out of the shadow to stand at the edge of the boards, leaning against one of the support poles.

He was in time to see Maddie emerge from the trees and ride into the small clearing in front of the cabin. His right eyebrow went up in a question mark as he realised that she wasn't alone. Another girl, of a similar age, was riding a few paces behind her. But where Maddie was slightly built and graceful in her movements, the other girl was a little overweight and looked uncomfortable in the saddle.

There were other differences. Maddie rode a sand-coloured Arridan gelding. It had fine lines and slender limbs, and a proud, intelligent face. It carried itself with dignity, stepping short and placing its hooves delicately with each pace. The other girl's mount was a placid-looking mare. A little taller than Maddie's horse, it was heavy-boned and had none of the Arridan's grace or fluidity of movement.

Their clothes were different too. Maddie wore fine woollen breeches, with knee-high riding boots and a purple short-sleeved jacket made from fine glove-quality leather. It was cinched at the waist by a belt made of connected silver discs, and a long dagger hung at her side, in a worked leather scabbard.

She wore a waist-length cape as well, off-setting it one side and leaving her right arm and shoulder unencumbered, an affectation that had become popular among wealthy young cavalry officers in the past few years.

Her companion wore a plain green linen dress, with a serviceable, but unadorned, woollen cloak over it. She looked around her with curiosity and a little uncertainty, while Maddie carried herself with confidence and an air of familiarity.

Gorlog's breath, Will thought to himself. She's brought her maid with her.

And not just her maid. Trotting obediently behind the two riders was a bay pack horse. Short-legged and barrel-bodied, it was festooned with leather valises hanging from the horns of its pack saddle. It looked to be carrying more weight than either of the two saddle horses.

Will took a deep breath. His first instinct was to bellow a tirade of angry questions at Madelyn, beginning with *What do you think you're doing?* then moving on through *Who the blue blazes is this with you?* and finishing with *What have you packed for? A twelve-month grand tour round the country?*

Instead, he controlled himself, waiting until Madelyn registered his presence on the verandah. She smiled winningly.

'Hello, Uncle Will. I didn't notice you there. You Rangers certainly can move quietly when you want to, can't you? I'll look forward to learning more about that in the next few weeks.'

Will noted the time frame she mentioned. She has no idea how long this is going to take, he thought. She thinks she's going to spend a couple of weeks running round the forest and then go home.

He bit back the furious phrases that were forming in his mind.

'You're late,' he said in a quiet voice.

She looked a little surprised, then shrugged. 'Am I? I had no idea. I was told to get here today. I didn't know there was any special time.'

'There was. The ninth hour. It was in your orders from Gilan.'

Maddie frowned, still not showing too much remorse over her late arrival. 'Orders?' she said. She looked at her maid. 'Rose-Jean, did Commandant Gilan give you any orders for me?'

The other girl looked confused, and a little worried. If Maddie hadn't noticed Will's irate expression, her maid definitely had. She was, after all, a servant, and accustomed to being alert for signs of displeasure from her superiors.

'No, my lady. He —'

'He would have given them to *you*, Maddie,' Will interrupted roughly. 'A letter. In a thick linen envelope.'

'Oh . . . that?' Maddie said. She laughed. 'Yes. I got that. I thought it was just a farewell letter — a going-away card or something. I haven't read it yet.'

'Perhaps it might be a good idea if you did,' Will said. His voice was dangerously low. Maddie didn't notice, but Rose-Jean definitely did. Her worried expression became even more concerned.

'Oh, I'll do it later!' Maddie said easily. 'I'm sure you can fill me in on anything I need to know.'

'Well, one thing you need to know is that you were due here over three hours ago. Where have you been?'

Maddie still wasn't getting it. Her maid looked around, wishing she could shrink behind something for protection when the storm broke — as she knew it was going to. She had no idea why the grim, bearded Ranger was so furious. Her mistress had told her that they were off for a holiday in one of the provincial fiefs. But now she was sensing there was a lot more to it than that.

'We stopped at the castle to see Arald and Sandra,' Maddie said carelessly.

'*Baron* Arald and *Lady* Sandra,' Will corrected her, placing slight emphasis on the two titles.

Maddie shrugged, grinning. 'To you, maybe. To me they're Arald and Sandra.'

Will's fury mounted even further. He was beginning to understand what Evanlyn and Horace had been going through with their daughter. But he controlled himself with an effort, speaking very slowly and deliberately. He didn't want a confrontation here with Madelyn, especially in front of her maid. He knew that the servant would be embarrassed and uncomfortable if there was a scene.

'No. To you they are Baron Arald and Lady Sandra. And you'd better get used to it,' he said.

Maddie cocked her head at him, a puzzled smile on her face.

'Uncle Will, I've always called them Arald and Sandra. You probably don't understand that. But as princess, I outrank them.'

Will took a deep breath. He looked briefly at the servant girl and saw the tension in her posture. He let the breath out and then said in a reasonable tone: 'Maddie, dismount, would you, and step this way?' He indicated that he wanted her to join him on the verandah of the cabin. She nodded and dismounted smoothly, passing her bridle to the servant girl.

'Hold on to Sundancer for me, would you, Rose-Jean?' she said. Then she walked across the small clearing and stepped up onto the verandah. Will took her elbow and led her a few paces further away.

'I must say, Uncle Will, you are behaving quite strangely. I've never seen you this way,' Maddie said.

When they were out of the servant's earshot, Will said quietly, 'Maddie, there are several facts that you need to get used to. You are not here for a glorified holiday —'

'Oh, I know that!' she interrupted, with a dismissive gesture. 'Mother and Father have some crazy notion that I'm supposed to learn —'

'Be quiet!' Will snapped. As before, he kept his voice low but there was no mistaking the intensity of his tone. Madelyn actually recoiled a half pace. Nobody had ever spoken to her that way in her life. Well, perhaps her parents had, but certainly nobody of any lesser rank.

'Uncle Will —' she began haughtily, but Will made a chopping gesture with his right hand that cut her off before she could say any more.

'Forget *Uncle Will*. Whether you realise it or not, you are now a member of the Ranger Corps and I am your mentor. As Rangers, we refer to each other by our first names. So you will call me Will — nothing more than that. I am not your uncle. I am not your godfather. I am your mentor and your instructor. You are my pupil and my apprentice. I will call you Maddie or Madelyn. We have no special relationship other than mentor and apprentice. Do you understand?'

Now Maddie's brows came together in a stubborn knot and she glared at the grey-bearded figure before her.

'I think you're presuming a little here, Unc . . . Will,' she corrected herself. 'Let's not forget that I am the Royal Princess of Araluen.'

'And let's not forget that I am a King's Ranger,' Will said evenly. He saw the brief light of puzzlement in her eyes and elaborated. 'I answer only to the King, or his representative. Nobody else. In this case, that's your mother.

'Although we rarely make a point of it, technically, I outrank everyone but the King or his representative.

That means barons, their wives, knights . . . and royal princesses.'

'That can't be right!' Maddie protested. 'I've never heard of such a thing!'

'As I said, we don't often make a point of it. But you can believe that I am right. What's more, your mother and father have given me full authority over you while you're undergoing your training. So your rank here means nothing to me, or to anyone else.'

Maddie's confident air began to desert her. She knew that Rangers did wield enormous, and often undefined, power and authority in the Kingdom. And while she wasn't entirely sure that what Will had said was true, neither was she sure that it wasn't.

'Now,' Will continued, in a more conciliatory tone, 'you will be staying here with me during your training, not in the castle. But your maid will not. Rangers don't have maids. And Rangers' apprentices definitely don't have them.'

He left Maddie with her jaw hanging open and stepped back down the verandah to speak to Rose-Jean.

'Rose-Jean,' he said, 'Madelyn will be living here in the cabin while she trains as a Ranger. Unfortunately, as you can see, we're rather cramped for space. Would you mind riding back to the castle and telling the Baron's seneschal that you will need accommodation there until such time as we can have you escorted back to Castle Araluen?'

Rose-Jean looked to her mistress, not sure how to react. If she obeyed the Ranger, she knew she risked Madelyn's anger. But she also knew that no wise person disregarded the instructions of a Ranger — especially such a senior one as the famous Will Treaty. Will sensed her dilemma and stepped forward, taking the bridle to Maddie's horse from her unresisting hand.

'It's all right, Rose-Jean,' he said soothingly. 'Just ride up to the castle. There's a good girl.'

'Rose-Jean —' Maddie began.

'Be quiet!' Will snapped, without turning to look at her. Then he gestured for the servant girl to leave. Coming to a decision, Rose-Jean wheeled her horse and trotted back up the path towards the castle. The pack horse watched her go, uncertain whether to follow. Then, in the absence of any definite instructions, it lowered its head and began to crop the short grass at the edge of the clearing.

Will proffered Sundancer's bridle to a very surprised and deflated princess.

'Put your horse in the stable behind the cabin,' he said. 'I'll take care of your pack horse.'

Then, as Madelyn moved forward to take the bridle from his hand, he added, 'But this will be the last time I do.'

Twelve

Once the horses were settled in the stable, Will showed Madelyn the small room that would be hers. Remembering his own first day, he had placed a vase of bright wildflowers in the room, just as Halt had done for him, so many years before. But it was going to take more than a bunch of flowers to help Maddie recover from the state of shock and hurt that had overcome her upon her arrival.

She went into the room and shut the door behind her. In his day it had been no more than a curtain, but he had decided that Madelyn might need a more substantial form of privacy while she was with him and had asked Redmont's carpenters to fit the door before her arrival.

He looked at the closed door, wondering whether to summon her out of the room. But he decided that she'd had enough surprises for one day and let her have a few hours to mull things over.

He prepared dinner — a savoury stew of chicken and potatoes — and as darkness fell, he lit lanterns in the main room of the cabin, and prepared a fire.

The warm, yellow light of the lanterns and the flickering flames of the fire cast a cheerful aura round the room. When he felt she'd had enough time to brood, he rapped gently on the door.

'Maddie,' he said. 'Dinner.'

In her room, hunger competed against pride and hurt feelings. After several minutes, hunger won and the door opened. She emerged with as much dignity as she could muster, taking her seat at the table while he served her.

She ate hungrily, noting with surprise how delicious the meal was. She had no idea that Will could cook so well. But the mood between them was still strained, and their conversation was limited to necessities — such as the occasional request for salt or bread to be passed. When she finished, she rose from the table.

'I'm going to my room,' she said. For a moment, she had considered asking permission, but stubbornly discarded the idea.

Will met her gaze, seeing the anger still there. Give her time, he thought, and nodded assent.

'Good idea. Tomorrow will be a big day.'

Maddie lay wide awake on the small bed for hours, listening to the night sounds of the forest around her, and fighting back the tears that threatened to claim her. This was all so different to what she had thought it would be.

Will — her loving Uncle Will for so many years — was being grim and distant. His disapproval of her was obvious.

But why, she wondered. What had she done wrong?

In truth, although she wasn't aware of it herself, Madelyn's arrogance and bumptiousness stemmed from a feeling of inferiority and a lack of self-esteem.

Her parents were renowned throughout the Kingdom. Horace, her father, was the most skilled knight in Araluen, feared by enemies and respected by friends. He was a larger-than-life figure, a true hero.

And her mother was no less so. She was a princess, of course, and was currently ruling the Kingdom in her father's place. But she too had earned the approval and respect of her subjects. Her life had been packed full of adventure and achievement.

Against this, what had Maddie done? What could she hope to accomplish? The more she measured herself against her famous parents, the more she found herself lacking.

Tears threatened once more but she knuckled her eyes furiously, forcing them back and refusing to let them fall.

I won't cry, she told herself furiously, and eventually, with that thought uppermost in her mind, she fell into a restless sleep.

She awoke to the sound of Will quietly clattering pots and pans in the kitchen. For a moment, she had no idea where she was and she looked around the little room, trying to place herself. For the first time, she noticed the bright posy of flowers on the windowsill, and the neatly folded towel on the foot of her bed. Hanging on a peg on the back of the door was a towelling gown — a bathrobe, she guessed.

She rose and opened the door. Will, busy in the small kitchen alcove, heard her and turned.

'Sleep well?' he asked and she nodded. She looked around the small cabin, taking in details for the first time. The previous night, she had been too shocked and confused to notice much. Now she saw there was just one large central room, with a kitchen alcove, and another bedroom leading off from it. Will saw her puzzled expression.

'Wash house is at the back,' he said. 'Breakfast in ten minutes.'

She nodded again, uncertain as to how to respond. His tone and manner were not as grim as the previous night. She decided to keep her reaction neutral. She went back into her room, retrieved the towel and the gown, then headed out the door.

Will's border shepherd was sprawled in the early morning sunshine on the verandah. She thumped her tail in greeting and Maddie stopped to scratch her ears.

'Hello, girl,' she said. 'What's your name?'

Sable, of course, didn't reply. But she stretched her head back, eyes closed in pleasure, to allow Maddie to fondle her chin and the thick fur under her neck. Maddie gave her a final pat and rose. She looked around her, taking in the sight of the little clearing. It really was a beautiful spot, she decided. The sun was just beginning to show over the tops of the trees, and the air was fresh with the scent of early morning.

She washed under the rudimentary shower bath in the wash house, shivering as the cold water hit. Then she towelled herself briskly, donned the bathrobe and returned to the cabin. Back in her room, she hesitated, wondering what she should wear. She had discarded her clothes on the floor the previous night but, of course, Rose-Jean wasn't here to pick them up and fold them, and lay out fresh clothes for the day ahead. In fact, her clothes were all in the valises, which were still in the stable.

Finally, she decided she'd don the clothes she'd worn the previous day. Dressed, she went back out into the main room.

Will looked up, nodding a welcome. He was laying a plate on the table.

'I didn't know how you'd like your eggs,' he said. 'I scrambled them.'

She wrinkled her nose. 'I don't like eggs at all.'

Will took a deep breath. 'You don't like eggs,' he repeated. She shook her head. 'How about bacon?' He glanced towards the cooking stove, where another pan was spluttering cheerfully on the hotplate over the coals.

Again, she shook her head. It struck him that it was a fussy little gesture but he held his temper.

'We have a special air-cured ham that's made for us by a pork butcher at Castle Araluen,' Maddie said. 'It's so light and delicate. It just melts on your tongue. But bacon?' She shivered dramatically. 'Yuck!'

'Well, we don't have any air-cured ham. Maybe later we could go shopping in Wensley Village and pick up some larks' tongues instead?' Will suggested, the sarcasm heavy in his tone. She shook her head, ignoring it.

'I like fruit,' she said.

Will heaved a small sigh of relief. 'Fruit is good,' he said. He selected a large, shiny apple from a bowl on the kitchen

counter and placed it on a plate in front of her. She looked
at it uncertainly.

'Apples aren't fruit?' Will asked.

Maddie made a small gesture. 'Well, usually, the servants peel it and slice it for me,' she said.

There was a long silence. They looked at each other.
She could sense that, once again, she had annoyed him.
Suddenly, he moved, taking the apple off the plate and
setting it on the rough wood of the table top.

There was a hiss of steel on leather as his saxe knife
leapt from its scabbard at his side. Then he brought it
down with a resounding *clunk*, chopping the apple into two
halves that oscillated gently on the table.

'Consider it sliced,' he told her.

Breakfast continued in a strained silence. Will, relenting
somewhat, produced a fresh loaf of bread, along with
butter and conserves made from raspberries. The conserve
had been a gift to him from Jenny and it was his favourite.
He wondered wryly why he was giving some of it to
Maddie.

She ate it with relish, realising how hungry she had
been. Will, for his part, ate the scrambled eggs and bacon
that he had prepared earlier. As Maddie finished her bread
and jam, he reached behind him to the coffee pot steaming
on the stove hotplate. Coffee would set everything right,
he thought. Nobody could maintain a sulk when they had
a cup of hot, sweet coffee before them.

'Coffee?' he said, already beginning to pour some of the
fragrant liquid into her cup.

'I don't drink coffee,' she told him.

Will's eyebrows arched in surprise. 'Why not?' he asked her. 'Everyone drinks coffee.'

'Not me. I don't like the taste. I'd prefer milk if you have it . . . please,' she added, after a pause.

He accepted that the last word was a major concession on her part. There was a jug of fresh milk cooling under a damp cloth. He fetched it and poured it for her, shaking his head as he watched the creamy white liquid filling her cup.

'How do they expect me to make a Ranger out of you?' he muttered.

She wasn't sure how she should answer that. Wisely, she remained silent. But the milk *was* good, she thought.

After breakfast, Will sipped his second cup of coffee. Perhaps there was something to be said for her not drinking the beverage, he thought, if it left extra in the pot for him. Maddie finished her milk and picked up all the stray crust and bread crumbs from her plate.

'That's excellent bread,' she said. 'Did you make it too?' She wasn't sure how far his cooking skills stretched. But he shook his head.

'There's a baker in Wensley who brings it over each morning. Actually, in the future, you can go fetch it and save him a trip. That can be one of your we-don't-have-a-maid duties.'

She sensed he was testing her and refused to rise to the bait. She simply nodded and he went on.

'In addition, you'll make your bed and tidy your room each morning before breakfast.'

He cast a meaningful look at her room, where the bed-clothes were still tumbled and twisted.

'Make my bed? I don't —'

'Yes, you do. Or did you assume the maid would be doing that for you?'

She set her jaw angrily. 'Well, I don't see why we should live like peasants,' she said. 'Rose-Jean could easily come down here each day and —'

'Rose-Jean is gone,' he told her.

For a moment she didn't comprehend. 'Gone? Gone where?'

'Back to Castle Araluen. There was a mail courier wagon leaving earlier this morning and I arranged for her to go with it. Couldn't have her stumbling around the countryside on her own, could we?'

'But . . . she was my maid. You had no right to . . .' She stopped, seeing the hard light in his eyes.

'Maddie, please understand, I have every right. She was your maid when you were the princess. Now you're a Ranger's apprentice. And Rangers don't have maids. I think I mentioned that.'

Will felt a grim twist of amusement as he recalled a similar conversation with Halt in his first few days as an apprentice. *What Ranger's apprentices do is the housework*, he remembered Halt telling him.

'In addition,' he added, 'you'll sweep this room each day after breakfast, and clean out the fireplace and stove firebox. And every Friday, you can take the rug outside and beat the dust out of it.'

She glared at him, eyes slitted. He pretended not to notice for a few seconds, then raised his eyebrows in a question.

'Did you have something to say?' he asked.

She answered very deliberately. 'May I enquire, who performed these tasks before I arrived?'

Will nodded as if the question was a good one. 'Actually, I did,' he told her. 'I can see now why Halt enjoyed having apprentices. Should have taken one on long ago myself.'

She said nothing, but rose and made her way into her room, making her bed in a series of brisk, angry movements. When she was finished, she looked around the room and saw that there was only one small curtained-off area for clothes storage. It wouldn't fit one-tenth of the clothes she'd brought with her.

'Where am I going to keep my clothes?' she demanded.

Will put his head round the door and gestured to the small curtained area. 'That should do you,' he told her.

She shook her head and gave a hollow laugh. 'That little space will barely fit any of the clothes I brought with me.'

Will waved a hand airily.

'Oh, don't worry about them,' he said. 'They're already on their way back to Castle Araluen with Rose-Jean.'

Thirteen

'Are you sure you're not being too hard on her?' Jenny asked.

Will considered the question for a moment, then shook his head.

'I think I have to be tough, Jen,' he said. 'She's spoiled and wilful and arrogant, and I'm going to need to shake that out of her if I'm to make a go of it.'

They were sitting under an awning in the outdoor eating area at the front of Jenny's restaurant. She gave him an appraising look, then nodded.

'Maybe. But don't overdo it, will you? I'm sure she's not a bad kid at heart.'

'Well, I'm trying to remember how Halt treated me,' Will said, 'and I'm being guided by that.'

'You said at the time that he treated you horribly,' she said with a smile. 'And you weren't even a princess.'

'Neither is she now. And that's what I have to remember. She's my apprentice and she has no more rights or privileges than any other apprentice. She gets no special treatment.'

'Just make sure that while you're not giving her any special treatment you're not leaning too far in the other direction,' Jenny warned him. 'Where is she now, by the way?'

'She's with Mistress Buttersby, being fitted for her uniforms,' Will said, jerking a thumb down the high street. 'At least, Mistress Buttersby is showing her how to alter the clothes so they fit. Maddie's going to have to do the job herself. She could be some time,' he added wryly.

Jenny looked at him. It was the first trace of humour she'd seen from her old friend for months. But she was wise enough not to mention it. She filed the thought away. She'd share it with Gilan when next he visited Redmont Fief — something he did more than was strictly necessary. She knew how much Will was hurting over the loss of Alyss and she thought it was a stroke of genius to assign Maddie to him as an apprentice. She glanced along the high street and pointed.

'Looks like she's coming now.'

Maddie was trudging up the shallow hill towards them, her arms encumbered with a pile of garments. Draped awkwardly over her shoulder was a familiar item — the mottled grey and green cloak that was standard wear for all Rangers and their apprentices.

'She looks a little overwhelmed,' Jenny added, smiling, as Maddie managed to drop a pair of boots and a leather vest into the dust. As she bent to retrieve them, she spilled more garments. She'd received three uniforms — woollen shirts and breeches, the leather jerkin and two pairs of boots — along with the cloak, and the mass of clothes was proving hard to manage.

'It's been an overwhelming day,' Will said. But he made no attempt to rise and move to her assistance. As Maddie came closer, boots, shirts and breeches balanced precariously, Jenny took pity and stood to move quickly to her side.

'Let me help,' she said. Maddie looked up gratefully and relinquished half the load. She followed Jenny into the restaurant and dropped the remaining bundle on a nearby table.

'She gave me the smallest sizes she had, but they're all way too big,' she said a little breathlessly.

Jenny smiled. 'Not surprising. After all, you're the first girl Ranger.'

'Did she show you how to take them in?' Will asked.

Maddie nodded. 'It's going to take me hours to get them all done.'

'Well, you only need one set for starters. That shouldn't take too long. You can get that done this evening after dinner,' Will told her. He wasn't sure if she'd been looking for sympathy, but if she had, she wasn't getting any from him.

Jenny and Will had been drinking pressed fruit juice. She signed to her waiter now to bring a third glass for Maddie, who accepted it eagerly and took a deep sip.

'Aaaah. That's lovely. Thanks,' Maddie said.

'It must be all very different and confusing for you,' Jenny said kindly. 'I hope Will isn't being too mean to you, Maddie. I'm Jenny, by the way.'

She held out her hand, smiling. Maddie regarded it uncertainly for a moment. She'd more or less come to terms with the strange relationship that now existed between her and Will. After all, as he'd pointed out, he was a senior officer of the realm and technically outranked her. But Jenny was different. Jenny was a commoner. She was a cook — really with no greater status than a servant at Castle Araluen might enjoy. Maddie wasn't sure that first-name terms were quite proper between them.

But Jenny had been friendly and welcoming, and Maddie didn't want to upset her. She tried to be tactful. Like most fifteen-year-olds aiming for tact, she was a long way wide of the mark.

'Um . . . I'm not sure that it's proper for you to call me Maddie,' she said apologetically. 'Really, you should call me "princess" or "your highness".'

Jenny's smile faded and she withdrew her hand. Will's face clouded with fury at Maddie's words. Jenny rose and said coldly, 'I'll bear it in mind.' She nodded briefly to Will. 'I'll see you later, Will. I've got work to do.'

She walked into the restaurant, her back straight. Maddie looked at Will helplessly and spread her hands in a defeated gesture.

'What? What did I do wrong now? I understand how it is between you and me. But do I have to let everybody speak to me as if I'm a nobody? After all, she's just a cook.'

'Jenny is one of your father's oldest friends. And mine. We all grew up together. And she's known your mother for years. If your mother feels it's all right for Jenny to call her by her first name, I don't see why you should be different.'

'But things were different back then. After all, when my mother met you all, she was travelling incognito. It would have been pointless for you to use her title. But I'm not. I'm —'

'You're a spoilt and arrogant brat who needs to be taught a lesson. I'd hoped it wouldn't come to this, but apparently it has. Follow me.'

He stood abruptly and swept out of the restaurant. Maddie went to follow, juggling boots, jerkin and shirts once more in a jumbled pile.

'And don't drop anything!' he snapped back at her.

She followed his fast-striding figure up the high street and along the woodland path that led to the cabin. Once there, Will slammed the door open and made his way to the desk against the far wall, rummaging through the papers there until he found what he was looking for.

She stumbled in after him, shedding items of uniform across the verandah and the living room. She paused uncertainly as he turned to face her, an envelope in his hand. He unfolded the single sheet of parchment, then held it out for her.

'Read this,' he said.

She read the first few words on the sheet and started with shock at their content. She glanced quickly to the bottom of the page and saw her mother's signature, and her father's, written above their individual seals. There was no doubt. This document was genuine. She went back to the top of the page and read on, feeling the blood drain from her face.

Let it be known that we, the undersigned, hereby renounce all ties with our daughter, Madelyn, and revoke all her titles and privileges as a princess of the realm of Araluen.

She is disinherited as a princess and as our daughter and is to be accorded no privilege or respect

*formerly due to her as a member of the royal family of
Araluen.*

*Until any further notice, she is to be known and
addressed simply as Mistress Madelyn Altman, or,
pending the agreement of Ranger Will Treaty to act as
her mentor, by the alternative title of Ranger's
apprentice Madelyn.*

*This is to take effect immediately, as of the date of
this proclamation, and will continue indefinitely until
such time as we may decide to reinstate Madelyn to her
former position.*

Given under our joint names and seals,
HRH Cassandra,
*Princess Regent of the Kingdom of Araluen and
    all its territories*
Sir Horace Altman,
Premier Knight of the Realm,
Royal Champion

The signatures were scrawled alongside the wax seals.
Maddie looked at the date. The order had been written the
day before she had left Castle Araluen to ride to Redmont.
All the time she had been on the road, she realised, she had
been disinherited — a common nobody. Her eyes filled
with tears.

'How could they do this?' she asked, her voice breaking. 'Do they really hate me so much?'

Will shook his head. 'They don't hate you. They're
simply at the end of their tether. They thought I might
need to have this document to make you understand how
serious this whole thing is. I was hoping I wouldn't have to
show it to you. But you made it necessary.

'I've been telling you, Maddie. You are no longer a princess. And you can no longer behave as if you are. You are my apprentice. You are no better than anyone else here in Redmont — not Jenny, not the stable boy at the castle, not the youngest of the Battleschool apprentices.

'On the other hand, you are no worse than any of those people, either. You're an equal among equals.'

Maddie frowned. 'But you said Rangers are among the highest ranking officers in the Kingdom . . .' she began uncertainly.

'Rangers are. Their apprentices are not. And you're not officially an apprentice yet. You'll have that as a courtesy title. But you will train for twelve months before you're assessed and accepted into the Corps.'

'Twelve months?' She was aghast at the prospect. 'Twelve months? I thought —'

'You thought this would all be over in a week or two. Then you'd ride back home, say you're sorry and convince your parents that you've seen the error of your ways and all would be forgiven. Right?'

'Well . . . yes. I suppose so,' she said. She realised how bad it sounded when he said it like that. She also realised that that was exactly how things had gone at least half a dozen times in the past. Her parents would punish her, she'd serve out the time for a day or a week, then apologise abjectly and things would go back to normal. And a few weeks later, she'd be back to her old bad behaviour.

'You've done it once too often, Maddie,' Will told her seriously. 'Cassandra and Horace have finally had enough. Whether you like it or not, I'm your only hope now.'

Her lip started to quiver and she felt a tear forming in

her eye. He noticed it but gave no sign that he had. She'd had a shock, he knew, perhaps the biggest shock of her young life. And now was not the time to let her brood on it.

He pointed to the items of uniform, scattered around the room.

'Gather this lot up,' he said. 'Find the best-fitting items. Just shirt, breeches and boots. No need for the cloak. Lace the boots up tight and be outside in five minutes.'

'Outside?' she said, stunned by the sudden change of subject. 'What . . .?'

'We're going for a run. I want to see how fit you are. Five minutes!'

Without waiting for a reply, he strode out of the door, banging it behind him. She heard his boots on the verandah as he headed for the stable at the rear of the cabin, heard Tug call a brief whinny of greeting to his master.

Then she realised that time was wasting and she still had to sort out the best-fitting items of her new clothing. Scrambling to gather them together, she dashed into her room.

She emerged some minutes later. Whether she had gone over her time limit or not she had no idea. But at least Will didn't comment. He was sitting astride Tug, waiting in the small clearing before the cabin.

'You're not running?' she asked.

He raised an eyebrow. 'I know how fit I am,' he said. 'I'll ride. You'll run. We're going to Foxtail Creek. It's a little settlement eight kilometres from here. Just a nice stroll there and back again.'

He indicated a path leading off through the trees. 'Get going.'

She set off through the trees, head back, arms swinging, legs pumping. She ran smoothly and evenly, setting a good pace. Her stride was balanced and light. Will edged Tug along behind her. The little horse twitched his ears quizzically.

How did she take it?

'Take what?' he asked. Maddie heard his soft comment and turned curiously. He waved her on. 'Keep going.'

Being disinherited. How did she handle it?

'How do you know about that?' This time, Will kept his voice low, so that it was almost inaudible.

I've told you. If you know it, I know it.

Not for the first time in his career, Will wondered whether his horse was actually talking to him, or whether he was simply talking to himself. He decided he didn't want to know the answer to that.

'Well, she wasn't thrilled,' he replied. Then he raised his voice. 'Walk for three hundred paces. Then run again,' he called.

Maddie nodded, without looking back. She slowed to a brisk walk, then, as she reached the three-hundred count, she began to run again. Will saw her shoulders go back and her head come up. There was a determined set to her body. He nodded approvingly.

'She's fit enough,' he said. 'And she's got some of her mother's steel in her.'

Tug rattled his short mane. *I knew she would have.*

'Oh really? And how did you know?'

I'm a Ranger horse. We understand good breeding.

And really, there wasn't a lot Will could say in answer to that.

Fourteen

Will awoke the following morning to the smell of bacon frying.

He frowned, sniffed the air experimentally and confirmed the fact. That was definitely bacon frying. His empty stomach rumbled in anticipation. He swung his legs out of bed, dressed hurriedly and opened the door into the main room of the cabin.

Maddie was standing expectantly by the stove, a frying pan in one hand and a large fork in the other. She smiled as he entered, rubbing the drowsiness from his eyes, smoothing his dishevelled hair.

'I made breakfast,' she announced. 'I didn't know how to scramble the eggs, so I fried them.' She waved him to a seat at the table.

'Well, this is a surprise,' he said, and she placed a laden plate before him. The surprise increased as he looked at the bacon, fried to within an inch of its life and reduced to flint-hard strips.

The eggs were not much better — she had burnt the bottoms and the yolks were hard and dried out. He looked at them uncertainly, then picked up his knife and fork, determined to eat them.

She had tried, he thought. She might not have succeeded but she had tried, and he saw the sentiment behind the gesture. It was her way of apologising, and a more meaningful way — if a not completely edible way — than simply uttering the words.

He put his fork into one of the strips of bacon and it promptly disintegrated into a mass of sharp little shards. Maddie was watching carefully, so he picked up several of them and put them in his mouth, sucking on them to soften them.

'Is it all right?' she asked. 'I've never cooked bacon before.'

'Remarkable,' he mumbled, past the splinters of bacon that filled his mouth. 'A very commendable first effort.'

He swallowed the bacon with some difficulty, then tried the hard, crisp-bottomed eggs. The flavour of burnt egg-white filled his mouth. He chewed and swallowed.

'I wasn't sure about those black bits on the bottom,' she said anxiously.

'They add flavour,' Will told her. He saw that she'd already collected the day's fresh loaf from the bakery. He hurriedly tore off a piece, slapped butter on it and wolfed it down. He put more butter on the hard egg yolks. At least that would soften them a little.

Maddie took a seat opposite him and he looked enviously at the plate of fruit before her — an apple and some plump, juicy strawberries. She also had a thick slice of buttered bread and jam. She took a deep draught of milk and a bite of bread and jam. He realised his own mouth was dry and clogged with the taste of burnt food.

He looked around for the water jug and a glass, but as he reached for it, she forestalled him.

'I made coffee,' she said.

Now that was a surprise. He'd detected no trace of the rich, fragrant aroma of fresh-brewed coffee. Although now she mentioned it, he was aware of a faint scent in the kitchen.

His old coffee pot was sitting on the stove hotplate, steam wisping from its spout. She picked it up, protecting her hand from the hot handle with a kitchen cloth, placed a mug before him and poured.

A thin stream of slightly discoloured hot water emanated from the pot into his mug. They both stared at it. Whatever it was, Will thought, it wasn't coffee. Maddie frowned as she realised the same thing.

'That doesn't look right,' she said doubtfully. 'I'm sure I did it correctly.'

'What did you do?' he asked, picking up the cup and inspecting the faintly brown liquid inside it. He sniffed it. There was a definite scent of coffee there. It was faint. But it was there.

'I filled the pot with cold water, set it to boil on the stove plate. Then, when it was boiling, I spooned in the coffee — three big spoonfuls. I thought that would be enough.'

'It should have been,' he said absently. Three spoonfuls should have produced a rich, dark brew. Not this insipid coffee impostor that confronted him. A thought struck him.

'Where did you get the coffee from?' he asked, thinking she might have reused old grounds. But she gestured to the pottery jar on the top shelf in the kitchen where he kept his coffee beans.

'From there. Where I've seen you get it.'

Realisation was beginning to dawn on Will. 'And you just . . . put three spoonfuls into the pot?'

She nodded.

'You didn't think to grind it first?' he asked gently.

Maddie frowned, not comprehending what he was saying. 'Grind it?'

'Grind it. Usually I grind the beans into powder. That releases the coffee flavour, you see.'

She was still holding the pot. He took it from her and hinged the lid back, peering inside. Once the initial cloud of steam had dissipated, he could see a raft of little round brown shapes floating on top of the water.

He started to laugh. He couldn't help it and, the moment he started, he knew it was a mistake. He forced himself to stop, but the damage was done. Maddie watched him, her face stricken, as she realised how badly she'd failed. She had wanted to cook him a good break-fast by way of saying 'let's start again'. But all she'd succeeded in doing was ruining his coffee. She now began to suspect that the bacon and eggs weren't exactly right either.

Will covered his mouth, forcing the laughter back.

'I'm sorry,' he said contritely, although he could see the disappointment in her face. He could see the way her chin was set and her lips were pressed together as she willed herself not to cry.

'I ruined it, didn't I?' she said. 'Not just the coffee, but the rest of it as well.'

'Let me put it this way . . . it's not the best. Eating the bacon is a little like chewing shards of pottery. And the eggs deserved a better fate.'

She dropped her gaze, totally crestfallen. She hated to fail.

'But I shouldn't have laughed,' he continued, in a gentler tone. 'You tried and it was a nice thought. Nobody's made me breakfast in months.'

'I'll bet nobody has ever made you a breakfast like that,' she said, her eyes down.

'I can't say they have. But how can I expect you to get it right the first time? Have you ever cooked eggs and bacon before?'

She shook her head, not trusting herself to speak. In her mind, she had seen Will coming to the table, surprised and delighted, wolfing down the meal and sipping contentedly at his coffee. It was to have been her way of apologising for her behaviour with Jenny — behaviour that even now made her cringe as she thought of it.

And now this . . . this unmitigated disaster. She felt Will's hand on her shoulder and she looked up. His eyes were very warm and gentle — like those of the Uncle Will she had known as a little girl.

'Maddie, you made the effort and that's the main thing. And while you might not have given me the world's best breakfast, you did something else for me — something far more important.'

She cocked her head to one side curiously. 'What?'

'You made me laugh. And nobody's done that in a long time.'

After breakfast — in Will's case a hastily revised one of bread, some slices of a ham hanging in the larder and a cup of properly brewed coffee — they stepped out into the small clearing in front of the cabin for Maddie's first session with the weapons she would be using for the next twelve months.

She watched eagerly as Will unrolled an oilskin to reveal them. He selected the double scabbard mounted on a thick leather belt first.

She had seen the peculiar double rig worn by Rangers before, of course. But she'd never had occasion to inspect the two knives that it held.

The saxe was first. It was the larger of the two, almost the length of a short sword. She'd had a saxe for some years, of course, but it was lighter and shorter than this. This was a Ranger's everyday weapon for close fighting — heavy-bladed and razor-sharp. She rested her forefinger lightly on the blade, testing the edge.

'It's sharp,' Will said, watching approvingly as she treated the weapon with respect and care. 'And it'll be up to you to keep it that way. If I ever inspect it and find traces of rust or a dull edge, you'll be running back and forth to Foxtail Creek for the rest of the week.'

She nodded dutifully. The saxe was a plain-looking weapon. It was unadorned and unornamented, made from plain steel and leather with a brass pommel and crosspiece. But as she held it, she felt the perfect balance in the weapon that made it feel light and easy to wield — in spite of the fact that the thick blade gave it considerable weight. She sensed that it had been made by a master craftsman and Will's next words proved her right.

'Our saxes are specially made for us,' he said. 'The steel is treated and worked so that it's tremendously hard. Parry a sword stroke with one of these and you'll leave a notch in the sword — while there'll barely be a mark on the saxe. Except your father's sword, of course,' he added.

She looked at him curiously, all the while working the blade of the saxe back and forth, getting the feel of it. 'My dad's sword? What about it?'

'It was crafted for him by the swordsmiths of Nihon-Ja. They use a similar technique to our weapon makers. Horace's sword is a masterpiece. It's harder and sharper than any blade in Araluen or the continent.'

'I didn't know that,' she said. Her father had never mentioned it to her.

Will dismissed the subject, gesturing for her to re-sheathe the saxe. She did so and he drew the smaller knife from its scabbard.

The blade was around twenty centimetres long. It was narrow where it joined the hilt, but widened rapidly, then angled in sharply to form a razor-sharp point. The tapering shape of the blade added weight at the point, which was balanced by the weight of the hilt — constructed of leather discs and with a small brass crosspiece. Again there was a brass pommel at the end of the hilt.

'You'll be learning to throw this,' he told her.

She pursed her lips. 'I've never thrown a knife,' she admitted.

Will shrugged. 'The principle is simple enough. You throw it so that it spins in the air just enough for the point to be facing the target when it reaches it. The further the target, the more times you spin it.'

He showed her how to vary the rate of spin by holding the blade further up or closer to the tip.

'Close to the tip and it's going to spin faster. Set your grip further up the blade towards the hilt and it'll turn more slowly through the air,' he said. She nodded, trying the different positions, miming throwing the knife. She could feel how the position close to the point would impart greater spin on the blade.

'That doesn't sound too easy,' she said doubtfully and he nodded at her.

'It's not. I said the principle was simple. The practice is definitely something else. Like everything a Ranger does, it requires practice, practice and . . .' He paused, raising an eyebrow for her to complete the statement.

'More practice?' she asked.

'Got it in one. That's the secret of most of our skills. When it comes down to it, throwing a knife is like cooking a perfect egg. The more you do it, the better you get — although the techniques are quite different.'

She replaced the throwing knife in its sheath. She weighed the double scabbard in her hand for a few moments, admiring the matched look of the two weapons and the plain, practical design. Deceptively plain, because, having examined them, she now knew that hours of painstaking, expert work had gone into their construction.

She set the knives down and looked expectantly at the oilskin wrap. There was another item hidden in its folds, a longer, slender item. And she thought she knew what it was.

'What's next?' she asked. She tried to keep her voice neutral, but Will heard the tone of expectancy in it. She was enjoying this session. She was interested in weapons. That was no surprise, considering her penchant for hunting. But that interest was a good thing and it would serve her well in the months to come, during the constant, repetitive actions of practice. A person needed that core of interest to keep practising and keep improving.

'What's next is our principal weapon,' he said. 'The bow.'

Fifteen

Her eyes were riveted on the bow as he unwrapped it. She frowned. It was like no other bow she had ever seen.

To begin with, it was short, perhaps only two-thirds the length of a normal longbow. And the shape was bizarre, to say the least. The centre section, comprising approximately two-thirds of its overall length, was a thick, dark piece of wood, with little apparent curve. In the centre of that was a grip made of soft leather, padded and shaped to fit the hand. But at either end, two spurs of wood were set, so that they stood out an angle to the front of the bow — projecting forward.

Will handed the weapon to her and she examined it closely. The two reverse spurs had been carefully shaped to fit flush to the ends of the centre section — which had also been carefully planed and angled. They had obviously been glued into place, then bound tightly with cord, which had been reinforced with more glue and several layers of varnish to prevent fraying.

At first glance, it seemed that the bow, which formed a wide, flattened W-shape, should be strung simply from one spur to the other, bending the bow into something that resembled the continuous curve of a normal longbow or shortbow. But as she looked more carefully, she could see the notches that would hold the string in place were shaped so that the bow would have to be bent back away from the direction of the two spurs. That way, she could see, the centre section of the bow would form one curve, with the two spurs curving back in the opposite direction at either end.

'It's a recurve bow,' Will said, after letting her study it for several minutes. 'The Temujai use them. I used one in my first few years as an apprentice. The recurved limbs give you a higher arrow speed for a lower draw weight. This one is about fifty pounds. You should be able to manage that after you build up your strength.'

He traced a finger down the outside edge of the bow. 'It's reinforced with deer sinew here to provide extra flex and recovery.'

'Who made it?' she asked. She was still turning the bow this way and that in her hands, admiring the workmanship that had gone into it. The wood had been shaped carefully and planed smooth. She could see the layer of sinew now that he pointed it out. But the whole bow had been varnished with a dark lacquer so that it had an overall dark brown tone. The lacquer was a matt finish, she noticed, so that there would be no reflections of light coming from it. The leather grip sat comfortably in her hand, although when the bow was unstrung, with the two recurved sections pointing outwards, it felt a little unbalanced.

'I did,' he told her. 'Halt showed me how to make one when I was an apprentice.'

'Could you show me?' she asked eagerly, and he nodded approvingly at her, once again noting her obvious interest in, and appreciation for, a good weapon.

'Time for that later. First you need to learn to shoot this one. Have you shot a bow before?'

She nodded dubiously. Archery was practised as a social sport by the ladies at Castle Araluen and she had joined in occasionally. But the bows they used were nothing like this one. They were simple longbows — made from lightweight staves with a draw weight of twenty pounds or less, for the less muscular frames of the women who shot them. From what he had said, this one would be more than twice as difficult to draw back.

'Nothing like this one,' she said. She turned it around, trying to work out how to string it. With the bows she had used previously, she had simply grounded one end and used her body weight to bend the stave, sliding the string up into its end notch. But she didn't like the thought of forcing one of those carefully constructed recurve ends against the ground. 'How do I string it?' she asked.

He reached out and took the bow from her.

'There are two ways you can do it. The first way is with a bow stringer, like this,' he said. He took a length of thick cord from his jerkin's side pocket and unrolled it. There was a small leather cylinder at one end and a wide loop, padded with leather, at the other. He slid the cylinder over the end of the bow where the string was already set in its notch, then placed the loop over the other limb, some thirty centimetres before the recurve began. The other end of the bowstring was already looped over the limb of the bow, with the string itself hanging in a loose curve.

Holding the bow with the string hanging down, he stepped onto the long loop of the heavy cord, pinning it to the ground, then began to force the bow upwards, using his back, arm and leg muscles to bend the limbs. The leather pad on the end of the bow stringer prevented its slipping down the limb as he applied increasing force. The bow creaked as the limbs bent further and further and, as they did, he slid the small loop of the bowstring up the limb, past the recurve, until it settled into the notch cut at the end of the bow.

'Always make sure it's properly seated before you release the pressure,' he said. 'You don't want it slipping out and the whole thing coming unstuck.'

He studied the string, satisfied that it was seated properly, then released the pressure on the bow stringer. He slipped the wide, padded loop over the end of the bow, removed the cylinder from the other end, and presented her with the weapon, now properly strung and ready for use.

'That looked kind of difficult,' she said doubtfully. She had seen the effort he had to make to bend the bow.

He shrugged. 'It's not easy. But you'll learn how to do it.'

She liked the way the bow felt now that it was strung. It was definitely balanced better than before. Tentatively, she pulled back on the bowstring and raised an eyebrow at the resistance. She'd heard archers talk about draw weights before, but it had meant little to her. Now she could feel how difficult it was to draw back a fifty-pound bow. She had a sudden spasm of doubt. She'd never manage this.

'It's a matter of technique,' Will told her, as if he'd read her thoughts. 'You'll need to use the big muscles in your back and shoulders and arms. I'm guessing that when you've shot before, you just pulled the string back with your arm?'

She nodded and he gestured for her to take up a shooting position with the bow. She held it at arm's length and he moved to correct her.

'Start with the bow hand close to your body, not extended. Then push with your bow hand and pull with the other. That way you're using the muscles of both arms, not just the string arm.'

She nodded thoughtfully, and brought the bow back close to her body. Then, with a co-ordinated effort, she pushed out and pulled back. The string came back almost two-thirds of its maximum draw before the increasing resistance defeated her. She let it down with a grunt of effort.

'I can't do this,' she muttered.

'Yes you can.' Will's reply was terse and left no room for argument.

She looked at him. If she was expecting any sympathy, there was none to be found. She realised then that if she tried, if she made an honest effort, Will would be understanding and helpful. If she simply decided to give up, it would be a different matter altogether. She took a deep breath and set herself to draw the bow again.

As she began, she heard him say: 'Think of pushing your shoulder blades together as you push and pull. That gets your big back and shoulder muscles involved.'

She did as he said and this time, she felt the string come back a little further, until her right thumb was a few centimetres from her nose.

'Good,' he said. 'Now try again and see if you can bring your thumb back to your nose.'

She did, exerting all the strength she could muster in her arms and her back. Fleetingly, her thumb touched against her nose. Then she let the string down again.

She shook her right hand. The string had cut painfully into her fingers as she hauled it back. Will noticed the movement and took something from his pocket, handing it to her.

'Can be painful, can't it? Try this.'

'This' was a patch of soft leather shaped rather like a small mitten. At the narrow end, a hole was cut in the leather, about the width of a finger. The patch widened out then formed into two pieces — one small, the other larger — with a notch cut between them. He showed her how to slip her second finger through the hole, so that the patch lay along the inner side of her hand. The smaller section corresponded to her first finger. The wider part covered her second and ring fingers. The gap in between separated them.

'The arrow goes here,' Will said, indicating the gap. 'The rest of it protects your fingers from the string.'

She tried it again, pulling the string back part way to experiment. He was right, the leather protected her fingers and she could see how the arrow would sit between them in the gap — with her forefinger above the nock and her other two fingers below it.

'Do you use one of these?' she asked.

He shook his head. 'They're a bit fiddly if you're in a fight. I have the tips of my gauntlets reinforced. We'll get some made up for you. But in the meantime, that tab will do nicely. Try it again. Remember, shoulder blades together.'

She raised the bow. Push, pull. Shoulder blades forcing together. Her thumb touched her nose fleetingly and she let the string down.

'I'm glad to see you know enough not to just release it without an arrow on the string,' he said gruffly.

She gave him a wan smile. She knew that dry-shooting a bow that way could cause damage to the limbs. 'Master-at-arms Parker always threatened the direst consequences for any lady who did.'

Will nodded. 'Good for him. And of course, the more powerful the bow, the more damage can be done. Let's see how you manage with an arrow.'

There were several arrows in the fold of oilcloth. He took one and handed it to Maddie, nodding with approval as she found the cock feather and set it out from the bow. He remembered how Halt had to teach him even the most basic facts about bows. She clicked the nock onto the string just below the marked nocking point and looked critically at the arrow.

'It's a little short,' she said.

He inclined his head. 'It'll be about the right length for you to draw back to your nose. No point in shooting a longer arrow than you can draw. All you're doing is adding weight without increasing the thrust behind it.'

She thought about that. It made sense. She took up her stance again, then hesitated.

'What's the target?'

Will indicated a hay bale some twenty metres away from them.

'That should do the job,' he said. She studied it, nodded and turned side on to it, bow down, arrow nocked to the string. The tight nock held the arrow in place, and the gap in the shooting tab fitted neatly where the nock was, with her index finger above it and her middle and ring fingers below. Much better with the leather to protect her hand, she thought. She began to raise the bow, then stopped.

'Do you have an arm guard?' she asked. She saw a slight look of disappointment cloud Will's face, then it was gone as he turned to rummage among the equipment in the oil-cloth. He found a leather cuff and handed it to her. She slipped it over her left arm.

'A bow like this would hit like a whip without an arm guard,' she commented.

He grunted and something in his attitude attracted her attention. She looked at him closely.

'Don't tell me,' she said. 'The first time you shot one of these, you didn't wear an arm guard, did you?'

He glared at her and she felt a wicked sense of delight.

'You didn't, did you?' she repeated.

He gestured stiffly at the target. 'Just get on with your shooting.'

She shook her head in mock disbelief. 'Boy, you must have been so dumb.'

'Any time you're ready to shoot will be fine.'

She set herself into the shooting position and raised the bow. As she did so, she couldn't resist one more sally.

'Bet you had one for your second shot.'

'Get on with it!' Will snapped at her.

She flexed her shoulder and back muscles, drew the bow as far as she could, sighted quickly and released. The arrow skimmed into the ground a metre before the hay bale.

She frowned, reloaded and shot again. Same result. She looked sideways at Will.

'What am I doing wrong?'

He inclined his head at her. 'Oh, do you think someone as dumb as me might be able to tell you?' he asked in a mock-sweet tone.

She sighed and rolled her eyes. There was no answer to that and she resigned herself to letting him have the last word. When he spoke again, his tone was brisk and businesslike.

'You're not used to the weight of the bow and you're too eager to release it. That means you're dropping your bow hand as you shoot and the arrow flies low. Hold steady a little longer. Not too long, or your arm will start to tremble. But keep it steady until after you've released. Release the arrow and count two, while you hold the bow in its shooting position.'

She tried again, straining to hold the bow steady for a few vital extra seconds. This time, as she released, she saw the arrow streak away and slam, quivering, into the left-hand edge of the bale. She grinned delightedly.

'Not bad,' Will said.

She reacted in a scandalised manner. 'Not bad? Not bad? My third shot ever and I hit the target! That's better than not bad.'

'If that had been a man,' Will told her, 'you would have grazed his left shoulder. If it had been a knight, he would probably have been wearing a shield there and your arrow would have glanced off while he kept coming. *Not bad* isn't good enough. *Not bad* can get you killed.'

They eyed each other for a few seconds, she glaring angrily, he with one eyebrow raised in a mocking expression. Finally, he jerked his head at the target.

'Twenty more shots,' he said. 'Let's see if you can progress to *halfway reasonable*.'

She groaned softly as she drew another arrow back. Already her shoulders and back were aching.

I shouldn't have made fun of him, she thought. But the realisation came too late, as it so often does.

Sixteen

The twenty arrows grew into forty. Then Will finally relented and let Maddie rest for the day.

That night, the muscles in her shoulders, back and upper arms ached and cramped as she tossed on her bed, trying to sleep. The strip of light under her bedroom door told her that Will was still awake. After an hour, she rose, tiptoed to the door and opened it a crack, peering through. Her mentor was sitting by the fire, with a sheaf of papers on his knee — reports from other fiefs, she knew. As she watched, he took a sheet and placed it in a leather folder on the side table by his elbow.

'Could be him,' Will muttered softly. Then he took up the next report, angling the page so that the candle light struck it directly.

Frowning thoughtfully, Maddie went back to bed.

'What was that all about?' she wondered. Somehow, she sensed it would be a mistake to quiz him on the matter.

The next day, after she had completed her housekeeping duties, Will had her at it again. She shot twenty arrows, rested for ten minutes, then shot another twenty. Again, her back and shoulders shrieked with pain. But she gritted her teeth and kept at it. By the end of the week, she sensed that it was becoming a little easier to draw the bow back to the full length of the arrow. Her technique was improving and her muscles were toughening. The pain was still there, but now it was a dull ache, not the searing cramps of the first few days. And it was decreasing with each passing day.

As she practised, she noted Will's continuing preoccupation with the regular reports from Rangers in other fiefs. He would sit, his back against a tree, scanning new reports as they came in. She knew by now that it was standard practice for Rangers to keep up to date with events around the Kingdom. But she sensed that this was something more than routine. Every so often, he would add a page or two to the growing file in the leather folder.

After two weeks, she found she could draw the bow with relative ease and hold it steady for several seconds. As this happened, she found her accuracy was improving and she was hitting in the centre of the bale more than half the time. Her misses and near misses were becoming less and less frequent.

As he saw her technique and strength growing, Will began to work with her on her accuracy.

'Don't try to aim down the arrow shaft,' he told her. 'You have to sense where the arrow will go. You need to see the entire sighting picture — the bale of hay, the bow and the arrowhead. Learn where the arrow will fly.'

She frowned. 'How do I do that?'

'There's only one way. You practise. Over and over again, so that aligning the shot to the target becomes an instinctive action. After a while, after seeing enough arrows fly, you'll instinctively know where to position the bow in the sighting picture. As the range increases, you'll also need to gauge how much elevation you give the arrow — how far above the target you need to aim to hit the centre.'

Of course, archery wasn't the only skill she was practising. He also set her to practising with her throwing knife and the saxe knife, using a pine board set against a tree for a target. As she became more proficient in putting the knives into the target from a short range, he moved her back so that she had to judge how to spin the knives twice on their way to the pine board.

At least, she thought, this didn't leave her with aching, cramped muscles. She had to admit, there was no sound in the world more satisfying than the solid *thunk* of a knife burying its point into the pinewood.

And nothing more frustrating than the vibrating rattle of an inaccurate throw hitting the board side on and bouncing harmlessly into the trees.

There were other lessons, too. Will showed her how the mottled, uneven design of the cloaks they wore helped them blend into the background of the woods around them.

'The mottling breaks up the regular shape of a person's body. There's nothing even. Everything is irregular and random, and the colouring matches the greens and greys of the trees and undergrowth.

'But the real secret is to stand absolutely still. Most people are spotted when they think they've already been discovered and they move. It's movement that gives us away. But if you stand perfectly still, you'd be surprised how close a searcher can be and still not spot you. Remember the basic rule: Trust the cloak.'

The words echoed in his own mind as he spoke them. He remembered the countless times Halt had said them to him. He found there was something surprisingly satisfying in passing this knowledge on to a younger person — particularly as he found Maddie to be eager to learn. The skills of a Ranger fascinated her. She was an adventurous spirit, like her mother, and she was more suited to learning about stalking and shooting than sewing and embroidery.

There were still some aspects of her attitude that needed correction. She had spent her life so far being spoiled and having people accede to her every whim. As a consequence, she liked to get her own way. If things didn't go well immediately, she could become impatient and frustrated.

And while she was a much more pleasant person than she had been initially, there was still a level of petulance there as well. Like her mother, Will thought to himself, remembering how Evanlyn had been in their first days together on Erak's ship and on Skorghijl.

But Maddie was also determined — which was possibly the reverse side of petulance, he thought — and that definitely won his approval. He noted that, even when she wasn't shooting, she would string the bow then spend twenty minutes to half an hour simply drawing the string back and slowly releasing it, building her muscle memory and strength.

He came upon her at the rear of the cabin one day, struggling with the thick stringer cord to bend the limbs of the bow and set the bowstring in place.

'There's another way to do that,' he said. 'And you don't have to carry a stringer round all the time.'

He held out his hand and she passed him the unstrung bow. He detached the stringer and handed it back to her.

'I think your strength might have improved enough for you to try this way,' he said.

She watched as he hooked one of the recurve spurs around the front of his left ankle, then stepped his right foot through the gap between the loose string and the bow. Then, with his left ankle holding the bow firmly in place, he used his weight and the strength of his back and right arm to bend the bow forward, using his right thigh as a fulcrum.

The bowstring slid smoothly up the limb of the bow and he seated it firmly in its notch. Then he straightened and handed her the strung bow.

'There,' he said. 'You unstring it the same way. Try it.'

She mimicked his position, then pushed against the bow limb to bend it so that she could release the loop of the bowstring from the top of the bow. She struggled at first, but found that by using the strength of her legs, her back and her newly tautened shoulder and arm muscles, she could bend the bow forward.

She smiled triumphantly at him. He nodded, unsmiling. But that didn't dampen her sense of achievement. She settled the bow firmly against her left ankle, then heaved at it to reset the string. She struggled over the last few vital centimetres, then felt a sense of accomplishment as the looped end of the bowstring slid home.

'Is that how you string your bow?' she asked. She realised that she had never seen him do this. He shrugged.

'Sometimes. It's easier with the recurve — the way it locks behind your ankle and stays in place. With a normal longbow, that can slip out at the most embarrassing time. But generally, I use this.'

He gestured to the back of his right boot, and she noticed that there was a loop of leather strap there, behind the heel.

'I put one end of the bow into that loop, then use my whole body to bend the bow over my back while I slide the string into place,' he said.

She nodded thoughtfully, seeing how it would work.

'So the idea is to use all your muscles to bend the bow — back, legs and arms?' she said.

'That's the best way to do it. Use everything you've got. Don't overwork one part. Most Rangers are small, after all. We need to use all the muscles we've got.'

She looked at him curiously. She had never thought of him as being particularly small. But now she realised that he was much shorter than her father — and most of the other knights and warriors she had known over the years. Shorter, perhaps, but no smaller around the shoulders and chest. She guessed that a lifetime of practising with his longbow, with its draw weight of eighty to ninety pounds, had developed those muscles to their current condition.

As he so often did, Will seemed to sense what she was thinking.

'There's something to be said for being small,' he told her. 'After all, the bigger you are, the more there is to hide.'

He nodded at the bow that she was still holding in her hand.

'Don't let me stop you practising,' he said, and strolled away. A bundle of reports had come in with the mail courier that morning and he needed to go through them.

She began to draw the bow, pushing in and out, drawing the string back. Now, she found, she could bring it back past her nose, until her index finger was almost touching the corner of her mouth.

'I may need to make you some longer arrows,' she heard him say. She looked up in surprise. She thought he had gone, but he had stopped at the corner of the cabin to watch her.

'Keep practising,' he said, then moved away once more.

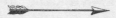

Usually she practised archery and knife throwing in the afternoon, with the mornings taken up by fitness training, distance running and camouflage skills. But on this day, Will changed the routine. They ate lunch together in the cabin — fresh bread, sharp, tangy cheese and apples. She washed hers down with cool milk, while he had coffee. He'd shown her how to grind the beans rather than just dump them in the pot and douse them with boiling water. He sipped the last few drops appreciatively.

'You're getting better at this,' he said. They cleared the table together and washed their plates. Then she reached for her bow and quiver, which were hanging from hooks beside the door. But he shook his head.

'Not today,' he said. 'Today I want to see how good you are with that sling of yours.'

'I'm pretty good,' she said confidently, although when she thought about it, she realised that she hadn't used the sling since she'd been at Redmont. Her days had been pre-occupied with the bow and her knives.

Will raised an eyebrow. 'And modest about it as well,' he commented.

She shrugged, hoping that she wouldn't disgrace herself when the moment came. She went to her room and took the sling and a pouch of shot from the chest that contained her belongings.

In the clearing outside, Will had set up five poles, each topped by a battered helmet he had scavenged from the discard pile at the Redmont Battleschool armoury. The five poles were at staggered distances, with the closest a mere twenty metres away and the farthest more than forty. There was no symmetry in their placement. The nearest pole was on the extreme right, the farthest in the middle of the line, with the others staggered randomly. She assessed the targets thoughtfully. This was a tougher test than Halt and Crowley had set for her at Castle Araluen. She'd have to assess the distance for each shot. She tied her shot bag onto her belt, selected one of the lead balls and set it in the sling's pouch, letting the weapon dangle from her right hand, swinging loosely. Will watched closely as she loaded the sling, then put out his hand.

'May I see?' he asked, pointing to the weighted pouch. She took out another shot and handed it to him, watching as he assessed its weight and heft.

'Lead,' he said. 'Your mother used stones, as I recall.'

She nodded. 'I used to use stones. I still would, at a pinch. But the weight varies and the shapes are irregular, and that affects your accuracy. This way, I know each shot is identical to the one before it. You wouldn't shoot arrows that were different lengths and weights, would you?'

He nodded, appreciating the point. 'Where do you get them?'

'I make them. I have a mould. I melt the lead and pour it in. Then I file off the little edges that form around the join in the mould.'

'Hmmm,' he said. He studied the shot and could see the file marks where she'd smoothed off its circumference. He approved of people making their own weapons and projectiles. Particularly someone who was a princess and could have handed off the task to the armourers at Castle Araluen.

'Right, five shots. One for each helmet. Let's see how good you really are,' he said. He placed a slight emphasis on the word 'really' and watched to see how she reacted to it. She glanced at him, her lips tightening into a thin line. A challenge had been issued and she was about to take it up.

'Which one first?' she asked. He screwed up his lips in mock consideration.

'Let's see. Those five helmets represent five Temujai warriors charging towards you, bent on separating you from your head. Which would you choose as the first target?'

The answer was obvious. 'The closest,' she said and he nodded, then gestured towards the line of helmets.

'Of course, by now he would have been upon you and your little sling wouldn't be doing you much good, would it?'

She took the hint.

He watched as she turned side on, advancing her left foot towards the target, letting the loaded sling drop back behind her extended right arm. She let it swing once, setting the shot in the pouch, then brought her right arm up and over in a near-vertical arc, whipping the sling over and releasing as she stepped through with her right leg.

CLANG!

The helmet she had selected as a target jumped in the air under the impact of the heavy lead ball and clattered on the ground, rolling from side to side. Almost immediately, she had reloaded the sling and cast again, this time at the helmet on the extreme left of the line.

CLANG!

The shot struck off centre and the helmet rotated wildly on the pole. But she was already lining up a third target. She cast again. But she was a little hasty and the lead ball whizzed past the helmet, missing it by thirty centimetres.

She hesitated, not sure whether to shoot at that target again.

'He's still coming at you,' Will said quietly. Quickly, she reloaded, cast again and sent the helmet jumping off the pole and spinning in the dust.

One shot left. She loaded, lined up the nearest remaining helmet and threw. The sling whipped overhead. The lead shot whizzed away and smashed square into the front of the helmet, putting a huge new dent in its battered surface.

She looked at him, her face flushed.

'How do you think that went?' he asked her, his face and voice devoid of expression.

She shrugged, trying not to look too pleased with herself. 'Well, four out of five. That's pretty good, isn't it?'

He regarded her for a few seconds in silence.

'There were five Temujai warriors charging you,' he said. 'You hit four of them. Presumably, the fifth one reached you. In that situation, four out of five isn't pretty good. It's pretty dead.'

She felt herself reddening with anger and embarrassment. He was right, she thought. In this world, four out of five wasn't good enough.

'Keep practising,' he told her.

'Until I get it right,' she said. But he corrected her.

'No. Until you don't get it wrong.'

Seventeen

Maddie was practising with her sling. It was a week since her first session and now Will had her working at it every day. First she would spend an hour with the bow. Then another with the knives. They would break for lunch and then Will would set her to practising the sling in the afternoon.

She was still using the five old helmets as targets, but each day, Will moved the poles so that they always formed a different pattern.

'No good getting to rely on one particular set of angles and distances,' he told her and she conceded the point. Her accuracy was improving. These days, she could usually manage to hit all five helmets three out of four times. But the perfect score that Will insisted on still managed to elude her.

She had noticed an interesting phenomenon. With each set of five shots, as she hit target after target, the nervous strain increased and her muscles began to tighten on that all-important final shot. As a result, she tended to rush the shot, to try to get it over with as quickly as possible. The usual result was a miss.

She mentioned this to Will and he nodded.

'It's a natural reaction,' he said. 'You can see that perfect score looming and the nerves begin to build up. Try to control it. Relax. Don't rush. We'll work on your speed later, but at this stage, it's better to take a little longer and hit every target, rather that rush through it and miss one.'

She was on her second set of five shots. Her first sequence had been perfect. Five casts for five solid hits. She had followed that up with four more hits and was now on her fifth. She paused, allowing her breathing to settle. She could feel the excitement, the temptation to rush and get it done with. But she resisted.

Better to hit the enemy late than miss him entirely, she thought to herself. She glanced covertly at Will. He was sitting to one side with his back against a tree, his legs stretched out in front of him. For once, she noticed, he didn't have that ever-present sheaf of reports or the leather binder. Thinking about it, she realised that it had been some days since she had seen the leather folder. His cowl was up, obscuring his face, and he appeared to be asleep. She was willing to bet that he was anything but.

She took another deep breath, settled herself, eyed the target and forced her muscles to relax. Then she whipped the sling up and over, stepping through with her right foot as she did so.

WHIZZ . . . CLANG!

The helmet leapt several centimetres in the air under the impact, then settled on the pole again, off centre and wobbling.

'That's ten shots for ten hits,' she said.

Will said nothing. She looked at him again. He hadn't moved. She sighed and moved forward to the target posts. Two of the helmets had been knocked off the poles and she replaced them. There were several lead shot lying in the dust and she retrieved them, studying them. They were distorted from the impact with the iron helmets, flattened on one side or with deep gouges scored in them from sharp edges on the helmets. She couldn't shoot with them again in that condition, but she could always melt them down and re-mould them. She picked them up and placed them in a pocket, then moved back to the shooting line.

She whipped another five shots away, moving smoothly and gracefully, controlling the power and speed of each shot.

Five hits.

She felt excitement mounting in her chest. Three rounds and not a single miss. She had never shot three perfect scores in a row before.

If I miss one now, I'll ruin it.

The negative thought stole into her mind like a thief. She angrily dismissed it, then paced up and down several times, breathing deeply, shaking her hands and arms to dispel the tightness that was beginning to take them over.

She rolled her neck and shoulders to loosen them. In her mind, she saw herself cast the next shot. She visualised a perfect cast, co-ordinated and accurate and powerful, seeing the blur of the lead shot as it flashed across the clearing to slam into the selected target.

See it. Then do it, Will had told her. She nodded to herself and, very deliberately, set a shot into the sling's pouch.

She advanced her left foot, letting her sling hand fall back and down to her right, the loaded sling swinging gently back and forth like a pendulum.

Will had her shooting at the targets in reverse order with each set of five. The first set, she would shoot at the nearest first, progressing to the most distant. Then for the second round, she would shoot at the furthest target first.

'Let's assume they're running away,' Will had said.

Then she would go back to the original order for the third round, then reverse it again.

She was on her fourth round now, so her first target would be the most distant helmet.

The hardest first, she thought, then again pushed the negative thought away. She blanked her mind, concentrated on the target, then smoothly whipped the sling over, releasing at just the right moment.

She knew it was a good shot the minute she released. She followed through to the target, her eyes glued to it.

WHIZZ . . . CLANG!

The helmet rotated madly and she smiled. From now on, the shots would become progressively easier as the range shortened.

WHIZZ . . . CLANG!

The second shot struck the helmet square on, the force of the shot actually knocking the pole from its vertical position. She reloaded, turning to stand side on to the next target, which was on the extreme left of the line.

WHIZZ . . . CLANG!

Another perfect strike. She reloaded. Two to go for a perfect score. Just two more shots. Her breath was coming faster and she felt her heart racing. She forced herself to calm down, relaxing all the muscles in her body, letting herself go limp. Then she loaded, addressed and cast.

WHIZZ-CLANG!

Slightly off centre, but still a killing shot. This time there was virtually no pause between the sound of the shot whirring away then striking the helmet.

Four out of four. Nineteen out of twenty. She had never before been this close to a perfect score. She fumbled in her pouch for another shot, then set it in the sling. She nearly dropped it and she realised her hands were shaking. She breathed deeply once more, pulling the air deep into her lungs, willing her heart to stop beating with excitement, striving for the calm she knew she'd need for the final shot.

And then, unexpectedly, finding it. Her breathing and pulse slowed and she saw that final shot in her mind's eye. Perfect, powerful and dead on line. Calmly, she took her stance, fixed her gaze on the target. Her instincts and the memory of hundreds of prior shots took over. She could do this. She let her weight settle back on her right foot, then whipped the sling through, letting the loose end slip through her fingers at just the right moment.

WHIZZ-CLANG!

The old helmet had a crack in it and the shot struck square on the fault. It punched a massive rent in the front of the helmet, penetrated, rattled against the back of the iron pot, then fell into the sand below. The helmet was knocked backwards, only staying on the pole by the barest margin.

She heaved in a huge, exultant breath. A wide smile formed on her face and she stepped forward to study the effect of that last, perfect shot.

Four rounds. Twenty hits. A perfect score. Will's words echoed in her mind: *Practise till you don't get it wrong.*

She had done it, she thought. She looked back at her mentor now. He was still leaning against the tree. But his cowl was pushed back and he was regarding her steadily.

'That sounded suspiciously like a perfect score,' he said.

She nodded eagerly. 'It was! Twenty out of twenty! I did it at last!'

'Hmmm,' he grunted, screwing up his face. 'Well, we'll see if you can do it again tomorrow.'

He scrambled to his feet and she looked at him, somewhat disconcerted. Was that all? We'll see if you can do it tomorrow? That was it? She'd practised for weeks to get it right . . . and that was it?

Will sensed her chagrin and his tone softened somewhat. 'Well done,' he said. 'But don't get carried away. I need you to be as good as you can be. And I sense you can be very, very good indeed.'

'Oh,' she said, looking at the ground and scuffing her toe in the dust. It was hard to stay offended when he said something like that. 'I suppose so . . .'

'So, keep practising for the rest of the week. Then we'll look at getting you a horse,' he said.

She actually took a pace back, looking at him in some confusion.

'I've got a horse,' she said. 'I've got Sundancer, remember?'

Sundancer was the name of the Arridan gelding she'd ridden from Castle Araluen to Redmont. He was stabled in the lean-to behind the cabin, with Tug.

'You need a Ranger horse,' Will said.

Maddie tilted her chin defiantly. 'One of those shaggy little ponies like the one you ride?' she said disparagingly. 'Sundancer could run rings around one of those four-legged barrels.'

'Is that so?' Will said, his eyes narrowing. 'Well, we'll see. And in the meantime, don't let Tug hear you say that.'

'Why not? Would his feelings be hurt?' she said sarcastically.

Will inclined his head and didn't answer for a second or two.

'Quite possibly,' he said. 'But more to the point, you might annoy him. And that's never a good idea.'

He turned away and started walking towards the rear of the cabin. She followed, hesitantly.

'Where are we going?' she asked.

'Let's get our horses saddled,' he said. 'We're going for a ride. I can't wait to see your horse run rings around my four-legged little barrel.'

As she followed him, she had the uncomfortable feeling that she'd just made a mistake.

'We'd better pack some provisions. We'll be away overnight,' Will called back to her.

'Where are we going?' she asked.

'Derrylon ford,' he said. 'It's only a day's ride away. We'll camp out and come back tomorrow. That should give Sundancer plenty of opportunity to run those rings you were talking about.'

Once again, Maddie had the feeling that she had made a mistake.

A big one.

Eighteen

They saddled the horses in the stable. Then Will took down a large canvas roll hanging on the wall and tied it in place behind his saddle. There was another, similar roll hanging next to the first and he gestured for Maddie to take it.

'Tie it behind your saddle,' he said.

She unhooked it and felt the weight, looking at it curiously. 'What is it?'

'Camping gear. Basically a waterproof canvas that forms a one-man tent, and a blanket for sleeping. Plus a few other odds and ends.'

She smiled cheekily. 'I thought we'd just roll ourselves into our cloaks and sleep under a bush,' she said. Will tested Tug's girth strap — the little horse was fond of taking a deep breath when the cinch was being tightened, then letting it out again once it was done so that the strap became loose.

'You can do that if you like,' Will said. 'I prefer to stay warm and dry. And it looks like rain.'

She tied the canvas roll in place. While she was doing so, Will led Tug to the front of the cabin, went inside and put together a sack of provisions — coffee, bread, cheese, apples, dried beef and a few vegetables. If they wanted fresh meat, he'd have Maddie get some with her sling, he thought. At the last, he placed his standard pack of spices, seasonings and cooking ingredients in the sack, then went out to join his apprentice.

There were two water skins hanging beside the pump. He gestured to them.

'You can fill them,' he said. Maddie moved to do so as he swung up into the saddle. Tug twitched his ears and looked at him inquisitively. Will shook his head.

'Later,' he muttered.

Maddie looked up from her task, soaking her sleeve with water as she took her eye off the gushing liquid. 'Did you say something?'

He shook his head. 'Just clearing my throat.'

She passed him a water skin and tied one to her own saddle bow. Then she mounted as well. Sundancer pranced a few steps, ready to run. He hadn't been out in a day or so and he was full of energy and enthusiasm — as was his rider. Tug, in contrast, stood solid and unmoving.

'Let's get going,' Will said. He urged Tug into a slow, easy lope. Maddie flicked Sundancer's reins and he started forward, eager to run. But she held him back, dancing a little with his head high, so that he matched Tug's steady pace.

'Is this as fast as we're going to go?'

Will twisted in the saddle to look at her. Sundancer was

longer in the leg than Tug and he had to look up to meet her gaze.

'I thought so,' he replied.

Maddie snorted disdainfully. 'No wonder it's going to take all day.' He made no reply, so she added, 'You know Sundancer is an Arridan thoroughbred, don't you?'

He nodded. 'Arridans are fine horses.'

'They're fast, too. I've heard people say they're the fastest horses on earth.'

Tug rattled his short mane and made an impolite belching sound. For a moment, Maddie looked at the little horse in surprise. It was almost as if he were responding to her claim. Then she dismissed the idea.

'They certainly can cover ground,' Will agreed calmly. They rode on in silence for a few minutes. Sundancer continued to pull at the reins. Maddie held him back. Tug loped on steadily.

He's like a rocking horse, Maddie thought, watching Tug's gentle, steady back-and-forth motion. She wriggled impatiently in the saddle. She could feel Sundancer's pent-up energy and she longed to let him run free – to show Will how a real horse could run.

'So where's this ford?' she asked.

Will gestured to the south-east. 'We follow the high road for twenty kilometres or so. Then we take a fork leading to Pendletown. After we go through the village, we continue on until we come to the Derrylon River. The road leads straight to the ford.' He paused, then added, 'It's all signposted.'

She nodded, noting the last statement particularly. It was almost, she thought, as if he was giving her tacit approval to go off on her own. Then she grinned at him.

'Well, I'll be waiting for you there.'

She clapped her heels into Sundancer's flanks, relaxing the restraining tension on his reins. Instantly, the gelding leapt forward, plunging and rearing for the first few metres, then gathering speed as he settled into his gait. His hoofs beat a rapid tattoo on the road's surface, raising puffs of dust with each stride.

Maddie's cloak and hair streamed out in the wind behind her and Will heard her delighted laugh.

'He's very fast,' Will said.

Tug turned his head and regarded him with his left eye. *Not as fast as Sandstorm.*

'No. Perhaps not. But there wouldn't be much in it.'

I beat Sandstorm.

'I remember. But you only managed it in the last few metres.'

The little horse snorted disparagingly. *I was foxing.*

'Of course you were.'

He felt Tug begin to pull against the reins, but held him in check.

Do you want me to catch him now?

Will shaded his eyes to look after Maddie. She and Sundancer were small figures in the distance. A cloud of dust was drifting in the air behind them. Then they rounded a bend in the road and were hidden by the trees. The gradually settling dust was all that was left to show where they had been.

'Not yet,' Will told him. 'Later.'

Maddie exulted in the rush of wind through her hair and the smooth, powerful strides of her horse. This was riding, she thought, and she urged Sundancer on to even greater speed. As she reached the first bend in the road, she turned in the saddle to look back.

Will and Tug were small figures in the distance now, plodding stolidly onwards. Well, she thought, what could you expect of a shaggy little barrel like that. Over the years, she'd heard people talk of Ranger horses with a certain degree of awe. Now that she'd seen one at close quarters, she couldn't understand what all the fuss was about.

'And he must be one of the better ones,' she said aloud. After all, Will was one of the most senior of all the Rangers. It stood to reason that he would have one of the better horses in the Corps — if not the best.

She felt a delicious streak of rebellion stirring within her. Will was so capable, so knowledgeable, so superior to her in just about every way. He could track game where there was barely a sign to be found. He could shoot with uncanny speed and unerring accuracy. And his knife work was almost superhuman — fast and deadly accurate.

But here was something she was better at. With a sudden moment of honesty, she amended that thought. Her horse was better than Tug, she thought. But then, if she had the intelligence to select a superior horse, why shouldn't she share in that superiority?

Sundancer would run Will's little grey pony into the ground, she told herself. And as she had that thought, she decided that she wanted their victory to be overwhelming. It wouldn't be enough to simply beat Tug and Will to this Derrylon ford. They would do it thoroughly, crushingly. If Will said it would take a day to reach the ford, she decided that she'd do it in half that time.

She leaned forward over Sundancer's neck.

'Come on, boy! We've got a point to make.'

Sundancer's ears went back and he tossed his head in delight. He loved to run. In fact, he lived to run. It had been bred into his bloodline for generation after generation. He lengthened his stride and accelerated.

Maddie yelled in delight. She had never felt him run so fast before! It was exhilarating and she gave herself over to the sheer, pulse-racing excitement of the ride.

Tug continued his steady, measured lope.

Dugga-dum, dugga-dum, dugga-dum went his hoofs on the hard-packed surface of the highway. From time to time, he would turn his head to look at Will. But his rider never responded to these hints. Finally, Tug decided to address the matter directly.

Tell me when you want me to start running.

'Trust me. You'll be the first to know.'

Dugga-dum, dugga-dum, dugga-dum.

It has to be said that, ordinarily, Maddie was not the sort of person who would allow her horse to overextend himself. Usually, she was careful to control her mount and ensure that he stayed within his own limits.

But the excitement of the ride, the exultation of the speed that she felt, and the temptation to show Will and his horse how superior Sundancer was, led her into error.

They had been galloping wildly for kilometres when she felt the Arridan horse's stride falter. Then Sundancer shook his head and plunged on. But now she realised how hard she'd been pushing him.

His flanks were streaked with foam and his sides were heaving like bellows as he dragged in huge lungfuls of air. She became aware that he was grunting loudly with each breath and instantly she was overcome with remorse. She reined him in, although he resisted her efforts initially. He was willing to plunge on until he dropped from exhaustion.

She drew back firmly on the reins, checking his mindless instinct to keep running, speaking softly to him, gradually increasing the pressure against the bit until he allowed her to bring him to a halt.

He stood, legs spread and breathing heavily, as she quickly dismounted, patting his neck and walking round him to make sure he was undamaged.

'You're all right,' she told him. Thankfully, she had caught her mistake in time.

She splashed some water from the water skin into her hand and held it near his muzzle. He pushed his soft nose against her hand and drank. She continued to let the water trickle into the cupped hand.

'Not too much,' she said. 'Not too fast.'

He snorted gratefully. She loosened the saddle girth and took a square of old blanket from her pack, rubbing him down and speaking softly to him. It had been a near thing, she realised. If she had kept going much longer, she could well have ruined her beautiful horse.

When he was rubbed down, she led him to the side of the road and let him crop the grass for a few minutes. Mentally, she kicked herself for coming so close to disaster. It wasn't Sundancer's fault, she knew. The blame lay squarely with her. She was the rider. She was the one who should have controlled him, harbouring his energy and strength.

She let him rest for some minutes, then took the reins and led him back onto the road. She'd walk for a while, until he'd cooled down properly and recovered. She stepped out and he followed her meekly. She turned and watched him for a minute or two, making sure there was nothing wrong with his gait — that he hadn't strained any muscles or ligaments in that mad, heedless gallop.

To her relief, he seemed fine. She smiled fondly, shaking her head in wonder as she thought of his amazing speed and willingness, grateful that there was no permanent harm done to him. She wondered how far behind them Will and Tug were.

'We're probably so far ahead that we could walk the rest of the way and still beat them,' she told Sundancer. He shook his head tiredly, plodding along behind her.

Then she became conscious of a noise behind them. A regular, rhythmic noise.

Dugga-dum, dugga-dum, dugga-dum.

She whirled round. Will and Tug had rounded a bend behind them and were cantering slowly towards them, still moving at that ridiculous, constant lope. Once more she had the thought that Tug ran like a rocking horse.

Be that as it may, she thought, he was a very consistent rocking horse.

Will drew up beside her. He didn't check Tug as they came level. Sundancer lifted his head at the sight of the smaller horse and dragged back against the reins, but she held him in check.

'Your horse looks tired,' Will said amiably, as he began to move ahead of her.

'He'll be fine,' she said defiantly.

He turned in the saddle to look back at her as he and Tug drew away.

'I'm glad to hear it,' he said. Then he faced the road ahead and called back over his shoulder, 'We'll wait for you in Pendletown.'

She glared at his back, then turned and began to tighten Sundancer's girth again. The Arridan, spent as he was, was moving nervously, eager to set off after Tug. She placed one foot in the stirrup, then stopped.

He wasn't ready yet. If she allowed him to run, she might injure him. Reluctantly, she took her foot out of the stirrup and loosened the cinch again. Then she resumed leading the horse at a walk.

At the next bend already, Will was surreptitiously watching over his shoulder. He saw her begin to mount, then saw her come to a decision and begin walking the horse once more.

'Good girl,' he said approvingly.

How's that? Tug, of course, was facing the road ahead and hadn't seen Maddie's moment of indecision.

'She won't mistreat her horse, even if it means losing the race. We'll make a Ranger of her yet.'

They rode on in silence for several minutes before Will spoke again.

'If only she drank coffee,' he said.

Dugga-dum, dugga-dum, dugga-dum.

Nineteen

'The thing is,' Will said, 'we need particular qualities in a horse.'

It was three days since they had returned from the ford. Sundancer was none the worse for the experience. Tug, of course, merely shrugged off the long ride as part and parcel of his everyday life. Today they were riding side by side, although as yet, Will hadn't said where they were bound. Maddie might have imagined it, but she thought Sundancer was showing a new level of deference to Will's shaggy little grey.

'What sort of qualities?' she asked.

'Speed, of course,' Will replied. 'And your Arridan has that. In the short haul, he's possibly faster than Tug.'

Tug shook his mane and snorted. Will smiled and leaned forward, patting his neck.

'I'd say he's definitely faster,' Maddie said. 'After all, he just ran away from the two of you the other day. You saw it.'

'Yes. I did,' Will said evenly. 'But Tug wasn't running then. He was just loping along conserving his strength.'

'So how fast can he run?' she challenged, turning sideways in the saddle to study the little horse. As before, she thought that he was a fairly unimpressive sight.

To her surprise, Will shrugged. 'I don't know.'

She looked at him sceptically. 'You've never seen him run?' she asked but he shook his head.

'I've seen him run plenty of times. And each time, he ran as fast as he had to. But I have no idea if that was as fast as he could go. In fact, I doubt it.'

Maddie frowned uncertainly. She wasn't quite sure that she understood him.

Tell her about Sandstorm.

Will considered Tug's suggestion, then nodded.

'Some years ago, we were in the Arridi desert,' he began.

Maddie nodded eagerly. 'Yes. Was that when my mother went off to rescue the Skandian Oberjarl?' She'd heard vague references to that event, but neither her mother nor her father had ever filled in any of the detail. Now she sensed that she was about to learn more about that adventure and she hitched herself around so she could watch Will as he continued.

'That was it. In any case, at one stage, I had to match Tug in a race against an Arridan stallion called Sandstorm. He was a real champion, the finest in the Bedullin herd.'

'Bedullin?' she repeated uncertainly. She wasn't familiar with the word.

'The Bedullin are a nomadic Arridi tribe. Great horsemen and wonderful horse breeders. One of their young men took a fancy to Tug.'

Actually, of course, it had been a predecessor of the present Tug who was involved in the race, but Will didn't want to get into that, or his belief that his horse's character transferred from one incarnation to the next. He wasn't sure that he could explain it properly if he tried.

'We were separated — by a sandstorm, ironically enough. The young Bedullin found Tug wandering in the desert and claimed him.'

Maddie glanced down at the little horse. 'Why?' she asked, undiplomatically.

Will looked at her for a few seconds, then shook his head. When he spoke, there was a hint of annoyance in his voice.

'Because they're great judges of horseflesh,' he said tartly. 'They look beyond the obvious.'

And I have a great inner beauty.

Absentmindedly, Will patted Tug on the neck again. 'Anyway,' he continued, 'Sandstorm was the pick of their herd. He was their ruler's personal mount. I convinced them that if Tug and I could beat him in a race, I would keep Tug.'

'Why didn't they just keep him anyway? Why did they have to race you?'

'The young man in question was having a hard time riding Tug. I agreed to help him if he won the race.'

She snorted disdainfully. 'Can't have been much of a horseman,' she said. 'What was so hard about riding him?'

He was about to answer, then he stopped himself. He felt a sudden, wicked impulse. Maddie was so sure of herself, so quick to denigrate Tug. It might be fun to prick that balloon, he thought.

'I'll tell you later. Anyway, Sandstorm took off like an arrow out of a bow. Tug went off after him, but over the first fifty metres or so, Sandstorm kept pulling away.'

'Well, of course he did,' she said, comfortable in her own certainty.

'The thing was, I was confident that Tug would outlast Sandstorm. Our Ranger horses are bred to have enormous stamina and I made sure the race was over a long distance, not just a sprint. In the second part of the race, we started to gain. We gradually drew up level with him, and we were running neck and neck, with barely three hundred metres to go.'

Will was looking into the distance, but in his mind, he was seeing that desert race course again, looking back over the many years that had passed.

'Tug was running faster than I had ever known him to. But Sandstorm was a great horse. He was matching us. We'd draw ahead a metre or so. Then he'd catch us and draw ahead in his turn.'

He paused, remembering.

Maddie's eyes were alight with the excitement of the tale. 'What happened?'

'Well, Tug sort of took over. He suddenly accelerated away from the other horse, leaving him standing. But Sandstorm made up the gap once more, and as he pulled level, I felt Tug falter in his stride.'

'You'd pushed him too hard,' she said, remembering how she had done the same thing with Sundancer three days previously. Then she frowned. Tug was here with them. Obviously, they hadn't lost the race.

'So I thought. But that slight falter was enough to make Sandstorm give it everything he had. He pulled away again, running like the wind.

'Then, he hit the wall, and Tug suddenly recovered and accelerated past him. I had no idea Tug could move as fast as he did. But even more amazingly, he had faked the other horse into overextending himself. That break in his stride had been intentional, to goad Sandstorm into too great an effort.'

Will grinned at his horse and leaned forward to scratch him between the ears.

'The thing is, we need horses that combine stamina and speed. A Ranger horse can move incredibly quickly, as you'll see later. But it can also keep up that constant lope you saw yesterday for hour after hour, with barely a rest.

'We need that. We travel alone. If we're ever in a tight spot, we need to know that our horses can outlast our enemies' horses — even if they have remounts available to them. We have just the one horse. We need to be able to rely on it.

'Our horses have to be smart and cunning. And be fast. And able to run all day without pause. That's the way they're bred. Our horse breeders have been breeding them that way for generations now.'

'So where are we going now?' she asked, although she thought she already knew. Will's words confirmed her suspicions.

'We're going to see Young Bob. He's our senior horse breeder. And he has your Ranger horse ready for you.'

Young Bob was something of a revelation. Bowlegged and slight of build, he ambled out from his cabin to meet them.

His skin was browned by years of exposure to sun and wind. He was almost completely bald, with just a few tufts of wispy white hair on either side of his head. When he smiled, Maddie saw that he had very few teeth left, and his face was wrinkled and creased with age. She couldn't begin to assess how old he might be.

Only his eyes were young. They were blue and bright and discerning. And clear. He knuckled his forehead to Will as they rode up to his cabin.

'Good day to you, Ranger Will.'

'Good day, Young Bob. Hope you're keeping well,' Will said. Young Bob nodded several times at that, as if considering the statement.

'Oh yes. Can't complain. Can't complain. Get the odd ache and pain now and then, of course, and my back sometimes gives me a terrible twinge . . .' He cackled with laughter. It was a strange, high-pitched sound but Maddie thought it was appropriate, coming from this gnome-like figure.

'But there I go, complaining, don't I?' Young Bob doubled up laughing, then stopped abruptly and turned that surprisingly shrewd gaze on Maddie. She felt she was being assessed.

'There's never been a girl apprentice before,' he said.

She nodded. 'I know.'

'So, how are you enjoying it? Do you like it?'

She hesitated. It had been some time since she'd even considered that question. The days had been too busy learning new skills and perfecting her shooting and slinging to ask herself if she was enjoying it.

'Yes. I am,' she answered after a pause. She was surprised to find that she meant it.

Young Bob tilted his head to one side to study her more closely. The smile faded as he looked at her, assessing her. He seemed to approve of what he saw.

'Good for you,' he said. 'It's a big chance you've been given. Make the most of it.'

'I plan to,' she said. She was conscious of Will's appraising gaze on her. Conscious, too, that she meant what she said. She did plan to make the most of this opportunity and she felt another quick sense of surprise as she realised it.

And suddenly, that smile split Young Bob's wizened face once more.

'Course, she can't be no Ranger without no Ranger horse, can she, Ranger Will?'

'That's what I've been telling her,' Will agreed.

'Then I'd best fetch one for her.' Young Bob turned away, hobbling quickly towards a large stable building that stood behind his cabin. He moved in a slightly sideways shuffle, hopping across the dusty ground.

When she judged he was well out of earshot, Maddie leaned over in her saddle and said softly to Will, 'Why do you call him Young Bob? He's positively ancient.'

Too late, he held up a hand to forestall her. But Young Bob turned back to face them, cackling once more.

'Cause my father is Old Bob — and he's even more ancient than me.'

He turned away again, resuming that strange, half-hopping gait towards the stables. He had gone another five metres when he glanced back over his shoulder at her.

'And he's the one who's deaf. I ain't.'

Maddie glanced at Will, holding her hands out, palm uppermost, in a helpless gesture. He shrugged.

The bent-over figure disappeared into the stable. A few seconds later, they heard a horse whinny from inside the large building. Tug instantly responded. Sundancer's ears pricked up and he looked around. He was a little unsure of himself in these surroundings. Tug, by contrast, seemed perfectly at home.

Young Bob emerged into the morning sunlight, leading a horse behind him. In spite of her misgivings about Ranger horses, Maddie leaned forward expectantly. This was to be her mount, after all.

Like Tug, he was stocky and barrel-chested, and somewhat short in the legs. His mane and tail were both long and his coat was on the shaggy side. But he'd been curried and brushed until his coat almost gleamed. And she felt a catch in her throat as she saw that he was a piebald — marked in irregular patterns of white and black. She'd always fancied piebalds.

Young Bob led the horse up to them. Tug whinnied again and moved forward to nuzzle the other horse. Sundancer stepped nervously, backing off a few paces.

'This here's Bumper,' Young Bob said.

'Bumper?' Maddie asked.

The horse breeder cackled again, patting the horse affectionately. 'Named him that when he was a foal. He used to like to bump into things — see if they'd fall over. He's over that now.'

As if on cue, the piebald butted him with his nose, causing him to stagger a few steps.

'Well, mostly, anyways,' he admitted.

Maddie was studying the horse, discerning the powerful muscles hidden under that well-brushed coat. Bumper looked at her and she saw the intelligence and empathy in his eyes. She felt a sudden rush of ownership — no, she thought, it was more like friendship.

'What do you think of him?' Will asked, his eyes intent on his young apprentice.

And for the third time in ten minutes, Maddie found herself somewhat surprised by her reply.

'He's beautiful,' she said softly.

Twenty

'**W**ell, slide down from there and I'll saddle him up for you,' Young Bob told her. 'I assume you'll want to use your own saddle?'

She nodded as she slipped from Sundancer's back. A saddle was a very personal item. She was used to this one and she was comfortable on it.

'Yes, please,' she said. Young Bob started to move towards Sundancer, but Will held up a hand to stop him.

'I think we'll let Maddie do her own saddling,' he said. 'May as well get started the way we mean to continue, and we don't have any stable hands to help us at the cabin.'

Maddie didn't mind saddling and bridling the horse. She'd been doing that for several years now. Young Bob hopped away towards the fence and retrieved a rope halter. He slipped it over Sundancer's neck as Maddie removed the bridle from the Arridan.

'Nice horse,' he said, looking approvingly at Sundancer's lines. 'Got a good turn of speed, these Arridans, and a nice nature too. Pity he's a gelding.'

Maddie slipped the bridle over Bumper's head. The little horse actually lowered his head to allow her to do so. She stopped and looked curiously at Young Bob.

'Why's that?' she asked.

'Would have liked to borrow him for a year or so. Use him in our breeding programme.'

'He's a bit fine in the limbs for a Ranger horse, isn't he?' Will asked. In the course of his career, he'd unhorsed many armed riders by the simple expedient of having Tug charge headlong into their horses. The Arridan's legs were too fragile for that sort of behaviour, he thought.

Bob scratched his nose thoughtfully. 'Mebbe so. But we could use the speed. Breed him with something a little heavier and you'd get speed and a good solid build as well.'

Maddie had the bit and bridle set now. Bumper moved his mouth open and shut, chewing until he settled the bit into a comfortable position. Maddie quickly unbuckled the saddle and heaved it off Sundancer's back, turning to carry it to Bumper.

The piebald pushed his neck forward to study the saddle. She felt his warm breath on her hands as he sniffed and snorted at it, his nostrils distending then contracting as he breathed in and out. After several seconds, he straightened up again and shook his head several times, as if giving her his approval.

She set it down, then fetched the saddle blanket from Sundancer's back. Once again, she allowed Bumper to study it, making sure that he gave it his approval. Then she spread it over his back, setting it smoothly and evenly, without wrinkles. She reached down and, with a slight grunt of effort, she hefted the saddle up and onto his back.

Bumper turned his head to eye her curiously. She grinned at him.

'All right?' she asked and he shook his mane several times. She reached under his belly to retrieve the hanging girth strap, then, pushing the saddle flap and stirrup up to expose the buckle end, she passed the girth through the buckle and heaved it tight. She hauled it in one more notch so that the saddle was firmly seated on the horse's back. She paused, watching Bumper to see if he was going to release any pent-up breath — she'd seen Tug's little trick when Will was saddling him over the past few weeks. But Bumper had no such guile in him. She patted his neck approvingly and he looked back at her again, moving his head up and down. For a moment, she could have sworn he was trying to speak to her. She shook her head, dismissing the thought.

She pulled the side flap and stirrup back down into position and looked at the two men who were watching her. There was something . . . expectant in the way they were looking. She glanced from one to another. She had the sensation that they knew something she didn't.

'Before you mount up —' Young Bob began, but Will quickly cut across him.

'Is there anything you want to ask? Anything you need to know?'

A look passed between the two of them. She cocked her head to one side and smiled. The smile was just a trifle supercilious.

'I have ridden a horse before, you know,' she said.

Will nodded. 'So you have.'

'And he looks pretty calm and placid.'

Will pursed his lips thoughtfully. 'Calm is accurate. I'm not sure that placid is the correct choice of word.'

She smiled indulgently, looking at Bumper, standing rock steady, without the usual fidgeting that horses often went on with when they had just been saddled.

'Oh, I think it's pretty accurate,' she said confidently.

Will made a sweeping gesture with his right hand. 'Then, if you're sure, go right ahead.'

She looked at Young Bob and he shrugged. She took the reins in her left hand and turned the stirrup so she could put her left foot into it. As she did so, Bumper turned again to study her. There was something expectant in his expression as well, she thought. Then she shook her head. Horses don't have expressions, she told herself.

She bounced once on her right toes. She noted that Bumper stood perfectly still for her. Often, a horse would try to sidle away as a rider tried to mount. She nodded at him.

'Good boy,' she said and swung herself easily up and into the saddle.

And all hell broke loose.

Bumper seemed to spring off the ground from all four feet, arching his back and throwing her off balance. Then he came down with a teeth-jarring crash and promptly put his head down, exploding his rump up into the air.

Maddie was a good rider but she'd never felt a horse buck like this before. In addition, she hadn't yet gained a firm seat and she felt herself sliding off to the right.

Bumper exploded away again in another of those spring-heeled leaps. But this time he went left, out from under her. She realised she would never regain her seat and kicked her left foot free of the stirrup. It was all too obvious that she was going to fall. Bumper started to rear back on his hind legs. She leant forward to compensate and realised, too late, that he was foxing.

His head went down again and his rear quarters shot into the air like a giant equine catapult.

She felt herself leave the saddle, soaring up and forward over the horse. She twisted in the air, hoping to land somehow on her feet. And she nearly made it. But she was too far off balance to manage it completely and she crashed into the dust of the saddling yard, the force of her fall driving the breath from her lungs.

Winded and groaning, she lay in the dust, desperately trying to drag air back into her temporarily empty lungs. She opened her eyes and realised that Bumper had moved to look down on her, a quizzical expression on his face. He snorted softly, blowing warm air onto her face. It was almost as if he were checking to see if she was all right.

She rolled onto her side and came up on one knee, looking around the saddling yard. Young Bob and Will were watching her with knowing expressions. Sundancer was looking quite alarmed. Tug seemed to be smiling quietly.

Maddie stood, a little shakily, and glared at them.

'You *knew* that was going to happen,' she said accusingly.

Will considered the statement for a second or so. Then nodded.

'Well, yes, as a matter of fact,' he said. He waited until Maddie had beaten some of the dust from her clothes, then went on. 'It's just you've been a little . . . condescending about our horses,' he said. 'I thought it might be useful if you saw they're not all solid and stolid and plodding. That they have a certain amount of fire in them.'

She rubbed her back painfully. 'You've got that right,' she said. She glared at Bumper, who approached her now and bumped her gently with his forehead. There was no sign of wickedness or contrary behaviour in his eyes. They were big and dark and liquid and friendly.

'Why did you do that?' she asked him.

''Cause he's been trained that way,' Young Bob told her.

She looked at him in disbelief. 'You've trained him to buck me off whenever I mount him?' She couldn't see much future in having a horse who behaved that way.

But Young Bob was shaking his head. 'He's trained to buck off anyone who hasn't used his permission phrase.'

She frowned at that and Will explained. 'All our horses have a code phrase,' he said. 'If you use it when you first meet a Ranger horse, he'll allow you to mount him and ride him with no problems. If you don't, he'll buck like Gorlog himself until he throws you off. Which, in your case, didn't take long.'

'Gorlog?' she asked. 'Who's Gorlog?'

'A very useful Skandian demigod,' he told her. But she was still absorbing the rest of what he'd said.

'So Ranger horses have some secret code? I've never heard of such a thing.'

'You've never heard of anyone stealing a Ranger horse, either.' Young Bob cackled in delight.

'Which has come in useful several times over my life,' Will told her.

Again, Maddie frowned, not quite believing them. It all sounded too far-fetched. 'So I have to say this . . . code word . . . whenever I mount up?'

Young Bob shook his head. 'Just the first time. After that, he'll know you.'

'So, what do we say?' She addressed the question to Will but he pointed to Young Bob.

'It's different for each horse,' Will said. 'You might as well know that for Tug it's "Do you mind?". There may come a time when you have to ride him, so it's worthwhile your knowing it.'

Maddie looked to Young Bob now. She still wasn't sure if she believed all this. She wondered if she was letting herself in for another bone-shuddering dumping from Bumper's back.

'So?' she said.

Young Bob frowned thoughtfully for a second or two, then replied, 'With Bumper, you say "Don't break me".'

Her eyes widened in disbelief. 'Don't break me?' she said.

Both Will and Young Bob replied in a triumphant chorus. 'Don't say it to us! Say it to the horse!'

'You whisper it in his ear just before you mount,' Will added. She recalled now that when she had gone to mount Bumper before, he had turned to her as if expecting something. Maybe, she thought, just maybe, they were telling her the truth.

She approached the little piebald again, crossing the reins and setting them on the saddle pommel. She stood for a second or two and, sure enough, Bumper turned his head to her. She leaned up on tiptoe and whispered in his ear.

'Don't break me.'

Bumper nodded his head, as if satisfied. Before he could change his mind, she put her left foot in the stirrup and swung up into the saddle.

She tensed, waiting, fearing the worst. Five seconds passed. Then ten. Bumper was as solid and unmoving as a wooden horse. Gradually, she realised that they had been telling her the truth.

Some day, she promised herself, she would get them back for this.

'Walk him round,' Young Bob told her. 'Get the feel of him.'

She touched Bumper with her heels and, instantly, he came to life. They walked, then trotted, around the saddling yard and she marvelled at the lightness and springiness of his step. She had thought the little Ranger horses appeared stolid and heavy. But once she was astride him, she realised how false this impression had been.

Bumper stepped lightly and eagerly. He responded to the lightest touch on the reins, the slightest pressure of her knees.

'Press with your left knee,' Will called and she did so — although now that she was aware of Bumper's response level, she applied only the lightest pressure.

Instantly, he danced sideways. She pressed with her right knee and he danced several paces the other way. Then she used both knees and he continued his straight-ahead progress.

What she had seen — or thought she had seen — and what she was experiencing were two completely different matters. Young Bob moved past her as she circled the yard and unhitched the gate, clearing the way to the open fields beyond.

'Take him for a run,' he said.

She urged the little horse through the gate and touched

her heels to his side again, loosening the tension on the reins.

The response was startling. Bumper accelerated like an arrow from a bow, so quickly that she was nearly left behind. But he sensed her momentary loss of balance and slowed, allowing her to regain her seat. Then he was off again, neck stretched out, legs reaching in great, bounding strides.

The speed was incredible. She had never ridden so fast in her life.

You didn't expect this, did you?

'No, I didn't,' she replied, shocked to find that she was talking to her horse — and, even more surprising, her horse had seemed to talk to her.

From the paddock, Will and Young Bob watched the horse and rider receding further and further into the distance.

'You've done well, Bob,' Will told him.

Young Bob was shading his eyes against the bright sun, watching Maddie and Bumper get acquainted.

'She's a good rider. Got a balanced seat and nice soft hands. You could see that from her Arridan's mouth.'

They fell silent for some minutes, watching the horse and rider, hearing the faint drumming of Bumper's hooves on the grass. Then, in a mock casual tone that didn't fool Young Bob for a moment, Will asked:

'I don't suppose Bellerophon is around, is he?'

Young Bob cackled with delight.

'Wondered how long it'd take you to ask! He's in the stable.'

Twenty-one

Maddie spent another two hours getting acquainted with her new horse. Bob took her through some of the basic commands that Ranger horses were trained to respond to — how to change gait on the rider's signal, how to press harder into the ground on each pace so that a tracker following the Ranger might not realise that his quarry had dismounted and the horse was now riderless. Plus there were basic movements that could come in useful in combat — sidestepping and backing up, rearing onto the hind legs, pirouetting in place, lashing out at an enemy with the front hooves and kicking back with both rear legs.

All Ranger horses came ready trained in these basic manoeuvres — and a lot more besides. Maddie delighted in Bumper's instant response to the hand, knee and foot signals that Young Bob taught her. It was almost as if all she had to do was think about the movement she wanted and Bumper responded before the thought was fully formed.

She continued to be amazed at his lightness of step. It was a constant surprise to see how quickly he moved, how rapidly he changed direction, and how he could accelerate from a standing start to a full gallop almost instantaneously.

Sundancer was a fine horse, there was no doubt about that. But Bumper seemed to be an extension of her own personality. He knew what she wanted of him, and did it, quickly and smoothly.

Maddie and Bumper ranged across the fields and through the woods, accompanied by Young Bob on a retired Ranger horse. Eventually, Bob decreed that she had learned enough for one morning and they rode back, cantering in that steady, loping stride until they were half a kilometre away. Then, at Bob's signal, Maddie gave Bumper his head and streaked away from him, her cloak and long hair streaming out in the wind behind her.

Going to have to cut that hair, she thought, then gave herself over to the sheer exhilaration of Bumper's speed and power and surefootedness.

She reined in as they drew closer to the cabin. She was surprised to see Tug standing in the saddling paddock, while Will rode bareback on an old grey horse, moving at a gentle canter around the field adjoining the saddling paddock. He saw her coming and waved, heading his mount towards her. Bumper whinnied a greeting and the old grey responded. As they drew closer, she could see that the hairs around his muzzle were white. But there was something vaguely familiar about him, she thought.

'Who's that?' she asked, as she reined in beside Will. He gave a faint smile and leaned forward to run his fingers through the horse's shaggy mane, tugging it affectionately.

'An old friend,' he said. 'Named Bellerophon. I like to see him whenever I'm out this way. But it's been a while. Haven't seen him since . . .'

The words faded and so did his smile. Instinctively, Maddie knew that he had been about to say *since Alyss died*. She covered up the awkward lull in the conversation.

'He looks somehow . . . familiar,' she said.

Will nodded and pointed to where Tug was standing in the saddling yard.

'He looks like Tug,' he said, and she nodded, seeing the resemblance now that he mentioned it. This horse was older, and his grey hair was white around the muzzle. But his whole conformation was the same. And he stood the same way, holding his head at a slight angle while he listened to them, just as she'd noticed Tug doing.

'He was my first Ranger horse,' Will continued. 'In fact, he was my first horse. I didn't have a wealthy mum and dad — and I didn't have a smart Arridan to ride on.'

Will tried the gibe as an experiment, to see if the reference to her parents, and the associated fact that they had disowned her, would produce an angry reaction. He was pleased to see that she smiled in return.

Interesting, he thought. Perhaps she meant what she said to Young Bob. Perhaps she is starting to enjoy all this.

'So how long ago was that?' Maddie asked.

Will shook his head. 'Longer than I care to remember. But I recall I was just as excited about him as you seem to be about young Bumper here.'

Bumper snorted and shook his mane at the mention of his name. Maddie leaned forward and patted his neck.

'He really is remarkable,' she said. 'You have no idea.'

'I'm sure I don't,' Will replied gravely.

Just then Young Bob cantered slowly up to join them. His face split in that now familiar smile as he eyed Will on Bellerophon's back.

'How does he feel?' he asked.

Will looked down at the horse, leaning a little to see the traces of the cruel scar that marked his right shoulder.

'Like I've never been away,' he admitted.

Young Bob chuckled. He'd grown up in the service of the Rangers and their horses and he always enjoyed seeing them reunited. 'He's still got quite a turn of speed on him, hasn't he?'

Will shook his head. 'I didn't want to push him too hard,' he said. 'I didn't want him straining anything or pulling any muscles.'

'Aaah, not that one,' the horse trainer said. 'He'd run at the drop of a hat, he would. And he'd show some of these younger ones his heels while he was at it.'

At which statement, both Bumper and Tug raised their heads and snorted and stamped a protest. Bellerophon looked from one to the other. Maddie could have sworn that he sniggered, if a horse could ever be said to do so.

They brushed and watered the horses, then had lunch with Young Bob. Will had brought fresh, crusty bread and sharp cheese, and several thick slices of ham. And Bob had crisp fresh lettuces and radishes from his small vegetable plot. Bob and Will drank coffee, sweetening it with large spoonfuls of honey. Maddie, as was her custom, drank milk.

Young Bob shook his head as he watched her.

'Don't know as I've heard of a Ranger who didn't drink coffee,' he said doubtfully.

Will shrugged. He was almost resigned to Maddie's dislike of the traditional Ranger brew by now.

'New times, Bob,' he said. 'I suppose we have to move with them.'

'Not me. Tradition is tradition, I say. Enough change that you've got a female apprentice, without her not drinking coffee. It's too much change, too quick.'

'Excuse me,' said Maddie, 'do you have to discuss me and my drinking habits while I'm sitting right here?'

The two men regarded her for several seconds. Then they looked at each other and replied in unison.

'Yes.'

Maddie rolled her eyes and reached for the tumbler of milk. She took a deep draught of the fresh, cool liquid.

'You don't know what you're missing,' she told Will.

'Nor do I want to,' he replied.

When they finished the meal, Will and Maddie cleared the table and washed the platters and knives they had been using. While they were doing so, Young Bob excused himself and went outside. He'd gone silent towards the end of the meal and Maddie looked curiously at Will.

'He's saying goodbye to Bumper,' he told her. 'Bob gets very attached to his horses. Sometimes I believe that he thinks they're only on loan to us. In a way, I suppose they are,' he added.

She moved to the window and glanced out. The little bowlegged man was standing by Bumper, his face almost touching the horse's. She could see his lips moving but she couldn't make out the words. Instinctively, she began to move towards the door, but Will stopped her.

'Leave them,' he said. 'You'll embarrass both of them if they see you're watching.'

She nodded, realising he was right, and moved back to the kitchen table. Will had washed the plates and she took a small towel and began to dry them, stacking them when she had done so. A few minutes later, Bob re-entered the cabin, his smile back in place.

'Just a few last-minute instructions for the boy,' he said. 'Wanted to make sure he wouldn't buck you off again — less'n you deserve it.'

They made their farewells to Young Bob, then went out to where their horses were waiting. They mounted and rode out, with Maddie leading Sundancer on a light halter. The Arridan seemed content to follow behind them. He didn't seem concerned that he had been replaced in Maddie's affections by the shaggy little black-and-white-patched horse. But then, he and Maddie had never had the close relationship that had already developed between her and Bumper. She chattered happily as they rode, extolling her new horse's many virtues.

For the most part, Will responded with monosyllabic grunts, but she seemed not to notice his lack of enthusiasm for the subject of her horse and his amazing qualities.

'He's so light on his feet!' she gushed. 'You'd swear they barely touch the ground when he's galloping. And as for his speed! Well, I've never seen a horse run as fast as he can. He really is quite incredible! One time, we came upon a ditch before I realised it was there and he simply gathered himself and seemed to fly over it! Honestly, it was like flying. One minute we were galloping, the next we were soaring over this ditch.'

Tug turned his head to look at Will. Will shrugged. Tug broke wind. But Maddie didn't seem to notice. Or if she did, she didn't understand that Tug intended the rude noise as a judgemental comment.

'And then Bob showed me how I could get him to pace harder, so that a tracker couldn't see if I'd dismounted. Did you know they could do that?'

'I seem to recall hearing it many years ago,' Will replied dryly. He sensed Tug was about to make another unpleasant noise and poked him sharply with his hand to stop him. Tug shook his mane.

'Yes, well, they can do it. And he showed me so many of his other tricks and little ways. Bumper really is quite amazing!'

Finest horse that ever lived.

Will squeezed Tug gently with his thighs to let him know he had heard. He thought Maddie might feel it was odd if he started having a conversation with his horse. Which was what made her next question all the more remarkable.

'Will,' she began, 'can I ask you a question?'

'You just did,' he replied, and felt an instant pang of nostalgia. How many times had that same exchange taken place between himself and Halt, he wondered? He was pleased to see that Maddie was just as thrown out of her stride by that reply as he used to be.

'What? Oh . . . er. Yes, I suppose I did. But anyway, can I ask you another . . .' She stopped herself in time as she realised she was leaving herself open to the same reply. She paused, then said, choosing her words deliberately, 'I'd like to ask a question if you don't mind.'

Will nodded assent. 'Go right ahead.'

'Well, it's just . . . I mean . . . this may sound silly, I suppose . . .'

'Wouldn't be too surprised by that.'

She glared at him. She desperately wanted to ask her question but was fearful that she might make herself look foolish. Will gestured for her to continue. She took a deep breath.

'I mean . . . do you ever get the feeling that your horse is talking to you?'

That caused Will to sit up straight in the saddle. He'd never discussed the communication he experienced with Tug. He'd long suspected that Halt and Abelard had a similar bond. But apparently, Maddie had felt it already with Bumper.

Perhaps we were right in selecting her for the Corps, he thought. Aloud, he replied: 'A horse? Talking? Are you serious?'

Maddie went very red in the face and looked away hurriedly.

'No. No. Just a silly notion, I suppose. Forget I mentioned it.'

He nodded. But he didn't forget it. The comment stayed with him long into that night.

Twenty-two

Maddie's training continued, but now there was an extra element added to her schedule. In addition to her other skill training, she now had daily sessions with Bumper, where horse and rider developed their already close relationship into a deep, intimate understanding.

Bumper was rapidly becoming, as she had previously observed, an extension of herself, responding to her slightest signal, instantly aware of what she expected of him. In turn, she learned to interpret the many signals the horse sent to her — warnings of possible danger, the presence of an unknown person or the approach of a potentially dangerous animal.

There were also fitness sessions, involving long runs through the surrounding countryside, or the obstacle course that Will had improvised for her. He alternated these with basic instruction in unarmed combat, teaching her to strike with the heel of her hand rather than a closed fist — 'A fist is an excuse to break your fingers,' he said —

and how to use an attacker's weight and impetus against him in a series of simple yet effective movements.

And there were tracking and camouflage lessons. Will and Maddie rode through the fief, looking for and identifying different animal tracks, following innocent travellers without making them aware that they were being tracked and standing, wrapped in her cloak, on the verge of the road, while travellers passed by, oblivious to the fact that Maddie was a few metres away.

'Trust the cloak,' Will told her repeatedly. 'And don't move. Even if you think you've been spotted.'

So her days were full and, at the end of each one, she was happy to roll into her bed, exhausted, and sleep soundly till the following morning, when the whole sequence would begin again.

She still went to Wensley Village each morning to fetch fresh bread and milk for the day. But now she rode instead of walking.

Will had previously banned her from riding Sundancer to the village. 'He's altogether too exotic for these parts,' he had told her cryptically. But now that she had Bumper, he lifted this restriction. 'A Ranger and her horse should do things together,' he explained.

Maddie wasn't quite sure what the difference was, but she was happy to ride Bumper, talking to him, patting him and generally enjoying his company, on her early morning excursions. Even a task as simple as fetching bread and milk became enjoyable in Bumper's company, she thought. Perhaps that was what Will had in mind.

So the sight of the small, upright figure, wrapped in her camouflage cloak, riding the shaggy black and white horse and with her bow across the saddle in front of her, became a familiar one in the village. Maddie was at first bemused, then a little flattered, as she realised that she had become something of a celebrity among the teenagers in the village. As a Ranger, she was a mysterious and intriguing figure — all the more so because she was the first girl to be taken on for Ranger training.

There was a group of half a dozen boys and girls roughly her own age in the village. They looked on her with some awe and a lot of respect — and envy. Their own lives were routine and circumscribed. Life in a small village held little in the way of excitement, whereas the new girl among them was an apprentice Ranger. She carried a bow, and they had observed on several occasions, when they had crept through the woods to watch her practise, that she knew how to use it.

As Maddie rode through the village, they took to calling to her and greeting her. From time to time she would rein Bumper in and stop to talk with them. She enjoyed their obvious hero worship — particularly that of the young girls. She wouldn't have been human if she hadn't. She found a quiet satisfaction and enjoyment in being a minor celebrity. But by now she had learned not to become too full of herself because of it.

Of course, in her time at Castle Araluen, she had had a circle of admirers and acquaintances. But she had sensed that most of them were more impressed by her title and her position than by her personal worth. At Araluen, she was the princess, and people around her vied for her attention and approval simply because she was the princess — not out of any real desire to be her friends.

Here, it was different. Aside from a small circle of people that included Jenny, Baron Arald and Lady Sandra, Halt and Lady Pauline, nobody knew Maddie's real identity. Will had thought it best not to reveal her royal lineage to others.

So Maddie enjoyed the admiration and the friendship of the young people of Wensley. From time to time, when her busy schedule permitted, she rode to the village and spent time with them, coaching some of the boys in archery, fishing in the calm waters of the river with them and playing games of hide and seek — which she invariably won, until the others banned the use of her cloak.

Will watched these activities with a careful eye. 'Don't get too close to them,' he cautioned. 'Rangers need to maintain a certain separation from the ordinary people. It helps if they hold us in a little awe. It maintains the mystique.'

Still, he thought, it was good for her to learn to relate to the common people — as opposed to the self-important sprigs of nobility who inhabited Castle Araluen. He was pleased to see that she didn't put on airs or graces any more. He could see she enjoyed being respected for her abilities and he saw no harm in that.

'Better to be respected for what you can do, rather than who your parents are,' he said to Jenny on one occasion. His friend looked at him keenly as he said it, watching the way his eyes followed Maddie as she laughed and joked with a group of local youngsters.

The lines of pain, graved in his face by Alyss's loss, were still evident. But they had softened, and the grim expression wasn't quite as grim as it had been. At times, she sensed, he was on the brink of smiling. There was a fondness in his eyes as he watched his goddaughter — one that he hastily disguised when she was aware of him.

She's doing him good, Jenny thought, smiling to herself. She had long forgiven Maddie's bumptious remark to her. The week after she said it, the girl had appeared on the doorstep of Jenny's cottage, a bunch of flowers in her hand and a remorseful look on her face, and apologised profusely. Jenny, warm-hearted and forgiving, accepted the apology instantly. Since then, they had become friends, with Jenny ever ready to listen to Maddie as she bemoaned her lack of talent with the bow — a totally inaccurate assessment of her ability, Jenny knew.

'If you want practice,' she had told Maddie, 'I can always use fresh game in my restaurant.'

In the following weeks, she had received a steady stream of rabbits, hares and wildfowl, either shot with Maddie's bow or brought down by her sling. It was evident that Maddie, who had spent her life having every whim catered for, was enjoying doing something for someone else.

And Jenny was more than content to be that someone else, so long as the game kept appearing on her doorstep.

It was a Friday morning. Maddie was riding back from the small dairy farm at the end of the village. A sack of warm loaves was hung across her saddle bow, the smell of fresh bread hitting her nostrils and reminding her stomach that she hadn't yet had breakfast. Two of the local teenagers waved her down and she checked Bumper, calling a greeting to them as they stepped out into the road.

'Morning, Gordon. Morning, Lucy,' she said. They

were two of her favourites. Lucy was the daughter of Mistress Buttersby, Wensley's seamstress. She was a gangly, freckled girl who was something of a tomboy. Gordon was dark-haired and had mischievous blue eyes. He was something of a rogue, although she felt there was no real harm or malice in him.

He glanced around now, making sure that nobody was listening, then spoke to her in a lowered voice.

'What are you doing tomorrow?'

She frowned, thinking. 'Nothing,' she replied. She had a free Saturday for the first time in weeks. Will was going to the castle to have dinner with Halt, Pauline and Baron Arald and Lady Sandra. 'Why?'

Lucy giggled. 'We're having a party,' she said, her tone conspiratorial.

Maddie cocked her head curiously. A party was no reason for their lowered voices and constant looking around. Something was afoot, she realised.

'Just a party?' she asked.

Lucy giggled again and Gordon grinned. He had a very attractive grin, Maddie thought. There was all sorts of devilment in it.

'A . . . special kind of party,' he said. 'Behind the stable at the inn. Lucy's bringing game pies and lamb on skewers. And we're going to bake potatoes in the fire.'

Lucy worked as a waitress in Jenny's restaurant. From time to time, Jenny rewarded her with choice bits of food from the menu. At other times, Lucy surreptitiously helped herself. Maddie guessed that this was one of those times, which would account for the knowing grins both her friends wore.

'And Martin's got a cask!' Lucy burst out, unable to contain herself. Then she dissolved in a fit of giggles.

'A cask?' Maddie asked, although she was beginning to understand what Lucy meant. 'A cask of what?'

'Of wine!' Gordon said triumphantly. 'Fine wine, it is, too. Will you join us?'

Maddie hesitated. She knew she shouldn't. But she had been working hard for weeks now, with very few breaks and little time to herself. She didn't know if she liked wine or not. But she knew she liked adventure and there was still a streak of the rebel in her. She deserved a chance to let her hair down, she thought. And nobody would know.

'Why not?' she told them.

Twenty-three

'I won't be too late,' Will said as he paused at the door. 'Halt and Pauline aren't night owls these days.'

Maddie looked up from her meal. Will had felt a little guilty, knowing that he'd be enjoying dinner from Master Chubb's kitchen at the castle. Maddie's cooking skills were improving, but they were still in the rudimentary phase. Accordingly, he'd arranged for a meal to be delivered from Jenny's restaurant.

She spooned another mouthful of the savoury spiced beef stew into her mouth, and nodded as she chewed and swallowed.

'I'll probably be asleep,' she told him. 'I'm looking forward to an early night myself.'

They'd had a long day, riding far afield and practising stalking and tracking, in addition to her normal daily work-outs with bow, knives and sling. She affected a yawn now.

Will took his cloak from the peg inside the door and swung it round his shoulders.

'Sable's here anyway, in case you need her,' he said. 'Keep the door bolted from the inside.'

Maddie nodded. There was a concealed release mechanism that could be used to unbolt the door from the outside, but a random visitor, or intruder, wouldn't know about that. She made a shooing gesture with her hand, seeing that Will seemed uneasy at leaving her by herself.

'Go along,' she said. 'I'll be fine.'

He came to a decision. 'All right then,' he said and went out.

Maddie heard his soft footsteps along the porch as he walked to the rear of the cabin, where the horses were stabled. Tug greeted him with a soft whinny. A few minutes later, she heard the little horse's hoofbeats as Will rode past the cabin and to the path that led to Castle Redmont. Once the hoofbeats faded away and she was certain he had gone, her feigned weariness dropped away and she began moving with greater urgency. Rising, she took the half-finished bowl of stew to the kitchen bench and scraped the contents into the scrap bucket. She was looking forward to the game pies and lamb skewers Lucy had promised and, tasty as the stew might be, she wanted to keep her appetite sharp.

She glanced into the scrap bucket and noticed that the beef stew was a little too visible, sitting on top of the other contents and making it obvious that she'd hardly eaten any of it. Taking the ladle from the pot that held the remainder of the stew, she moved the contents of the bucket around until the stew was mixed in and hidden from casual view.

She stepped back and surveyed her work, then nodded, satisfied. Going into her room, she took the saddle pack that she used to carry her camping gear, rolled it into a cylinder and placed it in her bed, pulling the blankets up around it. She tilted her head as she studied it. It looked too rigid and regular, she decided, so she pulled the blankets back, bent the pack in the middle, then rolled up a spare jacket and placed it at an angle at the bottom of the pack, so that the overall look was of a person with legs bent at the knee. Much more realistic, she decided, and pulled the blankets up again, tucking them high around the pillow to conceal the fact that there was no head resting there. If Will looked in on her when he arrived home, it would be a cursory look only, she thought. The pack and rolled jacket should pass muster.

She blew out the lantern in her room and hurried to the front door. It was second nature to her to swing her cloak around her shoulders as she went out. The simple latch lock clunked shut behind her. Without thinking, she turned towards the stable, then stopped herself. Will was riding Tug, which meant that he would put his horse back in the stable when he arrived home. If Bumper wasn't there, it would be a dead giveaway that she had gone out. She turned back. Bumper, who had heard her footsteps stop and turn away, whinnied once, a little reproachfully.

'Sorry, boy,' she said under her breath. 'You can't come tonight.'

Sable was lying, head on her paws, on the edge of the verandah. She rose expectantly. But Maddie waved a hand at her to stay.

'You too, girl,' she told her. 'Stay.' Sable lay back down again, covering the last few inches in a kind of slithering thud as her paws slid on the floorboards, and grunting softly as she did.

Maddie took one last look around. The lantern beside the door was turned low, which was how Will left it every night. That way, it cast just enough illumination over the steps and doorway in case of an unexpected visitor. Then she turned and hurried down the dark path through the trees, heading for Wensley Village.

She stayed in the shadows on the edge of the high street as she reached the village. Jenny's restaurant was one of the first buildings on the street. It was brightly lit and she could hear the loud babble of voices from inside. The restaurant was a popular spot in Wensley and on a Saturday night it was likely to attract patrons from the countryside around the village as well. She kept to the far side of the street as she passed, hugging the cloak around her as she moved through the shadows.

Trust the cloak, Will had told her repeatedly. She wasn't sure if it was intended to help her in such a devious mission as the one she was on.

So far as she could tell, nobody noticed her. That was hardly surprising. The restaurant patrons would be intent on their food and their conversation. And they were in a brightly lit room. It was highly unlikely that any of them might notice the dim figure slipping through the shadows across the street.

As she neared the village inn, the babble of voices from Jenny's restaurant died away, to be gradually replaced by another sound. There was a travelling minstrel in the inn, entertaining the people who had chosen to go there for the evening. As she listened, the music stopped and there was a burst of applause. Her friends had picked a good night for their party, she thought. There was plenty of activity in the village to mask any sounds they might make.

Looking at the stable situated beyond the inn, she could make out the dull glimmer of a small fire reflected from the walls. She let herself into the saddling yard. Lucy, Gordon and another friend, Martin, were sitting round a small fire in the rear of the yard, a spot that was hidden from casual observers in the street. If she hadn't known about the fire, she probably wouldn't have noticed the dull flicker on the walls.

But she did notice the delicious smell of grilling lamb. As she approached, her friends called a greeting to her.

'You're late,' Martin said cheerfully.

She shrugged an apology. 'I had to wait till Will left. He seemed to take forever.'

'Well, you've got some catching up to do,' Gordon told her. He took two sizzling lamb skewers from the fire, put them on a wooden platter and passed it to Lucy. Lucy added a small game pie to the platter as she handed it along. Maddie sat cross-legged by the fire and took the plate. The lamb smelled delicious and her mouth was watering already. Carefully, knowing the meat would be hot, she bit into it.

'Mmmmm! That's delicious, Lucy!' she said appreciatively. Her friend glowed at the compliment.

'They've been marinating for nearly eight hours,' she said. 'That makes them nice and tender.'

'Here,' Martin said, handing her a wooden mug. 'You can wash them down with this.'

Maddie took the mug. Her heart beat a little faster as she sniffed the contents. She could choose to say no now and there would be no harm done. Sneaking out to meet her friends was a minor thing. But drinking wine was another matter altogether. This was crossing a big boundary and, if she were found out, she had no doubt that she would be in trouble.

Gordon saw her hesitate and guessed the reason. 'He'll never know,' he said, grinning a challenge at her.

Abruptly, she decided, and took a deep swig of the wine. It tasted heavy and somewhat sour.

'Mmm, that's good stuff!' she said, wanting to appear sophisticated and knowledgeable. In truth, she had no idea whether the wine was good. She had drunk wine before, on special occasions at Castle Araluen, when official toasts were being drunk. But that wine had been heavily watered and tasted nothing like this.

'I only get the good stuff,' Martin agreed cheerfully. He had no idea, either. In fact, the wine was rather poor quality. But, like Maddie, he wanted to appear as if he drank wine all the time and knew what he was talking about. 'Here,' he added, 'have a top-up.'

He'd decanted some of the wine from a small cask into a jug. He reached across now and slopped more of it into her mug, winking conspiratorially at her.

'Bottoms up,' he said and for a moment she was confused, wondering what he wanted her to do. Then she realised he was talking about the mug. She tipped it and drank deeply. The second mouthful was less sour, although to be honest, she couldn't have said that she found it particularly enjoyable.

Lucy and Gordon drank deeply from their mugs too. Maddie took another bite of the lamb, then a large bite out of the game pie. The pastry was flaky and delicious and the spiced, rich filling seemed to explode flavour into her mouth. Maybe wine made food taste better, she thought. Perhaps that was why people put up with the sour taste.

As the evening went on, she noticed that wine seemed to have other properties as well. It seemed to improve one's ability to converse and to say witty things. She found herself laughing at Gordon's sallies, and replying in kind.

I've never been this amusing before, she thought to herself. She had just made a remark about the Wensley innkeeper, and his fondness for fried food. It seemed to be a hilarious observation. Her three friends laughed uproariously, and she only just managed to prevent a snot snigger as she joined them.

She peered owlishly across the fire at Gordon. His face seemed to be swimming in and out of focus. Must be the effect of the flames, she thought.

'Any wine left?' she asked Martin. He reached for the jug and overbalanced as he did so, narrowly avoiding falling sideways into the fire. They all howled with laughter. Maddie put her finger to her lips in a warning gesture.

'Shhhhhhh!' she said. 'Shomebody will hear us.'

She paused, a little confused, then added: 'Did I shay shomebody?'

'You shertainly did,' Gordon told her.

'And you shaid "shay" as well,' Lucy added, and they all exploded with laughter again. Maddie rocked back and forth, then lost her balance too. She toppled over sideways and lay on the stableyard earth. It seemed too much of an effort to sit up again, so she pulled her cloak around her and closed her eyes.

'Nobody can shee me,' she cackled. 'Trusht the cloak.'

Which profound witticism set them all off once more.

'What the blistering blazes do you think you're doing?'

Will's voice cut across their laughter, cold and angry. She opened her eyes and looked up. He was standing over her, his cloaked, cowled figure outlined against the dark night sky. She heard Lucy's quick gasp of fear. Ordinary village folk knew that Rangers were not people to be trifled with. Gordon's and Martin's laughter had died away and they sat staring fearfully at the dark figure confronting them. The shadow of the cowl hid Will's face, which made him appear more ominous. They had seen him before, of course, riding through the village or sitting in Jenny's restaurant. But here and now, in the dark, shrouded by his cloak and with the fury evident in his voice, he was a daunting figure indeed.

'Sit up, Maddie,' he ordered, his voice cold.

She scrabbled on the ground for purchase, became tangled in her cloak and finally managed to raise herself on her hands until she was sitting upright — although she swayed perilously.

All four teenagers peered anxiously up at the Ranger. Will held out his hand and snapped his fingers at Gordon.

'Give me that cask,' he demanded. Gordon hurried to comply, nearly dropping the wine cask in his haste. Will stepped forward and took it. He shook it experimentally. The cask was a little less than a quarter full and they could hear the wine sloshing around inside it.

Without warning, Will raised it over his head and

hurled it with all his strength at the ground. The cask split into pieces, small planks of wood rebounding upward, the remaining wine fountaining up in a liquid explosion. The movement was so unexpected, so violent, that again Lucy let out a small bleat of fear. The two boys started in fright as well. Will pointed a finger at the three of them, moving it from one to the other as he spoke.

'Your parents will be hearing of this,' he said.

Lucy rose on her knees, pleading with him, as tears began to stream down her face. 'Please, Ranger Will, don't tell my mam. She'll beat me something terrible if she knows.'

If her plea was meant to engender any pity in Will's heart, it failed dismally. He glared briefly at her, then nodded. 'Good,' he said. Then he looked down at Maddie once more, sitting, swaying slightly from side to side.

'On your feet, Maddie,' he said. 'We're going home.'

She rose awkwardly. If she had found it difficult to sit up straight, standing was even more so. She swayed, trying desperately to get her balance. But something was stopping her. Something was making the world spin around her. She realised she was kneeling on her cloak, pulled it free and staggered upright. Will jerked a thumb towards the entrance to the saddling yard.

'On your way,' he said. Then he glanced back at the others. 'You three get home as well. Right now!'

They obeyed, Lucy still sniffling piteously as she went. Once they had merged into the shadows, Will moved to where Tug was waiting for him. He swung up into the saddle with a creak of leather and pointed up the high street.

'Get going,' he ordered curtly.

Maddie felt tears rising to her eyes, but angrily shook them away. The world reeled as she shook her head and she staggered slightly. Then she began to make her way up the middle of the street. Several people were leaving Jenny's restaurant and they stared at the unusual sight of a girl in a Ranger cloak weaving awkwardly up the high street, followed by the grim figure of a mounted Ranger, occasionally urging her to get a move on. Maddie's face flushed with embarrassment. She had begun to enjoy a certain prestige in the village. Now she could feel the world watching her, judging her and finding her wanting. She was really nothing more than a silly little girl.

They passed through the village and entered the narrow path through the trees that led to the cabin. She stumbled once, then again, on the uneven ground. Then she fell, a sharp stone cutting into her knee and tearing her tights. She cried out with the pain, feeling hot blood flowing down her leg. She tried to rise and failed. Her head spun.

Then her stomach heaved and she was violently, helplessly sick. She knelt on hands and knees, retching until her stomach was empty and there was nothing more to throw up.

Will, on Tug's back, towered above her, watching her dispassionately as she alternately retched and sobbed.

'Best thing for you,' he said finally. 'Now get on your feet again.'

Hating him, hating herself even more, she managed to regain her feet and lurched down the dark path towards the cabin. Sable moved to greet her, tail wagging heavily, as she climbed the two steps to the verandah, holding on to the verandah post for balance.

Will clicked his fingers and uttered a command, and the dog slowly backed away, resuming her place on the verandah boards. Maddie felt a deep sob forming in her throat. Even Sable, ever-understanding, never-criticising Sable, was ashamed of her.

'Get to bed,' Will told her, as he turned Tug towards the stable at the rear of the hut. 'We'll talk about this in the morning.'

Twenty-four

Maddie woke with a raging thirst. Her mouth was dry and there was a vile taste in it — a combination of the regurgitated food from the night before and the sour aftertaste of the wine she had drunk. She groaned and sat up in bed, and promptly wished she hadn't.

The movement made her aware of a throbbing headache that pounded like a hammer against the inside of her skull. It seemed to be strongest behind her left eye, but the pain spread throughout the rest of her head as well, like a dark stain on a carpet.

She sank her head into her hands and moaned softly. Her eyes were dry and raspy, as if someone had thrown a handful of sand into them. Her stomach was empty and she had a queasy feeling — for a moment she thought she was going to throw up again. She fought the urge down and looked cautiously at her bedside table, where she normally kept a beaker of cold water. The beaker was empty, lying on its side on the floor. Vaguely, she recalled waking in the night and draining it, then falling back onto her pillow.

She needed water, cold water, desperately. She thought of the rainwater barrel that was set outside the cabin, by one of the downpipes from the roof. At this time of day, the water would be cold and fresh and delicious. And she would be able to plunge her head right into it, letting its cold, icy touch soothe her throbbing skull.

But first, she'd have to reach it.

She stood, carefully. Her head throbbed with the movement, then settled down to a steady, pounding ache. Her stomach heaved and she fought against the urge to throw up. Then, swaying uncertainly, she took a few steps to the door of her room. She leaned against the door jamb for several seconds, re-gathering her sense of balance, then opened the door and went into the small living room, walking gingerly, trying to minimise the impact of her feet on the ground. Every step reverberated through her frame and into her head.

Will was at the kitchen bench, with his back to her. He turned as he heard the door and frowned at her. She became aware that she was still wearing the same clothes she'd worn the night before, minus her cloak. Her tights were torn at the knee and matted with dried blood. There was a vomit stain on her left sleeve. What she couldn't see was that her hair was wildly disordered, standing up in all directions like a misbegotten bird's nest.

'Breakfast is nearly ready,' Will said. His voice was neither condemning or welcoming. His tone was completely neutral. She shook her head, then stopped quickly as the pain surged.

'Don't think I could eat,' she said, her voice hoarse.

He raised an eyebrow at her. 'I think you'd better. You'll need to get something in that stomach.'

The thought of her stomach made her gag. She swayed uncertainly.

'Need a drink,' she said. 'Water.'

He nodded slowly. 'I'm sure you do.' He jerked his head towards the door and she turned and made her painful way to it. For some reason, it seemed more difficult than usual to tug it open. The squeak of its bottom edge against the floorboards made her wince, but she got it open and made her way along the porch, one hand against the cabin wall for balance.

The water butt was almost full. It had rained the previous afternoon and the water would be fresh and clean.

And cold. There was a slight frost on the ground. The temperature had obviously dropped close to zero during the early hours of the morning. She stepped gingerly down from the verandah. It was a step of about fifty centimetres and normally she would manage it with ease. Today, it felt like leaping off a small cliff and her head pounded again as her feet thudded down onto the wet grass.

She groaned. There was a dipper hanging beside the water butt and she seized it eagerly, scooping up cold water and bringing it to her lips, letting it run across her foul-tasting mouth and tongue and down her parched throat. She emptied the dipper in one continuous draught and paused, breathing heavily, heart pounding.

For a moment, the dreadful thirst was slaked. Then it seemed as if she hadn't drunk at all and the awful-tasting dryness was back. She scooped up another dipper and drank, then another.

The cold water was delicious, but its soothing effect lasted barely thirty seconds. She looked at the water, then, setting her hands on either side of the barrel, she plunged her face into it.

The shock of cold was startling. But it seemed to clear her head and eyes. She reared back, throwing water in all directions, feeling it splash down inside her collar. She gasped and spluttered but she felt a little better.

For a few seconds.

Then the remorseless headache, the dryness and the surging, heaving stomach all made themselves felt again. She looked at the treeline, a few metres away from the cabin, and contemplated going into the trees to be sick in private. Maybe to lie down and sleep. She felt dreadfully tired.

Then she realised there would be nothing in her stomach but water, and the thought of the unproductive retching that would result was too much to bear. Her head would split apart, she thought.

'Come and eat something.'

Will was standing at the open door. She looked blearily at him. There was still no sympathy in his voice, but she could sense no condemnation either. She shook her head slowly.

'Couldn't,' she croaked. But he beckoned her inside.

'You need to,' he said. 'Trust me.'

She looked at the edge of the porch. Normally, she would bound up with a light-stepping movement. Today, her legs were like lead and the thought of bounding any-where made her quail. Head down, she trudged along to the steps and climbed heavily onto the porch.

Will had set out a simple breakfast for her. He had toasted two pieces of flat bread and covered them with butter and fruit jam. There was a beaker of milk beside them.

She sat, letting her head rest in her hands for a minute or so. She sensed Will standing behind her chair. He leaned past her and pushed the plate of toasted bread closer to her.

'Go ahead,' he said. 'The sugar in the jam will help. And the milk should settle your stomach.'

She took a sip of the milk. It had been left on the window ledge overnight and it was cold and soothing. She looked at the toast and jam and was struck by conflicting feelings. On the one hand, she was ravenous. On the other, the thought of putting anything into her rebellious, uncertain stomach seemed too much of a risk. Then the milk made its way through her system and she felt the uneasy heaving sensation in her stomach lessen.

Tentatively, she took a bite of toast. The jam was made from berries and its sweet sharpness filled her mouth, fighting the vile sour taste that lingered there. She took another bite, then another sip of milk. Will was right. The food and drink was calming her stomach, and dispelling the bitter taste in her mouth.

It did nothing for the headache, of course. That continued to pound away. Now it had moved its focal point to her temples and they throbbed painfully. She realised she had begun to sweat heavily as well. She looked up at Will with bleary eyes. He was watching her, but still he retained his neutral expression.

'Why do people do this?' she said. Her voice was still a croak, in spite of the palliative effects of the milk.

'Because they're stupid,' he replied shortly. Then he turned away, satisfied that she was going to survive.

'Hurry up and eat,' he said over his shoulder. 'Then you need to change and bathe. Your clothes stink.'

She lifted one sleeve to her nose and sniffed cautiously. He was right. Her clothes reeked of stale woodsmoke and roasted meat, overlaid by the sour smell of vomit and spilled wine.

'Ugh,' she murmured. She finished the toast and milk. Feeling a little better, she collected fresh clothes and a towel from her bedroom and made her way to the bath-house behind the cabin. She looked hopefully at the little stove that was used to heat bath and shower water, but it was unlit. It was going to be a cold shower bath this morning, she thought miserably.

Eating and bathing, albeit in cold water, did a lot to improve her condition. But she was still a long way from feeling better. Her head still pounded and she was sweating heavily. Plus her arms and legs ached, for some unknown reason, and her jaw was sore as well.

Must have slept tensed up, she thought, as she made her way back to the cabin, where Will was waiting impatiently on the porch.

'Archery practice,' he said briefly, pointing to the path that led to their archery range. Maddie groaned. The thought of concentrating on a target while she heaved back against the fifty-pound pull of her recurve bow was not a pleasant one. Then she shrugged mentally. She hadn't really expected Will to give her an easy day, just because she was feeling poorly.

She shot dreadfully. Her hands trembled as she tried to nock the arrows to the string, and she found it almost impossible to focus her vision and maintain a good sighting picture. She released prematurely, snatching at the bowstring as she did so, trying to will her shot into the centre without using any of the technique she had learned to make it happen.

Arrows glanced off the edge of the target, flying at random angles into the trees. After fifty shots, she hadn't managed to hit the centre of the target once. Her arrows bristled accusingly at the very edge of the target. Only three of them had managed to get into the circle outside the centre. Will snorted in disgust.

'I think you need a task that requires a little less skill,' he said. 'Follow me.'

He led the way back to the small open space before the cabin. Off to one side was a large stack of logs and an axe.

'Those logs are too wide for our stove,' he told her. 'Split them into smaller pieces.'

She stowed her bow and quiver, now short half a dozen arrows that she hadn't been able to find. She knew she'd spend the next few nights making replacements. Then she made her way back to the yard. Will was sitting in a canvas chair on the porch, reading reports sent in by Gilan. She paused as she came level with him. Idly, she noticed that there was no sign of the leather folder.

'How did you know I was gone last night?' she asked.

He glanced up from the report he was studying.

'If you plan to sneak out,' he told her in a cold voice, 'try to remember not to take your cloak.'

Her mouth opened in a soundless O. She remembered taking the cloak off its peg as she left the cabin. It was second nature to don it whenever she left the cabin.

'Sneaking out was foolish and disobedient,' Will continued. 'Taking your cloak was just plain stupid. I don't know which I found more disappointing.'

She hung her head in shame. She hated it when he was like this — cold and dispassionate. In the time she had been with him, she had felt him warming a little to her, becoming more encouraging as she strived to learn the skills a Ranger needed. Now, it seemed, she was back where they had started, all because of one foolish incident.

She guessed that was all it took to destroy trust.

'Those logs aren't going to split themselves,' Will said, looking back to his report.

She trudged across to the woodpile and began to split logs. It seemed her throbbing head was splitting along with them. But she continued doggedly, fighting the waves of nausea that assailed her, groaning softly as the impact of the axe resounded through her body with each blow. Will watched her from under lowered brows. He nodded once as he saw her fighting the pain and the nausea to keep going. She had discarded her cloak and her jerkin. Her linen shirt was dark with sweat.

After forty minutes, he called a halt. She lowered the axe and sank gratefully onto the tree stump she was using as a chopping block.

'All right,' he said briskly. 'One quick pass through the obstacle course and you can take a break — after you've done your laundry, that is.'

She looked at him in horror. The obstacle course was a fitness training area Will had built. It included, among other things, high log walls that one had to scale and drop down the other side, narrow logs over pits filled with mud, and worse, rope swings across the stream and a net set thirty centimetres from the ground under which she would have to crawl. And it was all done against a timer, so that 'one quick pass' was a misnomer. If she didn't finish before the timer ran out, she would have to do it all again.

The thought of it made her ill. The reality, when she came to it, was even worse. She fell from the narrow log across the mud pit and had to crawl out of the vile-smelling, glutinous mud, her clothes now heavy with it. Consequently, she was short on the rope swing and fell into the waist-deep water. The sand in the timer had long run out before she finished, and Will gestured wordlessly to the start once more. She staggered back to it and began again. She didn't notice that, this time, he turned the sandglass on its side to stop the grains trickling through from top to bottom.

She lurched and floundered through the course and finally staggered up to him, covering the last ten metres on her hands and knees after she fell, seeing with relief that there were a few grains remaining in the upper half of the sandglass. She slumped full length on the ground.

'Up,' Will said briefly and she groaned as she dragged herself to her feet.

'Why are you doing this to me?' she asked piteously.

He regarded her for several seconds before he answered. 'I'm not doing this to you, Maddie. The wine is. Bear it in mind.'

She stood, exhausted, hands on her hips, head hanging low. 'I'm never going to drink wine again,' she said.

He continued to study her. 'Let's hope not.' Then he turned towards the cabin, gesturing for her to follow. She trudged behind him, head aching, stomach roiling once more. The dreadful taste was back in her mouth.

As they stepped up into the cabin, she became aware of a familiar smell. Familiar, but now strangely attractive. It was the rich aroma of fresh coffee. While she had completed the course, Will had returned to the cabin and brewed a pot. He sat her down now and poured a cup, placing it before her.

'I don't drink coffee,' she said automatically. But the enticing smell was filling her nostrils and she wondered if maybe she was mistaken. Will added milk and several spoonfuls of dark honey, stirred it and handed it to her.

'Drink it,' he ordered and she wondered briefly if this was a further part of her punishment. Then she sipped at the hot, sweet drink, feeling it course through her weary body, easing her throbbing head, revitalising her, refreshing her with its wonderful, restorative aroma and rich taste. She sipped again, deeper this time, then put her head back and sighed appreciatively.

'Maybe I could get used to this,' she said.

Will raised one eyebrow. 'There might be hope for you yet,' he said.

Twenty-five

Somehow, Maddie got through the rest of that gruelling day.

She showered again in the wash house. This time, she had time to light the little stove so that the water was hot when it cascaded down on her. She gasped and spluttered as she tipped the bucket to send water gushing down on her. But the hot water on the back of her neck helped to dispel that dreadful, pounding headache.

By the time she towelled off and dressed in fresh clothes, it was only a dull remainder of its former self.

Will watched her as she walked back from the wash house. He felt that perhaps she had learned her lesson. Hangovers had a way of teaching people that drinking alcohol was not a good idea. After working her so hard in the morning with the log splitting and the obstacle course and the archery practice, he relented somewhat and gave her an easier afternoon. He set her to the task of doing their laundry — she had gone through two changes of clothes that day and her discarded garments were stained with sweat, and worse. She also had to repair the rip in the knee of her tights and wash away the dried blood there. Then he introduced her to the Courier's code — based on a grid of letters — and set her several exercises to do.

The figures on the page blurred in and out of focus a little, and the headache surged again as she concentrated on them. But all in all, it was preferable to the violent exertions of the morning.

Maddie finished a set of code exercises and handed them to him. He went through them quickly, made a few corrections, then grunted. She was a little disappointed. Normally when she did well on an assignment — and she felt she had done well on this one — he would mutter a few words of praise.

But not today.

I've lost his trust, she thought miserably, and she wondered if they would ever attain the level of warmth that had been beginning to develop between them. Probably not, she thought glumly.

They had one bout of contention that afternoon. The sun had sunk below the trees and Maddie lit the three oil lamps that provided light to the cabin. As she adjusted the wick on the final one, Will spoke.

'There's one thing,' he said. 'I want the names of your companions last night.'

She looked up fearfully. His face was grim and determined. But she couldn't comply with his order.

'I . . . I can't do that,' she said. 'I don't care if you punish me, but I won't betray my friends.'

He studied her grimly for several seconds, then he nodded slowly.

'Well, I applaud your loyalty to your friends, if not your wisdom,' he said. 'But I assume it wasn't you who procured that cask of wine last night?'

She shook her head. She felt she could go that far without betraying the others. But she wasn't going to tell him who had brought the cask to the party.

'Whoever did should be punished,' he said and she shook her head once more.

'I'm not going to tattle on them,' she said.

'Hmmm,' he said grimly. In truth, he didn't need her to tell him the names. It would take him less than half an hour to find them. The faces of the three were imprinted on his memory. He would know them when he saw them, and he would report them to their parents. They needed to be disciplined, just as Maddie had been.

But he was pleased that she hadn't tried to curry favour with him by informing on them. The loyalty might be misguided, but her refusal showed a strength of character.

'You have to realise, Maddie, that as Rangers we need to maintain a certain sense of . . . aloofness from people.'

She cocked her head. 'Aloofness?' she queried.

'There's a mystique about the Rangers,' he told her. 'And we need to maintain it. You need the respect of those around you. It's fine to have friends, but let's say one day you need to discipline one of those kids who was with you last night. Or order them to do something. You need them to think of you as Maddie, the Ranger, and obey you immediately, without thinking. They can't see you as Maddie, the silly girl who fell down drunk with them one night.'

She considered this. 'You're saying I can't have friends?'

He started to say no, then reconsidered. 'In a way, yes, I am. You can be friendly with them, but you can't let them become too familiar with you. It's one of the sacrifices we make as Rangers. Our friends tend to be other Rangers.'

'But my mother and father are your friends,' she pointed out and he nodded, accepting the point.

'Our friendship was forged through a lot of dangerous times. We had to depend on each other and trust each other. My life was often in your father's hands. And your mother's,' he added. 'That's a better basis for friendship than sneaking around drinking stolen wine behind the stables.'

'I suppose so,' she said. She could see his point. She enjoyed the prestige and respect she had earned as a Ranger's apprentice. She had seen how people looked up to her. And she could see how a stupid escapade like the night before could destroy that respect.

'It's time to grow up, Maddie,' he said.

'I suppose it is,' she replied.

She went to bed early that evening, shortly after they had finished a simple meat of grilled beef strips and boiled, buttered potatoes. Will also prepared a salad of some bitter green leaves, lacing it with a light, astringent dressing.

It was all simple, nourishing food, calculated to drive away the last remnants of her terrible hangover. As she finished and took her platter to the kitchen basin, Will gestured to the coffee pot.

'Like a cup?' he asked.

She hesitated, then remembered the wonderful sense of relief that she felt from that milky, sweet coffee earlier in the day. 'Why not?' she said.

He turned away to hide a slight smile as he poured a cup for her, then added milk and honey.

She drained the cup, marvelling at the way the liquid eased the last remaining vestiges of her headache. Then she yawned.

'I think I'll turn in.'

He nodded. He had turned his chair toward the open fire and he was staring into the twisting, writhing flames.

'Night,' he said.

She made her way to her room, yawning continuously. Her bed had never felt so welcoming.

It was well after midnight when she woke. The moon had slid across from one side of the cabin to the other, its light now slanting through the window in the opposite direction from where it had been when she fell asleep.

She wondered what had woken her. Something had intruded on her sleep, she was sure. She lay still, holding her breath for a few seconds. Then she heard it. The low murmur of voices.

She sat up, quietly laying the blankets to one side. One part of her mind registered the fact that the dull headache was finally gone. She looked at the gap under her bedroom door. There was no slit of light showing there. The lamps were obviously out in the living room, although she could make out a dull flicker thrown by the dying coals in the fire.

She turned her head and listened keenly. There it was again. Voices. Or, more correctly, one voice, pitched low and almost inaudible. If it hadn't been for the silence of the early morning, she might never have heard it.

She rose and made her way to the door, easing it open. The hinges were well greased and made no sound — Rangers liked it that way. She smiled at how quietly she could move now. After months of training with Will, she had learned to step lightly, avoiding obstacles and learning where the floorboards that might give off a warning creak were to be found.

She stepped silently into the living room, then frowned as she saw that the front door to the cabin was open.

That was unusual. Will always made sure the door was locked from the inside when he retired for the night. Moving back into her bedroom, she reached to where her scabbard hung from a peg and silently drew her saxe from it. Then she made her way to the front door, avoiding the three loose floorboards that were set to create a loud screech of wood on wood and warn of any intruder.

The murmuring voice could be heard more clearly now. It seemed to be coming from the end of the porch — the spot Sable usually occupied. Maddie glanced cautiously around the open door, ready to recoil instantly if anyone was looking in her direction, careful not to touch the door itself. The bottom of the door dragged against the floorboards of the cabin. Originally, she had thought of this as sloppy workmanship, until Will explained that it was another alarm device, in case someone tried to enter. Unlike the interior doors, this one was designed to be noisy. To open the door silently, one had to lift it on its hinges.

Which was obviously what Will had done. She could see him sitting, with his back to her, on the edge of the porch. Sable was sitting beside him, leaning her warm body against his, her tail moving in slow sweeps on the porch floorboards as Will talked to her, pouring out his troubles.

'. . . I miss her so much, girl. I wake up in the morning and think she'll be there. Or walk into a room and expect to see her. Then I remember that she's gone, and my heart wants to break all over again.'

He's talking about Alyss, Maddie realised. Suddenly she felt like an intruder, listening in to Will's private thoughts. She wanted to turn away and creep back to bed. But she couldn't bring herself to do it. Curiosity got the better of her.

'She was everything to me, girl. Everything.'

Sable's tail swirled in a sympathetic thump against the boards. Will put his arm around her, pulling her closer to him, burying his face in the thick fur of her ruff.

'Oh god how I miss her. It's like there's a huge hole in my life. But I can't cry for her. I've never cried for her and that hurts so much. Why can't I cry, Sable?'

Again, Sable twitched her heavy tail in understanding. Will fell silent for a minute or so.

'Pauline says the pain will gradually grow less. It'll be easier to bear. But when will that happen? It seems to be just as fresh, just as deep, every day that passes.'

Maddie, embarrassed by her eavesdropping, turned to move away. But Will's next words stopped her.

'Thank heavens for Maddie. At least she gives me something to take my mind away from the pain and the grief. She's the one bright spot in my life.'

Me, she thought. I'm a bright spot in his life?

'If she gets past this current nonsense and settles down, she could be an excellent Ranger. She's smart. She thinks fast and she's an excellent shot already — particularly with that sling of hers. She could open the way for a whole lot of girls to follow her into the Corps. It's a shame I've only got her for one year.'

Maddie shook her head in wonder. She had no idea that Will thought of her so highly. He had certainly given her no sign of it.

'Well, it's late, girl. I'm for bed. Thanks for listening.'

Maddie heard the heavy thump of Sable's tail on the boards once more. Then she heard the scraping sounds of Will coming to his feet. Moving silently, she fled across the room to her door. She had it almost closed when she heard Will lifting the front door to re-enter the cabin. Then the soft *clack* as the latch closed. Faintly, she heard the *slither-thump* of Sable sliding her forefeet out before her as she slipped down to a lying position.

Maddie waited till Will had crossed to his own room. As he closed the door carefully, she matched his action, so that any slight sounds of her own door latch engaging would be covered by his.

She lay carefully on the bed and pulled the blankets up to her chin. It was a chilly night and she was cold all over. She shivered once, then relaxed. She lay for a long time with her eyes open, thinking over what she had heard.

Eventually, she went to sleep. But a firm resolve had formed in her mind. She would make amends for her behaviour with the three village teenagers. She would never let Will down like that again.

And she would regain his trust in her.

Twenty-six

In later years, Maddie often reflected on how the smallest event can have the most profound result. Four days had passed since she had woken with that blinding, nauseating hangover. Her young, fit body had expelled the poisons she had drunk on that dreadful night and now she was back to normal and ready for any activity.

Although she felt physically better, the memory of the hangover persisted, and she had vowed never to drink alcohol again.

She had apologised profusely to Will for the way she'd acted and he had nodded silently, accepting her words. But, like him, she knew that they were just words, and words were easy. Deeds were more difficult and she had resolved to show him how true and heartfelt her words of apology were. She applied herself to her training and her lessons with a new diligence.

He noted this, but said nothing. He would wait to see how long this new energy and application would last. It was early days yet.

They were finishing lunch one day when there was a knock at the cabin door. Several minutes before the knock, Tug and Bumper had both sounded an alert from the stable as they sensed someone approaching the cabin. Whether it was an enemy or not, they had no idea, so their warning was a neutral one. On the other hand, Sable was outside in her usual position at the end of the porch, and she had made no sound. That indicated to Will that who-ever was approaching posed no danger.

He rose and moved to the door. At the last moment, he twitched his cloak aside to free the hilt of his saxe. Then he seized the latch left-handed and threw the door wide open. The movement was intentionally sudden, designed to give him an immediate view of the entire porch area — just in case someone was lurking to one side, out of sight. The animals may have detected no threat, but they were animals. They weren't infallible.

On this occasion, however, they were proved correct. The person standing outside the door could hardly be described as threatening. He leapt back in surprise as the door flew open, startled by the unexpectedly sudden movement.

He was a small man, shorter than Will and painfully thin. His arms were like sticks, although there was sinewy muscle there. He obviously earned his living by hard labour. He was stoop-shouldered and his hair was begin-ning to recede from his forehead. His face was lined.

Maddie estimated his age at around sixty, and weathered by years of hard work in the outdoors — in rain, hail or shine. He wore a farmer's smock — threadbare and patched in many places — and carried a shapeless felt hat in his hands.

'What can I do for you?' Will asked.

The man bobbed his head nervously. He had never been in such close proximity to a Ranger and he found the experience somewhat unsettling.

'Aah . . . hmmm . . . sorry to trouble you, Ranger. Didn't mean to disturb you or nothing . . .' he said uncertainly.

Will decided not to reply with the obvious — *If you didn't mean to disturb me, why did you knock on my door?* He felt that such a reply would confuse the man even further and make him more nervous than he already was.

'Did you need help of some sort?' Will asked.

The farmer considered the question, rotating his hat several times as he did so.

'Name is Arnold, Ranger. Arnold Clum of Split Oak farm.' He gestured over his shoulder with a jerk of his head. 'Off to the south there some ten kilometres.'

An impressive name for what was probably an unimpressive farm, judging by the state of Arnold's clothes and his obviously meagre diet. Will realised that Arnold, like most countrymen, was going to take the long way round answering the question.

'Been farming there most of my life,' Arnold Clum continued, confirming Will's suspicions about roundabout answers. 'It's not a big farm, mind you. Just a small holding. We grows a few vegetables — not too many. The soil is rocky out there. And we keeps some sheep. Mostly though, we depend on the hens. The wife keeps them.'

Maddie had risen from the table and moved to stand slightly behind Will. Arnold Clum noticed her and bobbed his head, tugging at a nonexistent hat brim. The hat, after all, was in his other hand.

'Afternoon, miss,' he said politely. He stared at her, confused. She was dressed as a Ranger, but she was a girl. He found the two facts hard to reconcile.

'Maddie is my apprentice,' Will said, by way of explanation. 'You can call her "Ranger Maddie".'

'Ah, yes, well . . . afternoon, Ranger Maddie,' Arnold said.

Maddie smiled at him. She decided she liked being referred to as Ranger Maddie. She felt it gave her a certain cachet — although she wasn't totally sure what cachet might be. It was a term she had heard used once and she thought it might have something to do with prestige.

'We've got maybe twenty, thirty hens and one rooster,' Arnold continued, focusing his attention back on Will. 'Keeps us in eggs, of course, and from time to time we kill one for the pot. Nice to have a bit of meat from time to time,' he added. Unconsciously, he licked his lips at the thought of a chicken going into the cook pot. His expression was so wistful that Will was willing to bet 'from time to time' was no more often than once a month.

'Chickens can be useful that way,' Will said, hoping to move the narrative along a little faster.

Arnold Clum nodded several times. 'Aye. Right handy beasts, chickens can be. Raise 'em virtually anywhere, you can.'

'I've never tried,' Will said.

Arnold shrugged and looked up at him, his head tilted sideways.

'Aye, well, you should. Dead easy, chickens is. Just need a small patch of ground for them to scratch around in. They like scratching around. Then you can feed them any sort of scraps and —'

'Are you having some problem with your chickens?' Will asked.

Arnold stopped in mid-sentence and stared at him, mouth slightly open. 'How'd you know?'

Will sighed. The man had said he needed help and obviously his chickens were the most important creatures in his life. It was a logical guess. And it was a further logical step to assume that the problem was with some kind of predator. After all, if the chickens were sick, he would hardly have come to a Ranger for help. An apothecary was a better bet.

'Something's taking your chickens?' Will asked.

Arnold's mouth dropped open a little wider. 'You Rangers are uncanny!' he said. 'It's true what they say. I turn up here asking for help and straight away you know there's some critter taking my chickens — and eating my eggs.'

Not quite straight away, Will thought. But still, the loss of chickens and eggs would be a serious matter for someone like Arnold. Judging by his undernourished frame, he got little enough to eat as it was.

'Seen it a couple of times — usually on dusk,' Arnold said. 'About the size of a small dog, it is. And quick as a snake. I've got no way of stopping it. I've got an old spear, but I'm no great shakes with that. Comes and goes as it pleases, it does. Not frightened of me one bit. My wife, Aggie, she said to me, *Arnold, go fetch the Ranger. He'll know how to deal with this!'*

'Probably a weasel or a stoat,' Will said thoughtfully. He could imagine the problems Arnold would have, trying to kill a fast-moving creature like that with an old spear and his shaky hands.

'Mebbe so,' Arnold agreed. 'But he's a big 'un. Mind you, so he should be, with the number of my eggs he's been eating!' He added the last with a little heat.

Will nodded sympathetically. 'Well, we'd better see what we can do. We'll come out this afternoon. No need for you to lose more eggs. Now, let me know how to get to your farm.'

Arnold gave him directions, then departed. He was riding a raw-boned plough horse with no saddle. The horse looked as ragged and threadbare as his owner.

'Thought I'd let him go ahead of us,' Will said to Maddie. 'Farmers love to talk when they meet someone new and I thought we'd spare ourselves that.'

'Is it really worth our while?' Maddie asked. 'I mean, riding all that way for just a few eggs?'

'It's just a few eggs to us. To him it's a matter of eating or going hungry. And looking at him, I'd say he's done plenty of that.'

Maddie pursed her lips thoughtfully. 'Oh. I see.'

'This is part of what we do, Maddie,' Will told her. 'We help people in trouble. Whether it's tracking down high-waymen or arresting killers — or saving a farmer's eggs. Rangers are here to serve the people.'

'I hadn't thought of it that way,' she said. 'So, should we get moving?'

Will shook his head. 'Not just yet. I wouldn't want to catch up to him. I'll help him, but I don't want to have to listen to him.'

Twenty-seven

They reached the farm an hour before dusk. They rode into the yard and looked at the small, dilapidated farmhouse. It was made from bark slabs and wattle and daub, with a thatched roof that was barely higher than Maddie at the edges. A spiral of smoke curled from the chimney.

Maddie made a move preparatory to swinging down from the saddle, but Will put out a hand to stop her.

'Wait till we're invited,' he said quietly.

Maddie took note. As a princess, of course, she had never felt the need to be invited. She had always assumed she was welcome wherever she went. But now, she waited as Arnold and a woman who was obviously his wife emerged from the farmhouse.

'Welcome, Ranger, welcome. This here's my wife, Aggie. Aggie, this is the Ranger, and Ranger Maddie.'

Aggie performed a slight curtsey, the action curtailed by years of hard work and an aching back. She was as thin as her husband and her hair was grey. Like Arnold, her face was lined by years of working hard and going short.

'Welcome, Rangers. Step down, please. Would you like tea? Summat to eat, perhaps?'

'Thank you, no, Mistress Aggie,' Will said. These people had little enough. He didn't want to deprive them by sharing their meagre provisions. 'Let's take a look at this henhouse of yours.'

He and Maddie dismounted. As was their custom, they left the reins of their horses trailing. Ranger horses didn't need to be tied up. They'd stay put as long as their riders were here.

Arnold and Aggie Clum led them to a sizeable enclosure set some fifteen metres away from the house. It was two and a half metres high and made of narrow willow wands, set vertically into the ground and intertwined with horizontal strands. Every two or three metres was a more substantial fence post. Inside it was a ramshackle roosting house, constructed of odd bits of timber and bark. An angled ramp ran up to it, allowing the hens access.

The structure was intended to contain the hens and keep them safe at night. Not that it had seemed to work, Maddie thought.

They entered the enclosure and Maddie stooped to peer inside the henhouse. There were rows of brooding boxes inside and she heard the faint cluck of hens as the sound of her movement disturbed them.

Arnold pointed to the fence farthest from the farmhouse.

'Comes up and over there, quick as you please. Nothing I can do to stop him.'

Will moved to the point the farmer had indicated. There was a water trough at that point and it wasn't totally watertight. A slow trickle ran from it, wetting and softening the ground. He studied the tracks in the mud and beckoned to Maddie.

'Look at that. What do you think?'

She frowned. He had shown her dozens of tracks in the past months. She wasn't sure.

'A weasel, maybe?' she said. She was half guessing, because she knew it was a predator of some sort and a fox could hardly have climbed that fence. Will drew his saxe and pointed to the tracks.

'See there? There are claw marks there at the front of the paws.'

She looked at him, wondering what he was getting at. He realised he hadn't explained this to her before, so he continued patiently.

'It's a pine marten,' he said. 'Like a weasel or a mink. But with one difference. A marten's claws only retract halfway. So you can see the marks of the claws in his tracks. Looks like a big one too.'

'He's big, all right,' Aggie said with heartfelt venom in her voice. 'And right quick too.'

'Well then, we'll see if we can slow him down a little,' Will said.

They found a spot against the farmhouse where the top of the chicken-run fence would be silhouetted against the evening sky, and settled in to keep watch. They waited as the light faded. Arnold had told them that the marten had become increasingly bold over the past week, raiding the chicken house every day or two. It had been two days since he'd last appeared, so chances were good that they'd see him tonight.

Will had his bow. When Maddie went to fetch hers from the bow case beside her saddle, he shook his head.

'This time of year, he'll have a good rich pelt,' he said. 'An arrow broadhead will tear it up and ruin it. So use your sling. I'll keep my bow ready in case you miss.'

Maddie glanced at him, her chin going up. 'I don't plan to miss,' she said.

Will shrugged. 'Nobody ever does.'

It was chilly after the sun set and Maddie longed to wrap herself in the warm depths of her cloak. But Will shook his head.

'He may not be frightened of humans,' he said, 'but Aggie and Arnold say he's quick as a snake. We'll only have seconds for you to hit him and we can't afford to waste time untangling ourselves from our cloaks.'

Accordingly, she pushed the cloak back on either shoulder to free her arms and stood with a shot already loaded into the sling. Will kept an arrow nocked to his bow. Behind them, the dark bulk of the farmhouse would help conceal them from view.

The sun had dropped below the treetops but there was still light reflecting from the clouds when Will gently nudged her. A dark shape was scurrying out of the bushes and across the cleared ground of the farmyard. It was low to the ground and moving fast. Maddie touched his hand to let him know she had seen the predator. Then she watched as the marten scurried to the hen enclosure and swarmed up the fence. Inside the henhouse, she could hear the worried clucking of the hens as they sensed the arrival of their nemesis.

Maddie laid her right arm back, letting the shot dangle in the pouch of the sling.

The marten hesitated at the top of the fence, getting his balance on the swaying willow wands, as he prepared to transfer from climbing to descending. As he did so, Will made a gentle clicking sound with his tongue. The marten's head came up as he searched for the source of that sound, and Maddie whipped the sling up and over, stepping into the shot as she released.

The light was poor and it was a small target. But Maddie had hurled hundreds, if not thousands, of shot over the past months, in all conditions: in bright sun, in semi-darkness, in pouring rain. The lead sphere smashed into the savage little predator and hurled it backwards off the top of the fence. It fell to the soft ground outside the enclosure with a dull thud. For a moment or two, its back legs quivered. But that was simply a muscular reaction. The marten was dead.

'Good shot,' Will said quietly. He was impressed. It had been a difficult shot and Maddie had managed it perfectly. He knew there was a big difference between practising with a lifeless target and being faced with a split second shot at a live, fast-moving quarry. In a louder voice, he called to the elderly couple in the farmhouse.

'She got him.'

The door opened and a shaft of light fell out across the farmyard as Aggie and Arnold emerged. Maddie was already moving towards the lifeless form at the base of the fence.

'Be careful,' Will called. 'Make sure he's dead. Those things can bite through your gauntlets.'

She waved a hand in acknowledgement and approached the animal more carefully. She drew her saxe and prodded it experimentally. But there was no reaction.

He was a big one, she saw, more like a small dog than a large cat. Obviously, the diet of chickens and eggs agreed with him. The pelt was thick and lustrous as well. She knelt beside the marten, re-sheathed her saxe and took out a small skinning knife from her belt pouch. Quickly, she skinned the animal, slicing the thick, shiny fur away from the body.

Will watched approvingly. Skinning was an art she had already been skilled in when she came to him.

She rose and walked back to where they were waiting for her, the pelt hanging from one hand. Then she held it out to the farmer's wife.

'Here, Mistress Aggie. You can make this into a fine neck warmer or hat for the winter.'

'But it's yours,' Arnold protested. 'You killed him. The pelt is yours.' That was the rule of hunting, he knew. The successful hunter kept the pelt for himself. Or herself.

'And I'm free to do as I please with it.' Maddie smiled, holding the pelt out. Hesitantly, Aggie took it. 'You'll have to peg it out and salt it,' Maddie continued. 'You know how to do that, don't you?'

'Oh aye. I know how to do that all right,' Aggie said. She looked admiringly at the pelt in her hand. It was a fine piece of fur. Pelts like this were for the gentry, for the rich. Not for poor farmers like her. 'Thank'ee, Ranger Maddie. Thank'ee. This is a pelt fit for a fine lady, this is.'

She ran her work-worn hand over the soft fur. She could make a bonnet from it. Or she could trade it at the next market day for two good wool coats for her and her husband. Maddie's gift would keep them both warm this coming winter.

'You *are* a fine lady,' Maddie told her. She glanced at Will. 'Shall we go now?'

They rode back to the cabin in silence. Will studied the young girl beside him in some detail.

She had come to him as a bumptious, self-centred and selfish princess, thinking only of herself and her own enjoyment. Gradually, he had watched her transformation. Of course, the episode with the wine was a step back. But everyone made mistakes, he thought. Smiling, he recalled several from his own days as a trainee. But her unpremeditated gesture this evening, handing over the valuable pelt to the poor farmer's wife, showed a growth and a maturity that gave him a warm glow. Finally, he spoke.

'That was a nice thing you did.'

She glanced at him. 'Did you see her clothes? They were thin and threadbare and patched. At least now she'll have one warm item for winter.'

He nodded. 'Yes. She will.'

But the old Maddie, Princess Maddie, wouldn't have even noticed the state of Aggie's clothes, let alone made the connection that she would be cold in winter.

I think she's going to work out just fine, he thought to himself.

Tug shook his mane and snorted. *I always knew she would.*

Twenty-eight

The little cabin in the trees was still hidden from sight when Tug raised his head and let out a cheerful whinny. Bumper looked up at the sound. Almost instantly, an answering whinny came from the direction of the cabin.

'We've got company,' Will said.

Maddie looked at him inquiringly but he said no more. He thought he'd recognised the strange horse's sound but he wasn't totally sure. No sense in voicing an assumption only to have it proven wrong.

As it turned out, he was right. They rode into the clearing and saw a bay mare standing before the porch. She turned her head as they approached and whinnied again. Both Bumper and Tug responded.

Maddie looked at her horse, puzzled. 'How does Bumper know her?' she asked.

Will glanced at her. 'Ranger horses tend to recognise each other. Even if they've never met.'

'That doesn't make a lot of sense,' said a cheerful voice from the end of the porch. 'How can you recognise someone you've never met?'

Will shrugged. 'Why ask me? I'm not a horse.'

You don't have the legs for it, Tug commented dryly.

Gilan was sitting at the end of the porch, fondling Sable's ears. The dog had her head to one side, eyes closed and a blissful expression on her face. Sable loved to have the thick fur around her ears and throat patted and smoothed.

Will dismounted and glared in mock disappointment at Sable.

'Some watchdog you are. You should have torn him to pieces.'

Sable thumped her tail on the porch boards in agreement. Gilan gave her a final pat and rose to his feet.

'Hello, Maddie. How's your training going?'

She gave him a wan smile as she dismounted. 'Well, some days I think I'm getting there. Then others I know I'm not.'

Gilan raised an eyebrow and looked at Will. He had never heard such self-deprecation from Maddie before. Perhaps this idea of Halt's was working out. Will saw the look and guessed its meaning. He gave a brief nod.

'Should I take the horses to the stable?' she asked and Gilan's surprise went up another notch. Maddie volunteering to do menial work was something else he wasn't accustomed to.

'Yes. If you would,' Will told her. 'Blaze too.' He glanced at Gilan. 'I assume you'll stay with us? Or did you want to sleep at the castle?'

'No. I'll stay here if I'm welcome,' Gilan said hastily. 'Too much fuss and formality at the castle.'

'And we're closer to The Heaped Platter here, of course,' Will said.

Gilan allowed himself a grin. The Heaped Platter was the name of Jenny's eating house in Wensley Village.

'Well, yes,' the Commandant replied. 'I thought I might slip over there for breakfast in the morning.'

'She'll be glad to see you,' Will said, and for a moment, a hint of sadness tinged his expression. Jenny and Gilan might not have married, but they still had each other.

He led the way inside and moved to the kitchen bench, filling the coffee pot from the large jug of fresh water. He didn't ask if Gilan wanted coffee. He was a Ranger. Rangers always wanted coffee.

As Will began to grind coffee beans, the rich aroma released by the grinding filled Gilan's nostrils. His mouth watered at the thought of fresh coffee. He sat at the table, pushing aside a stack of papers that had been left there. Glancing idly at them, he recognised several of the weekly reports he sent out to Rangers throughout the country. There were several letters as well, and beneath them was a leather folder, with more papers inside. He tapped his finger on it.

'What's this?' he asked. Will looked round and saw the leather folder. His face took on a slightly embarrassed look.

'Oh . . . just an idea I was working on. It's not important now.' He took the folder and shoved it into a bookshelf along one wall of the living room. There was an air of finality about the gesture, Gilan thought. He shrugged. He had merely been making idle conversation.

'So, how's it working out with Maddie?' he asked, changing the subject. Will, who had resumed his coffee grinding, turned to face him.

'Surprisingly well,' he said. 'She's quick and keen and she's eager to learn. She loves the outdoor life and a little freedom. My guess is, she was rebelling against all the restrictions at Castle Araluen. Now that she's not a princess any more, she seems to be taking more notice of people around her.'

Gilan pursed his lips with interest. 'Did you use the letter?' he asked. He was aware of the letter that Cassandra and Horace had sent to Will, disinheriting their daughter.

Will nodded, turning back to the task of making coffee again.

'Had to. She needed a jolt. Needed to know she was nothing special. And it worked.'

'How so?'

Will paused to consider, while he set the pot on the stovetop. He opened the firebox and tossed in several pieces of wood, then opened the draught at the bottom of the stove.

'Well, today is a good example. A local farmer was having trouble with a marten, stealing his eggs and killing his hens.'

'So you took care of it?'

'Maddie did. Knocked it down with her sling. She's a dead shot with that thing, by the way. Then she slipped over and skinned it in a few minutes.'

Gilan looked impressed. 'Be a good pelt at this time of year.'

Will nodded as he dropped a handful of coffee into the boiling pot. 'It was. It was a beautiful pelt. And that's the thing. The farmer and his wife were as poor as church mice. Their clothes were thin and ragged. She gave the woman the pelt. Said she wanted her to have something warm for winter.'

Gilan nodded. 'As you say, it sounds as if she's taking notice of other people's needs. Which is a good quality to have in a Ranger.'

'She's always been a good kid at heart,' Will said. He'd decided not to say anything about the episode with the wine. 'She just needed to remember it.'

Gilan stroked his chin thoughtfully. The news about Maddie was interesting — and gratifying. Appointing a girl as an apprentice Ranger had always been a risk. But it appeared to be working out.

But even more interesting was Will's attitude and manner. There was a sense of muted enthusiasm as he talked about his apprentice and her abilities. The haunted look, the tension, the morbid obsession with revenge that had been so much a part of him over the past months seemed to have gone. He wasn't back to his original, cheerful self. But he was definitely improving.

Looks like Halt knew what he was talking about, Gilan thought. Then he wondered why he was surprised by the revelation. Halt usually did know what he was talking about.

He waited while Will placed a cup of steaming, rich coffee in front of him, then said, 'So, do you think she's ready to go on a mission with you?'

He said it casually, but it was a crucial point. Will, torn by grief and fixated on the idea of hunting down Jory Ruhl, had spurned the last two missions Gilan had assigned to him. Gilan felt a surge of relief as he saw his friend considering the point, then nodding.

'Yes. I'd be happy to take her along on a mission. Be good for her at this stage of her training.'

The door opened and Maddie entered. They both turned and fell silent, as people do when the subject of their conversation suddenly appears. Maddie noticed their sudden lack of conversation and looked anxiously from Will to Gilan. Had Will been telling the Commandant of her fall from grace, she wondered?

'I gave Blaze an apple,' she said tentatively. 'She seemed to think that was totally inadequate, so I gave her another.'

'She'll be your slave for life,' Gilan said easily.

Maddie relaxed a little at his friendly tone. She glanced anxiously at Will and, sensing the cause for her concern, he gave a slight shake of the head. He pointed to the cup on the table.

'Coffee's made,' he said and she sat gratefully, cradling her cup in both hands.

'I drink coffee now,' she told Gilan.

He nodded gravely. 'Just as well. It's a condition of becoming a Ranger.' He saw the look of relief in her eyes and he'd noticed the quick glance that passed between her and Will. Will's face was deadpan. So deadpan that Gilan knew there was something he wasn't being told. Then he shrugged mentally. If Will had decided not to tell him, it was probably none of his business, he thought.

'Will says you're ready to go on a mission with him,' he said. 'What do you think?'

She glanced once at her mentor, then looked back to Gilan.

'I'm ready,' she said. 'What's the mission?'

Gilan was pleased with her reply. No hesitating. No uncertainty.

'It's in Trelleth Fief,' he said. 'The Ranger there has been killed.'

Will's head snapped up instantly. 'Killed? Killed by whom?'

Gilan shook his head uncertainly. 'There's no one suspected. He fell from his horse and his neck was broken.'

'So it was an accident?' Maddie said.

Gilan looked at her sceptically. 'Possibly. Indeed, that's the way it looks. But I don't believe in accidents — not when it's a Ranger who's died.'

Will was frowning thoughtfully. 'Who's the Ranger at Trelleth?' He paused and corrected himself. 'Or rather, who was he?'

In a small force like the Ranger Corps, everyone knew each other, at least by sight and name. Of course, there were some closer relationships within the ranks as well.

'It was Liam,' Gilan told him. 'Remember him?'

Will nodded sadly. He'd been present at Liam's graduation, the day he was presented with his silver oakleaf. It had been the year that he and Halt and Horace had travelled to Hibernia to track down the cult leader, Tennyson.

'Yes. He was a good type.'

'He was indeed. He was one of the brighter ones among the younger crop of Rangers. We'll miss him badly.'

'So what do you want us to do?' Will asked.

'Go up to Trelleth and ask around. See if you can find

anything suspicious about his death. As I say, I'm always suspicious when a Ranger dies.'

Will glanced at a map of Araluen on the wall of the cabin. Trelleth was a medium-sized fief on the eastern coast of the country. Gilan followed the direction of his gaze.

'The baron there is called Scully. He sent a carrier pigeon with news of Liam's death. The man who found Liam's body is a farmer,' he said. 'Name of Wendell Gatt. His farm is a large one, about five kilometres south-west of Castle Trelleth.'

Will's eyes remained fixed on the map. Like Gilan, he distrusted accidents. Particularly in a coastal fief like Trelleth. Coastal fiefs were vulnerable to outsiders — smugglers, pirates and the like. A coastline presented too many opportunities for intruders.

'We've nothing to keep us here,' he said. 'We'll start out tomorrow.'

Gilan nodded approvingly. 'The sooner the better,' he said. The phrase might well have been the official Ranger motto, Will thought. 'Check it out and see if it was just an accident.'

Will turned his gaze from the map to look at his old friend. 'And if it wasn't?'

Gilan made a small hand gesture. 'Find out why someone wanted a Ranger dead. And who that some-one might be.'

Twenty-nine

They left the following morning, shortly after an early breakfast. Gilan had coffee with them, but he planned to have breakfast later, at Jenny's eating house. He promised to let Jenny know they were gone so she could arrange to feed and water Sable each day.

They rode north-east, at the usual Ranger travelling pace — cantering for twenty minutes, then dismounting and walking briskly for ten, leading the horses. The horses could maintain this pace hour after hour and it ate up the miles to their destination.

They camped out that evening and reached Trelleth Fief early in the afternoon of the second day. There was a border sign to let them know they were entering the fief, but even more telling was the scent of salt on the air.

'I can smell the sea,' Maddie said.

Will nodded. He remembered the first time he had noticed that fresh, tangy scent. He had been riding to his first Ranger Gathering. He sighed quietly. It seemed like such a long time ago. Then, he shook his head in realisation. It *was* such a long time ago.

'What do we do now?' Maddie asked. She was curious to see how an investigation like this would be carried out.

'We'll look at the scene first,' Will said. 'We'll find this farmer . . .' He hesitated while he searched his memory for the name.

'Wendell Gatt,' Maddie supplied.

He looked at her, a little annoyed. 'I know,' he said.

She gave him an innocent look. 'Just trying to be helpful. I thought maybe you'd forgotten.'

'I don't forget things.'

Ilah! Tug gave one of those explosive snorts that indicated his derision. Will decided it was best to ignore him. You could never get the last word with a creature who could snort, stamp and shake his mane the way Tug could.

'We'll look for a hamlet or a farmhouse and ask directions to Gatt's farm,' he said.

A few minutes later, they came upon a small group of buildings. There was a blacksmith's forge and a run-down-looking tavern, plus a few houses to accommodate those who worked there. As they approached, a man wearing a leather apron, and with soot stains on his bare arms, emerged from the smithy to greet them.

They learned that Gatt's farm was a few kilometres further along the road they were travelling. Will thanked the smith and turned Tug's head back towards the road, but the man called after him.

'Rangers, are you?'

Since their cloaks, bows and shaggy horses made it obvious that they were, Will was disinclined to answer. He was still smarting over his momentary inability to remember Gatt's name, and Maddie's intemperate haste in supplying it. She might have given him a minute or two to recall it, he thought. As a result, he was not in a mood to be chatty, particularly since the smith's question indicated that he was puzzled by Maddie's garb and was looking for some explanation.

'No. We're travelling seamstresses,' he said shortly, and set Tug into a canter, with Maddie hastily following.

The smith twisted his mouth into an ill-tempered expression and he wiped perspiration from his forehead with the hem of his leather apron.

'Only asking,' he said irritably as the two riders clattered away.

Several hundred metres later, Maddie drew alongside Will as he allowed Tug to slow down to a trot.

'Shouldn't we call on the local baron first?' she said, adding tactfully, 'This Baron Scully?'

She was vaguely aware of the dictates of protocol. She had been present when her father and mother had visited fiefs in the past, and she knew it was normal procedure to make their presence known to the local baron when they did so. She was beginning to learn, however, that protocol and normal procedure had little to do with the way Rangers operated.

Will grunted disdainfully. 'We'll do that later. Local barons have a habit of getting in the way when something out of the ordinary has happened in their fief. They know we report directly to the crown and they often want to make sure there's nothing that puts them in a bad light.'

Maddie was somewhat surprised at this. She had never been aware of this clash of power or purpose between barons and the Rangers who worked in their fiefs.

'Not all of them, surely?' she said.

Will relented a little. 'Well, no. The majority of them are good men. Arald at Redmont, for example, is an excellent baron and he's good to work with. But you do get the occasional one who's inclined to stand on his dignity and exaggerate his own importance. I don't know this Scully character, so I don't want to take the chance he's one of those — at least not till we've had a preliminary look around.'

They arrived at the Gatt farm a few minutes later. The contrast between this property and that of old Arnold Clum could not have been more marked. The farmhouse and barn were large, substantial buildings, in excellent repair and recently painted.

The fences were straight and well built. And the farmyard itself was a model of order, with the ground swept, tools piled neatly and a wagon standing in front of the barn. The wagon body was freshly painted as well. The undercarriage was in good repair and glistened with fresh grease. Several horses were in the home paddock and they crowded curiously along the fence to view the newcomers. A single dairy cow was tethered some distance away.

As they approached the house, a door opened from what was apparently the kitchen and a woman emerged. She was in her forties, tall and obviously well fed. Her clothes were fresh and clean and of good quality — even if they were homemade. They were without the array of patches that Aggie Clum's threadbare garments had boasted.

She had been baking. She brushed a stray lock of hair away from her face, leaving a smear of white flour there.

Will and Maddie halted their horses. Forewarned now, Maddie made no move to dismount.

'Good afternoon,' Will said. 'Would you be Mistress Gatt?'

'I am,' she said, glancing curiously at Maddie, then back to Will again. 'Welcome to Gatt farm. Will you care to dismount?'

'That we would,' Will said. He swung down from the saddle and Maddie did likewise.

'My name is Will Treaty,' he said. There was no need to mention the fact that he was a Ranger. That was obvious from his clothes and equipment. 'This is my apprentice, Maddie.'

Maddie, watching the woman closely, saw her eyes widen slightly at the mention of Will's full name. He was a figure of some renown in Araluen, she knew — the legendary apprentice of the legendary Ranger Halt, who had gone on to equal or even surpass his mentor's reputation. Mistress Gatt gave a hurried curtsey.

'Would you care for a bite to eat, Rangers?' she asked. She glanced curiously at Maddie as she said the word 'Rangers'. It was a reaction that Maddie was rapidly becoming accustomed to. 'I've got a mutton stew heating for the men's dinner and there's plenty to share.'

Will shook his head. 'Thank you. But we won't trouble you. Perhaps a drink of water to settle the dust?' He inclined his head towards a well-kept pump close by the kitchen door and she hurriedly gestured towards it.

'Of course. Help yourself. What brings you to Gatt farm? Is it because of the other Ranger? The one who . . .' She hesitated, not sure whether to say 'died' or 'was killed'.

Will nodded. He worked the pump handle and drew a dipper of water, took a long drink, then wiped his beard with the back of his hand, passing the dipper to Maddie.

'Yes. I understand your husband found the body,' he said.

She nodded several times. 'Aye, Wendell found him. But there was nothing he could do for him by then. The man was dead several hours, he said.' She glanced out to the fields. 'He and the men are bringing in the last of the hay today. He'll be in for his dinner in an hour or so. Would you care to wait for him?'

Will shook his head. 'No. We'll go and find him now. I have a few questions I need to ask him.'

Mistress Gatt shifted her feet uncomfortably as he said the words. She looked worried. Will hastened to reassure her.

'I'm sure there's no blame attached to your husband, mistress. I'd just like him to show us where he found Liam — the Ranger.' He added the last for clarification. The worried frown disappeared from her face and she pointed across the fields.

'He'll be two fields down in that direction, beyond the small spinney of trees.'

'Then we'll talk to him there,' Will said. He gestured for Maddie to follow and they re-mounted their horses. He touched one finger to his forehead.

'Thanks for your help, mistress. Best get back to your baking before it burns.'

He'd noticed a delicious smell on the air. It was obviously bread or a pie just on the brink of being overdone. Her mouth formed a quick O of surprise. She'd forgotten all about her baking. She turned and hurried back into the farmhouse as they trotted away.

'Well, she was certainly helpful,' Maddie observed as they rode across the fields.

'Let's hope her husband is the same,' Will replied.

As it turned out, Wendell Gatt was a good deal less helpful than his wife had been. He was a big, florid man, dressed in breeches and a blue linen working smock. Like his wife, his clothes were of good quality and in excellent condition. Gatt had three farm labourers working with him, gathering the last of the hay into bales.

He shook his head emphatically when Will asked if he'd show them the spot where he found Liam's body.

'Too busy. Work to do here. We've got to bring in this hay before the rain comes.'

'We'll only need you for half an hour or so. Surely your men can continue without you?' Will said reasonably.

'No. No. No,' Gatt replied. 'Wouldn't trust them to do the job properly. They need to be watched constantly.' He said it loud enough for the men to hear him. Two of them cast annoyed looks at him. The third ignored him.

Will looked at them and touched Tug with his heels, walking the little horse towards the farm workers.

'Who's the senior man?' he asked. One of them raised his hand. He was about forty years old and thickset. He looked quite capable, Will thought. After all, hay baling wasn't too complex a task.

'That would be me, sir,' the man said. 'Lionel Foxtree, I am.'

'Well, Lionel Foxtree, do you think you're capable of continuing this work unsupervised? Your master will be away for several days.'

Hearing this, Gatt exploded with indignation. 'Several days? You said half an hour!' he shouted.

Will turned in his saddle to look at him. His eyes were cold.

'Well, that was when I simply wanted you to show us where Ranger Liam died,' he said. 'But since you've refused to help us in the investigation, I'm going to have to arrest you and have you charged. That could take a day or two. Even a week.'

Gatt spluttered furiously as he searched for words. The farm workers turned away, but not before Will could see the smiles on their faces. Gatt was obviously a man who liked to get his own way.

'Arrest me?' he said. 'You can't arrest me! I'm a free man!'

'Actually, I can arrest you. I'm a King's Ranger. You've refused to help me in an investigation, which is pretty much the same as impeding said investigation. I don't want to do it. I'd prefer it if you'd simply show us where you found Liam. But if you force me to, I will arrest you.'

Their gazes locked. Gatt's was hot and angry. Will's was cold and unmoving. Finally, the farmer gave way.

'Oh, all right! Have it your own way! I'll take you to where I found him!'

'That's the spirit,' Will said. He gestured to a saddle horse that was tethered to the tail of the hay wagon. 'And there's a horse for you, right there.'

Thirty

Containing his annoyance as best he could, Gatt led them to the spot where he'd found Liam's body. It was on a narrow but well-defined track, fringed on either side by scattered, low bushes. The ground was soft and easy underfoot, but not so much that it might cause a horse to stumble or lose his footing. Will swung down and studied the ground.

'Had any rain lately?' he asked.

Gatt shook his head. 'Not since I found the body. But the ground is usually soft in these parts, except in high summer, when it tends to dry out.'

'Not high summer now,' Will said to himself, moving along the trail. It ran in a straight line here. There seemed to be no reason why Liam should have fallen from his horse.

'Where exactly did you find the body?' he asked.

Gatt walked his horse forward several metres. 'Here. On the side of the trail. Just past those two trees.'

There were two sizeable trees, standing out from the general vegetation of bushes and shrubs in the area. They were about five metres apart, standing one on either side of the track. Will glanced at them. There were no low, over-hanging branches that might sweep an incautious rider from his saddle.

'Figure he fell off his horse and broke his neck,' Gatt said.

Will pursed his lips. 'Unlikely,' he said. All Rangers were excellent riders.

Gatt shrugged at the uncompromising reply. 'Maybe his horse stumbled . . .' he essayed.

Tug, standing a little apart, shook his mane violently. *Ranger horses don't stumble.*

'Or maybe he'd been drinking,' Gatt added.

Will turned a cold gaze on him. 'Liam didn't drink,' he said and Gatt shrugged.

'If you say. It was just a suggestion.'

Will didn't answer. He was pacing back along the trail from where Liam's body had been found, checking the horse's tracks. With no rain in recent days and with the soft condition of the ground, they were still clear to see. Maddie had dismounted and was kneeling beside one of the trees, studying its trunk low to the ground.

Will turned to Gatt abruptly. 'Thanks for your time, Farmer Gatt. We'll trouble you no longer. You can get back to your work.'

Gatt looked surprised, and his bad mood lifted a little. He'd expected the Ranger to keep him here for hours, asking pointless questions. Now he found himself free to go about his business. But perversely, his curiosity was piqued. He'd noticed the way Will had been studying the tracks.

'So have you found something?' he asked. 'Any clue as to what happened?'

Will shook his head. 'Probably as you said. His horse stumbled and he fell. Just an accident.'

'Oh . . . well then . . .' Gatt still hesitated. He didn't want to be left out if there was something significant to be known.

Will nodded to him. 'We won't bother you further,' he said.

'Right. I'll be off then,' Gatt said. He turned his horse away and set it into a lumbering trot, heading back to his farm. As he rode away, he turned in his saddle several times to look at them. Will waved to him as he did. Finally, when he had rounded a bend in the track and was lost to view, Maddie spoke.

'So did you find something?'

Will nodded, and gestured for her to join him. They walked back down the track for ten metres and he pointed to the ground. 'Look at the tracks Acorn left.'

'Acorn?' Maddie asked.

'Liam's horse. See here, as they lead up to these trees, his gait is smooth and even. From the length of his stride and the depth of the hoofprints, I'd say he was at a full gallop. But as he passes the trees, the tracks are all over the place. He's lost his balance and he definitely stumbled.'

Tug snorted and Will looked quickly at him. 'It happens,' he said. Maddie was down on one knee, studying the tracks, and didn't see that he'd addressed the comment to the horse. Instead, she rose and turned towards the nearest of the two trees.

'I noticed something on one of the trees,' she said. 'It may be nothing but you should see it.'

'Or it may be something,' Will said. He followed her and looked where she was pointing. There was a faint scar in the bark of the tree, about half a metre above the ground.

'Something cut the bark here,' she pointed out.

Will raised his eyebrows. 'Well spotted.'

She glanced up at him. 'I didn't think anything of it until you mentioned that Acorn seemed to lose his footing.' She turned quickly and walked to the opposite tree. 'Let's see if there's a corresponding mark on this one.'

There was but it was very faint. If they hadn't known to look for it, they might never have seen it. Will reached forward to touch it. There was a small piece of thin white thread sticking to the bark. He plucked it free.

'Could be fibre from a rope,' he said. He looked up and down the track, then at the tree opposite them. 'So let's say Liam is galloping along this track full tilt . . .'

'Chasing someone perhaps,' Maddie suggested and he nodded.

'That's not unreasonable. And let's say someone else has stretched a rope across the track between these two trees. Acorn hits it and stumbles, only just retaining his footing.'

'But the stumble is enough to throw Liam clear of the saddle and he pitches onto the ground up here . . .' Maddie walked quickly to where Gatt had told them he found Liam's body. 'And he's killed in the fall.'

'That would explain the marks on the trees,' Will said thoughtfully. 'As Acorn hit the rope, it would have cut into the bark with the impact.'

They looked at each other in silence for a moment. Then Will spoke.

'Someone wanted Liam dead,' he said quietly.

Maddie pursed her lips. 'They couldn't be sure the fall would kill him,' she said.

'True. But he would have been incapacitated — knocked out or winded by the fall. And they would have been ready to finish him off.'

'Of course we can't be sure,' Maddie said. 'It's just a few jumbled hoofprints and a faint mark on a tree. That could have been caused by anything.'

'We need to have a close look at Acorn. If he hit that rope at any sort of speed, there'll be bruising or cuts on his legs,' Will said.

'Where would he be now?' Maddie asked.

'Most likely in the stables at Castle Trelleth,' Will said. 'The horsemaster would have taken him in to care for him after Liam's death.' He leaned back, stretching his back muscles, cramped from so much stooping and kneeling.

'Time we paid a call on Baron Scully,' he said.

In the event, he visited the castle alone, leaving Maddie at the small Ranger cabin set in the woods below the castle.

'Don't know this Scully person,' he said. 'But there's always the chance that he's been at Castle Araluen and he might recognise you. If that's so, then he'll want to entertain you at the castle. And then the whole countryside will know about your presence here in the next twenty-four hours.'

Maddie nodded, understanding. 'And that would make it difficult for us to investigate,' she said.

'Very difficult. It's better if we can keep a low profile. Plus I don't want too many people knowing who you really are. It's a matter of your safety.'

'That's fine by me,' Maddie said. She was becoming weary of the way people stared at her when they realised she was a girl — and an apprentice Ranger. If the fact that she was a princess was added in, the curiosity would get out of hand. 'I'll stay in the cabin.'

'Take a look through Liam's papers while you're here,' Will told her. 'There might be some clue as to what he was on to.'

Ranger cabins were all built to two basic designs. Liam's was almost identical to the one Maddie shared with Will and she felt comfortable there. As Will had instructed, she went through the papers on Liam's small desk to see if there was any clue as to the reason for his death. But she found nothing. It was almost dusk when she heard Bumper whinny from the stable behind the cabin. Then Tug answered and a few minutes later Will rode up through the trees.

'Well, we've got our answer,' he said. 'Acorn was limping when they recovered him. He had a cut on his right foreleg. The horsemaster said he assumed Acorn had stumbled and injured himself, throwing Liam off. But it could have been caused by his hitting a rope.'

'So Liam's death was definitely no accident,' she said.

'It would appear not. Now all we have to do is find out why someone would want to kill him. He must have chanced upon something. Must have seen something going on.'

'Should we tell Gilan?' she asked and he nodded.

'I'll send a message pigeon from the castle tomorrow. But I know what he'll say. He'll want us to nose around and find out what's going on. No sense in having crowds of people coming in here to investigate. That'll just tip our hand to whoever killed Liam. Better for us to do it quietly.'

He paused, then a thought struck him as his gaze fell on the desk and the papers crowded there.

'Anything in his papers?' he asked.

Maddie shook her head. 'Nothing I could see.'

'Hardly surprising. If he was on the trail of something, he wouldn't leave his paperwork in full view. He'd have it well hidden.'

Maddie glanced round the little living room. There seemed to be nowhere that would serve as a hiding place.

'Where would he do that?' she asked.

In answer, Will rose and paced along the centre of the living room floor, his eyes down, studying the boards on either side. He stopped, staring at one point off to the left. Then he stepped towards it, went down on one knee and drew his saxe knife.

He rapped on the boards with the hilt, working in a semi-circle. On the fourth rap, the boards sounded hollow and he gave a small grunt of satisfaction. Then he inserted the tip of the saxe into a narrow join between two boards and levered.

There was a groan of wood rubbing on wood, and a small trapdoor was levered open, exposing a hidden, wood-lined cavity below the floor. He looked up at Maddie.

'All our cabins have a strongbox,' he said by way of explanation. 'It's just a matter of spotting where it is.'

He reached into the cavity and produced a thin sheaf of papers, enclosed in a folder and wrapped with a green ribbon.

'Now what do we have here?' he said.

Thirty-one

They moved to the table and sat side by side as Will laid out the contents of the hidden strongbox.

The first item was a rough map of the area surrounding Castle Trelleth. It had been quickly sketched, presumably by Liam, and showed little in the way of geographical features. But there were three villages marked on the map, all some distance from the castle. Beside each, a person's name was neatly written.

Maddie leaned forward, elbows on the table, and looked at the name nearest her.

'Boyletown, Peter Williscroft,' she said, reading from the map. 'Who's Peter Williscroft and what does he have to do with Boyletown?'

Will shook his head. 'And who's Carrie Clover, and what is she doing in Danvers Crossing? And what does Maurice Spoker have to do with Esseldon?'

They looked at the map for several seconds, as if expecting the answer to become clearer.

'Maybe they're the headmen of those villages?' Maddie suggested.

Will tapped the name on the second village they had mentioned. 'Carrie Clover would be a woman,' he said.

Maddie grunted. She'd never heard of a village electing a head woman, although it was possible.

'Maybe she was his wife?' she suggested.

'Maybe.' Will didn't sound convinced. Again they sat silently, considering the puzzle. Finally, Maddie spoke.

'What else was in the strongbox?'

There were two other sheets. Will unfolded the first and smoothed it out. It was a list of the three villages marked on the maps, with details of the relative sizes of each.

'All about the same size,' he said. 'Large villages. Not large enough to call a town. Or to have any elected law officers.'

As villages grew into towns, they became more organised. Sheriffs were appointed to keep the peace. And a town watch was usually recruited to carry out the sheriff's orders. Smaller villages tended to do without such hierarchy.

'That might be significant,' Maddie said. 'What's that final sheet?'

Will unfolded the third piece of paper and his eyebrows rose as he read its contents. He moved the list of villages aside to study the map once more, then sat back, thinking hard.

Maddie leaned over to study the final sheet of paper.

'These are the names of the people from the three villages,' she said.

'And they're not headmen or councillors,' Will replied. 'Look: Peter Williscroft, twelve, and a date that's three weeks ago. Then Carrie Clover, fourteen, and another date. Five days after the one for Peter Williscroft.'

'And Maurice Spoker, four days after Carrie. He's eleven,' Maddie said.

'What do the dates mean?' Will said.

'Maybe they're birthdays,' Maddie suggested.

Will screwed up his lips, looking doubtful. 'Maybe. If so, they were all born around the same time. But in different years.'

'Maybe something happened to these children,' Maddie suggested.

Will looked at her. 'Like what?'

She shrugged. 'I don't know. Maybe they died. Or went missing. Something like that.'

'Possibly. It's a dangerous world, after all. There are wolves in this part of the country. And you still see the occasional bear.'

'Let's assume I'm right for a moment,' Maddie said, 'and they're dead or missing. Why hasn't anyone seen a link between three children from three villages in the same fief who have gone missing in the space of two weeks?'

'They're probably unaware of it. Look how widely separated they are. The people in, say, Danvers Crossing are probably upset about Carrie Clover. But they'd have no idea that two other children of similar ages have disappeared from two other villages. There's not a lot of communication between villages like this.'

'How did Liam know?' Maddie asked.

Will shrugged. 'It's part of a Ranger's job to know what's going on in a fief. We travel round the villages, collecting news and information, looking for unusual events. He probably saw this pattern across the three villages.'

'And someone killed him before he could do anything about it,' Maddie said.

Will held up a cautioning hand. 'That's assuming that these three are missing, or dead, or that something bad has happened to them. There could be a lot of explanations for those dates.'

'Such as?'

'Such as I don't know.'

'But think about it, Will. It must be something like that. After all, Liam went to the trouble of hiding those names and dates in his strongbox. So they must mean something important. And somebody killed him. He must have been asking questions about those three kids and whoever took them found out about it — and arranged his accident.'

'It's a reasonable hypothesis,' he admitted, 'but that's all it is.' Maddie had a vivid imagination and he needed to rein it in. All too often with a situation like this, there was a temptation to arrange the evidence to suit the theory, and ignore any that didn't fit.

'Let's not jump to any conclusions,' he continued. 'I think it's time we did a little investigating. I'll need to get some equipment from the castle first thing.'

'A handcart?' Maddie said, looking at the shabby little vehicle that Will had brought from the castle. 'What do we want with a handcart?'

'It's to carry all our worldly belongings,' Will told her. 'We're posing as an itinerant worker and his daughter. I'll be looking for work and you'll be tagging along with me.'

He paused, then reached into the cart and tossed a patched, ragged dress to her. 'While I think of it, you'd better dress the part.'

Maddie regarded the tatty garment with distaste. 'Do I have to wear this rag?' she asked.

Will nodded. 'Bit of a giveaway if you're wearing a Ranger cloak and carrying a bow,' he said. 'We don't want people to know who we are. All too often, country folk clam up when they see a Ranger. What we have to do is go into these villages and nose around. Odds are you'll have better luck with the local kids than I will with their parents. Kids tend to talk to other kids, while they'll be more wary around adults.'

'What about our horses? What will we do with them?' Maddie asked.

'When we reach a village, we'll hide them in the woods close by. A farm worker would hardly own one horse, let alone two. Mind you, Tug's not going to be too pleased about all this. He's going to have to pull the handcart for us and that may well be beneath his dignity.'

Indeed, Tug was incensed when he saw the small cart.

You expect me to pull that? I'm not a cart horse, you know.

'And I'm not an itinerant farm worker,' Will told him. He'd glanced around to make sure that Maddie was out of earshot before he answered the horse. 'But we're undercover, and it's an excellent disguise.'

I'm not letting people see me pulling this.

'You don't have to. We'll unharness you when we get close to the villages. You can wait for us in the woods.'

And who'll pull the cart then? Tug wanted to know.

'I will. It's a handcart, after all. And people will see me doing it.'

People will see you? Lots of people?

'Dozens of them, I should think. I'll even wear a big straw hat with a raggedy brim.'

That sounds fair to me.

As it turned out, Tug pulled the little cart easily. It was quite light and even with Will on his back, he wasn't over-burdened. His pride was another matter, however, and he snorted angrily at Will whenever they passed anyone on the road.

Danvers Crossing was the closest village and Will selected it as their first destination. They stopped on the road about two kilometres before they reached the village. They found a small glade some ten metres in from the road with plenty of fresh grass and shade for the horses. Will unhitched Tug from the wagon. There was a large water skin hanging from the rear tray of the cart and he used it to fill a leather bucket for the two horses.

'I'll come out to check on you tonight,' Will told the horses. 'For now, stay silent.'

The last two words were a command taught to all Ranger horses. It ensured that Bumper and Tug would remain in hiding in the glade when people passed by, and make no sound. Both horses nodded their heads several times, understanding the command. Then Will took hold of the cart's two shafts and started out down the road to Danvers Crossing, Maddie tagging along beside him.

As he reached up to place an old straw hat with a ragged brim on his head, Will was convinced he could hear Tug sniggering.

Thirty-two

Danvers Crossing, as the name suggested, was situated on the banks of a small river. Maddie had expected that the crossing might be a shallow ford, but the river was deep and the current swift. Crossing was effected by means of a large flat-bottomed punt, which ran on thick rope cables set on either bank.

It was a pleasant-looking village, with its groves of willows stooping down to the water and providing cool, shady retreats along the bank. The gurgle of the river was ever present in the background. Maddie found it to be a soothing sound.

Aside from the punt, the village itself was typical of its kind, with a blacksmith, a tavern, a small tannery, a lumber yard with a sawpit and a seed and grain merchant's shop. Set by a river as it was, it was logical that Danvers Crossing also boasted a flour mill, the massive grinding wheels driven by the fast-flowing river. Farms from the surrounding countryside would bring their grain to the mill to be turned into fine-ground flour.

In addition to these businesses, there were the villagers' homes — most of them small structures, and all of them single storey, built in the ubiquitous wattle and daub method, and with steeply sloping thatched roofs. They stood on either side of the main street. Side lanes between them led to barns and sheds and other outbuildings. All in all, there were about thirty such dwellings.

The tannery stood at the near end of the village street. Maddie wrinkled her nose as they trudged past it.

'Yuck. What's that dreadful smell?' she asked.

Will, bent to the shafts of the handcart, looked up at her. 'You don't want to know,' he said.

There was a sizeable space between the tannery and the first of the village buildings proper. The next was the smithy, and they could hear the dull clink of hammer on metal, and the rhythmic roar of the bellows as the black-smith's assistant kept a constant draught under the bed of glowing charcoal. It was a logical arrangement, and one that could be found in most villages. Businesses like the tannery, with its unpleasant smell, and the smithy, with its inherent risk of fire, were kept at arm's length from the houses, the taverns and inns.

A few villagers were on the street and they glanced at the newcomers with interest and, in some cases, suspicion. One or two of them nodded and Will replied by touching his hand to the battered hat he wore.

As they moved further into the village, he glanced up and saw the two-storey building that stood in pride of place by the riverside.

'That'll be the tavern,' he said quietly to Maddie. 'In a place like this, it'll also serve as the inn, I imagine. We'll head there first.'

Danvers Crossing was too small to boast a separate tavern and inn, as he had suspected. The building by the river served both purposes, with a long tap room, where meals were also served, and bedrooms for rent on the upper storey. There was a grassy bank outside where the tavern keeper would set up tables in good weather, so that patrons could enjoy their ale and their food in sight of the river.

Will brought the cart to a stop outside the tavern and straightened up gratefully, stretching the stiffness out of his joints and massaging the small of his back with his fists. The handcart was a little low for comfort. As a result, the person pushing it was forced to adopt a crouch. He took off his hat and wiped his forehead. Maddie waited impatiently as he slowly surveyed the village and the river.

'What now?' she asked, and he glanced at her, shaking his head slightly.

'Take your time,' he said. 'Country folk never hurry. Just relax and smell the roses.'

She looked around. 'Roses? I don't see any roses. The only thing I can smell is horse manure.'

There was a stableyard and stable beside the tavern. Obviously, it was for use by the tavern's patrons. Equally obviously, there had been more than a few of them, and their horses, in recent times.

'Figure of speech,' Will said. 'I can hardly say *Relax and smell the horse dung*, can I?'

Maddie allowed a half smile to twist her lips. 'The two thoughts don't really go together.'

Will nodded absently. 'Well, we've relaxed enough. Let's go in.' As they headed for the door, he said, 'Leave the talking to me.'

'You've told me that — several times,' Maddie replied.

He glanced at her. 'Just making sure it's sunk in,' he said, and led the way inside.

The tavern was dark inside, with only a small window in the side wall to provide daylight to the tap room. There were four lanterns hanging from the central ceiling beam and a fire flickered in the massive grate to one side. That was for cooking as well as providing warmth, Maddie realised.

The roof beams were low, and even Will, who was not the tallest of men, had to stoop as they made their way into the tavern, approaching the bar. The tavern keeper looked up at them with mild interest. He was busy wiping out a row of tankards.

'Something to drink?' he inquired. 'And maybe a bite to eat?'

Will frowned at him. 'Yes to the drink. Ale for me — small ale, that is.'

Small ale was ale and water mixed in equal proportions. That is, the proportions were equal if the tavern keeper was honest. All too often, small ale was more water than ale. But it was cheaper, as well, which was why Will ordered it.

'What about food?' the innkeeper asked again, as he placed a tankard in front of Will. 'We've a good chicken stew today. Chicken with dumplings and farm vegetables and a good crusty loaf for three pennigs a serve.'

Will pursed his lips, considering. 'We'll share one,' he said. The price was actually more than reasonable, but he was playing the role of an itinerant worker and such men had to watch their coins.

'Be an extra coin for a second plate and spoon,' the innkeeper replied.

Will scowled at him. 'Hmmmph!' he snorted. 'I suppose I've no choice. All right then.'

The innkeeper gestured to Maddie. 'Will she want something to drink? I've fresh cider if she wants.'

'Water will do her fine,' Will said, maintaining his penny-pinching character. The innkeeper poured Maddie a beaker of water and shouted their food order to an unseen worker in the kitchen behind him. He leaned his elbows on the bar as Will and Maddie sat opposite him.

'Travelling through?' he asked.

He was friendly enough. Probably wondering if he could rent them a room, Will thought.

'Travelling, yes,' Will replied. 'Whether we go on through depends on whether I can find work here.'

'That might be a possibility,' said the tavern keeper. 'What sort of work are you looking for?'

Will shrugged. 'Anything. I can turn my hand to most things. Farm work, fencing, repair work, carpentry. You name it.'

'Not much farm work at the moment,' the innkeeper said. 'But I've got a few repairs need doing round the tavern here. Carpentry and some painting.'

Will looked up at him, interest in his eyes at the prospect of work. 'Well, I'm your man for that.' He held out his hand. 'William's the name. William Accord. This here's my daughter, Maddie.'

They shook hands. 'Good day to you, Maddie,' said the innkeeper. Then, speaking to Will again, 'My name's Rob. Rob Danvers.'

Will raised his eyebrows in interest. 'Danvers? Is the village named for you then?'

Rob Danvers shook his head. 'My great-grandfather,' he said. 'He built the first punt across the river. Mind you, in those days, there were all sorts of brigands and bandits in these parts. Not like today.'

'Aye, things have quietened down in recent years,' Will answered. 'So how many days' work do you think you'd have for me?'

Danvers shrugged. 'Two or three, maybe. But you'd have a good chance of picking up more if you're here in the tavern — and I put in a good word for you. You could rent a room here for you and your daughter, be right on site.'

Will wrinkled his nose at the idea — and the expense. 'Rather sleep in your stables if that's no problem to you,' he said.

Danvers shrugged. 'Suit yourself. Be cheaper that way. But a good deal draughtier.'

'We'll rug up,' Will told him. 'By the way, while I'm working, I'll need someone to look after Maddie here. I don't want her running wild all over the place. Any of the village women be prepared to do that sort of thing?'

A young girl emerged from the kitchen with their food. Will took a bite, chewed and swallowed before he spoke again. Maddie piled into hers with gusto. After a long morning on the road, the chicken stew was delicious. She glanced up at Will's next question.

'Someone in the next village said there was a family here whose daughter had moved away. Maybe they'd be interested?' Will paused, pretending to search for the name. 'Clover, it was. Said their girl was about Maddie's age.'

Rob Danver's face clouded over. He stood up abruptly.

'Carrie Clover didn't move away,' he said shortly.

Will raised his eyebrows in surprise. 'So she's still here then?'

Danvers shook his head. 'She disappeared. Some weeks back. Just disappeared one night.'

'Run away, did she?' Will asked.

The innkeeper paused, then replied. 'I wouldn't be too surprised. Her parents didn't treat her so well. You'd often see her with bruises on her face. Or red eyes from crying. Pity too. She was a likeable little thing.'

'Maybe she met a boy and ran off with him? Wouldn't be the first time.'

But Danvers shook his head once more. 'Had a boy she was sweet on. He's still here. No, you ask me, she got tired of the beatings and ran off.' He leaned forward, conspiratorially, 'Unless, of course, someone took her.'

'Took her? What for?'

Danvers shook his head. 'Don't know. Maybe for ransom?'

'Is her family well off then?' Will asked, but Danvers shook his head, negating his own theory.

'Father's a ploughman. Just manages to make ends meet. He'd never be able to pay a ransom.'

'Then why abduct her, if you knew there was no chance of any ransom?'

Danvers moved his head back and forth as he pondered the question. He hadn't really considered his theory in any depth before. He was simply used to saying, in darkest tones, that 'somebody took her'.

'Dunno. But she's gone, that I know.' He paused. 'Was I you, I wouldn't go asking the family about it, neither. Clover's a bad-tempered type. Likely to fly off the handle if he thinks you're blaming him for her going.'

Will considered the point for a few seconds, then nodded his head in agreement.

'Thanks for the warning,' he said. 'If I run across him, I'll make sure I don't mention it.' He paused, as if digesting that thought, finished off his meal, then glanced at Maddie.

'Well, come along, girl. Eat up and let's get our things into the stable. Like as not it'll rain before dark.'

He swallowed the last of his beer, nodded to Danvers and turned for the door, Maddie following.

Thirty-three

They spent a further two days in Danvers Crossing, but learned little more about the fate of Carrie Clover.

While Will applied himself to the repairs and painting at the tavern, Maddie wandered through the village and attempted to make friends with the local youngsters. They proved to be neither friendly nor unfriendly. But they showed a certain interest in her as an outsider.

It was easier for Maddie to raise the subject of the missing girl. Will, having discussed it already with Danvers, could hardly continue to show interest in her. To do so might have invited unwelcome attention and questions as to why he was so concerned. He could only spend his evenings in the tavern and listen to the conversations around him, hoping that someone else might bring up the topic. Unfortunately, this didn't happen.

Children, however, tend to be more forthright than adults, and Maddie could simply ask them about Carrie's disappearance, under the pretext of having heard her father discussing it with the innkeeper. She waited until she had mixed with the village children on two separate occasions, then bluntly raised the matter.

'My da told me some girl disappeared from around here,' she said. 'Told me to go careful around the village, lest the same might happen to me.'

She was sitting by the river late in the afternoon with half a dozen of the locals, ranging in age from eight to fifteen. The children exchanged uncomfortable glances and for a moment nobody replied. Pretending not to notice their reluctance, she ploughed on.

'So what happened to her? Where'd she go?'

The children exchanged glances again. Then one of the older boys spoke.

'That'd be Carrie Clover,' he said.

Maddie shrugged. 'Didn't say her name to me. So she ran off, did she?'

There was a general shaking of heads among the group. Then a younger boy, about ten and with blond, unruly hair, answered her.

'Didn't run off. Was taken, more like.'

Maddie leaned forward, feigning surprise. 'Taken? Taken by who?'

'You shut your mouth, Clem,' the older boy said quickly. He looked at Maddie. 'We don't talk about it.'

'Why not? What took her?' she asked. It seemed logical to press the question.

The boy glanced around the rest of the group. They all wore wary expressions, except for the young boy, Clem, who was smarting at being reprimanded in front of the stranger.

Finally, the older boy replied. 'She was taken by a river wight.'

Maddie was watching the rest of the children and she saw a few surprised expressions, hastily covered up.

'Aye, Simon's right. It was a river wight took her.' One of the girls, who was a few years younger than Maddie, agreed, nodding her head emphatically.

'And what's a river wight?' Maddie asked. She'd never heard the term before and she was genuinely puzzled.

The older boy, Simon, hesitated a few seconds, and she had the distinct impression he was formulating an answer to her question on the spot.

'It's a river spirit,' he said. 'An evil river spirit. They lurk in the deep water, then suddenly dash out and seize anyone who gets too close to the bank.'

'We're close to the bank now,' Maddie pointed out.

Simon glanced at the river and realised she was right.

'Aye, we are. We should move afore one of us is taken.' He started to rise, gesturing for the others to do the same. Belatedly, they all came to their feet.

He's lying, Maddie thought. He's making this up as he goes along. But why?

Clem, the young boy who had spoken first, shook his head dismissively.

'River wights! Ain't no such th—' he began muttering. But the girl who had agreed with Simon grabbed his arm and dragged him aside. She spoke to him in a fierce whisper.

'You shut your yap, Clem! Remember what the Story-man said . . .'

She spoke a little louder than she intended, and Maddie overheard the words. Her mind was racing. The story man? Who or what was the story man? Having heard the word only once, she didn't realise it was a name, rather than a description. But she pretended she hadn't heard the girl's words.

Simon rounded on the girl. 'Shut up! Both of you shut up!' He realised Maddie was watching him and continued. 'Now, best we all get on home. It's bad luck to talk about river wights.'

The others all mumbled agreement and the group broke up, heading for their homes. One or two of them glanced back at Maddie as she remained by the river. She stepped closer to the bank and peered into the smooth, fast-running water, trying to see if there was, in fact, a river wight visible. Then she realised that she had no idea what such a creature might look like. A cloud passed across the sun and the river, so cheerful and sparkling, was suddenly transformed into a dull, leaden grey. A frisson of fear assailed her and she turned away from the river, hurrying back down the village main street to the stable where she and Will were staying.

'What's a river wight?' The question burst from her lips the moment Will entered the stable an hour later. He'd finished work for the day. In fact, he'd finished all of the tasks that Rob Danvers has set for him and no other work had eventuated.

He looked curiously at her. She was sitting with her back against one of the handcart's wheels. Her face was pale and she looked bothered.

'A river what?' he asked and she shook her head impatiently.

'Not what. Wight. A river wight. It's some kind of creature.'

He shook his head, pursing his lips. 'Not that I've ever heard. There are barrow wights. Or some people say there are. They're supposed to be spirits that hang around ancient graves. Although I can't say I've ever encountered one.'

He paused, as an unpleasant memory stirred in his mind. There was an occasion many years before, when he was riding to fetch Malcolm to heal the mortally wounded Halt. He'd sensed something then as he rode past some barrows, as the ancient grave mounds were called. It seemed to be some malign presence. But he'd passed it off as imagination, triggered by nerves and weariness.

'This was a river wight,' Maddie insisted. The idea of it seemed to be troubling her.

'Where did you hear about it?'

'The local children. They said Carrie Clover was taken by a river wight.'

That got his attention.

'They said it dragged her into the river,' Maddie continued.

'They saw it?' Will asked quickly. There could have been some creature in the river, he thought — a large fish of some kind. Or a bear. Some bears could swim, he knew. He'd never seen one do so, but he'd heard people say they could.

'No. They didn't see it. In fact, I think they were lying about it.'

'What makes you think so?' Will asked.

Maddie paused, unable to explain it fully. 'Just a sense I got. One of the younger boys didn't believe it. He was pooh-poohing the idea and an older girl made him stop. Simon, the oldest boy, told me the story about the river wight. But I just felt he was making it up.'

'And the young boy didn't believe it?' Will asked and she nodded. 'That's odd. Normally, you'd think the younger ones would be more likely to believe tales about monsters in the river.'

'Doris, the girl who told him to shut up, said something about a story man.'

'A story man,' Will said slowly. 'Maybe he's the local raconteur or spinner,' he suggested.

'They didn't say. She said, "Remember what the story man said." Then Simon yelled at her and told *her* to shut up.'

Will sat down, thinking about what she had told him. He glanced up and saw Maddie's anxious face.

'But there's no such thing as a river wight, is there? Not really?' she said.

'No. I've never heard of one and I've been around a lot of rivers in my time. It's just a story,' he said reassuringly. As he said the word 'story', he wondered about this story man character. He decided he'd ask in the tavern later, and see if there was a local storyteller — or spinner, short for yarn spinner, as such men were often known. Villages like this often had such people. They helped keep the oral history of the village and its people alive.

'It's your turn to check on the horses,' he said. They had taken it in turns to slip out of the village after dark and make sure the horses were all right. Maddie looked out of the unglazed stable window. The sun was setting and the shadows were lengthening across the village. To reach the clearing where Tug and Bumper were hidden, she'd have to walk part of the way beside the river.

She twisted her hands together nervously at the thought of it — and the thought of dark creatures that might be lurking beneath the surface. Simon had been lying. She was sure of that. But even so, there *could* be such a thing as a river wight, even if it hadn't been one that took Carrie Clover. After all, Will had simply said he'd never heard of such a creature. He hadn't said definitively that they didn't exist.

'Will you come with me?' she asked in a small voice.

Will turned to her in surprise. He was used to Maddie being confident and self-assured. Obviously, this talk of evil river creatures had got to her. He was about to laugh at her fears, then realised that she was young, and it was getting dark and imagination could be a terrible thing, no matter what logic might tell you. He sighed. He'd had a hard day and he'd been looking forward to a quick nap in the straw before heading into the tavern for supper.

Wearily, he rose to his feet, brushing loose strands of straw off his clothes.

'Of course I will,' he said.

The horses, as ever, were delighted to see them. They were even more delighted to find the apples that their owners had secreted in their pockets.

There was plenty of grass for them to graze on, but Will had brought a small sack of oats as well. He assumed that grass on its own would be a boring diet. He'd certainly find it so, he thought. The horses seemed to agree as they munched happily on the oats. He patted Tug's muscular neck as the little horse put his head down to the oats.

'We'll be heading off tomorrow, so eat up,' he said. Maddie overheard him.

'We're leaving?' she said. She had been smoothing Bumper's coat with a stiff brush. She knew her horse enjoyed the attention.

'There's no more work, so there's no reason to stay. I'll see what I can find out about this story man tonight. But unless there's something important comes up, we'll move on to the next village.'

Maddie nodded. She cocked her head. In the near distance, she could hear the rush and gurgle of the river. When they had first arrived, it had seemed so cheerful and friendly, she thought. Now, she wasn't so sure.

'I won't be sorry to go,' she said.

Later that night, nursing a tankard of small ale, on the pretext of having a nightcap before going to sleep, Will broached the subject with Danvers.

'Do you have a spinner living in the village?' he asked, trying to sound casual.

Danvers shook his head. 'Village isn't big enough to support one,' he said. 'From time to time we get itinerants passing through. As a —' He was about to add something but, at that moment, a rowdy group of ploughmen called loudly for more ale. He shrugged apologetically and moved away. He was caught up serving for some time and Will finally finished his drink. He had no further reason to stay in the bar, so he quietly left, heading for bed.

He wondered briefly what the innkeeper had been about to say, but decided it was probably unimportant. The important question had been answered. There was no local storyteller.

Thirty-four

Esseldon wasn't quite as big as Danvers Crossing. It wasn't situated on a river, so there was no flour mill, and none of the associated buildings and services, such as storage silos and sack makers. Nor, of course, was there a ferry service.

But it was a pleasant little village, built along the usual lines, with one main street, and houses and businesses ranged along either side. At the far end of the village, at the crest of a small hill, stood the ever-present inn. No matter how small a settlement might be, there was always a place where the locals could gather to relax and to eat and drink. And accommodation where travellers could spend the night.

As before, Will asked for, and obtained, permission to sleep in the inn's stable. He had been well paid by Rob Danvers, and with the money he'd earned, he could have afforded a room at the inn. But he was maintaining the character of a wandering labourer. Such a man wouldn't waste valuable coins on fancy accommodation. A roof over the head and clean straw to bed down on were enough for such people.

When it came to work, however, the news wasn't good. Jerome, the innkeeper, shook his head dubiously when Will raised the subject.

'No farm work,' he said. 'The harvests are over so there's no work in the fields now for a few months. And if there's any repair work to be done, most farmers do it themselves. As do I. You can ask around, of course, but don't expect too much.'

Will nodded glumly. 'Thought as much,' he said. 'Well, I'll spend maybe a day or two and see what's on offer. Best get our things into the stable.'

He seized the handles of the handcart and put his weight to it, wheeling it into the stableyard, then into the small stable itself. He looked around, pointing to a pile of fresh straw in a bin.

'Let's get some of that spread out so we can sleep on it,' he said.

Maddie found a wooden pitchfork and began to heave bundles of straw onto a dry portion of the hard earth floor, working so enthusiastically that a cloud of fine straw particles rose in the air, visible in the beams of sunlight that made their way through gaps in the stable wall. Aside from one elderly draught horse, the stable was unoccupied. After she had moved a suitable amount of straw, and sneezed several times in the process, Will took the pitchfork from her hand. It was midafternoon. By now, if Esseldon was like most villages, the local children would have been released from their chores and be relaxing in the few hours of spare time they'd have before their evening tasks had to be done.

Of course, in a village as small as this, there was no school. If the children had any formal instruction, it came from their parents. In most cases, that meant they had little formal learning. The ability to read and write was rare.

'Why don't you head out and get to know the local kids?' he suggested.

She dusted herself off, went to sneeze, then suppressed the urge with a forefinger pressed up under her nose.

'Should I ask about Maurice Spoker?' she asked. Maurice Spoker was the Esseldon boy mentioned in Liam's notes. Will considered this for a few seconds, then shook his head.

'Not right away. You can always do that tomorrow. Use the same story — that I'd heard about his disappearance in the tavern and warned you to be careful. For the moment, see if there's been any sign of a storyteller here in Esseldon.'

He frowned. There obviously had been a spinner in Danvers Crossing. The children had mentioned him, after all. And as Maddie told it, he seemed to make them nervous. It was odd that Danvers knew nothing about him. Then a thought struck him. He had asked if there was a spinner living in Danvers Crossing. Perhaps the story man was an itinerant. Maybe that was what Rob Danvers had been about to say when he had been interrupted.

'In the meantime, I'll do the rounds of the houses in the village, seeing if there's any work to be had.' He paused, looking at his bandaged left hand, which he had gouged painfully when a chisel slipped the day before. 'With any luck, there won't be any.'

Maddie nodded and headed out the stable door. She assumed that there would be a place where the local children gathered — the common or the village green, perhaps. She found that the latter was the favoured place. It was an open, grassy space set in the middle of the village, where any resident could graze cows or sheep or run hens or ducks. There was a pond in the middle that was used for watering the animals.

As she approached, she could see half a dozen young people on the grass. One of them stood up as she came nearer, drew back his arm and threw a rock into the pond.

Maddie watched as it splashed into the water. There was a small wooden raft drifting on the pond's surface. It was obviously the target he had aimed at. The others jeered or cheered as his throw missed by a metre. He grinned and sat down. Another boy stood in his place, viewed the floating target carefully while he weighed a rock in his hand, then drew back his arm and threw.

His cast went well wide of the target and again a chorus of jeers rose from the others. He glanced back and saw Maddie approaching. He said something to the other children and they all turned to look at her. She waved shyly and sat on the grass about five metres away from them, drawing her knees up.

The group decided that there was no further purpose in staring at Maddie and went back to what they had been doing. Obviously, there was a contest going on among the four boys in the group. A younger boy stood now and threw in his turn. His stone raised a splash a few centimetres from the target, setting it rocking. The two girls cheered. The other boys glared at him. The fourth boy stood and threw, but he was in too much of a hurry. His stone landed short, skipped once, then sank. The younger boy laughed.

Maddie was idly fingering her sling, which she wore tied around her waist. She looked around and saw several smooth stones in the grass beside her. Picking two up, she rose and walked closer to the group, as the first boy stood to throw again. His throw was closer this time, and again, the target was set rocking. He became conscious that Maddie was standing close by and looked at her curiously.

'Good shot,' she said, pointing to the target, bobbing up and down in the centre of a widening circle of ripples. 'Can I have a go?'

'Girls can't throw,' he said. He didn't say it in a scornful or derogatory way. It was a simple statement of fact as he saw it.

Maddie smiled. 'I'm a girl. And I can throw.'

She had the attention of the entire group now. One of the other boys shook his head, a tolerant smile on his face. The two girls, she saw, were quite interested in her assertion. They didn't look as if they believed her, but they were willing to see her try, hopeful that she might live up to her claim.

'Let her have a go, David,' one of the girls said.

The boy looked at her, then back at Maddie, and shrugged, standing aside.

'Why not? But it'll cost you two pennigs to compete. First one to hit the target wins it all.'

She continued to smile at him while she reached into her belt purse and produced two small copper coins. She handed them to him.

'You'll be sorry to lose them, I'm sure.' The boy smiled.

Maddie shook out the sling and set a stone into the pouch. She stepped forward quickly, before anyone could see exactly what she was doing. She set her left foot forward, letting the sling hang down at the end of her extended right arm, then swung it up and over as she stepped into the shot. The rock whizzed away with enormous speed.

The water around the float erupted as the rock smashed into it, sending splinters of wood and a large water spout into the air.

The village children sprang to their feet, amazed at the power and accuracy that Maddie had just shown. The youngest boy, whose throw had been the closest to the target so far, was wide eyed as he looked at the smashed float. Then he noticed the sling dangling from Maddie's right hand.

'What's that?' he said. She held the sling up for them to see.

'It's a sling,' she said. She smiled at them. 'Don't worry, I won't take your money. I had an unfair advantage.'

David stepped closer, frowning as he held out a hand for the sling. She passed it to him.

'It's just a few pieces of cord and a leather pouch,' he said.

'Yes. But it gives you a lot of extra power when you throw. Do you want to try it?'

He nodded and she showed him how to load a stone into the pouch, then stand side on, with his right arm stretched back and the sling hanging down behind him.

'Let it swing back and forth a few times to get the feel,' she said. 'Then whip it up and over and, when it's pointing at the target, release the end.'

His first few attempts were wildly inaccurate, as he released either too early or too late. The stones flew high into the air above them, or splashed wildly into the pond a few metres from the bank. But gradually, he began to get the hang of it.

'Try to feel as if your forefinger is pointing at the target as you release,' Maddie told him. He did so and sent a stone whizzing through the air, raising a large fountain of spray to the left of the remnants of the little raft. He turned to her with a delighted smile.

'This is terrific!' he said.

'With a bit of practice, you'll start hitting what you're aiming at,' she told him. Instantly, the young boy who had thrown closest to the raft reached out for the sling.

'Let me try!' he said. Maddie coached him in the correct technique and he let fly. His cast was better than David's first attempts. He threw another three stones. Two of them slammed into the water close to the shattered target. On the third, he became over eager and swung too hard. As a result, he released late and the stone thudded into the ground, short of the edge of the pond.

Maddie looked at the girls. 'Do you want to try it?'

They looked at each other hesitantly. 'Can girls do it?' one asked.

David jerked his thumb at Maddie. 'Well, she's a girl and she can do it all right!' He grinned. So the two girls, Eve and Joscelyn, took their turn with the sling. Eve quickly grasped the principles and was soon hurling stones with considerable power and accuracy. Joscelyn wasn't as quick to pick it up, but she managed several reasonable throws. All of the children were fascinated by the simplicity of the weapon — and the power they could achieve when they cast.

'We could hunt with this,' David said, admiring the sling before handing it back to Maddie.

She nodded. 'Yes. You can easily take rabbits and birds with a sling.' She looked around at them. 'Tell you what, let's meet again tomorrow and I'll show you how to make one. Just bring some leather thongs and a scrap of leather for the pouch.'

There was a general chorus of excitement and agreement. Maddie put the sling away and they sat on the grass in a companionable group.

That's it, she thought. They've accepted me. She stretched her arms over her head and let her gaze wander round the picturesque little village.

'So, what do you do for entertainment here?' she asked.

David shook his head and the others mumbled incoherently. Obviously, life in Esseldon wasn't overly exciting.

'Nothing much,' he said. 'Nothing happens here.'

'Oh. That's a shame. So you don't have a story man or anything like that?' she said casually. In spite of her apparent nonchalance, she was watching them closely and she saw the startled reaction that galvanised the group. They looked at one another, then at her. There was a sudden start of fear in their eyes.

'What do you mean — a story man?' Joscelyn asked.

David shot a glance at her, too late to stop her asking.

Maddie shrugged. 'You know: a spinner. Someone who tells ghost stories at night round the fire.'

There was a long silence. The discomfort among the other children was almost palpable. She continued, maintaining her innocent air.

'We just came from Danvers Crossing. The kids there said a travelling storyteller came through some weeks ago. Told really good, scary stories, they said.' She pretended to take keen interest in the lacing of her shoe.

Again there was an awkward pause. Then Eve said, in somewhat stilted tones, 'We don't have anything like that here.'

Maddie shrugged. Her manner said it was of no great importance.

'Oh? Well, that's a pity, but never mind.' She looked up, gauging the level of the sun over the trees in the west. 'I'd better be going. I'll see you tomorrow. Don't forget to bring the thongs and leather and we'll make some slings.'

Now that she had changed the subject and seemed to have lost interest in the concept of a storyteller, the mood lightened and the group enthusiastically agreed to meet again next day for sling-making lessons.

Maddie rose and dusted some loose grass off her dress. She wound the sling around her waist and fastened it there, then waggled her fingers in farewell.

'See you tomorrow then. Same time?'

There was a general chorus of farewell and she turned away, striding across the thick grass towards the inn and the stable where she and Will were staying. As she went, she muttered softly to herself.

'That storyteller was here all right. I'd bet my life on it.'

At the time, she had no idea that she might be doing exactly that.

Thirty-five

'No. We don't have a storyteller in this village,' the innkeeper said in response to Will's casual question.

'Pity,' Will said, taking a sip of his coffee. 'My daughter could use a bit of entertainment. It's hard for her, travelling all the time, with nothing to do and no permanent friends.'

The innkeeper nodded sympathetically. 'I can understand. Pity you didn't get here sooner. We had a travelling spinner come through here some weeks back. The kids loved him.'

Will looked up, feigning no more than polite interest.

'Heard tell of a travelling spinner in Danvers Crossing recently,' he said. He rubbed his jaw, pretending to think. 'What did he call himself, now?'

'The Storyman, was it?' Jerome suggested. Will mentally slapped his forehead with his hand as he realised that Storyman was a name.

'That's him,' he said. 'The Storyman. Of course.'

'Colourful type, he was. Wore a bright blue cloak and scarlet shoes.' The innkeeper frowned, remembering the man. 'Seemed a little odd. But I suppose that goes with the job.'

'Odd?' Will's interest was aroused but he didn't show it. 'How do you mean?'

Jerome made a dismissive gesture. 'Oh, not in a bad way. Just . . . theatrical, I suppose. He wore bells on his wrists and ankles so you could hear him coming. And he acted out his stories with great enthusiasm, I'm told.'

'You didn't see him at work?'

Jerome shook his head. 'He entertained the children. I remember giving my nephew a coin for him. He'd sit down with them by the pond on the village green and tell them stories.' He grinned at the memory. 'Ghost stories, I think. I recall the children were often a bit pale when he'd finished.'

'Well, children love a good scare now and again,' Will said. 'When was he here, do you recall?'

Jerome threw back his head, looking at the ceiling while he considered the question. Finally, he replied.

'Must have been two, maybe three weeks ago. It was a few days before the Spoker boy disappeared.'

Will frowned, looking a little concerned. 'A boy disappeared? Does a lot of that go on round here?'

Jerome shook his head, recognising a parent's natural tendency to worry. 'Lord, no! Never happened before that I recall. If you ask me, young Maurice simply ran off. His da used to beat him too often for my liking.'

Will drained his coffee, setting the mug down on the bar. He nodded good night to the innkeeper.

'Well, I'm for my bed. Got a long day tomorrow. Going to visit some of the outlying farms and see if there's any work going.'

'No luck in the village?' Jerome asked and Will shook his head, a dejected expression on his face. Jerome smiled sympathetically. 'I'm not surprised. Times have been hard and people don't have any extra money to spend.'

'Well, I certainly don't and that's for sure,' Will said. He hesitated, then said uncertainly, 'Matter of fact, I was wondering if I could ask a favour?'

Jerome's eyes narrowed. Favours usually involved money in his experience, and Will's next words bore out his assumption.

'I could be gone for a night or two. Wonder could I move Maddie into one of your rooms while I'm gone. I'd feel safer about her that way. I wouldn't like to leave her sleeping in the stable, what with children disappearing and such.'

'It was only one boy went missing,' Jerome said defensively. Then he saw the worried look on Will's face and he relented. It must be hard being a sole parent and travelling round the countryside, he thought. And he had several rooms unoccupied.

'All right then,' he said. 'She can take the attic room. I'll charge the same as I'm charging for two of you in the stable.'

Will heaved a sigh of relief. 'Thanks for that. It'll stop me worrying about her while I'm gone.'

Privately, he resolved to bring some game back for Jerome's kitchen. The innkeeper was a likeable fellow and his gesture was a generous one. He turned away for the door.

'How long will you be gone?' Maddie asked, when he told her of the new arrangement.

'A day or two. I thought I'd ride over to Boyletown and see if this Storyman character has visited there as well.'

He'd explained the confusion over the travelling spinner's name. Maddie had a similar reaction to his. Once you knew it was a name, everything seemed clear.

'We know he was at Danvers Crossing, then he came here.' Will paused, frowning. 'Wish we'd thought to find out when he was at Danvers Crossing. Jerome said he was here shortly before the local lad went missing.'

'And Jerome told you Maurice Spoker's parents mistreated him,' Maddie said thoughtfully. 'Just like Carrie Clover's father.'

Will's eyes narrowed. 'Yes. The coincidences are beginning to mount up, aren't they?'

Maddie nodded agreement. 'So what do you want me to do while you're gone?'

'Keep talking to the local kids. See if you can find out more about this blue-cloaked, red-shoed storyteller. Jerome seemed to think they loved him.'

'Not the impression I got,' Maddie said.

'Well, see what you can dig up. But be careful. Don't push it if they're reluctant.' A separate thought struck him and he added. 'Oh, by the way, while you're staying in the room, you might make yourself useful. Make your bed and offer to help out in the kitchen.'

'I'm not a good cook,' Maddie pointed out.

'I was thinking that your efforts might lie more in the area of dishwashing,' Will told her.

Maddie recoiled in mock horror. 'I don't know if I'm trained for that.'

He raised one eyebrow at her. She'd seen him do that before and found herself wishing that she could do it. She resolved to practise the expression.

'I'm sure you'll pick it up,' he said. 'It's not alchemy.'

As it turned out, Maddie didn't need to ask any further questions about the mysterious blue-cloaked Storyman. She met the other children as arranged the following afternoon and they sat on the grass as she showed them how to fashion their slings. She had brought a small knife with her and she lent it to them so they could cut the leather thongs to length, then fashion the pouches. There was only one other person on the common — a farm worker, judging by his patched work smock and a shapeless old hat. He was leaning on a fence, idly watching them. He had a small bundle wrapped in a spotted cloth at his feet.

As the group sat in a semi-circle, heads bent to the tasks of cutting, shaping and tying, David caught her eye, rose to his feet and jerked his head in an unmistakable gesture for her to follow him. She rose and they moved away from the others. She looked at him expectantly.

'Did you want to say something?' she asked.

He glanced around. She could see he was nervous. No, she corrected herself. He was more than nervous. He was scared.

'The Storyman,' he said finally. 'Don't go asking about him any more. And above all, don't mention him to your da.' He paused, then added anxiously, 'You haven't said anything to him, have you?'

She shook her head. 'No. But why not?'

'He told us things. And he said we should never repeat them to any grown-ups, or something bad would happen to us.'

Maddie's eyes widened. 'What things did he tell you?' she asked, her voice wavering. David's nervousness was getting to her.

He shuffled his feet. 'At first it was just normal stories. Some funny ones and some scary ones. They were all good fun and we all enjoyed them. Mostly they were stories we'd heard before, like the Ogre of Alden Pass and the Great Green Troll of Tralee.'

Maddie nodded. These were well-known folk tales. They varied in detail with each different storyteller, of course, but they were always essentially the same, and were calculated to give children a good healthy scare — without causing too much concern.

'But then he told us about the Stealer in the Night,' he said, his voice becoming very quiet.

'The Stealer in the Night?' Maddie repeated. Even the name sent a shiver of fear down her spine. It seemed so sinister, so evil.

David nodded, licking his dry lips in a nervous gesture.

'The Stealer is a mysterious spirit, dressed all in black, and wearing a black mask and cloak. He materialises in a village and takes children.'

'Takes them where?' she asked. Her heart was beating a little faster as his tale unfolded. She leaned closer to him, dropping her own voice. 'What does he do with them?'

David shrugged. 'Nobody knows. He takes them away and nobody ever sees them again.' He glanced round once more and Maddie did likewise. The other children were all intent on making their slings.

'The thing is, the Storyman said if we were ever to see him, we were to say nothing. Just pretend we'd seen nothing. And he said we must never, never tell a grown-up about the Stealer in the Night.'

'What would happen if you did?' Maddie asked, her voice now barely above a whisper.

'If we did, he said the Stealer would know. And he'd come after anyone who told. He'd come in the night and carry them off as well and they'd never see their family again.'

There was a long silence between them. Both of them were wide eyed. David's fear was contagious and Maddie found herself wishing she was back in Redmont, in the cosy little cabin in the trees. She heard a slight noise and looked round nervously. The farm worker she had noticed earlier had left his position by the fence and moved closer to them. He was sitting on the grass, cutting thick slices from a piece of cheese he had taken from the bundle. He caught her eye, nodded and smiled pleasantly as he ate some of the cheese. She wondered if he'd heard what they had been discussing. She decided he was probably too far away, but she lowered her voice anyway when she spoke again.

'Do you think that's what happened to Maurice Spoker?' she said.

David recoiled half a pace. Unaware of the nearby farm worker, he raised his voice in surprise. 'How did you know about Maurice?'

Maddie realised she'd made a mistake mentioning Maurice Spoker. She made a warning gesture for David to lower his voice again, glancing meaningfully at the nearby farm worker, and continued. 'My da heard about him in the tavern. He told me about it. Said this boy called Maurice Spoker went missing and to take care I didn't get about on my own after dark. Do you think he was taken by the Stealer in the Night?'

David hesitated. Her explanation seemed to have satisfied him. Then he nodded slowly.

'What else could it have been?' he said.

Thirty-six

The Stealer in the Night tore the leg off a chicken and stripped the flesh with his teeth. He grimaced. The bird wasn't properly cooked and the meat was red and bloody close to the bone.

He glared at the gang member who had been responsible for cooking the chicken, which had been stolen from an outlying farm the night before.

'Harold! This bird is raw!' the Stealer snarled. 'Where did you learn to cook?'

Harold, a black-haired, heavy-set man, returned his glare sullenly. 'Never said I was a cook,' he replied. He'd spitted the bird on a green branch and suspended it over their fire. But he didn't wait for the flames to die down to hot coals and soon the outer skin was blackening and charring. Assuming that the inside meat would be the same, he'd taken it off the fire and served it to his leader.

The Stealer threw the leg bone into the bushes. Then, his anger mounting, he grabbed the rest of the chicken carcass and sent it spinning after the leg.

'Get me some cheese and bread,' he ordered. 'Even you couldn't mess that up. And some ale as well.'

Harold muttered angrily to himself. But he kept the comments down. Bitter experience had taught him that the Stealer had a vicious temper — and an uncertain one.

The leader of the kidnappers was dressed all in black, the colour he wore when he entered households and stole children away. He was above average height and well built — although he was running to fat and had thickened round the middle. His hair had once been blond — almost white. Now it was a dirty grey colour. It hung to his neck and was matted in thick strings. The Stealer didn't believe in washing it too often.

His features were regular. His chin was strong, although the same tendency to fat was becoming apparent around his chin and neck. His would have been a handsome face except for the eyes and mouth. The eyes were pale, tinged with yellow. They were like a wolf's eyes, he had been told once — although the man who told him regretted those words a few minutes after uttering them. They were cold, cruel eyes and they were matched by the thin-lipped mouth that turned down at the corners. Nobody could remember seeing him smile.

Harold placed a wooden platter before him, with a hunk of strong cheese and the end of a loaf of bread. The Stealer grunted, drew his belt knife and cut himself some of the cheese.

'Where's the ale?' he demanded. His follower turned hurriedly back to the supply table and drew a mug of ale from a small cask. The Stealer grunted again when it was placed in front of him. The words 'thank you' didn't seem to be part of his vocabulary.

They were in the camp that was their temporary head-quarters. There were nine men, including the Stealer himself and the blue-cloaked Storyman. In addition, there were five children, with ages ranging from ten to fourteen, chained together underneath a large tree. The Stealer glanced at them now. They were huddled under the tree, where a torn piece of canvas was stretched over the branches to provide them with cover in the event of rain. The kidnappers themselves shared small two-man tents, except for the Stealer. As leader, he demanded a tent to himself. It was larger than the low-standing tents his followers slept in, and where they made do with sleeping blankets on the ground, he had a small folding camp bed.

The gang had been abducting children from small villages throughout Trelleth Fief for several months. They targeted small villages, remote from one another and with little or no communication between them. That way, by the time one village where a child had gone missing found out that there were others in the same fief where a similar thing had happened, the Stealer and his men would be long gone.

The system he'd devised worked admirably. The Storyman entered a village, gained the trust of the local children and targeted a child for kidnapping. He selected boys or girls who were mistreated by their parents. That way, when they disappeared, they were usually assumed to be runaways. Their parents might search for them, but there would be no organised hue and cry.

Once he'd engaged the children in a village and selected a target, the Storyman changed tack. His stories, at first amusing and entertaining, took on a darker, more sinister nature. He described the fearsome person known as the Stealer, a figure from the shadows, who stalked through the land seeking out children and stealing them away to his realm in the netherworld. He warned the children that if the Stealer should visit their village, they were to say nothing about him. They were never to discuss him with their parents, or any other adult.

If they did, the Stealer would know, and he would wreak terrible vengeance on them.

The Storyman was an accomplished raconteur. By the time he moved on from a village, the children were usually terrified out of their wits

That way, when one of their number disappeared shortly after, they said nothing. It was a clever stratagem. In many cases, in poor villages like the ones they preyed on, several children would sleep in the same room. If by chance a child woke and saw the black-clad figure, the fear engendered by the Storyman would ensure that he or she remained mute. Mute and terrified. The children knew if they interfered, if they said anything about him or tried to raise the alarm, they would disappear along with their companion.

The Stealer's gang had been operating this way for the past twelve months, moving from one fief to another, changing their area of operation frequently, so that no word of their activities ever reached the authorities.

Once they settled in a new area, they would begin abducting children. Then, when they had sufficient prisoners — usually ten or twelve — they would move on to the next phase of their operations.

The Stealer heard hoofbeats and looked up. One of his scouts had ridden into the camp. The man was dressed in a patched farmer's smock and wore a shapeless felt hat. He would pass virtually unnoticed in any of the villages or hamlets the gang had passed through. He looked around, saw the Stealer sitting hunched at his table and strode across to him.

'We may have trouble brewing,' he said briefly. He sat down opposite his leader and turned to yell at the man who had served the Stealer. 'Harold! Get me some ale here!'

Harold mumbled to himself. But he moved towards the cask and selected a mug from the table. There was a distinct ranking order in the gang and he was close to the bottom of it.

The Stealer frowned.

'Where?' he asked. The scout held up a hand for him to wait while Harold handed him a mug of ale, foam slopping over the brim. The scout didn't seem to care. He upended it and drank thirstily, then slammed the mug down with a satisfied grunt.

'Esseldon,' he said, and belched. The Stealer frowned. They'd hit Esseldon recently. He glanced towards the group of prisoners under the tree, trying to pick out the one he'd abducted from that village. But after they'd been operating for a few weeks, the faces all blurred and he couldn't be sure which one it was.

The fear that the Storyman struck into the hearts of the village children was usually enough to prevent any mention of the Stealer reaching the ears of their parents.

Usually.

But there was always the chance that a child, braver or more foolish than the others, might talk. If that happened, the villagers would be alerted to the presence of the Stealer in their area and might well mount a search for the missing child. And in that case, the gang would have to move on to a new fief to avoid discovery. To gain early warning of such an occurrence, the Stealer had his scouts make regular visits back to the villages where they'd already struck to make sure that their secret was still secure.

In Esseldon, apparently, someone had been talking.

'May be nothing,' the scout continued. 'But there's a young girl been asking questions.'

'One of the locals?' the Stealer asked.

The other man shook his head. 'No. She's travelling through with her da. He's looking for work and they've been staying at the inn. But I heard her quizzing one of the local kids about the Storyman — and about the boy we took out of that village. She's learned nothing so far, but I thought you ought to know.'

The Stealer massaged his jaw between the thumb and fingers of his right hand. There was always the chance that one child might talk. And now, it seemed, his extra pre-cautions in sending the scout back to check things in Esseldon had proved worthwhile.

'I think we'd better let this girl know what happens to people who ask awkward questions,' he said thoughtfully. Then he turned and shouted towards the group of men sitting on the grass around the camp fire.

'Benito! Come here. I've got a job for you!'

Yes, he thought, Benito was the one to send. He'd been injured in a fight some years before, struck by a blow to the throat that left his voice little more than a harsh whisper. Benito was bitter and angry about the injury and he was usually only too glad to undertake the task of frightening any child who disobeyed the Storyman's instructions.

He walked to the table now, touching one knuckle to his forehead in a sign of respect for the gang leader.

'What is it, *Jefe*?' he asked, using the Iberian term for boss or chief. Benito's Iberian accent overlaid the harsh whisper of his voice. The combination was usually enough to frighten any child.

'There's a girl in Esseldon asking questions. Robert here can tell you what she looks like and where to find her,' the Stealer told him, indicating the scout. 'Go in there tonight and frighten her off. Or kill her,' he added carelessly.

A cruel smile stole over Benito's swarthy features.

'That will be my pleasure, *Jefe*.'

Thirty-seven

Early in the afternoon, long before the shadows began to lengthen, Maddie slipped away from the village and walked out to the spot where Bumper was waiting. Will had taken Tug, of course, so her black and white horse was alone in the small clearing a little way off the road. She had worried about this, but Bumper seemed quite content with his own company.

She brushed him down and fed him two apples. A small stream ran near the clearing and she took the water bucket and filled it for him. Of course he could have drunk from the stream, but it was visible from the road and there was a chance that he might be seen by any casual passers-by.

Or any who were not so casual, she thought, considering the stories she had been told in the past twenty-four hours. She was glad she had visited Bumper while it was still full daylight. She would have been too nervous to walk out to the clearing after dark. She hurried back to the village while there was still plenty of light.

After sunset, troubled by the story of the evil and mysterious Stealer, Maddie was glad to spend the night in the inn. The attic room she had been given had a stout door with a good lock on it. That gave her a certain sense of security. But she was still nervous and tended to jump at any unexpected noise. The sound of footsteps on the stairs would make her freeze, head cocked to one side and listening attentively. Even though logic told her they probably belonged to Jerome or his wife, or another member of the inn's staff, she would keep one hand close to the hilt of the saxe knife, hanging over the bedhead, until she heard them move away again.

As Will suggested, she offered to help in the kitchen and her offer was gladly accepted. Aside from anything else, it gave her a few hours in the company of other people, and the noise and bustle of the busy kitchen was a welcome change from the little room at the top of the stairs.

Jerome watched approvingly as she bundled her hair up under a head scarf, donned an apron and began scraping the greasy platters, then plunging them into a large iron cauldron of soapy water suspended over the kitchen fire. She would then scrub them thoroughly with a long-handled wooden brush. After a few minutes, her face was red and damp from the steam and her arms were coated with soap suds up to the elbows. When the washing-up was done, she busied herself sweeping the kitchen and the tap room. She was still at it when the last customers made their way out, calling their farewells to the innkeeper. A few of them muttered pleasantries to her as well. They'd seen how hard she had been working and they admired such industry.

It was still relatively early when the tavern emptied out. It was a weeknight, after all, and country folk went to bed and rose early.

Jerome entered the tap room as she finished sweeping and put the broom away in its cupboard. He moved to the front door and shot the two heavy iron bolts across to lock it — one near the top and the other at the bottom of the door. He glanced at her and smiled reassuringly.

'I'll bolt the kitchen door too, once Emma and Ted have gone,' he said. He assumed she might be nervous with her father away and he wanted to reassure her. He liked her. She had worked hard through the night. Even though he would charge Will for a night's accommodation in the stable — after all, their handcart and their belongings were stored there — he decided he would pay Maddie a few coins for her work.

Maddie smiled at him. The doors were solid oak, with the inside reinforced by a second layer of planks, set diagonally to the outside layer. The tavern, after all, held a lot of valuable items — wine and ale and food, not to mention the money that had been paid across the bar during the evening. It was probably the most secure building in the village.

The cook and the kitchen hand, Emma and Ted, said their goodnights and left for their homes. Jerome went into the kitchen and locked the door that led into the stable-yard. He moved around the big, low-ceilinged room, pinching out the candles and blowing out the one large lantern that hung from the central beam. The only light now came from the fireplace. The fire had been banked down and cast flickering shadows into the corners. That left only Jerome and his wife, Tildy, in the inn with Maddie. The innkeeper and his wife had a small suite of rooms that took up half the first floor of the building, leaving room for an additional three bedrooms for guests. Maddie's room was on the next floor up, under the sloping ceiling of the attic.

'Time for bed, Maddie,' Jerome told her. 'Be careful with your candle now. Make sure it's out before you go to sleep.'

After the cheerful noise and bustle of the evening, the inn seemed strangely silent as Maddie mounted the stairs to her room. She carried a candle with her, in a pewter tray, shielding its open flame with her free hand as she went upstairs. The inn was riddled with draughts and the night was cold.

The attic was positively icy. None of the heat from the ground floor seemed to penetrate here and she shivered as she pulled her dress over her head. She hesitated, then delved into her pack and took out her breeches and jerkin, pulling them on over her shirt. There was a thick pair of socks in there, and she pulled them on too. When she finally lay down and pulled the two thin blankets up to her chin, she felt passably comfortable, if not exactly warm. The wind had risen during the night and it whistled round the upper floors of the inn, seeking out the many cracks that would give it entry and shaking the walls and rattling the small attic window with its heavier gusts.

'A good night to be inside,' she told herself. Of course, the wind set off a myriad of small noises, with the timbers of the house creaking and groaning as they moved and rubbed together. Just as she would become accustomed to the pattern of sounds, a new one would arise and set her teeth on edge. Then she would listen for several minutes, lying tensed under the blankets, until she was sure the new noise was nothing sinister.

Lying wide eyed while the wind pounded the walls, she reached up behind her head to where the belt holding her saxe was hanging over the head of the bed. She unhooked it and placed the weapon under her pillow, her hand resting on the hilt.

Comforted by the feel of the heavy weapon, she finally nodded off.

And woke.

Her eyes shot open, but other than that, she showed no movement. Apart from a momentary hesitation, her breathing remained the same — deep, even and rhythmic. Will had trained her to wake at the slightest sensation that danger might be present, but to do so with the smallest possible outward signs. Hurriedly, she closed her eyes again, leaving only the smallest slit between her eyelids to see through.

She sensed a presence in the room. Someone, or something, was standing by her bed. She was lying on her right side, facing away from the door, her right hand touching the hilt of her saxe under the pillow.

Whatever or whoever was in the room was behind her, out of her field of vision. She didn't know how she knew it was there. She could hear no breathing, no small movements. Outside, the wind still battered at the window and walls.

But she could *sense* something there. Something close. Something malevolent.

'You awake, girl. I know you awake. Don't move. Don't try to turn over. And leave whatever is under your pillow where it is.'

The voice was a hoarse, croaking whisper. The speaker sounded foreign — Maddie could detect an accent and he had said 'you awake', rather than 'you're awake'. She lay rigid under the blankets, not daring to move. She wanted to whip over, drawing the saxe as she went, and strike out. But she couldn't find the will to do it. Now she heard a low rustle of clothing as the speaker moved slightly. How did he get in? The front door and the kitchen door were bolted solidly. And her room was locked as well.

She realised there was no future in trying to answer that question. He was here, and that was all there was to it.

'You been asking questions, girl,' the voice croaked. 'That not healthy. Not healthy for you. Not healthy for that village boy you've been talking to.'

Her heart lurched with fear — for herself, and for David. David was vulnerable and virtually unprotected. His parents were simple villagers. Probably brave enough, but not fighters.

'You know what happen to people who talk about the Stealer. You don't want that happening to your friend. Or to you. So keep you trap shut. Understand?'

She said nothing, not knowing whether to admit she was awake or not. The silence became unbearable.

'I said, *understand*?' the intruder repeated. Obviously, he wanted a response. She tried to speak but her mouth was dry with fear. Finally, she managed to say, in a voice that was barely above a whisper:

'I understand.'

Again, she heard a slight sound of movement. Then to her relief, she realised that the man was moving away from her.

'Make sure you do,' that horrible voice continued. She heard the soft click of her door latch as he carefully lifted it. He was going, she thought, and relief flooded through her. The hinges squeaked as the door opened, then he spoke again.

'Don't look after me. And don't try to follow me. I'll know if you do. And the Stealer will come for you one dark night.'

She shivered. The faceless threat of the Stealer, the horror of the very name, made her blood run cold. The door closed quietly and the presence, whoever it was, was gone.

For at least twenty seconds, she lay motionless, paralysed by fear. Then, slowly, fear began to be replaced by anger. She wasn't a helpless child, to be frightened by a voice in the dark. She was an apprentice Ranger! She had been trained to use her saxe, her throwing knife, her bow and her sling. She had been trained to fight without weapons if necessary. She was a member of a proud and highly skilled Corps. And she was its first female member! If she were to lie here now, quaking under the blankets at the sound of a croaky-voiced foreigner who didn't dare show his face, and who threatened her with some vague character out of a horror story, she would be letting down the Corps. And she would be proving that all those doubters (and she knew there were many) who said a girl didn't have what it took to make it as a Ranger were right!

It was the last thought that galvanised her into action. She swung her legs off the bed, bringing the saxe out from under the pillow. She was already dressed. The cold night air had seen to that. She started for the door, then hesitated. Her sling and the saxe's scabbard belt were looped over the bedhead. Along with the scabbard, the belt held her shot pouch, with twenty lead shot nestled inside. She scooped both up, putting the belt over her shoulder and sheathing the saxe as she did so. The sling remained in her right hand, ready for action. As she opened the door, her left hand was scrabbling in the shot pouch for one of the smooth, heavy lead projectiles.

She loaded the shot into the sling and made her way softly down the stairs, placing her weight to the sides, close to the walls, to minimise movement and creaking. In the tap room she glanced round quickly. The window was gaping open, its simple lock bent and distorted. That was how the intruder had entered, she realised. The front door was also slightly ajar. She hurried across to it now, went to throw it open, then hesitated.

Her heart was racing and she realised that it would be foolish to plunge headlong out the door. The intruder could be watching and waiting to see if she had followed him. Instead, she opened it a crack and slipped through the opening, staying close to the wall, in the dark shadow of the low-hanging eaves.

She glanced around the street, eyes straining for some sign of movement. Nothing. She cursed quietly. Had he escaped in the time that she was lying, quaking in fear, under the blankets? She didn't see how he could have. She hadn't taken that long to gather the resolve to come after him. Her eyes raked the shadows of the street and she thought she saw a blur of movement forty metres away, in the narrow alley between two houses.

As she did, she felt a stabbing pain in her stockinged foot as she trod on a sharp stone.

Gasping in pain, she bent over to seize her foot in a reflex action — and saved her life by doing so.

Something heavy whirred over her head and thudded into the wood of the door frame behind her. Now she could see her attacker more clearly. He was a dark shape in a gap between two houses and as she watched, his arm went back, preparing to throw another projectile.

Her training clicked into place. She straightened up and reacted to the threat without thinking. Arm back, step forward, then whip the sling over and through. The lead shot flashed away on its journey and, a fraction of a second later, she saw the man's arm jerk forward as he threw in his turn. Instinctively, she dropped flat to the ground.

The shot, with the extra impetus of the sling to propel it, hit its target first. She heard an ugly, meaty smack and a muted cry of pain from her attacker as it struck home. Then the dark figure staggered, threw out his arms and crashed over on his back. A second later, the projectile he'd thrown slammed into the door behind her, a metre and a half above where she lay prone.

She rose, her eyes intent on the dark shape on the ground. Automatically, she loaded another shot into the sling and moved towards him, placing her feet carefully, making as little noise as possible. She felt horribly exposed as she moved into the open street, where the pale moonlight suddenly seemed to be as bright as day. She followed a curving path as she approached him, looping out to the right, then coming back in. That way, if he was foxing and suddenly sat up, she wouldn't be where he expected her to be.

A part of her mind wondered at the effortless way she had carried out the sequence of actions. Responding to the attack, dropping flat, now moving in a half circle to approach him, the sling dangling, ready for use, from her right hand and slightly behind her. They were all things that had been dinned into her head over and over again in her lessons with Will.

The man didn't move as she got closer. She paused a few metres away. She could see no sign of movement, no sign that he was still breathing. She realised that at close range, the sling would be useless. She stuffed it quickly into a pocket and drew the saxe. The soft whisper of steel on leather and wool was strangely comforting.

She circled round him, staying out of reach of his arms and legs, and moved closer. She knelt by him and she could see the wound on his forehead. His eyes were wide open and staring and she knew he was dead.

For a moment, she was numb with horror. Then her stomach lurched as she realised that she had killed a man. She wanted to be ill but she controlled herself with an effort, and sat back on her haunches to study him. She had reacted instinctively when she hurled the shot at him. It was an automatic reaction — and one of self-preservation and self-defence. She hadn't had time to think of the possible result. The man had already tried to kill her with the first missile he had thrown. He was about to throw a second. If she hadn't retaliated, it was she who would be lying dead now. She remembered how his second missile had whizzed overhead, remembered the vicious thuds as both missiles had slammed into the inn doorway.

It had been him or her. As she considered the fact, remembering how he had threatened her and tried to terrify her to gain her silence, and then twice tried to murder her, she found she couldn't regret her actions. She had done what she had to do.

He was dressed all in black. A black woollen skull cap. Black trousers tucked into black felt boots, and a black woollen shirt under a short, waist-length cloak with a high collar. A black leather belt around his waist held a long, curved-bladed dagger in a sheath. He had dark hair and a dark, drooping moustache — uncommon among Araluan men — and his skin was swarthy.

Under the cloak, she could see a leather strap crossing his chest diagonally. She moved the cloak aside with the point of her saxe and revealed a flat leather satchel hanging by his left side. It was impossible to remove it easily, encumbered as it was by the cloak and the fact that he was lying on the strap where it crossed his back.

She slipped the saxe under the strap and sliced easily through it, then tugged the satchel clear.

Inside were a few personal effects: a few coins and a small, short-bladed knife that might be used for eating, an iron spoon, a flint and steel. Her interest was piqued by two cross-shaped items. She took one out carefully and examined it. It consisted of a heavy brass disk, with four blades set around its circumference at right angles to each other. The blades were approximately eight centimetres long. Their edges were smooth but the points were razor-sharp.

'A quattro,' she muttered. She had seen one once before, in the armoury at Castle Araluen. They were an Iberian weapon — an assassin's weapon — designed for throwing. With four blades spinning rapidly through the

air, it was almost certain that one would strike and penetrate the target. She realised that this was what had
whizzed over her head and thudded into the tavern door.
She shook her head slowly. Thank providence for that
sharp stone in her foot, she thought.

As she replaced the quattro, she heard the rustle of
paper and discovered a second compartment at the rear
of the satchel. She pulled it open and looked inside. There
was a single folded sheet there.

'We'll look at that later,' she said softly, then stood, considering what she should do about the dead man.

In the end, she decided to leave him where he lay.

If she roused the village now, there would be questions
asked. How had she managed to overcome a grown man —
and one armed with a long dagger and a pouch full of
quattros? What was she really doing here? What was in
the papers she'd found on him?

Inevitably, her real identity, and Will's, would be discovered. It would become obvious that he was not a
harmless itinerant worker but a King's Ranger. And that
would give a warning to the Stealer and his gang that they
were being pursued.

If that were the case, they might slip away to another
fief and Will and Maddie would lose track of them.

If she left him here, his friends might well wonder what
had become of him. They might hear that he was found
dead in the village high street. But they would have no
idea how it had come about. They might suspect. But they
wouldn't know.

Coming to a decision, she scanned the surrounding
ground, finally catching a dull gleam of metal in the

moonlight. It was the lead shot she had hurled at him. She retrieved it, then turned and walked quickly back to the inn, pausing to prise the two quattros from the timber of the door frame. Then she slipped back upstairs to the attic, after locking the front door.

She was awoken early the following morning by a hubbub in the street. Peering out her narrow window, she saw a small crowd gathered round the black-clad figure on the ground. He had been discovered by a dairyman, on his way to bring his cows in from the village green for milking. He had raised the alarm and now eight or nine villagers clustered round the mysterious dead man. They wondered aloud where he had come from and what had happened to him. His black clothing and weapons indicated that he had been up to no good.

Eventually, he was placed on a litter and carried to one of the houses. They would arrange a burial later.

His presence, his purpose and his death were a mystery. And in a small village where extraordinary events rarely happened, it would be a topic of conversation and specula-tion for months, perhaps years, to come.

But among all the theories that were discussed, nobody ever associated him with the young girl in the attic of the inn.

Thirty-eight

By the time Will returned Tug to the little clearing outside Esseldon and resumed his farm worker's garb, it was well after dark.

He hurried back along the road to the village. Unlike Maddie, he wasn't nervous about the dark shadows under the trees that lined the road. But he was no fool and he knew that dark forces were at work in this part of the world. As a result, he kept his hand near his saxe knife as he strode along. His bow was unstrung and, along with the quiver, concealed inside a canvas wrapping.

The lights blazed in the inn and there was a babble of conversation coming from the crowded tap room. It was the end of the week, and the villagers were relaxing after six days of hard work.

He stowed his bow and quiver in the bottom of the handcart. The stable was dark, the lanterns unlit. Maddie, of course, had slept in the inn the previous evening. It was logical to assume that she was there now.

He made his way to the main building, pushed the door open and was greeted by the noisy babble of voices and the smell of good cooking, woodsmoke and spilt ale. A few people looked up, recognised the itinerant farm worker who had been in the village for several days and lost interest in him. By now, they all knew his story, prosaic as it was. Jerome was behind the bar, passing two full tankards to a customer. He caught sight of Will, smiled and beckoned him over, drawing another foaming tankard of ale as Will crossed the crowded room, threading his way between tables and chairs and their noisy occupants.

Jerome placed the tankard on the bar in front of Will.

'You're back!' he said cheerfully. 'Any luck?'

Will grimaced. 'Not a skerrick. No work at any of the farms for an honest man.'

'How about a dishonest one?' Jerome grinned.

Will shook his head, managing a faint smile in return. He took a deep draught of the ale before he replied. As he'd told Maddie, he didn't make a habit of drinking ale but it would be out of character for a farm worker to refuse a drink.

'None for one of them either,' he said. 'It's hard pickings these days.'

'It's a bad time of year to be looking for casual work,' Jerome agreed. 'And you missed all the excitement here.'

Will cocked his head curiously. 'Excitement? What's been going on?'

'Man found dead in the street — just a little way down the road.'

'Who was it?' Will asked.

But Jerome shrugged. 'That's just it. Nobody knows. Nobody'd seen him before until Neville Malton found him yesterday morning, sprawled in the middle of the road with a huge wound on his forehead.'

That detail definitely got Will's attention. There were several weapons that could leave a mark like that on a man, but the one that sprang to his mind was a sling. He glanced round the room for some sign of Maddie. Then he turned back to Jerome.

'What did he look like?' he asked.

'Big feller. Dark looking. I'd say he was a foreigner. Had one of those long, droopy moustaches that foreigners wear. And he was all in black. Up to no good, I'll be bound, and someone went and settled his hash for him.'

At that moment, the door to the kitchen banged open and Maddie appeared, laden with four platters of steaming roast meat and vegetables. She wended her way through the crowd to the table that had ordered the food. The four men sitting there cheered as she set the platters down, joking with her and thanking her for saving them from death by starvation.

They were cheerful and friendly and meant no harm. Maddie smiled at them, a little wanly. She seemed bothered by something, Will thought. Then she looked up and noticed him at the bar, and he saw relief flood across her face.

'That's a good girl you've got there,' Jerome said, noticing the byplay between them. 'A hard worker and good with the customers. I won't be charging you for that room she's been in. And I'll toss a few coins into her purse as well. Matter of fact,' he added, 'you can use the room tonight if you choose.'

'Thanks. We may do that,' Will said.

Maddie was looking meaningfully at him, and now she jerked her head towards the door that led to the stableyard. The message was obvious.

He drained the last of his ale. 'I'll just go and say hullo,' he said, and turned to follow Maddie out of the stableyard door.

'Tell her to take a good long break,' Jerome called after him. 'She's been working hard all evening. Best waitress I ever had,' he added, thinking to himself that it was a pity that Maddie and her father wouldn't be staying long in the village.

As he followed Maddie into the cool air outside, Will smiled wryly to himself. Maddie, the royal princess, the superior, snobbish young lady of Castle Araluen, had found her vocation as a serving maid.

Might be a new career for her if Evanlyn and Horace don't reinstate her as a princess, he thought, and gave a short bark of laughter. He paused, surprised. It was the second time recently that he'd laughed out loud, he realised. He shook his head and strode quickly to where his apprentice was waiting for him.

He stopped a few paces from her. Her face was pale and her lip was trembling. As she looked at him, her eyes welled with tears.

'Uncle Will, I killed someone,' she said.

Her shoulders began to shake and she began to sob uncontrollably. He gathered her in, wrapping his arms around her and muttering soothing noises as he did so. The fact that she had called him 'Uncle Will' spoke volumes for her state of mind. She was still a child, he realised, in spite of all her self-confidence and bravado. And she had been forced to do the most terrible thing a person could do —

take the life of another. He had no doubt that circum-
stances had forced her to do it. He also had no doubt that
she was talking about the mysterious black-clad stranger
who had been found in the street.

'Hush now, my girl,' he crooned softly to her. 'Hush
now. I'm here and everything's going to be all right. Can
you tell me what happened?'

Gradually, between the vast, gulping sobs that were
shaking her, she described how she had woken in terror to
the presence of an intruder in her room. How he had
threatened her, and then how the terror had been gradually
replaced by anger and indignation.

'You followed him?' Will said, as she described how she
had gone down the stairs, her sling ready. She snuffled
back a tear and nodded.

'Yes. I thought I should.'

He had released her when he asked the question, but
now he pulled her into his embrace once more.

'My god but you're a brave girl,' he said, marvelling at
her courage.

She continued with her tale, describing how the sheer
chance of the stone under her bare foot had saved her life,
as the quattro whirred over her head. Then she told him
how she saw the man preparing another cast and let fly
with her sling, a fraction of a second before he could release
his missile.

'Let me get this straight,' Will said. 'He threw a quattro
at you. He was about to throw a second, and you retaliated,
just in time.'

She nodded tearfully. 'I didn't think what would
happen. I just let fly. Then I fell flat,' she said.

Will nodded sympathetically. 'Of course you didn't think. You acted as you've been trained to act. You reacted to a threat. There's no blame here attached to you, my sweet.'

'But he —'

'He was obviously working with that filthy Stealer. He tried once to kill you as you came out the door. And he was trying to kill you again when you threw. And you say he had another two of those weapons in his satchel?'

She nodded, not saying anything. Will made a dismissing gesture with one hand.

'Then you acted in self-defence and there's no blame in that. None at all. If you hadn't, I have no doubt he would have tried again to kill you with those remaining quattros.'

'I suppose so.' She had told herself this over and over since the event. To have someone else say it, and particularly Will, was enormously comforting.

'Dry your tears now. I know it's a horrible thing to face, but it was something you had to do. You had to do it or you would have been killed. Are we clear on that?'

She nodded, wiping the back of her hand across her face to dry her tears.

'I so wanted to talk to you. I couldn't tell anyone and I felt so . . . dreadful,' she said in a small voice.

Will nodded at her, comforting her. 'I shouldn't have left you. If anyone is to blame for this, it's me. But I want you to put this out of your mind now and don't think any further on it, all right?'

'All right. But it's just —'

'No. No more. Put the thoughts aside.'

'But . . . he had a sheet of paper on him. I think it might be important.'

Will's head snapped up at those words. 'Paper? What is it?'

'I'm not sure. It could be a map of some kind. It's in my room.'

He took her hand and led her towards the inn. 'Then let's have a look at it.'

'But . . . I've got work to do . . .' she protested.

He shook his head. 'Let Jerome and his wife do it. He said you should take a long break. So let's take it.'

'What did you find out in Boyletown?' she asked as they headed for her room.

'The Storyman was there all right — a couple of days before Peter Williscroft disappeared.' Will paused, then added, 'And the boy was being mistreated, just like the others.'

'By his father?'

He shook his head. 'An older brother. He used to bully him continually. Nobody was surprised when Peter went missing.'

They reached the top of the stairs and he pushed the door open, standing aside to let her enter the little room.

'Now let's see what's on this paper you found.'

Thirty-nine

They studied the single sheet of paper, frowning as to its possible meaning. There was one word written on it: *Pueblos*.

And six crosses drawn, each one numbered. Will scratched his head. There was something about the arrangement of three of those crosses that looked familiar.

'What does *pueblos* mean?' he asked, more to himself than to Maddie.

But she answered. 'I think it's Iberian. I just can't place it. Does it mean horsemen?' She frowned. Her schooling at Castle Araluen had included a basic study of foreign languages including Gallican and Iberian. But she hadn't paid a lot of attention to those lessons — or any other lessons she had been taught, for that matter.

'The benefit of a classical education,' Will muttered.

Maddie was still frowning, rubbing her forehead furiously as she strained for the elusive meaning of that word.

It wasn't horsemen. It was on the tip of her tongue. It was . . .

'Villages!' she said triumphantly. '*Pueblo* means village in Iberian!'

And suddenly, Will knew why the arrangement of three of those crosses was familiar. He scrabbled in his inner pocket for Liam's map and spread it out beside the sheet from the intruder's satchel.

He took a stick of charcoal from his belt wallet and quickly drew lines connecting the three villages of Danvers Crossing, Boyletown and Esseldon on Liam's map. The lines formed a narrow, oblique triangle. Then he took the sheet that Maddie had found and connected the first three villages marked there. He found himself looking at the same triangle.

'These are the villages where children disappeared,' he said, leaning back.

Maddie pointed to the sheet she had taken from the stranger. 'And there are three others,' she said.

Will frowned and drew a line from village number three, which represented Boyletown, to the farthest village marked on the stranger's chart. The line ran east of north-east. He measured the length with finger and thumb, then compared it to the distance between Esseldon and Boyletown, calculating quickly.

When Will had visited Castle Trelleth, he had obtained a detailed map of the fief. He took it out now and unfolded it, running his finger in an east-north-east direction until he came to a village that corresponded roughly with the one on the chart Maddie had found in the intruder's satchel.

'Willow Vale,' he said.

Maddie craned over his shoulder to see the map. 'Why that one? Why not four or five?' she asked.

'Because it's number six. So it's the last one they plan to visit. Maybe they haven't been there yet. It's a day's ride from here,' he said thoughtfully.

'Or a night's ride,' she put in. 'After all, we don't know how much time we've got.'

'In which case, we don't have any time to waste.'

They retrieved their bows, quivers and cloaks from where they were hidden in the handcart. Maddie went into one of the empty stalls and changed from her patched old dress back into her breeches, shirt and jerkin. She tossed aside the thin-soled sandals she'd been wearing and hauled on her soft leather boots.

When she finally donned her cloak once more, she heaved a sigh of satisfaction. It was good to feel like a Ranger again.

Staying in the shadows, they made their way out of the village. Nobody saw them or challenged them and, once away from the open space of the main street, they settled into a steady jog towards the clearing where they had left their horses.

'Will Tug be up to the trip?' she asked as they paused for breath. 'After all, you've been riding him all day.'

'He's a Ranger horse,' Will replied. 'He could keep going for another two days if I asked him to.'

They set off again, reaching the clearing five minutes later. Tug and Bumper heard them coming, recognised them and whinnied a welcome. They quickly saddled the horses and mounted, then Will touched Tug with his heels and headed out onto the road, Maddie and Bumper close behind them. They settled into a smooth canter, side by side. The only sound was the rhythmic drumming of their horses' hooves on the packed earth surface of the road. Behind them, a small cloud of dust rose and drifted in the shafts of moonlight that broke through the trees. Eventually, it settled until there was no sign that they had passed.

After half an hour, they slowed the horses and dismounted. They gave them a quick drink of water from the canteens they carried, pouring it into a folding leather bucket. Then they began leading the horses, walking beside them for ten minutes to let them rest. They would continue this pattern throughout the night, alternately riding at the mile-eating lope the Ranger horses were trained to, then walking to rest them.

It was easier to talk now that they weren't cantering.

'What I don't understand,' Maddie said, 'is why these people are stealing the children. There have been no ransom demands. And in any event, the parents are poor for the most part and could hardly afford to pay much. So what's the point?'

It had been bothering her for some time. One thing Will had taught her was to always look for a reason behind a crime. The question to ask was 'who benefits?'. In this case, she could see no advantage for anyone — unless the Stealer and his group were simply doing this for the sake of evil itself.

'I don't think the idea is to ransom the children,' Will said now. He had been giving the matter considerable thought and there were several clues now apparent.

'I think we're looking at a slave ring.'

'A slave ring?' Maddie stopped in surprise and Bumper, caught unawares, lived up to his name and bumped into her.

'Think about it,' Will said. 'You said the man who broke into your room was foreign. He had a chart with an Iberian word on it and those quattros are an Iberian weapon.'

'Is that significant?' Maddie asked.

'It is when you consider that there's a very active slave trade in Iberion,' Will told her. 'And children in their early teens are particularly sought after.'

'I didn't know the Iberians kept slaves,' Maddie said. But then, she thought, she didn't know much about Iberion and its people anyway. She just had a general, vague impression that slavery was a thing of the past on the main continent.

'They don't. The Iberian king has outlawed the practice. Apparently his religion forbids keeping slaves. But it doesn't say anything about trading in them, so he permits his people to capture slaves and sell them on to others. There's a small but active fleet of slave ships operating out of Magala harbour in south Iberion.'

'Who buys them?' Maddie asked.

'Generally, they're sold in the market in Socorro.' He looked at her and she returned the gaze blankly. 'Have you never studied geography?' he asked her. 'What do they teach kids these days?'

He paused. The words struck a strange chord of memory in him. He seemed to recall Halt saying something similar to him when he was first apprenticed to his old mentor. He shook his head to clear the thought. It seemed that the older he became, the more words and events began to repeat themselves.

'I learned a lot of needlepoint,' Maddie said acidly. It had always been a sore point with her that she was told to embroider when what she really wanted to do was go hunting in the forest.

'Hmmph. Remind me to call on you when I rip my shirt,' Will said. Then he continued with his lesson on the slave trade. 'Socorro is a city-kingdom on the west coast of Arrida. It has a big slave market — one of the biggest on the Arridi continent. Slaves are bought and sold there and transported from there to all corners of the hinterland.'

'And you think that's what's happening here?' she said.

He shrugged. 'It makes sense. The Stealer, the Storyman and their gang are operating in remote villages, where word of the children's disappearance is unlikely to get out to the wider world. Who knows how many children they've abducted? They pick kids who are mistreated, and likely to run away. That deflects attention further. People assume that the kid has finally rebelled against the constant mistreatment and run off.'

'But how do they know who those kids are?' Maddie asked.

Will tapped his finger alongside his nose in a knowing gesture.

'That's where the Storyman comes in. He visits a town, gains the confidence of the children and spots a likely candidate. After all, it's a sad fact that you can usually find a badly treated child in most villages. He then frightens the children into silence, so they say nothing about the questions he's been asking. He leaves town and, some time later, the Stealer comes in and abducts the child the Storyman has singled out for him. The other kids say nothing, because they've been told if they do, they'll be the Stealer's next target. And the kidnapped child is so petrified by the Stealer's terrible reputation – as described by the Storyman – that he or she goes along without protest. It's quite an ingenious system when you look at it.'

'That's horrible,' Maddie said, thinking over what he'd said.

'That doesn't make it any less ingenious,' Will told her.

She turned to look at him. 'That's what's so horrible about it. So what do you plan to do when we reach Willow Vale?'

'I'll find out if the Storyman has visited recently, and if there's any child in the village who's badly mistreated by his or her parents.'

'How do you plan to do that?' she asked.

Will's expression turned bleak. 'I have my ways,' he said. 'Come on. It's time we got mounted again.'

Forty

Fernald Creasy, the owner of The Tubby Duck, Willow Vale's small inn, rubbed his eyes and yawned. He had unwisely spent too much time keeping his customers company the previous night.

In other words, he had drunk far too much ale. As a result, he had staggered off to his bed without bothering to clear away the dirty platters and half-filled tankards that littered his tap room. Nor had he scrubbed out the cooking pots in the kitchen.

Of course, his kitchen hand should have done that. But he was a sly boy and once he saw Fernald happily raising his fifth tankard with a group at the central table, he had taken the opportunity to slip away. Now it was early morning, just after sunrise, and Fernald was faced with the task of cleaning up last night's mess.

He piled a tray with dirty platters, knives, spoons and tankards and went back into the kitchen, yawning continuously. His head throbbed painfully and he vowed he would never drink again. He glanced around the kitchen with a look of distaste. The work table was littered with food scraps and more dirty plates and cooking pans. There was a lot of work to be done before he could return to his bed. And the tap room wasn't halfway tidy yet, he thought morosely.

He muttered angrily to himself. There was no room on the wash bench for the tray he was carrying. The bench was already piled high with detritus from the previous night.

He turned to place the tray on the long kitchen table.

A cowled figure was standing less than a metre away from him, silent and sinister in the dim light of early morning.

Fernald dropped the tray in fright, sending its contents clattering and clashing on the floor. He was sure there had been nobody in the kitchen when he'd entered from the tap room. And he'd heard no sound of anyone arriving.

'By the Black Troll of Balath!' he exclaimed, putting his hand to his heart, which was working overtime with fright. 'Where did you come from?'

'An interesting curse,' Will said. 'Don't think I've heard the Black Troll invoked in many a year. You must follow the old religion.'

Fernald rubbed his face with one hand as his heart rate gradually slowed to a gallop. He glanced down and saw a half-empty tankard of flat ale on the table. He picked it up and drained it, grimacing at the stale flavour.

'I don't hold with these new gods,' he mumbled vaguely. Then, shaking off the distraction, he continued. 'Who are you? And how did you get in here?'

'I'm a King's Ranger, as you've possibly guessed. And that back door lock wouldn't keep out a determined three-year-old. Now sit down. We need to talk.'

Will shoved Fernald towards a bench and the innkeeper sat down — aware that his knees were shaking still with the shock of the Ranger's sudden appearance.

Why me, he thought. What have I done?

And the answer was, quite a lot, actually. Fernald was adept at giving his customers short measure in their food and drink. He wasn't reluctant to water his ale from time to time. And on occasions, he had slipped unwary customers a few worthless lead discs among their change. He wondered how the Ranger knew about these things.

'I need information,' Will said. 'First of all, have any children disappeared from the village recently?'

Fernald frowned, not grasping the question. 'Disappeared? What do you mean?'

'Gone missing. Run off. Haven't been seen around.'

'Oh . . .' Fernald thought about that for several seconds, then he shook his head. 'No. Can't say I've heard of anything like that,' he said finally. Will felt a quick surge of satisfaction. They had arrived in time. Unless . . . He hesitated before he asked the next question. It was crucial.

'Can you think of any child who might run off — given the opportunity? Someone whose parents tend to mistreat them?'

Before he had finished, Fernald was nodded eagerly.

'Oh, aye. Young Violet Carter. Nice young thing. Only thirteen years old. But her parents are always fighting and they take it out on Violet. Poor girl can't seem to do a thing right sometimes. I've even let her stay here some nights, it gets so bad.'

Right, thought Will. It was all falling into place.

'Where does she live?' he asked.

Fernald made a vague gesture towards the high street outside. 'Third-last house from the far end of the street. House with a blue door — although that could use a lick of paint. The yard behind is piled with old broken bits of carts — wheels, shafts and harness. Can't miss it.'

'You're doing well, Fernald,' Will told him.

How did he know my name, the innkeeper wondered, forgetting that it was painted on the sign hanging outside his front door.

'Now I've got one more question. Has there been a travelling spinner through Willow Vale in the last few days?'

'You mean the Storyman?' Fernald said, and Will's own heart rate accelerated. 'Rum cove in a blue cloak and red shoes? Yes, he was here. Left two days ago. Why? What has he done?'

Will ignored the question. He had a deep feeling of satisfaction that his hunch had paid off. Willow Vale was on the list. The Storyman had been here. But the Stealer was yet to come. And there was a likely candidate for abduction in the person of Violet Carter.

He'd taken a risk revealing his true identity and asking these questions so directly. But time was short and direct action was called for. Now he had to ensure that Fernald remained silent about this meeting for the next few days. He couldn't hope for much beyond that. But by then, the Stealer may well have been and gone.

'Fernald,' he said, 'you've told me what I need to know. But nobody else can know that I've been here. And nobody else needs to know what we've been discussing. Is that clear?'

Fernald nodded eagerly, sensing that this grim figure was about to leave him to his cleaning. What a tale this would make in the bar, he thought. Then the Ranger's next words dispelled that thought.

'I mean it. You will tell nobody that I have been here. You will tell nobody what we've talked about. Understand?'

'Eh? Oh yes. Of course! Goes without saying!'

Will stepped a pace closer, holding Fernald's eyes with his. Fernald instantly dropped his gaze away.

'Don't do that!' Will snapped and Fernald jerked as if he had been stung. 'Look at me. Look at my eyes.'

Fernald did. He didn't like what he saw there. The brown eyes were dark, almost black. And they were boring into his without any sign of pity or compassion. They were dark, threatening holes.

'If I find that you have breathed a word of this to anyone — even a hint to anyone at all — I will arrest you and put you in the deepest, wettest, worst-smelling dungeon in Castle Trelleth. Understand?'

Fernald mouthed the word 'yes'. But no sound came. Rangers, he thought. You should never mess with Rangers.

'What's more,' Will continued, 'I will keep you there for the next five years, and in the meantime, I'll have your licence as an innkeeper revoked.' He saw a flicker of doubt in Fernald's eyes. The innkeeper wasn't sure what the word meant. 'Cancelled,' Will clarified. 'Taken away.'

Understanding and fear dawned in Fernald's eyes, as he envisioned a future where he was penniless, unable to earn a living. Running an inn was all he knew. Without The Tubby Duck, what would he do? Will's next words made the possible future even bleaker.

'Then I will come back here and have this building torn down, brick by brick, plank by plank, and ploughed under. So when you do finally get out of prison, there will be nothing here for you. Do you doubt I have the authority to do all that?'

Fernald shook his head. Rangers could do anything they wanted to, he knew. It would be nothing to a Ranger to have him thrown into a dungeon and his inn, his lovely inn, razed to the ground.

'No, sir,' he managed, in a small voice.

'Then remember what I've said.'

Fernald didn't trust himself to speak. He could feel tears welling up at the thought that his beautiful inn might be destroyed at the whim of this implacable, pitiless figure.

Will glared at him for several seconds. In fact, he hated to bully the man like this. But it was essential that there should be no word of Will's presence, or of his questions, being bandied around the village. Even now, the Stealer might have men watching Willow Vale, listening for the slightest hint of danger. After all, somehow they had known that Maddie had been asking questions. If he could maintain secrecy for a few days by frightening Fernald, then he was willing to do so.

For a moment, he wondered if he would be willing to carry out his threat if the innkeeper talked about his visit. He decided that, all things considered, he would.

It was past midnight. Will sat comfortably in the long grass behind the Carter house. As Fernald had told him, the rear yard was littered with broken carts and their fittings. They made weird shapes in the light of a low sickle moon.

Maddie was across the high street, watching the front of the house. Will expected that if the Stealer made an appearance, he would do so from the fields behind the village, where the surrounding trees would give him a convenient, concealed approach and escape route. He was hardly likely to come down the main street itself. But it was as well to make sure, and Maddie was positioned where she could see the part of the street that was hidden from Will's view.

He leaned his back against a tree stump. His cowl was up so that his face was in shadow, and his cloak was gathered around him. He remained motionless, knowing that the cloak and absolute stillness were his sureties against being seen. From anything further than three metres away, he was totally invisible. Even close to, he blended into the tree stump itself, appearing like a pile of fallen branches, or a large, irregular bush.

This was the second night they had kept a vigil over the Carter house. By day, they had stayed back in the trees, hidden from sight. After the first night, Maddie had been impatient, fretting at the long hours of inactivity.

'He's not coming,' she said. 'We've missed him.'

Will shook his head. 'This is a large part of what we do,' he told her. 'Watching and waiting. Be patient. It's only been one night. He could come tomorrow. Or the next night. But he's coming.'

'How can you be so sure?' Maddie asked.

He considered the question in silence for a few moments, then gave her an unblinking look.

'I don't know. I just am. It's a hunter's instinct, I suppose.'

Now as he sat here waiting, that instinct was telling him that tonight would be the night.

Forty-one

He heard them before he saw them.

There was a faint sound of movement through the long grass and low-lying bushes behind him. Instantly, he froze. He lowered his breathing rate so that no movement or sound was perceptible.

He resisted the almost overpowering temptation to turn and look. Instead, he strained his ears, listening to the faint rustling and swishing of clothes through the grass. Two of them, he thought. He couldn't say how he knew that. It was just the result of years of experience, years of stalking and waiting for prey.

The men, assuming they were men, were only a few metres behind him now, and several metres off to one side. Their attention would be focused on the Carter house, he knew. The odds were well against their seeing him, sitting huddled in the cloak. The wind was sending clouds scudding across the sky, alternately concealing then revealing the moon.

The men paused for a few seconds, presumably study-ing the house and the village itself.

'No one around,' said a voice. It was startlingly close to Will, and only his discipline and training stopped him from starting in surprise. The voice couldn't be more than two metres away.

They were on the move again and they slid past him, almost close enough to reach out and touch. There were two of them, as he had guessed. One was wearing a dark cloak. The other was all in black. As he moved, Will saw that there were long, uneven strips of diaphanous black cloth trailing from his arms and shoulders. They swirled and stirred in the wind, giving him the appearance of a tat-tered, unearthly being — a creature from the graveyard.

As the cloaked man crouched, the tattered figure pro-duced a tight-fitting hood and pulled it over his head. He glanced sidelong at his companion and Will could see that the mask covered his face and was marked with lines of white paint, delineating what looked like a skull. Finally, he donned a wide-brimmed, floppy black hat, looking for all the world like some tattered, ghostly scarecrow. He bent low and began moving through the long grass towards the house. He would be a terrifying sight to any child who woke and saw him. Will imagined the throat-closing fear that would assail young Violet in the next few minutes. He was tempted to stop this abduction, and save her the horror of it all. But he knew that if he caught these two, the rest of the gang would fade away — with the chil-dren they had already abducted. Much as he hated the idea, he had to let poor Violet endure the next few hours. The slaving gang must have a hideout somewhere. If he could track them to it, he and Maddie could release all the captives and destroy the gang once and for all.

The black figure was by the house now, almost lost in the shadows. Will wondered if Maddie had seen the two men and hoped that if she had, she wouldn't try to signal him. They had devised a simple signalling method, but it could only be used when the kidnappers were not placed where they could see Will or Maddie. The evil-looking intruder was standing at the side window of the house. Mentally, Will nodded, although there was no actual movement of his head. He had reconnoitred the house the previous evening, looking for possible points of entry. The side window was the most suitable. Its lock was weak and primitive and the window itself was shielded from the sight of any passer-by in the village high street.

The cloaked man, crouched only five metres away from Will, moved nervously, shifting his weight from one foot to the other. Obviously, he was keyed up, watching and waiting for something to go wrong.

The black tattered figure eased the window open. He put one leg over the sill and slipped inside the house. Again, his companion shifted nervously, waiting for a shout, a scream of fright, an uproar from the darkened house. But there was nothing.

Minutes passed. Will focused on the open window — now a dark square hole in the side of the house. Then he saw movement. A small figure in a white nightshirt clambered over the sill, followed by the black, predatory scarecrow. He held her by one arm, never letting her loose. As they made their way across the field to where Will and the Stealer's companion waited, Will saw her stumble. Her abductor heaved her to her feet and Will could see she had a sack over her head.

The cloaked man stood to greet them. He uttered a low laugh as he saw the frightened girl stumbling awkwardly in the grip of the tattered figure.

'Get that sack off her head,' the Stealer told him. 'We'll move faster if she can see where she's going.'

'How did it go?' his friend asked.

The black figure shrugged. 'She had a brother who woke up as I went into the room. But once he saw who I was, he shut up quick smart and pretended to go back to sleep. I told him if he raised the alarm, or told anyone what he'd seen tonight, I'd come back for him and cut out his eyes. Scared the living daylights out of him.'

The cloaked man was busy undoing the sack and removing it from Violet's head. She was a pinch-faced little girl, with badly cut brown hair. She was gagged with a thick piece of cloth and Will could see tears running down her face. But she remained silent, her large, frightened eyes moving from one man to the other.

The Stealer was dragging off his skull mask now. He let out a sigh of relief as he shook his head to loosen his hair, which had been matted down under the tight mask.

'That's better,' he said. 'I must say, Victor does a good job getting those kids scared of the Stealer. That's the third time I've had one wake up and just freeze in terror.' He laughed softly.

Scum, Will thought. Victor, he assumed, was the name of the Storyman, who sowed such terror in the hearts of the children of these villages.

'Full marks to you. The Storyman idea was yours, after all. He's just doing what you told him to do, Jory.'

In spite of all his discipline and training, Will's head snapped round at the name. Fortunately, the two men were facing away from him and the movement went unnoticed. But then the Stealer turned back, running his fingers through his hair and scratching his scalp. At the same moment, a cloud that had been obscuring the moon scudded away on the wind and the pale light fell on his face.

It was a face Will had never forgotten. He had seen it only once before, as he stood, helpless with rage, on the edge of a river, and watched a punt slide away from the bank. But it was burned into his memory as if with a hot iron.

The Stealer in the Night was Jory Ruhl.

Beneath the concealing folds of the cloak, Will's hand moved to the hilt of his saxe, closing around it. A savage rage filled his heart and he wanted to leap to his feet, throw back the cloak and strike at the man who had been responsible for Alyss's death, but he held himself back with an enormous effort. Deliberately, he slowed his breathing and gained control of the blind, unreasoning fury that threatened to overwhelm him. He had finally found Ruhl — ironically, when he was no longer looking for him. And Ruhl had no idea that he had been discovered.

But if Will killed Ruhl here and now, he would never find the missing children from Danvers Crossing, Boyletown, Esseldon, and who knew how many other villages in the fief. Will knew he could track the kidnapper back to his base. Presumably, it would be somewhere on the coast, where an Iberian ship could embark the captured children and take them off to the Socorro slave market.

Will would follow Ruhl to the coast, release the children and, if possible, destroy the ship.

Then he would kill Ruhl.

As the red rage slowly abated, he became aware of what Ruhl and his assistant were saying.

'Well, she's the last one,' Ruhl said, jerking his thumb at the weeping little girl. 'That makes ten and that's how many we contracted for with Eligio. We'll collect the others and head for Hawkshead Bay. The ship is due in three days.'

His companion nodded assent. 'It's been a successful month,' he said. 'We only drew a blank in two villages.'

'It would have been a better month if that Ranger hadn't started snooping. That wasted four days of our time.' The Stealer produced a length of rope from his pocket, pulled the girl's hands behind her back and began to tie her wrists together.

Liam, Will thought. If he'd had any doubts that the slavers were the ones who had killed the young Ranger, they were dispelled by Ruhl's words. That's something else you'll pay for, he promised.

'And I still wonder what happened to Benito. He was supposed to scare off that girl but he's disappeared,' Ruhl continued.

The cloaked man shrugged. 'I always thought he was unreliable. He's probably drunk somewhere, or in jail. He was always getting into trouble.'

'Well, it's one less to share the profits with,' Ruhl said. He tugged the rope around Violet's wrists, testing the knot. The girl gave a small cry of pain. 'Be quiet,' he ordered her. Then he continued to his companion: 'Let's go. We've stood here long enough.'

He grabbed the young girl's arm and dragged her along beside him as he jogged across the grassy field to the dark line of the trees. The other man followed.

Will waited until they had disappeared into the forest. He'd have no trouble tracking them and besides, he knew they were heading for a place called Hawkshead Bay. He wondered briefly about the man they called Benito.

'Probably the one who tried to kill Maddie,' he said to himself.

When he was sure they were gone, and he could no longer be seen, he stood up from his hiding place. His knees ached with the movement, having been bent in one position for several hours.

'I'm getting too old for this,' he muttered. He had no idea that he was repeating a sentiment that Halt had expressed many times.

He took his flint and steel from his belt pouch. Turning his back to the direction Ruhl had taken, he spread his cloak wide to form a screen. Then he struck two sparks from the flint in quick succession.

It was the signal he had devised with Maddie before they began their vigil. Even though the spark was tiny, it showed up clearly in the darkness. The spread cloak shielded it, in case Ruhl happened to still be in sight and glance back at the house.

A few moments later, he saw a dark form slip out of the alley where Maddie had been concealed. Staying in the shadows cast by the eaves of the buildings on the far side of the street, she moved quickly to the left for about twenty metres. At that point, she became lost to his sight. Minutes later, she crept silently out of another alley, parallel to the one beside the Carter house. She made her way to where Will stood, waiting.

'I saw them,' she said. 'Did they take the girl?'

Will nodded. 'Yes. And now they're heading back to their lair. It's at a place called Hawkshead Bay.'

'Do you know where that is?'

He shook his head. 'Not yet. We'll check the map and see if it's marked there. If not, we'll simply follow Ruhl's tracks.'

She looked at him, slightly puzzled, her head to one side. 'Ruhl? Who's Ruhl?'

'He's the Stealer,' Will told her. But something in his voice caught her attention.

'Do you know him?' she asked.

Will nodded grimly. 'He's the man who killed my wife.'

Forty-two

Dawn was four hours away and Will decided they
should get a few hours' sleep before they set out after
Ruhl and his gang.

'We can't track them in the dark and we've been up for
hours keeping watch the past two nights. We might as well
get some sleep while we can,' he said. 'They won't be
moving too fast. Ruhl said they were going to collect the
other children they've abducted. That'll slow them down.'

Maddie yawned. She didn't disagree with his assessment of the situation.

They returned to the clearing where they had hidden
the horses and rolled out their blankets on the soft, springy
grass. Maddie was asleep almost as soon as she closed her
eyes. The tension of the nights spent on watch, and the
events of the previous few days, had left her emotionally
and physically exhausted.

She awoke to what she now considered to be the
delightful smell of fresh coffee brewing. She sat up and saw

Will sitting beside a small fire, the map of Trelleth Fief spread out on the ground beside him. He heard her moving and looked up, gesturing to the coffee pot in the coals at the edge of the fire.

'Get yourself some coffee,' he said. 'And there's bread there to toast as well. No sense setting out on an empty stomach.'

She propped a slab of bread up on a stick close to the heat of the coals, then poured a cup of coffee. They had no milk but by now she could drink it black, so long as it was sweetened with plenty of honey. She sipped it appreciatively, turned the toast as it was on the point of burning and hunkered down opposite him.

'Did you find Hawkshead Bay?' she asked.

He nodded, jabbing a finger at the chart.

'A little south of here,' he said. 'I can see why they called it Hawkshead Bay.'

She peered at it, frowning. 'Doesn't look like a hawk's head to me,' she said, rubbing her eyes.

Will raised an eyebrow in her direction. 'That could be because you're looking at it upside down,' he said patiently. 'By the way, your toast's burning.'

She grabbed at the toast and burnt her fingers, dropping the slightly blackened slice of bread onto the grass. She muttered a very unladylike oath. That sent both of Will's eyebrows soaring.

'Not the sort of language one expects from a princess,' he said. 'Where did you hear that particular expression?'

'From my mother,' she replied shortly.

Will nodded. 'That would explain it.'

'Besides, I'm not a princess any more, as you've pointed out.'

He glanced quickly at her. He was pleased to note that there was no bitterness in her tone and she seemed to be merely stating a fact, not complaining about it.

She actually prefers this to her former life, he thought, mildly surprised by the realisation. Then he thought, why not? At least these days there was a sense of purpose to her life, and a sense of accomplishment that had been lacking in her time at Castle Araluen.

She retrieved the toast and spread butter on it, crunching into it with gusto. There were a few blades of grass clinging to it but she picked them out of her mouth, craning her head around to view the chart from Will's perspective.

'Hmmmph,' she admitted reluctantly. 'I suppose it's a little like a hawk's head now I look at it this way. How far away is it?'

'It's about a day's ride on the main road,' Will said. 'The kidnappers will probably take longer. A day and a half, maybe two days. They'll be moving on foot and they'll have to avoid other travellers. Be a little hard to explain how you happen to be travelling with a group of young prisoners. By the same token, the highway runs through half a dozen towns and villages and they'll have to bypass them.'

He pointed to a track marked on the map. 'There's a track here, running south. It's a little bit of a diversion, but it links up with another road that runs east — and that road is a direct route, while the highway winds and twists and loops around to take in those other villages.'

'Wouldn't it make sense for the kidnappers to take that path?' she asked.

But Will shook his head. 'They were heading east when they left the village. That would indicate they're taking the highway. As for this track, it may not even be on their maps. The Castle Trelleth cartographer is pretty painstaking. He puts in a lot of detail that other people would leave out.'

'So if we take that path, we should make it to the coast before they do?' Maddie said.

'Yes. That way we can scout the area and see what's what. There must be some sort of camp there and there may be other members of his gang waiting. Plus I heard him say he was expecting an Iberian slave ship in a few days. Always a good idea to get a look at the scene of the battle beforehand.'

She glanced up at him. 'Is there going to be a battle?'

Will's face was grim as he replied. 'Oh, I think there might be.'

They finished their breakfast, rolled their blankets and tied them behind the saddles. Tug and Bumper were both restless and excited. They were keen to get moving again after days of enforced inactivity.

It was good to be in the saddle again and Maddie enjoyed the feeling of Bumper's enthusiastic gambolling beneath her. Tug eyed the younger horse with a superior smirk.

'You're just as excited as he is,' Will said softly. Tug tossed his head. In fact, both horses, sensitive to their riders' mood, recognised the fact that whatever Will and Maddie had been searching for over the previous week, they seemed to have found it. Accordingly, they reacted to their riders' new sense of purpose. They sensed that action lay ahead of them — and Ranger horses were bred for action.

They cantered south and a little west until, an hour before noon, they reached the road that led east to the sea. Will stepped down from the saddle to inspect the ground, checking to make sure nobody had passed this way recently. It was one thing to assume that Ruhl and his men wouldn't take this path. But it was wise to make sure.

'A cow and a cowherd went through here,' he said. 'Maybe two days ago. Since then, there appears to be nothing.'

'You didn't think Ruhl would come this way,' Maddie pointed out.

Will gave her a long look before replying. 'And now I know he didn't,' he said. He swung up into the saddle and they cantered along the path, occasionally being forced to lie low over their horses' necks to avoid overhanging trees.

'Looks like not too many people use this track,' Maddie commented.

Will said nothing.

Eventually, the path emerged from the thick forestland that comprised nearly two-thirds of its length. They found themselves cantering in open fields and past farmsteads, with occasional stands of timber dotted around. And before long, Maddie smelt that heady salt smell once more that told her they were nearing the sea.

In the midafternoon, they reached the coastal highway. The road was raised slightly above the surrounding terrain, with drainage ditches on either side. Will gestured for Maddie to remain on the lower ground off the road, out of sight. He dismounted and climbed up to the road, looking north and then south.

'All clear both ways,' he said. Then he jerked his thumb south. 'Hawkshead Bay is three kilometres that way. Let's go.'

The countryside changed once more. The green pastures and carefully tended fields gave way to coarse heathland, where scrubby bushes grew barely waist high and trees were few and far between. Will grimaced as he surveyed the land.

'Not a lot of cover,' he remarked.

Maddie glanced at him. 'So we'll see them coming,' she pointed out.

'I'm more concerned that they'll see us going,' he remarked. 'Remember, it won't just be us. We'll have ten children with us. They'll be a little hard to conceal.'

She pursed her lips. She hadn't thought of that. She began to look from side to side, marking any places where there might be useful cover. Inland, about half a kilometre from the road, a row of low cliffs rose up from the heath. At their base, boulders were tumbled untidily. The cliffs were obviously unstable and prone to landslides from time to time. She could see several dark holes that could well mark the openings to caves. That meant it might be possible to find a useful hiding place.

In case they needed one. And she was beginning to think they might need one before too long.

The highway swung south to run close to the coastline. More cliffs here, she saw, falling away to the ocean below them. They were made mainly of clay and fell sheer to the water, looking as if they had been cut with a blade. The sea, running over a sandy bottom, was shallow and clear green.

'Pretty,' she said. Will followed her line of sight and grunted.

'Not if you were a sailor,' he said. 'That water's shallow for almost a kilometre out to sea. You'd need to wait for high tide to land.'

He had memorised a few landmarks from the map so he'd know when they were approaching Hawkshead Bay. Now, as they passed the final one, a small pond by an equally small copse of low trees, he called a halt.

'We'll leave the horses here,' he said. 'We'll go ahead on foot to see what's what.'

They left the horses concealed in the trees and made their way through the waist-high gorse to the next headland. Beyond that, according to the map, lay Hawkshead Bay.

As they came level with the edge of the cliff, Will moved his hand in a palm downward gesture. Maddie went into a crouch, then, following her mentor's lead, she dropped to hands and knees, crawling forward through the coarse undergrowth.

If there were people in the cove, it would be asking for trouble to simply walk to the edge of the crest in full sight.

Will stopped and beckoned her forward. She crawled through the bushes, making as little noise as possible, until she was level with him. Hawkshead Bay was spread out before them.

The cliffs were lower here, around ten to fifteen metres high, and they sloped more than the knife-edged vertical cliffs they had been passing. Unlike those cliffs, which were basically clay, these were formed from rock and sand, interspersed with tufts of seagrass and bushes. At their base was a semi-circular beach of coarse sand.

The tide was running in and she could see it forming corrugated ripples in the shallow sand bottom. The water was shallow for at least a quarter of a kilometre out to sea.

In the centre of the beach, well above the high-water mark that was delineated by tangles of driftwood and seaweed, were four large tents. The canvas was weathered and grey and it was stretched over timber frames. They'd been here a while, she thought. This was a permanent camp.

There was a large fireplace ten metres away from the tents — far enough so that smoke from the fire wouldn't be a problem — and a rough wooden table and benches set under a canvas roof supported by a timber frame. The four sides were open.

She counted two men moving about the camp site, although there could have been others concealed in the tents. Four tents would seem to indicate at least sixteen men in the camp, she thought. Then she reconsidered. The hostages would have to be kept somewhere.

As she had the thought, Will nudged her and pointed to the cliffs on the left-hand side of the bay. She peered in the direction he was indicating and made out a dark opening in the rock, at ground level. As she looked more closely, she could make out a barred timber door across the opening.

She revised her thinking. That was where the hostages were kept, she realised.

Will had told her about Ruhl's statement — that they had taken ten prisoners. She wondered how many of them were already in the cave, and how many were on their way here with the Stealer and the Storyman.

Will leaned closer to her. 'There's a track leading down the cliff to the left of the cave. See it?'

Even though the nearest slaver was over a hundred metres away, and intent on bringing the dormant fire back to life, he barely breathed the words.

Maddie scanned the cliff and could make out the track. It ran down through the rocks at an angle, switchbacked several times, then ended at the beach, twenty metres from the dark opening that marked the cave. She raised a thumb to indicate that she had seen it.

'When we get the kids out, that's where you'll take them. Back up to the top of the cliff,' he told her.

She turned quickly to look at him. 'That's where I'll take them? What'll you be doing?'

He patted the smooth wood of his longbow, lying in the grass before him.

'I'll be making sure nobody sees you leaving.'

Forty-three

In the late afternoon, the slave party finally arrived.

As Will had predicted, the captives trudged wearily along the middle of the road, their hands bound in front of them, and a heavy rope linking them together tied round their necks. There were six of them and they all looked dispirited and dejected. Ruhl and two of his men rode on small ponies, chivvying the captives along, urging them to move faster. Will recognised Ruhl and the cloaked man who had been with him when they had abducted Violet.

The Storyman was recognisable as the third of those riding. The blue cloak, wide hat and red shoes marked him out. In addition to those three, there were six other men in the party.

As the party passed close to where Will and Maddie were concealed in the long grass by the cliff's edge, they could hear the tinkling bells on the Storyman's shoes carrying to them on the slight breeze.

Violet and the other captives looked thoroughly cowed. Will noticed that they cringed away whenever the Story-man rode close to them. Once, he heard the blue-cloaked figure laugh as the other girl in the party, whom Will took to be Carrie Clover from Danvers Crossing, flinched away from him with a frightened cry. Will's lips set in a tight line.

The other men in the slaving party were heavily armed with an assortment of spears, clubs and axes, and two had swords thrust through their belts. They were a hard-bitten lot, bearded and unkempt, and dressed in rough leather and wool. Each of them had a short, knotted length of rope, which they used to urge the captives on to greater speed.

'Nine of them,' Will whispered.

'And at least two more in the camp,' Maddie said.

'And there'll be more still in the ship's crew when it arrives. At least another half dozen.'

Maddie chewed her lip thoughtfully. The odds were tilting a little too far in the enemy's favour, she thought. Consequently, she was surprised by Will's next comment.

'The good news is, we have more than enough arrows,' he said grimly.

Ruhl and the other two horsemen dismounted to lead the way down the cliff path. The line of prisoners followed them. It was obviously difficult going with their hands tied, and with the heavy rope linking them. If one slipped, the two on either side would be dragged down as well. They struggled awkwardly down the rough track. The other men brought up the rear. The track was too narrow to allow them to walk beside their prisoners. At least it meant they couldn't beat the children with the knotted ropes.

Slipping, sliding and stumbling, the line of captured children finally made their awkward way to the level ground. Ruhl and the other two horsemen formed up to bar their way, preventing their moving out onto the beach and directing them along the base of the cliff towards the cave.

The two men already in the camp looked up to watch as the party made its way down the rough track. Maddie was interested to see that nobody else emerged from the tents. It would appear that the gang so far totalled eleven men. The man who had been tending the fire took a large key ring from one of the posts supporting the open-sided tent. Picking up a heavy club that was leaning against the table, he began to walk in a leisurely manner over to the cave door.

'Get a move on, Donald!' Ruhl shouted roughly. 'We haven't got all day!'

'And welcome back to you, Master Ruhl,' the man replied in a bad-tempered tone. Nonetheless, Maddie noted that he quickened his pace.

The new arrivals milled uncertainly by the barred gate to the cave, not sure what was to happen next. Will could see now that the rope joining them passed through metal rings on heavy boiled-leather collars, each one fastened with an individual lock. The man with the keys unlocked the barred gate. Apparently someone inside the cave made an attempt to come out because he snarled and prodded with the club into the darkness.

Satisfied that the cave's inhabitants were settled, he then turned to the first prisoner in line and unshackled the collar, prodding the boy with his club to drive him into the cave.

Ruhl watched as the man called Donald repeated the process for the next two prisoners. Then, satisfied that things were moving smoothly, Ruhl moved to the eating enclosure, tying his horse to one of the uprights and glaring at the other man who had been in the camp and who now stood staring vacantly at his leader.

'Bring me a drink, curse you, Thomas!' Ruhl snarled. 'I've been in the saddle all day!'

'Not a lot of love lost between them,' Will murmured as the man hurried to fetch Ruhl a dark jug and several tankards. Ruhl poured a large measure and drank deeply, sighing with satisfaction as he finished. The Storyman and the other rider dismounted and joined him. In the hierarchy of the gang, the three of them were obviously on the top rank. Ruhl was the undisputed leader, and the Storyman and the cloaked man were his lieutenants. The others were simply the rank and file.

Ruhl and his two cohorts relaxed and drank, laughing from time to time as they talked, while Donald and the other men shoved and cursed at the children, forcing them into the cave.

'Must be getting crowded in there,' Maddie ventured.

Will glanced sidelong at her.

'Ten prisoners in all, you said,' she continued. 'You'd need a pretty big cave to keep them all comfortable. And most caves tend to be small.'

The last prisoner was shoved roughly into the cave, then the barred door was slammed shut behind him and locked. From their vantage point on the clifftop, they could hear the rattle of the heavy key. One of the three who had been guarding the prisoners en route to the cove gathered up the heavy rope and leather collars. The man with the keys, Donald, returned to the central area of the camp, replacing the big key ring on the post whence he had taken it.

'Get some food ready,' Ruhl ordered.

Obviously Donald and the other man, Thomas, were detailed to look after the menial work around the camp site. Will filed that information away. If it came to a fight, they could be left till last. They were unlikely to be particularly aggressive or quick witted. Men like them did as they were told. They rarely thought for themselves. And, from what Will had seen of Ruhl so far, he seemed to be a man who would discourage individual thinking among his subordinates.

The camp settled into what seemed its normal routine. Around seven in the evening, the man Ruhl had called Thomas took food and water to the cave. Donald accompanied him, unlocking the barred door and making sure none of the occupants tried to escape. The tide had turned and was beginning to run in once more, creeping slowly up the beach and covering the wide expanse of rippled sand that had been exposed by the low tide.

Maddie and Will remained watching until the bearded Ranger touched her shoulder and jerked a thumb back towards the small stand of trees where they had left the horses.

'Looks like they've settled in for the night. We might as well get some rest ourselves. We'll come back before dawn and figure a way to get the kids out.'

'Just us, against eleven men?' Maddie asked.

Will gave her a long, grave look, then nodded. 'Just us, against eleven men.'

They crept back to the copse of trees, although there was really no need for stealth. The slavers were all asleep in their tents and the beach was at least twenty metres lower than the ground on which they stood. They watered the horses and unsaddled them. Then they had a cold meal of dried beef, fruit and flat bread. Maddie lifted the battered old coffee pot and raised an eyebrow at Will. But he shook his head.

'No fire,' he said briefly. 'They might smell the smoke. Or they might decide to have a look around the area.'

They drank water from their canteens. There was no running water in the vicinity and the small pond they had passed was slime-covered and stagnant. They rolled out their blankets. Maddie looked at Will.

'Should we set a watch?' she asked and he nodded.

'We should keep an eye on the beach to see if anything happens,' he said. 'I'll take the first four hours.'

She calculated quickly. That meant that Will would be standing watch twice during the night, to her once. She shrugged. That was only fair, she thought, as she crawled into her blankets.

She watched his dark figure ghost away into the night. A few minutes later she was asleep. She wasn't concerned about anyone catching her unawares. Bumper and Tug would give adequate warning if someone approached the little camp.

But just to be on the safe side, she slept with her sling twined around her right hand and her shot bag beside her head.

Forty-four

Maddie awoke just before dawn. She glanced at Will's bedroll but saw that it was empty. He was still at the cliff, on watch over the cove. She threw off her own blankets, dashed cold water over her face from her canteen and pulled on her boots.

Bumper saw her moving and gave a low rumble of noise. She looked at him and his ears pricked up. He sensed that she was going somewhere and wanted to go with her. She shook her head and put her finger to her lips.

'Not now, boy. And keep silent.'

He shook his mane and lowered his head again, going back to cropping the short grass. She thought he looked a little disappointed, then wondered if she was being fanciful. Could a horse express disappointment, she wondered. Then she dismissed the thought, realising she could be here all day debating it and never get a satisfactory answer.

She strung her bow then donned her belt, heavy with the double scabbard for her saxe and her throwing knife.

The weight of the knives was counterbalanced by the pouch of lead shot on her other hip. Finally, she slipped her quiver over her head, adjusting it so that the arrows lay easy to hand over her right shoulder. Then she donned her cape, opening the small flap on the right shoulder that allowed access to the arrows.

She moved to the edge of the copse of trees, paused and sank to one knee while she scanned the ground around her. She did it as Will had taught her: first taking a wide overview, then searching one small part at a time, until she was sure there was nobody in sight.

Staying in a crouch. she planned her path where the scrubby ground cover was highest, and headed for the clifftop, where Will was keeping watch.

She moved slowly and smoothly, placing each foot carefully, testing the ground underfoot before she put her full weight on it. If she felt a twig or a branch, she would carefully move her foot to a clear spot, then proceed.

Speed is the enemy of stealth, Will had told her. *You're better to move slowly and silently than to rush about making noise.*

She saw the tall grass moving to her left. The pre-dawn air was still, with no sign of a breeze. Instantly, she froze in place.

Trust the cloak, she thought. That and *stay completely still* were the two principal mantras of unseen movement in the Ranger Corps.

She didn't even turn her head, swivelling her eyes instead to focus on the spot where she had seen movement. After some thirty seconds, a large fox slipped out of the long grass and padded away, belly low to the ground, long bushy tail streaming behind him. He hadn't even noticed her.

'I must be getting better at this,' she said to herself. She wished Will could have seen how the fox was unaware of her presence. She could tell him about it, of course. But that wasn't the same. It would seem like boasting.

It is boasting, she realised.

When she was forty metres from the cliff edge, she dropped silently to her hands and knees, staying below the tall grass. Even though she knew where Will was keeping watch, she could make out no sign of him. She raised her head to scan the terrain ahead of her. As she did so, she incautiously placed her hand on a clump of stiff, dry grass, causing a slight, rustling *snap!* as it broke.

She paused. The sound had been so small that she was sure nobody would have noticed it. Then, ten metres away, in the spot where she knew Will was keeping watch, she saw his hand rise briefly above the top of the grass.

He'd heard her. He knew she was coming. And he'd signalled her to let her know.

She crawled forward, careful to make no more unnecessary noises. When she was two metres from Will's position, she was able to discern the mottled cloak that covered him. He turned and she could see his bearded face in the shadow of his cowl. It was uncanny how still he could remain, she thought. If she hadn't known to look for the cloak, she would probably never have seen him, even as close as she was.

'Anything happening?' she whispered.

'Aside from you blundering about like a lost elephant?' he asked, in the same low tone.

She nodded, accepting the rebuke. 'Aside from that.'

He tilted his head towards the rim of the cliff, a metre or so away from them. 'Take a look,' he said. Then he added, unnecessarily, she thought, 'Carefully.'

She checked the direction of the sun. It was low and out to sea and a little to her left. She pulled her cowl forward to make sure her face was well in its shadow, then inched toward the cliff edge. Keeping her head below the level of the surrounding grass, she carefully parted several strands and peered through.

There was a ship on the beach.

She was about fifteen metres long, lean and narrow waisted. She was built for speed, Maddie thought. The hull was painted a dull black. She was built to be unobtrusive as well, she added mentally. She was pierced for six oars, three on either side. The square sail was loosely furled on the yardarm. From what she could see, it was made of black canvas.

Behind the mast, in the centre of the deck, was a wooden cage. It stretched back for about a third of the ship's length, ending a few metres from the steering platform.

Will had edged up beside her, moving so silently that she had no idea he was there until she saw him in her peripheral vision.

'See the cage?' he said softly. 'That's where they'll keep the slaves. There'll be iron rings and shackles in there to keep them secured.'

'When did she arrive?' Maddie asked.

'About two hours ago. She came in on the making tide. It's starting to ebb now.'

She noticed that the ship was canted slightly one side, as there was insufficient water under her to float her. The water was receding fast and already the bow was high and dry on the sand.

'We'll need to get a move on if we want to stop her,' she said, but Will shook his head.

'She'll need high tide to go out again, and that's not due until six or seven hours after noon. She'll go out on the ebbing tide once there's enough water to float her. And she'll wait until it's dark, just in case there are any ships patrolling.'

Even as they were speaking, Maddie noticed, the water had receded to the last oar port on the black hull.

'How many in the crew?' she asked.

'Seven. Six rowing and one helmsman. They're in the mess tent.'

She changed the direction of her gaze. Up until now, her attention had been totally distracted by the ship.

'You should have noticed that yourself,' Will admonished her gently.

She bit her lip. He had taught her when she was viewing a scene to scan the entire area first, and to avoid focusing on any one object. Now, the first time it mattered, she had neglected to make an all-round sweep of the beach, concentrating instead on the black ship. The mess tent was the open-sided shelter on the beach. She studied it and could see the legs of a number of men sitting at the rough table. Their upper bodies were obscured by the canvas roof. She could hear a low murmur of voices, and occasional laughter. The cook fire was alight, and a column of smoke spiralled lazily into the air.

She frowned. I'm going to have to do better, she thought. She realised that there was more to being a Ranger than being a crack shot with a bow or being able to move silently. A Ranger's main job was to observe and report.

Sensing her annoyance, Will touched her arm.

'Don't worry,' he said. 'Learn from it. For the moment, take a good look at the layout of the camp, and where the cave and the cliff path are. Study it until you're sure you can picture it all in your mind. Then we'll get back to our own camp site.'

She nodded, then settled down to study the beach below her, taking particular notice of the cave with the barred door and the rocky path that led down the cliff. She noted distances, angles and available cover between the path and the cave, then did the same with the cave and the tents. Finally, she set the relative position of the ship in her mind. When she was convinced that she had it fixed firmly in her memory, she squirmed back from the cliff edge and nodded to Will.

'Got it,' she said. He looked at her a moment, head slightly to one side.

'How far from the cave to the mess tent?' he asked.

She saw again the picture of the beach she had engraved in her memory. 'Thirty-five, maybe forty metres.'

He nodded. 'And to the sleeping tents?'

'Another ten.'

'How far to the ship?'

'A hundred and ten metres. And she's a little to the right of the camp.'

'Can you see the ship from the cave entrance?'

She paused, frowning. She hadn't been expecting that question. Then she answered carefully.

'I don't think so. The mess tent and the sleeping tents are in between those two points.'

'Good girl.' He touched her arm, then gestured behind them. 'Let's get back to where we can talk comfortably and we'll go over the plan for tonight.'

'Do we have a plan for tonight?' she asked.

'We certainly do.'

'Is it a good plan? Will I like it?' she asked, grinning cheekily.

Will regarded her solemnly for several seconds.

'It's a great plan. You're going to love it.'

She thought about the situation. There were two of them, and now that the ship's crew had added another seven men to the enemy, it was two against eighteen. They were pretty long odds, no matter how many arrows they might have.

Whatever the plan was, she doubted that she was going to love it.

Forty-five

Will cleared a patch of dirt between them and sketched with the point of his saxe.

'Here's the cliff path, with the cave at the bottom of it —' he began.

'The cave is about ten metres from the path,' she corrected him and he glared at her. She shrugged. 'You said for me to study every detail. That's a detail.'

'Very well.' He amended his sketch. 'Happy now?' She nodded. 'Here's the path. Here's the cave. The tents are here.' He indicated their position. 'And the ship is here, down the beach.'

He glanced up at her. 'Any corrections?' he asked, a little acidly.

She made a small disclaiming gesture with one hand. 'No. That looks fine.'

'Now, the tide will start coming in about four hours after noon. It'll be full by seven and then it'll start to ebb. My guess is, the Iberians will want to go out on the ebbing tide when it's full dark. That'll be about an hour after high tide. They'll still have enough water under their keel and the tide will take them out.'

'Why will they wait till dark?' Maddie asked.

'There are patrols. The Skandians station a ship on the east coast for the King's use. She patrols these waters, keeping an eye out for smugglers, pirates . . . and slavers. The Iberians won't want to run into her, so they'll wait for dark. You noticed the ship is all black?'

She nodded.

'That's because they prefer to travel by night. Now the cave is on the left-hand side of the bay as you look out to sea. The ship is a little to the right of the middle of the beach. I plan to work my way down the cliffs on the right side of the beach, and get within a hundred metres of the ship —'

'What if there's no way down?' she interrupted.

He looked at her for a long moment, took a deep breath, then answered. 'There is. I reconnoitred and found one while you were snoozing. Now don't interrupt.'

'You've always said I should have an inquiring mind,' she said.

'I have. But not an interrupting one. If you want to inquire, wait till I finish. Now, once I'm down the cliff, I'm going to start shooting fire arrows at the ship.'

'Fire arrows?'

He glared at her again.

'That wasn't an inquiry. It was more a statement,' she said apologetically.

'I'll let it pass. Yes, I'll start shooting fire arrows. If there's one thing puts the fear of the hereafter into a sailor, it's fire on board his ship. Ships are full of tarred rope and dried-out canvas and pinewood. They burn at the first hint of a flame.'

'So they'll go running down the beach to their ship to put the fire out?' Maddie asked

Will nodded. 'And my guess is, Ruhl and his men will help them. If they lose that ship, all their work goes for nothing. Once they're all bunched around the ship, I'll pick off a few of Ruhl's men. That'll lessen the odds.'

'They'll come after you as soon as you do that,' she said. There was a worried tone in her voice as she thought about him facing eighteen men on his own.

He shook his head dismissively. 'That's the idea. I'll lead them away, heading back up the cliffs to the south-west. And they won't come too fast. Nothing slows a man down like the thought that he might be running into an arrow at any minute,' he added grimly.

'What do I do while all this is going on?' she asked.

He tapped the point of his saxe on the dirt map again, at the spot where the path was indicated.

'I want you at the bottom of the path before I start. Once they head down the beach to the ship, you have to let the kids out.' He paused and glanced at her appraisingly. 'Do you know where the key is?'

She nodded. 'It's on a hook on one of the mess tent support posts.'

'Good girl. You get them out of the cave and lead them back up the path. Then head north as fast as you can. With all the commotion at the ship, odds are nobody will notice you going.'

'And if they do?'

'Well, that's where all that practice with your bow and your sling will come in handy. Don't let them get close. They're killers and they won't give you a second chance. If they're coming at you, don't hesitate to shoot them.'

She thought about his plan for some moments. It seemed logical. It was simple enough, but Will had often told her that simple plans were the best. There was less to go wrong.

'All right. And do we meet up again back here?' she asked finally.

But he shook his head. 'You leg it north as fast as you can. I'll take Ruhl and his men out to the south-west. Then I'll shake them off and double back to join up with you.'

He sounded confident. But she knew it wouldn't be as simple as he was making it out to be. He sensed her concern.

'If something goes wrong, head for Ambleton. It's a large town on the highway, about fifteen kilometres up the coast. There'll be a sheriff there and you should be safe. I'll catch up with you eventually.'

She looked at him doubtfully. 'Make sure you do.'

'Trust me,' he said. Then he added, 'There's another thing. Once I get a fire started on the ship, there's a better than even chance that the Iberians won't wait around. They may well launch her and take her out to sea. After all, if they lose her, they're finished.'

'And it'll be ten or eleven hours before the tide will let them back in,' Maddie said.

'Exactly. So that will cut down the numbers we're facing. Any questions?'

She looked at him. He was putting himself at enormous risk, she knew. Her part in this was dangerous, but he was the one exposing himself to the enemy, in order to lead them away from her and the prisoners as she made their way north. But she couldn't think of a way to express this to him, so she finally answered.

'No. It all seems clear.'

'Good. Well, we've got five hours before we need to start moving. Might as well get some rest.'

He settled back, his head pillowed on his saddle, arms crossed on his chest, and pulled his cowl over his face. Maddie's stomach was churning with the anticipation of the night to come. Her nerves were taut as a bowstring.

'How can you sleep at a time like this?' she asked but the only answer was a low snore. She looked at him suspiciously. In the time she had been with him, she had never before heard him snore.

'You're faking,' she said.

'No. I'm really fast asleep,' came his voice from under the cowl.

Will rested for several hours. As the shadows began to lengthen, he rose and stretched. Then he fetched the case that held his spare arrows and the saddle bag where he kept his equipment. He unlaced the top of the case, glanced inside, then brought out half a dozen arrows. Maddie moved closer to watch him. The arrows were all wrapped in an open weave cloth just behind their broadheads.

'What are they?' she asked curiously. She hadn't seen them before. He glanced up at her.

'Fire arrows,' he said. 'It makes sense to always have a few prepared. The cloth behind the broadhead changes the weight distribution. So when I make them, I re-balance them to make sure they fly the same as a normal arrow. I've also made them a little longer than my normal arrows so I can get a full draw. Obviously, once the tip is on fire, I can't draw one of these all the way back to the bow.'

'Do you always carry some with you?' she asked.

He nodded. 'If I started making them up now, I'd be fiddling around getting the balance right.'

'It pays to be prepared,' she said thoughtfully.

'Exactly. You never know when you're going to need something like this,' he said, holding up one of the arrows. He took a small wooden cylinder from his equipment bag and unscrewed the lid. The cylinder was really a wide-mouthed jar containing oil and he slid three of the arrows into the oil, then set the cylinder down carefully, leaving the oil to soak into the cloth-wrapped tips of the arrows. After several minutes, he withdrew them, inspected them to make sure they were completely saturated, then wrapped the tips in a piece of oilcloth to stop the flam-mable oil evaporating. He placed the other arrows into the oil jar and repeated the process.

Maddie watched him, fascinated. Once again, the thought occurred to her that there was more to being a Ranger than shooting straight and moving silently.

'How are you going to light them?' she said. 'If you start striking a flint and lighting a fire, they'll spot you before you can get a shot away.'

'I'll take a dark lantern,' Will said. He showed her a small metal lantern with a candle inside. There was a shutter at the front that opened and closed, alternately blocking or releasing the light from the flame.

She shook her head in admiration. 'You've thought of everything,' she said. But Will looked up at her and shook his head solemnly.

'I doubt it,' he said. 'No matter how thoroughly you plan, no matter how much you think you know, you've never thought of everything.'

Forty-six

Maddie crouched at the top of the path leading down to the beach. The kidnappers and the ship's crew were gathered in the mess tent, finishing their evening meal. The table was brightly illuminated by half a dozen lanterns. That'll make it easier to remain unseen, she thought. If the men were looking into the light cast by the lanterns, their night vision would be ruined.

Most of them were seated round the table. Donald and Thomas, the two men who had been in the camp when she and Will first arrived, prepared and served the meal. They then sat on the ground with their own food, a few metres away from the fire.

The kidnappers and the sailors seemed to be in good spirits. Their conversation was noisy and animated, and laughter broke out frequently. She guessed they had good reason to be content. They had ten captives to take off to the Socorran slave markets.

The moon rose over the ocean, bathing the water in silver light. The black outline of the ship stood out in stark contrast. Water was lapping around the hull, and the ship was no longer canted to one side.

There was no sign that the captives in the cave had been fed. Presumably, they were given only one meal a day. Ruhl wasn't the type to waste money feeding his prisoners more than they needed to stay alive.

She waited, squinting at the moon with her hand held out at arm's length, until it was four finger widths above the horizon. That was the time she had agreed with Will. By now, he'd be making his way down the cliffs on the northern headland of the bay. She moved in a crouch to the beginning of the path. She paused, checking the men in the mess tent once more. But they were busy eating. And, judging by the raucous laughter that came more frequently with each passing minute, they were drinking as well.

She set her bow to one side. It would only be a hindrance as she made her way down the path and, in the dark, she'd probably need both hands free. She wound the sling around her right hand and started down the track to the beach.

The footing was uneven and she went slowly, testing each step. Once she was below the level of the clifftop, she would be all but invisible against the dark cliff face. But if she were to slip and fall, the chances were high that she'd be heard. And someone might come looking to see what had caused the noise.

Her foot slipped as she stepped on a loose layer of pebbles. Several of them clattered over the edge of the path, bouncing off the rocks below. She froze, her heart in her mouth. To her, the skittering pebbles sounded as loud as an avalanche. Her left hand went to the shot pouch, ready to select and load a lead ball into the sling.

She waited a full minute. But there was no sign that anyone had heard her. Taking even greater care, she set off again, a black, uneven shadow sliding slowly downwards, barely visible against the dark background of the cliff.

She reached the first switchback, where the path angled back on itself. The ground was rough and strewn with small boulders here and she picked her way carefully around the turn. She glanced back over her shoulder at the mess tent. The slavers were still intent upon their food and drink. A loud burst of laughter rang out.

'Keep making noise,' she said under her breath. 'That way, you won't hear me.'

The second stretch of the track was more even underfoot. She'd been crouching on the rougher ground higher up to maintain her balance, but now she straightened and moved faster until she reached the second switchback. She picked her way carefully around it. There was only twenty metres to go now and she'd be at the bottom. She forced herself to concentrate. With the end of the track in sight, it was tempting to relax and rush. Yet she continued her slow, careful pace, crouching once more, feeling the ground twist underfoot as she stepped on larger rocks, occasionally sinking into unexpected dips and ruts in the track. One was deeper than it looked and she jarred her back as she stepped into it. She grunted in surprise, then froze. But there was no reaction from the men at the mess tent table and she continued, finally stepping down onto the level ground at the foot of the track.

Now she had to wait once more. As Will had once described it to her, a Ranger's day seemed to be made up of hours of waiting followed by a few minutes of frantic, frightening action.

She waited now for those frantic minutes to come. Her stomach was a tight knot. The tension was almost unbearable. She had no idea whether Will had reached the rocks at the base of the northern cliff yet. He could have fallen and injured himself. If the path he had found was anything like the one she'd traversed, one incautious step could have left him lying with a broken ankle. Or unconscious.

The longer she waited, the worse the picture in her imagination became. What would she do if Will didn't fulfil his part of the plan? If he was incapacitated somewhere on that cliff path, how could she get the children away?

It was too late to go for help. Ambleton was the nearest settlement of any size. By the time she got there and brought help back to Hawkshead Bay, the slavers and the children would be long gone, heading for the Socorran slave market and a life of misery.

Could she somehow set fire to the ship, then double back up the beach to release the children? She discarded the idea almost as soon as she thought of it. The chances that she could make it across the open beach unobserved were slim to none. And she needed Will to draw off the pursuit to the south while she got the children safely away.

She thought of another option. She had two dozen arrows in her quiver and there were eighteen men sitting round the table. She could simply start shooting at them. She'd take them by surprise, possibly drive them off in panic.

Then she considered the plan realistically. She might get two of them, even three if she was fast enough. But they weren't simple villagers to be frightened off by a surprise attack out of the darkness. They were ruthless men with an investment to protect. They were armed and, she assumed, experienced fighting men. They'd go to ground, taking cover behind the tents or the table, or the large rock outcrops that dotted the beach. Then they'd begin to move to outflank her, and sooner or later, she'd be overwhelmed.

Besides, she thought bitterly, she'd left her bow at the top of the cliff.

She sighed. There was nothing she could do if Will didn't make it to the rocks on the south side of the cove. She'd have to watch helplessly while the children were herded aboard the ship and taken away.

Then she saw it. A flash of light, briefly visible among the dark jumble of distant rocks. Will must have opened the shutter on his dark lantern to light one of the fire arrows. Then it was gone as he closed the shutter.

But now she thought she could see a pinpoint of light among the rocks. She realised it was the glowing tip of one of the fire arrows. She glanced back fearfully at the slavers. But they were sitting in a circle of bright light and hadn't noticed the brief flash from the rocks.

As she watched, the yellow pinpoint arced up into the night sky, then curved down towards the black ship. It seemed to strike close to the base of the mast. There it remained, still visible, but not growing any larger for the moment. It must have hit in a clear section of deck, where there was nothing flammable to catch alight. The arrow would burn itself out and the ship would remain unharmed.

She cursed silently.

Another pinpoint briefly soared, then descended. This one travelled on a higher arc that seemed to end in the middle of the vessel's loosely furled sail.

And this time, it was seen by one of the slavers.

'What was that?' The blue-cloaked figure of the Storyman, who was sitting facing the ocean, suddenly sat up straight, pointing towards the ship.

Ruhl looked at him with idle curiosity. 'What?' he demanded. He was replete with good food and wine and not in the mood to be disturbed.

The Storyman continued pointing and the others turned, casually, to look at what he was indicating.

'It was a light,' he said. 'Looked like a falling star. And it came down on the ship. There's another!'

He added the last two words in a shout as a third fire arrow soared briefly across the cove. Even as it struck near the base of the mast, yellow flame suddenly flared in the sail, as Will's previous shot finally ignited the tarred canvas.

'Fire arrows!' the Iberian captain shouted. 'Someone's trying to burn *La Bruja*!'

Chairs crashed over backwards as the men leapt to their feet. The Iberian crew were the first to react, sprinting across the sand to save their ship. Another source of flame was visible at the base of the mast now, then a fourth point of light soared across the sky and struck the side of the hull.

The fires in the sail and at the base of the mast were burning steadily. But they were yet to attain the fierce, uncontrollable rage that would spell the end of the ship. An unbidden memory of her Iberian classes strayed into Maddie's mind as she watched.

'*La Bruja*. The witch,' she murmured. That was the name of the ship.

'Help us!' the Iberian captain stopped and yelled at the slavers, who were standing uncertainly by the table. He beckoned furiously with his arm, waving them to follow. Already his own crew had reached the ship and were dashing sea water on the flames at the base of the mast. The sail, gradually beginning to burn with more intensity, was out of their reach.

'If we lose the ship, we lose everything!' he shouted and that seemed to penetrate the stasis that gripped Ruhl and his men.

'Come on!' the Stealer shouted, and led them running down to the ship. The captain was yelling at his men, ordering them to let the yardarm with its burning sail fall, then smother the flames with buckets of water.

As they did, another fire arrow hissed down, landing in the bow of the ship, where coils of tarred rope were lying ready for use. The flame shot up, licking at the tar, melting it, then igniting it.

'Put that out!' the captain yelled at Ruhl and his men. His own crew almost had the burning sail under control. As Maddie watched, they heaved a still burning remnant over the side into the sea. There was an immense hiss and a cloud of steam. Realising that there was nobody paying any attention to the camp site, she darted out from the shadows and ran towards the mess tent with its abandoned table and overturned chairs. In her haste, she went to the wrong upright and had a moment of panic when she saw there were no keys hanging there. Then she re-oriented herself and saw them hanging on the next post. She seized them and turned towards the cave.

In the bow of the ship, the coil of rope had begun to burn fiercely, and the flames spread to a spare sail furled and stowed along the bulwark. Ruhl and his men beat at the flames with their jackets and cloaks. Unfamiliar with the layout of the ship, they didn't know where to lay their hands on the buckets that the sailors were using. The captain realised this and sent two of his men forward, laden with half a dozen buckets. The men began to hurl sea water on the flames, slowly bringing them under control.

Ruhl searched frantically for the source of the arrows.

'Who's shooting at us?' he screamed in fury. As he said the words, another arrow hissed down. But this wasn't a fire arrow. It was a war arrow and it buried itself in the chest of the man beside him.

The slaver staggered under the impact of the heavy shaft, then fell across the burning sail, extinguishing some of the flames. Ruhl looked around, in time to see another fire arrow arc up from the rocks. It was Will's final fire arrow, but there was no way the panicked men on the ship could know that.

'They're in the rocks at the base of the cliff!' Ruhl shouted, pointing to the spot where he'd seen that curving light begin. He felt the deck of the ship lurch under him and looked around to see the captain severing the anchor rope with a small axe. *La Bruja* began to move. Ruhl ran down the deck, grabbing the captain's arm.

'What are you doing? Are you mad?'

The captain glared at him. His face was smeared with ash from the burning sail and his arm was red and blistered where the flames had seared him as he had helped throw it overboard. He was in no mood to argue with Ruhl. He knew how quickly fire could claim his ship.

'I'm getting her out of danger. She's a sitting duck here and I'm not risking her!'

The ebbing tide was moving the ship faster and faster. Ruhl looked around in desperation.

'They're in the rocks!' he shouted. 'The archers are in the rocks! We can catch them!'

'Then do so! I'll leave two of my men with you.' The captain glanced down the deck, assessing his crew. 'Enrico! Anselmo! Go with Señor Ruhl!' He looked back at Jory Ruhl. 'You'd better go if you're going. We'll return tomorrow.'

Ruhl hesitated a moment, then came to a decision. He leapt over the bulwark, landing in waist-deep water, yelling at his men to follow. He heard a series of splashes behind him as he waded ashore. Glancing back, he saw his men and the two Iberian sailors forcing their way against the tide behind him.

He staggered onto dry sand, then stumbled, saving his life. An arrow sliced through the air just over his head. He looked at the rocks. He had no idea how many archers were hidden there but he realised that he and his men were armed with nothing but knives.

'Get your weapons!' he shouted as an arrow slammed into the upper arm of the man nearest him. The slaver cried out in pain, but it was a glancing blow and the arrow tore free. One of his companions quickly bound the flesh wound with his neck scarf.

'He's okay!' he called to Ruhl.

The Stealer nodded, then, crouching in an unwitting attempt to avoid further arrows, led his men up the beach to the camp.

Forty-seven

Maddie had reached the barred gate that closed the entrance to the cave. She was fumbling with the keys, searching for the correct one. Inside the cave, she heard a querulous voice cry out. Obviously, the prisoners thought the time had come for them to be taken to the ship. They could see only a dark, cloaked figure at the entrance. One of them began to cry.

'Quiet!' she hissed. 'It's all right! I'm here to help you. I –'

She became aware of running feet behind her and whirled around. Ruhl and his men were racing back up the sand towards her. For a moment, she thought she'd been discovered and she reached into her shot pouch to load her sling.

Then she heard Ruhl issuing a string of orders.

'Get your weapons! Brad, bring your crossbow! They're in the rocks at the base of the cliff. Spread out, use cover as much as you can!'

Maddie pressed herself against the dark rock face beside the gate. Inside, one of the children was still crying. She could hear another making soothing noises and trying to comfort his companion. She wished fervently that they'd both shut up. All she needed now was for Ruhl or one of his men to come and see what was happening.

The Stealer was still yelling orders and she turned back to the cave, hoping that the slavers wouldn't hear her above his shouting.

'Quiet!' she hissed again. 'Quiet or I'll come in there and whip you!'

She was reluctant to threaten the obviously terrified children that way, but it seemed to have the desired effect. The crying died away to a few desperate muffled sobs. She shrugged. She'd make it up to the unfortunate child later.

In the rocks at the base of the cliffs, Will had been studying his handiwork with grim satisfaction. The black ship was now halfway out of the bay, drifting on the outgoing tide while her reduced crew struggled to get a pair of oars in the water.

He'd had a moment of panic when Ruhl had led his men back to the tents. At the time, he feared that someone had spotted Maddie. Then he heard the slaver yelling orders and realised they were fetching their weapons before coming after him.

'Should have thought of that,' he muttered. It was one of those unforeseeable things that can spoil a plan. He hoped they hadn't caught Maddie napping. Then he saw the slavers heading back down the beach again, rushing from cover to cover.

He thought about whittling their numbers down a little but rejected the idea. If he made things too risky for them now, they might stay in cover close to the camp, and that would ruin Maddie's chances of getting the children out. He needed to let them reach the rocks, needed them to follow him as he led them away.

'Time enough to reduce their numbers tomorrow,' he said and began to make his way up the rough path to the clifftop.

Without thinking about it, he moved silently and swiftly, as he had practised for so many years. Then he realised that this wasn't the time for stealth. He wanted them to see him and to follow him. There was a small pile of rocks on the edge of the path and he nudged them over with his boot, sending them clattering and bouncing down the cliff face.

Ruhl heard the noise, looked up and saw the dark figure halfway up the cliff.

'There they go!' he yelled, pointing the way. Then he led a rush towards the base of the cliff. One of his men, armed with a crossbow, stopped and knelt down to aim. He aimed the weapon at the dark figure on the path and tripped the trigger.

Will heard the all too recognisable slamming sound of a crossbow releasing and dropped flat to the ground. A second later, the heavy quarrel buzzed overhead and screeched off the rocks, its iron point striking sparks where it hit.

The crossbowman stood. He had seen his target drop to the ground as he shot.

'I got him!' he yelled in triumph.

Ruhl snarled at him. 'You missed him, you fool! There he goes again!'

The dark figure was back on his feet, moving quickly to the crest of the cliff. As Ruhl urged his men on, the crossbowman paused to reload. He put his foot into the stirrup at the front of the short, stubby bow, and heaved back on the thick string with both arms. Will turned as he reached the top of the path. The crossbowman was in the open, straining at the heavy string on his weapon. Will hated crossbowmen. He nocked an arrow, drew back and released, sending a shaft flashing down the cliff face.

It struck the crossbowman full in the chest. He gave a shriek of pain, then staggered back and fell, dropping his weapon. Ruhl paused to take it from his lifeless hands, and dragged the quiver of short, heavy quarrels free. Then he glanced back up to the top of the cliff. But the dark figure, who had been briefly silhouetted when he turned to shoot, was gone.

'Come on!' he yelled, leading a renewed rush. 'There's only one man!'

As he ploughed up the path, it occurred to him that it might be only one man, but the casual ease with which he had picked off the crossbowman might prove to be a problem.

The lock on the gate was stiff and Maddie wrestled with it for what seemed like a lifetime before it suddenly sprang free. She dragged the gate open and was met by a chorus of frightened voices. In the darkness, she sensed rather than saw the children inching back — away from her.

'It's all right. I'm a friend. I'm here to help you.'

She tried to make her voice calm and reassuring. But the tension and excitement made it come out like a high-pitched, nervous shriek. She realised that they could only see her as a cloaked silhouette against the lights on the beach. She swung her cloak off and held her arms out.

'Look! I'm a girl! I'm a Ranger and I'm here to help you. Come on now.'

Her eyes were becoming accustomed to the darkness in the cave and she could make them out now — a group of dim shapes huddled together. One, a boy who was taller than the others, stepped forward suspiciously.

'You're not a Ranger. Girls aren't Rangers,' he said.

She took a deep breath. She wanted to grab his nose and drag him out of the cave. But she knew if she did that, she'd never get the rest of them moving. They'd huddle together and cry. She forced herself to be calm, forced her voice into a lower, more normal, register.

'Well, I am. My name's Maddie and I'm apprenticed to Will Treaty.'

There was a low murmur of recognition. Everyone had heard of Will Treaty. She realised the power of the name and invoked it again.

'Will wants you to come with me and go back up the cliff. He'll meet up with us tomorrow, after he's finished off the Stealer and his friends. Now come on.'

They hesitated still and she took the tall boy's arm. 'What's your name?' she asked.

'Tim. Tim Stoker.'

'Well, listen to me, Tim. I need you to help me. Take charge of the little ones and get them up that path. I'll bring up the rear to make sure no one follows us. All right?'

She made her voice as calm and reassuring as she could, looking steadily into his eyes. She saw his back straighten as he accepted the job she'd give him.

'All right,' he said. Then he turned to the others. 'Follow me, everyone. Do as the Ranger says. It's all right. She'll look after us.'

Nervously, reluctantly, they began to move out of the cave, the tall boy leading the way. Maddie stood to one side, ushering them out, pointing them towards the cliff path, shoving them gently on their way. Moving with a maddening lack of speed, they began to climb the rough track behind Tim Stoker.

The Storyman was a coward.

He was more than happy to frighten young children with tales of the Stealer in the Night, and the terrible things that would follow if they told their parents one word about him. But when it came to following a skilled archer up a dark cliff, that was another matter altogether.

He too had noticed the casual ease with which Will had brought down the man with the crossbow. He'd seen another gang member dropped cold on the deck of the ship, and a third spun around by an arrow through the arm. He wasn't going to chance that he'd be the next victim. It was one thing to terrify helpless children. Facing a skilled and determined warrior was another matter altogether.

He hesitated at the base of the cliff. He looked back uncertainly towards the camp, then narrowed his eyes. Something was moving on the path by the cave where the prisoners were confined. He strained his eyes and uttered a low curse. There was a line of figures wending their way up the path.

He turned back to alert his companions. But the nearest was halfway up the cliff, and Jory himself was already scrambling over the crest. He came to a decision. Let Jory and the others take care of the lone archer. He'd recapture the prisoners, who had somehow escaped.

He turned and began to run back towards the camp site.

Will saw the first figure come over the crest of the cliff, crouching low to avoid an arrow. He snorted disdainfully. If he wanted to, he could drop the man easily, crouching or not. But that wasn't his task at the moment. He had to lead them away to give Maddie a chance.

He started to run through the waist-high scrub. Then he stopped, grabbed a nearby bush and shook it violently, kicking at its lower branches to snap them.

Ruhl heard him. He looked in the direction of the sound and saw the dark figure moving away.

'This way!' the Stealer yelled, then added, 'Spread out! Don't make an easy target!'

Will nodded in satisfaction. He'd keep making noise and letting them see him until dawn. Then, when he'd led them far to the south, he'd start moving more cautiously and double back to meet Maddie.

Maddie heard feet pounding on the beach as the Storyman approached. She was a few metres from the cave, ready to intercept any pursuit. The last of the children was halfway to the first switchback, some five metres above the beach. She shrank back against the rough cliff face, pulling the cloak around her. She took a shot from her pouch and loaded it into the sling.

The Storyman burst into sight from behind the tents and ran past without seeing her, moving too fast for her to react. He plunged up the path after the children, eating up the distance with his long strides. They began to cry out in terror as they saw the frightening blue-cloaked figure chasing them. The last in line, a girl, tried to run and slipped on the loose shale. Then the Storyman was upon her, his cloak swirling around him like the wings of some evil night creature. He dragged her upright, shouting furiously at her. The girl cried in terror, held fast in his grip.

Maddie hesitated. If she threw now, the shot might well hit the girl.

'Didn't I tell you what would happen if you disobeyed? Didn't I? Didn't I?' The Storyman shook the girl violently and she screamed all the louder as her terror grew.

'Leave her alone! Let her go, you coward!'

The young voice cut through the Storyman's shouting and the girl's sobs. It was Tim Stoker, the tall boy Maddie had ordered to lead the way. He came plunging back down the cliff path now, shoving past the other children, sliding and slipping on the loose rocks. Off balance and unable to stop, he blundered awkwardly into the Storyman, who released the girl, throwing her back against the cliff face. He grabbed Tim's collar instead, reaching with his free hand to a draw a long-bladed knife from a boot sheath.

'Defy me, would you? Let's see how brave you are when I cut you, you little swine!'

His arm went back, preparing to bring the blade across the boy's throat in a long slashing movement. Maddie knew she had to risk a shot now. If she hesitated, Tim would die.

She whipped the sling over and forward. The lead ball caught the moonlight, glinting once as it flashed towards its target. Then it smashed home below the Storyman's raised right arm.

He gasped with the shock and the sudden, savage pain as the heavy lead ball splintered a rib. He dropped the knife and released his grip on Tim's collar. He drew in a breath to scream and the action caused him more agony as the jagged ends of the fractured rib grated together. He screamed even louder, clasping both hands to his shattered side. He turned, stumbled on the uneven footing, then realised that there was nothing but air beneath his right foot.

For a moment, he seemed to waver, tottering off balance as he slowly leaned further over the drop. Then he fell, landing with a sickening crunch on the rocks below.

Maddie was already moving up the path. She gently caught hold of the young girl and helped her to her feet.

'Come on, my dear one. You're safe now,' she said.

The little girl looked up at her, wide eyed. Then, slowly, a smile spread over her face as she realised that the terrifying Storyman was gone.

'I am. I'm safe now,' she repeated.

Maddie patted her shoulder and gently shoved her on her way up the cliff once more. The other children, who had been frozen in place, slowly began to move again.

'Faster!' Maddie urged, with an edge on her voice. 'You've got to move faster.'

She turned back to help Tim Stoker to his feet. He had been sprawled on the rocks when the Storyman had released him. His face was white with fear as he remembered how close he had come to dying.

'You're a brave boy,' she told him. It didn't occur to her that he was only a few years younger than she. 'Are you all right?'

He nodded, not trusting himself to speak, knowing his voice would quaver uncontrollably. She put a hand on his shoulder and urged him up the path after the others.

'Get moving, Tim. We have to get out of here.' She realised that it might help if she gave him a further task. 'Keep them moving. Get them to move faster. Can you do that for me?'

His eyes were huge, the fear still in them. Then he gradually brought himself under control and nodded.

'Wh-where's the Storyman?' he asked. He still wasn't sure what had happened. One moment he was staring at that long knife as it prepared to slash down at him. The next, he was sprawling on the rocky path. Maddie squeezed his shoulder reassuringly.

'You don't need to worry about him any more,' she said. 'He's dead.'

'Dead?' he repeated, wanting to be sure. She nodded emphatically.

'Stone dead,' she said, suddenly aware of the unintended irony. Tim studied her face for a few seconds, then turned away, starting up the cliff.

'I'll keep them moving,' he said. She watched him go and let out a long, pent-up breath. Then, just to make sure, she moved to the edge of the cliff and peered over.

The Storyman was a dark shape on the rocks below. His cloak fluttered in the breeze. He had landed on his back across an upthrusting rock and now his body was twisted at an unnatural angle. There was no sign of movement.

'Tell that in one of your stories,' she said savagely. Then she started up the path after the children.

Forty-eight

Maddie reached the top of the cliff path to find the ten former prisoners huddled together, waiting for her. She retrieved her bow from the long grass where she had left it earlier that evening. She shook her head at the thought of it. It seemed to be days since the time when she had started down the path, not hours.

'Let's move away from the cliff edge,' she said. She was conscious that, at any moment, Ruhl might give up his pursuit of Will and return to the camp to find his prisoners gone. There was no sense in standing against the skyline so that they could be seen from the beach.

The children shuffled a few metres away from the cliff, then stood in a half circle, watching her expectantly. There were six boys and four girls. She judged their ages to range from around ten to fourteen. She scanned their faces and saw a mixture of fear, bewilderment and relief. She took a few deep breaths. The adrenaline was still coursing through her veins following the encounter with the Storyman and she knew that when she was excited or tense, her voice tended to go up into a shrill register. She had the good sense to realise that would be anything but encouraging for the children watching her.

'All right,' she said, when she was sufficiently calm. 'Here's what's happening. You were captured by a slaving gang.'

'We were taken by the Stealer in the Night. He's a spook,' one of the younger girls corrected her. At the mention of the name, the others looked around nervously. Unconsciously, they moved closer together.

Maddie shook her head and continued in a patient tone. 'He's not a spook and you don't have to be frightened of him any more. He's just a man — but he is a very bad man and he's a slave trader. He was going to sell you all as slaves.'

'He said he was going to lock us away in a dark, dark dungeon and rats would eat our toes and ghouls would drink our blood in the night and he'd take out our eyes if we ever disobeyed him.' That was one of the younger boys. The others all mumbled agreement. Maddie made a calming gesture.

'He just said that to frighten you,' she told them. And it worked, she thought to herself. She paused, remembering the calming power of Will's name when she had used it earlier that evening. Fight a spirit with a legend, she thought.

'Now, tell me, how many of you have heard of Will Treaty?'

Ten hands raised in unison and, in spite of the gravity of the situation, she had to smile. *Everyone* had heard of Will Treaty.

'Well, Will Treaty is my master, and he's going to help us.'

Predictably, they all looked around to see where he was and she added, with a little asperity, 'He's not here now. He's gone to chase the Stealer and his men away.'

That wasn't exactly the way of it, she thought, but it was close enough for the moment. She decided the exact truth could stand a little colouring.

'And when he catches the Stealer, he's going to kill him,' she told them. That seemed to give them a certain amount of encouragement. They liked the idea of the famous Will Treaty killing the Stealer who had caused them so much pain and terror.

'How will he kill him?' asked the boy who had spoken earlier. She looked at him, realising that, being a boy, he wanted grim and gory details. But she didn't think the time was right for that.

'Never you mind. He'll find a way.'

'I hope he *hurts* him!' the boy said viciously. 'I hope he really, really hurts him.'

'I'm sure he will, and we'll ask him all about it when we see him,' she said. Then she clapped her hands together to get their attention away from the Stealer and his imminent, painful demise. 'Now!' she said briskly. 'We have to get moving. We can't stay here and we have to get to Ambleton as fast as we possibly can. The bigger ones can go on foot. But you smaller children can ride.'

She put her fingers in her mouth and gave out a low whistle. She heard a brief whinny in reply, then Tug and Bumper trotted out of the dark. She and Will had brought them forward earlier in the evening, sensing that some of the smaller children might need to ride.

Will had declined to take Tug with him.

'I'll want to let Ruhl keep me in sight when I'm leading him away. If I'm mounted, he'll give up. Or he'll realise I'm faking if I don't make a clean getaway. Better to leave both horses with you. They can help with the children.'

She assessed the group now, selecting the youngest of the children.

'You three,' she said, pointing to a boy and two girls who looked to be about ten years old. 'Do you want to ride on Will Treaty's famous horse, Tug?'

Tug rattled his mane and looked approvingly at her. *I always knew I liked you.*

But of course, Maddie didn't hear him. The three children stared round-eyed at the stocky grey and nodded their heads.

'Come on then.' She lifted the first girl to place her in the saddle. Then she had second thoughts. She set the girl down and moved to face Tug, searching her memory for the code phrase Will had told her so casually on the day she was given Bumper. Finally, it came to her.

'Do you mind?' she said softly. She hoped the phrase would be acceptable for a third party. Tug's intelligent eyes met hers. His head went up and down two or three times.

She had been pretty sure he wouldn't buck off a small child, but it paid to make certain.

She picked the girl up again and boosted her into the saddle. Maddie kept one hand on her arm as she looked warily at Tug.

'Don't do anything silly, will you?' she said. Tug turned his head to look her in the eyes. She could almost swear that if he could have raised an eyebrow, he would have.

But he didn't buck or plunge. Heartened, she picked up the second child, a boy this time, and lifted him onto the horse's back as well. Again, Tug stood steadily and she knew it was all right. She boosted the third child up. Even their combined weight was a light load for the hardy little horse, she knew. She nodded her thanks to Tug and moved to stand by Bumper.

'Do you want to ride this horse?' she asked another of the younger ones.

The little girl nodded, then asked, 'Whose famous horse is this?'

Bumper neighed. The sound was amazingly like a snigger. She thought quickly.

'Have you heard of Will Treaty's famous friend, Sir Horace, the Oakleaf Knight?'

The girl nodded.

'This is his horse.'

I most certainly am not! I wouldn't want a big lump like him riding me.

She moved closer to Bumper and whispered, 'Just go along with it, will you? And how do you know my dad is a big lump?'

He's a knight. They're all big lumps. But all right, hoist her up.

'Don't break her, all right?' She wasn't sure if Bumper needed to hear his code phrase as well but she said it anyway.

Oh really!

She lifted the little girl into the saddle and looked around for another small child. Tim Stoker raised a hand to catch her attention.

'Miss Maddie?'

She rolled her eyes. She felt positively ancient. 'Maddie will do, Tim. What is it?'

'Rob here has a bad leg. The Storyman burnt him with a hot iron.'

He indicated another boy, around his own age. Rob was shorter than Tim, and a little stockier. If he rode on Bumper, she wouldn't be able to put a third child on him as well. But she shrugged. The remaining children were all older and bigger. She gestured to Rob.

'Up you go then, Rob. Mind that leg.'

She helped him put his foot in the stirrup. His right leg, she saw now, was heavily bandaged. He swung gingerly up into the saddle, sitting behind the girl.

She turned to face the remaining five children.

'All right, we have to go now. And we have to go quickly. I know some of you aren't feeling well and you haven't been properly fed for days — or even weeks. But I want to ask this one effort from you. If you become too tired, let me know and you can ride one of the horses for a while. All right?'

Mutely, they all nodded.

'Then come on. We're going to jog for ten minutes, then walk for twenty. We've got a lot of ground to cover and we've got to do it as fast as possible. Ready? Let's go.'

She led the way, jogging steadily, with Bumper on her right and Tug on his far side. The children hesitated, then followed in a ragged formation. Their feet rustled and shuffled through the coarse grass. Then they reached the high road and the going was easier. They had been badly treated and ill fed, she knew. But they were children and she knew that children were usually fit. They'd manage. They'd have to manage. She was aware of someone beside her on her left. She looked around and saw Tim jogging there. He was frowning.

'Maddie?' he said, his voice jerky and staccato as his feet hit the road.

'What is it, Tim?'

'If Will Treaty is chasing the Stealer, why do we have to get away from here?'

She opened her mouth to answer, then hesitated, looking round. None of the others seemed to have heard his question.

'Just keep that thought to yourself, will you?' she said.

She saw the understanding dawning in his eyes. He nodded once, then dropped back to his former place.

The night wore on, and Will continued his game of cat and mouse with the slavers, letting them get closer to him, tantalising them with a quick sight of him, then moving quietly and surreptitiously away. It was a fine line to tread, keeping them on the hook without letting Ruhl know that he was doing so intentionally. But once the pattern was set and Ruhl accepted it, there was no risk that he'd give up the pursuit.

He recalled all he knew about Ruhl. In the days following Alyss's death, he had interviewed as many of his former victims as he could. And he'd interrogated the members of his gang that he'd caught.

He had built up a picture of a cruel, ruthless and pitiless man. Intelligent, but with a fatal flaw. He could not stand to be crossed or thwarted. If that ever happened, Ruhl would be overcome with a blind, unreasoning rage and desire for revenge.

'Much like I was,' he muttered to himself.

That rage would often cloud Ruhl's judgement and lead him to hasty, ill-considered decisions.

This was how Will believed that if he could spoil Ruhl's plan to get the children away, the slaver would pursue him unrelentingly and single-mindedly, intent only on revenge. And so it was proving.

As the dark hours slipped away, Will led the pursuit farther and farther south, knowing with grim satisfaction that Maddie was herding the children in the opposite direction as fast as their legs, and the two horses, could carry them.

He glanced at the sky to the east. The first vague fingers of light were stealing above the horizon. Here and there, an occasional bird began calling, predicting the coming dawn.

'Time to make myself scarce,' he said. Once daylight came, it would be more difficult, with the lack of real cover available in the area. He let himself be seen once more, hearing the shouts of his pursuers. Then he crouched, staying just below the long coarse grass, and turned hard to the right. He covered two hundred metres this way, then dropped to the ground, pulling the cloak around him. He drew the saxe from its sheath and held it ready, hearing the rustling blunder of the slavers off to his left. He'd done this so often before that he knew that they could pass within a few metres of him and never be aware of his presence. The only way they might discover him was if one of them chanced to tread on him. He gripped the saxe a little more firmly.

If that happened, it would be bad luck, slaver.

He listened as they trampled through the long grass and low bushes, passing him by. The nearest pursuer passed twenty metres away. He waited till the noise of their passage dwindled, then died. Then he rose, still in a crouch, and began to ghost his way back towards the north.

Forty-nine

awn was several hours behind them and the children
straggled wearily along the road. They walked with
heads down and lowered eyes, looking only at the next
metre of hard, dusty road that lay ahead of them.

Maddie had abandoned the attempt to alternate jogging and walking. They simply couldn't maintain that
pace and when she set them jogging, the weaker ones
dropped behind, until they were moving in a long, uneven
line that stretched for a hundred metres along the road.
And the longer they jogged, the longer that line became, as
the rearmost children dropped further and further behind.
Before long, she realised, without her on their heels to urge
them along, they'd begin to drop out and collapse by the
roadside.

Aware of the possibility of pursuit, she kept casting anxious eyes to the horizon in the south, looking for the first
sign of the slavers coming after them. Although she had
immense confidence in Will's ability to lead them away,

she was conscious of something he had told her over and over again during her training.

Any plan can go wrong, he'd say, *and most of them do, sooner or later. Always be prepared for things to go wrong. If they do, you'll be ready for them. If they don't, you'll be pleasantly surprised.*

It was because of the fear of pursuit that she wanted them close, where she could see them and protect them if danger approached.

So now they walked, trudging along, feet dragging. And she moved continually around the little group, urging the slower members on to greater efforts, pleading with them, cajoling them, threatening them — anything to keep them putting one foot in front of the other. She was tired herself, but she was too keyed up to notice the fact.

'Come on, Julia,' she said to one of the older girls for perhaps the hundredth time. 'If the little ones can keep going, so can you.'

Julia, predictably, burst into tears and stopped walking, head down, hands knuckling her streaming eyes.

'It's not fair,' she wailed. 'I want to ride. It's my turn to ride.'

Maddie had been alternating the riders, giving each child a turn to rest on horseback for fifteen minutes at a time. Julia, she knew, had been in the previous group and had dismounted, complaining about the fact, only five minutes previously. Her turn wouldn't come again for another twenty-five minutes at least.

Maddie glared at her. 'Keep moving,' she ordered.

Julia pouted. 'Why can't Rob walk? He's been riding the whole time. It's not fair.'

Maddie thought grimly that if she heard Julia utter the phrase *it's not fair* one more time, she would slap her. Rob was the boy with the burnt leg. He had offered to take his place among the walkers but he limped so badly and he was so slow that he held the entire group back. She had decided he should continue riding, while the other nine alternated places.

'Rob has a bad leg,' she pointed out.

Julia glared at her. 'Well, *both* my legs are sore so I want to ride too.'

Rob had overheard the exchange. Everyone had. He leaned down towards Maddie now.

'I'll walk for a while,' he said. 'She can take my place.'

Maddie looked up at him, her face grim. 'No, she can't,' she said firmly. 'There's nothing wrong with her legs. She's just being selfish.'

Julia sniffed. The tears were going to start again, Maddie thought. She moved closer to the girl and spoke in a low voice that only Julia could hear.

'See that mound over there, beyond the bush with purple leaves?' she said. Julia turned and looked at the spot she had indicated. The mound was nothing remarkable. It was just a small hillock. The girl nodded, frowning a little, wondering why Maddie had pointed it out.

'Well, that's an old burial mound. There are a lot of them in these parts.'

Julia's eyes widened at the words 'burial mound'. She looked at the mound, then back at Maddie.

'There are —' Maddie sought for a properly frightening word and remembered her conversation by the river at Danvers Crossing '— grave wights in there. You know what a grave wight is, don't you?'

Julia shook her head. She didn't know, but she didn't like the sound of the word.

'A wight is an evil spirit that lives in a grave. They have long teeth and terrible claws and they attack people passing by and drag them into the grave to become wights like themselves.'

Her imagination was taking wings now. So was Julia's. Her face was pale.

'But wights are afraid of one thing only . . .' She paused, then nodded her head towards Bumper and Tug. 'Horses. They can't stand to be around horses. So as long as Bumper and Tug are with us, we're safe.'

'Are you sure?' Julia found her voice at last. It was a very small voice.

Maddie nodded confidently. 'I'm positive,' she said. 'But here's the thing. If you don't stop whining and complaining and wanting special treatment, I'm going to leave you here on your own. And once the horses are out of sight, the grave wights will come out after you.'

Julia gave a mewling squeak of fear. Tears were flowing down her cheeks again. But these weren't the same as the previous self-pitying tears. Now she was genuinely fearful. Maddie sighed unhappily. She felt incredibly guilty at using scare tactics to keep Julia going and she despised herself for doing so.

I'm no better than the Storyman, she thought. But she was only young herself, barely a few years older than Julia, and she too was close to exhaustion. On top of that, she was at her wits' end to find a way to keep the other girl moving. Over the course of the morning, she had pleaded and cajoled and begged. But Julia was sunk deep in her own welter of self-pity and nothing Maddie had tried could motivate her. She saw that her scare tactics had finally got through and, reluctantly, she decided to continue. It could be a matter of saving the girl's life, after all.

'Now you'd better keep going,' she said. 'You'd better keep walking. And you'd better stop complaining. Or I'm going to leave you behind for the wights. Understand?'

Julia looked into Maddie's eyes. She could see no sign of pity there, only the harsh determination to do as she was threatening. Julia wiped her eyes with the back of her hands and nodded.

'Then GET MOVING!' Maddie roared at her.

Galvanised by the shout and the fear of grave wights, Julia stepped out smartly, overtaking the line of walking children and making her way to the very front. She kept looking repeatedly over her shoulder to the mound of earth, as if expecting to see spectral forms rising from it at any minute. But she kept walking, and with renewed energy.

The boy Tim had been an interested audience to this exchange between Maddie and Julia. He stepped closer to Maddie now. His eyes were red-rimmed with weariness and his face was caked with a thin layer of dust where it had settled on the perspiration, then dried. But in spite of that, he smiled.

'Grave wights and burial mounds?' he said softly. 'Looks like an ordinary old run-of-the-mill hill to me.'

Maddie shook her head wearily. 'She asked for it.'

Tim nodded. 'And she got it.'

It was an hour after dawn when Jory Ruhl realised he'd been duped.

There'd been no sighting of that cloaked, dark figure since well before first light. They had blundered on, heading south, looking for another glimpse of him. During the hours of darkness, these had come frequently enough, so that they could keep track of the direction he was taking. He had rarely been more than a hundred and fifty metres ahead of them, sometimes closer.

Now he had disappeared. There was open ground before them, covered with that ubiquitous long, coarse grass, and Ruhl could see for three kilometres. But there was no sign of the man they were pursuing.

Ruhl began to curse violently. The man had obviously given them the slip after that final sighting, encouraging them to keep hurrying south while he slipped away in another direction.

One of his henchman, the dark-cloaked man who had accompanied Ruhl on the raid at Willow Vale, hurried over.

'What's wrong?' he asked.

Ruhl turned on him furiously. 'That blasted archer has tricked us! He's led us on and then backtracked in another direction, curse him!'

The cloaked man looked around uncertainly. 'Are you sure?' he said, and instantly suffered the penalty for doubting Jory Ruhl. The Stealer swung his fist backhanded and struck the man, sending him staggering.

'Of course I'm not sure, you fool! If I was sure, I'd know where to find him!' he screamed, flecks of spittle flying from his lips. Instinctively, his follower backed away. He'd seen what Ruhl could do in a rage like this.

'All right, Jory, take it easy,' he pleaded, his hands up in a placating gesture. But Ruhl was beyond any calming down.

'Why am I surrounded by incompetents?' he demanded. 'Didn't any of you think he might have slipped away? Didn't anyone notice that we haven't seen hide nor hair of him for over an hour?'

Didn't you? the cloaked man thought. But he was wise enough not to voice the question.

Ruhl looked around his followers and realised one was missing. There was no sign of the Storyman.

'And where the blazes is Victor? I'll wager he's skived off to the camp and is sitting around drinking ale and doing nothing! That's just what the lazy swine would do! Typical of him! Typical of all of you, you useless bunch of incompetents.'

Nobody could tell him what had become of the Storyman, and Ruhl stormed up and down, screaming abuse and insults at his men, cursing them for not noticing his absence, and for not realising that their quarry had given them the slip. They had all seen how unpredictable Ruhl could be in this sort of mood. They all gave him room, moving away from him. And they all avoided making eye contact.

All except one — one of the Iberian sailors who had joined their group when *La Bruja* had slipped out on the ebbing tide. He stepped forward, meeting Jory's gaze steadily.

'*Jefe*, I think you may be right,' he said.

Ruhl turned on him with withering scorn. 'Oh, you do, do you? How very perceptive of you. And what do you propose to do about it?'

- 411 -

The man shrugged, ignoring the sarcasm and the rage. 'In my country, before I was sailor, I was hunter.'

'Well, let's give three cheers for you, you ignorant Iberian peasant!' Ruhl replied. He went to turn away angrily, but the man raised his voice a little and continued.

'I was a *perseguidor*, a —' he searched for the Araluan word, then found it '— a tracker. I could follow the tracks animals made.' He indicated his feet, then the ground below them. 'And men,' he added.

Ruhl's rage dissipated as quickly as it had begun. He turned back, looking at the man with narrowed eyes.

'Are you a good . . . *perseguidor*?' he asked carefully.

The man shrugged. 'I was the best in my province,' he said simply. 'I think I can find where this man has gone.'

Slowly, very slowly, a smile began to broaden over Ruhl's face.

The dark-cloaked man shook his head. The smile was possibly more unpleasant than the red-faced screaming, spitting bout of rage that had preceded it. Not for the first time, he found himself wondering about his leader's sudden changes of mood, the way he could go from screaming fury to total calm in a blink of an eye — and back again.

There was something very wrong in that mind, he thought.

Fifty

'**I**'m going to have to give them a real rest soon,' Maddie muttered to herself.

She'd just called a ten-minute break, and the children sank wearily and gratefully to the ground on the side of the road. Maddie helped Rob down from the saddle. He thanked her and limped to the roadside, sitting down carefully to avoid jolting his throbbing leg.

Even he was exhausted and he'd been riding the entire time. The others were silent, almost catatonic. For hours, they'd concentrated on placing one foot in front of another, until it seemed there was nothing else in their lives. Maddie went to unhook the water skin from Bumper's saddle. Suddenly, the effort seemed too much for her and she leaned her head against the black and white coat for a few precious seconds. Her legs ached. Her feet were sore. There was a blister forming on her right heel and, for the moment, she could go no further.

Why don't you ride for a while?

She looked up. Bumper had turned his head to look at her. His big brown eye was full of sympathy and concern for her wellbeing. She shook her head.

Can't. I have to keep going or they'll think they can stop.

Bumper trembled the skin and muscles of his shoulder, as horses do. To Maddie, it looked suspiciously like a shrug — and she knew horses couldn't shrug. Once again, she reached up for the water skin. It was less than half full by now, even though she had been doling it out as sparingly as she could manage since they'd been on the road. There was another skin hanging from Tug's saddle, but she'd used that first and it was virtually empty.

She took a swig of the lukewarm, leather-flavoured water, then slung the skin over her shoulder and began moving among the exhausted children, passing the skin to them, making sure that nobody took more than his or her fair share.

She'd just taken the skin back from one of the youngest girls when Tim Stoker, who was standing in the middle of the road, at its highest point, called softly to her.

'Maddie. Someone's coming.'

Her heart missed a beat and she hurried to stand beside him. He was shading his eyes with his right hand, peering away to the south, and she began searching in the same direction.

There was a figure just cresting the horizon. That would be the direction she could expect Ruhl and his gang to come from — if they had given up the chase after Will.

It would also be the direction from which she might expect Will. But she was conscious of his teaching — *always expect the worst and you won't be disappointed.*

She looked at the children. None of them, aside from Tim, showed any interest in the distant figure. They sat on the roadside, heads down, elbows cradled on knees.

They were at the end of their tether, she knew. If that figure in the distance was a forward scout, if Ruhl's men were just over the horizon, she would never get them moving fast enough to avoid recapture.

She scanned the horizon again. There was no sign of any other men following the first and hope began to grow in her heart. Nevertheless, she unslung her bow and eased the string in and out a few times to stretch her muscles. And she pushed back the flap in her cape that protected her arrows from bad weather.

'Who is it?' Tim asked.

She squinted, trying to see the figure more clearly. He was bare headed, she saw, and that wasn't a good sign. Will would normally have the cowl of his cloak up. Her hand moved in an automatic gesture and selected an arrow from her quiver, nocking it to the string of her bow with practised ease.

'I don't know,' she said. But as the figure came closer, she could make out more detail. He was carrying a massive longbow and she could see the fletching of a sheaf of arrows visible above his right shoulder. The knot that had formed in her stomach began to unravel and, as the figure stopped and waved, holding the longbow above his head, she started to laugh.

'It's Will,' she said, with a huge sense of relief. She called to the children. 'It's Will Treaty. He's here to take you home!'

Most of them were too exhausted to show any reaction. One or two looked up at the word 'home'. But Tim was grinning at her, the relief obvious on his face. He alone had been aware of her fear that they might be followed by the kidnappers and he shared her sense of relief as she recognised the figure striding towards them.

Maddie moved closer to Tim and put her arm around his thin shoulders. She shook her head and laughed again. Will was here and now everything was going to be all right.

'You've done well to get them this far,' Will told her approvingly.

She shrugged. 'I didn't think so. We've still got a long way to go.'

They had agreed to give the former captives a long rest, to help them regain some energy. They made a simple meal of flat bread, smoked meat and dried fruit, sharing it out among the hungry children and using up all their supplies in the process.

'We can always get more at Ambleton,' Will said.

Maddie sighed happily. She was delighted to be free of the responsibility of guiding the children to safety. Will was so capable, so experienced. Everything was all right now that he was here. She felt a huge burden lift from her shoulders as she turned the responsibility over to him.

'Are you sure Ruhl and his men aren't around?' she asked.

He shook his head. 'They're miles away. I doubled back on them just before daylight and cut across country to catch up to you. Last I saw of them, they were still chasing their tails and heading south.'

He bit off a tough piece of smoked meat and chewed it thoughtfully to soften it.

'Unless one of them's a tracker,' he added. 'But the way they were blundering around all night, I doubt there's anyone among them who could follow a trail. I had to keep showing myself to let them know where I was.'

Maddie settled back, the last trace of doubt wiped away by his confident statement.

'So we can take it easy?' she said. He regarded her for a few moments.

'We can take it a little easier,' he corrected her. 'It never pays to take too much for granted. We'll let the children rest for another hour, then get them moving again.'

'*Jefe!* Here! Here is where he doubled back!'

The Iberian was on one knee, studying the ground. He pointed to a line of almost invisible depressions in the long grass. Already the stalks were beginning to recover and stand upright once more. Ruhl could barely see the difference that the tracker's experienced eye had recognised. The Iberian reached forward to a scrubby bush, where a grey thread of cloth was snagged on a branch. In the dark, and confident that his departure had gone unnoticed, Will had been a little careless.

Ruhl smiled. It was not a pleasant sight.

'Well done, Enrico,' he said. 'Keep us after him and there'll be gold for you when we catch him.'

Enrico smiled in return, his teeth white against his olive skin. '*Sí, Jefe,*' he said. 'Enrico will find him. Just follow me.'

Ruhl waved an arm and his men fell into line behind him. Enrico quartered ahead of them like a hunting dog, bent double, studying the ground, following the almost invisible traces that their quarry had left behind. The man had made no attempt to cover his tracks, the *perseguidor* thought. Although in long grass like this, there was little he could have done. And only an expert tracker would have noticed the slight traces that he left.

For a moment, he lost the trail. Then he picked it up again. The man had angled off to the left. He waved to Ruhl.

'This way, *Jefe*. I have him!'

'Time to get them moving again,' Will said. They had rested by the side of the road for over an hour, eating and drinking. Maddie and Tim had refilled the water skins in a small stream that cut under the road through a culvert, and there was no need to ration the water any further.

If they stayed much longer, Will reasoned, with the heat of the day growing as the sun passed its zenith, they'd never get the children moving again.

As it was, there were grumbles and complaints as he and Maddie moved among them, rousing them and getting them back onto the road once more. As before, the smallest children and Rob rode on Tug and Bumper.

While they were assembling on the road, a young boy who was riding on Tug called out to Will.

'Will Treaty, did you kill the Stealer?' he wanted to know.

Will glanced at Maddie, a question in his eyes.

She shrugged. 'I told him you were going to. He's a bloodthirsty little wretch and he wants details.'

Will turned to the boy, looking up at him where he sat on Bumper's saddle, in front of Rob.

'Not yet,' he said, and, seeing the boy's disappointed face, added, 'But I plan to. Any day now.'

'Can I watch?'

Again Will looked sidelong at Maddie.

'I told you. He's a proper ghoul,' she said softly.

Will shook his head and looked back at the little boy. 'I don't think that would be appropriate. But I'll tell you all about it.'

'Oh . . . all right then.' The boy looked properly crestfallen.

Will shook his head, then called to the group assembled on the road. 'Come on, let's get moving! Pace it out there!'

Still dozy from napping in the warm sun, they began to shamble northward. Will strode to the head of the line, goosing the leaders with the tip of his bow.

'Come on! You can move faster than that! Shake it up! Get a move on! Show a little speed!'

Maddie smiled to herself. They were the same exhortations he had used on her when she was running the obstacle course back at Redmont Fief. And he'd poked her backside with his bow more than once, too. It was strangely pleasant to see other people suffering the same treatment.

But it was effective. The children gradually shook off their torpor and began to stride more purposefully down the road. Will moved along the line, repeating his demands for greater speed. There were still some who grumbled or complained. Predictably, Julia was the loudest.

'It's not fair,' she whined. 'My feet hurt. I've been walking all day and I've got a blister.'

She sniffed loudly and artfully wiped a tear away. But if she thought that Will would be more inclined to pity her because he was a male, she was mistaken.

'Dry your eyes, princess!' he stormed at her. 'No time for tears here. Or do you want me to leave you behind?'

By chance, they happened to be passing an area where there were more hillocks and humps in the surrounding ground, similar to the one Maddie had pointed out to her earlier. Julia took one look at them, went pale and accelerated, marching briskly to the head of the column and striding ahead of the leaders. Will was a little puzzled by her swift reaction. Maddie said nothing. She still felt guilty about the way she had frightened Julia and she thought Will might think less of her for doing so.

As the afternoon wore on, their initial speed and enthusiasm gradually drained away and Maddie and Will were kept busy urging them along, demanding greater speed.

'How long can we keep pushing them like this?' Maddie asked, as she and Will stood by the side of the road, watching the children file past. Once again, their heads were down and their shoulders were sagging. 'They look just about done in.'

Will shook his head. 'They've still got plenty in reserve,' he said. 'They're all farm children and they're used to hard work. Point is, they don't feel any urgency any more. There's no threat so they'll try to drag the chain to have an easier time of it.'

'Kids,' she said critically, shaking her head.

He looked at her, amused by her attitude. She was only

a year older than the oldest of them, he thought. She was really not much more than a kid herself. Yet she was showing levels of stamina and resolve and responsibility that did her credit.

It didn't occur to him that her behaviour was also a testament to the way he'd trained her and to her respect for him.

'Come on!' he roared. 'Get a move on, you lazy lot!'

Those nearest the two Rangers looked up sulkily. But the column began to move a little faster, led by Tim Stoker in the front rank. Will nodded towards him approvingly.

'He's a good kid,' he said and Maddie agreed.

'He was a big help before you turned up,' she said. 'He was the one who took on the Storyman when he caught up with us.'

She had told Will the bare facts of the confrontation with the Storyman but she hadn't gone into detail. She didn't want to dwell on the fact that she had killed him. Or on the savage pleasure she had felt at the time. Such feelings still made her vaguely uncomfortable.

'Maddie! Will Treaty!'

It was Rob, seated on Bumper. He had turned back when Will had yelled for greater speed. Now he was staring beyond the two Rangers, to the horizon in the south.

'What is it, Rob?' Maddie asked. But there had been a shrill note in his voice that made her fear the worst.

'Someone's coming,' he said.

Fifty-one

Rob had seen them first, from his slightly elevated position on Bumper's back. But within a few seconds, they were visible to Maddie and Will and the other children.

For the moment they were just dark figures against the skyline. Maddie tried to count them but as they moved she lost count. There seemed to be almost a dozen of them and they were coming from the south, bunched together on the road.

One of them was slightly in the lead and he waved the others on. Even from a distance, Maddie fancied that he was pointing to the small group ahead of them.

Frightened cries rang out among the children. They had thought they were safe. Worse, they had been assured they were safe. Now they were in danger again and they looked at Will and Maddie with distrust. They had no doubt who was following them.

'It's the Stealer!' one of them said and, as the words were spoken, the others whimpered in fear.

'You told us he was gone!' That was one of the older boys, and he shouted the words at Will.

The Ranger met his accusing eyes steadily.

'I thought he was,' he said evenly. 'Apparently I was wrong.' He turned back to watch the pursuing men, frowning as he concentrated his gaze on the man leading them, recalling how he had been crouched, peering at the road, when they had first seen the slavers.

'Seems I was wrong about them having a tracker too,' he said in an aside to Maddie. 'Looks like that fellow in the lead has been following our trail.'

Maddie looked at him, panic clutching at her throat. 'What do we do?' she said. Her voice threatened to betray her and rise into a high-pitched quaver. She fought against it, forcing herself to remain calm. Will reached out and took her wrist, squeezing it firmly. The contact calmed her down. She drew in a deep breath and looked him in the eyes.

'I'm all right,' she said.

Will nodded. 'Good. Now here's what you do. You run. Get these kids running as fast as they can. I'll stay here and hold off Ruhl and his thugs.'

She glanced fearfully around the open terrain that surrounded them.

'Here?' she said fearfully. 'You can't stop them here! You've got open ground on either side, with nothing to protect your flanks. They'll outflank you and kill you!'

He nodded approvingly at her assessment of the situation. 'Seems like you've learned a lot about judging terrain,' he said. 'But I'm not going to try to stop them. And I'm not planning to let them outflank me. I just want to slow them down — although maybe I'll be able to pick off a few of them. Then I'll fall back and do the same thing over again. And I'll keep doing it for as long as it takes for you to get away.'

As he was talking, he walked to where Tug was standing and unbuckled the arrow case hanging from his saddle. He took an extra dozen arrows and crammed them into his back quiver.

Tug snorted nervously. *I don't like this.*

'I'll be fine,' Will said softly. Maddie assumed he was talking to her to reassure her.

'Let me stay with you,' she said impulsively. 'Together, maybe we can hold them off.'

He shook his head. 'Together we'd still be outflanked. And it'd be twice as hard for two of us to slip away unseen. Besides, I need you to get the children to safety. If we leave them on their own, they'll give up after a few kilometres. You'll have to drive them, Maddie. Keep them running. Force them. Threaten them. Scream at them. But keep them running.'

He glanced up at the sky, noting the position of the sun, where it was beginning its slanting journey down in the west.

'It's a few hours till dark. If you're still ahead of them at sunset, look for a good hiding place off the road. Let them rest up for a while, then get them running again before daybreak.'

'But . . . what about their tracker? He'll be able to find us,' she said.

Will raised an eyebrow. 'When they get closer, he's going to be the first one I look for,' he said.

She looked fearfully at the dark figures on the road behind them. Already, she could see they were getting closer.

'They'll kill you,' she said miserably, tears welling in her eyes. Will shook his head.

'Nobody's done that yet,' he said. 'And a lot have tried. Now get going!'

He snapped the last three words at her, galvanising her into action. She reached out and touched his arm and he nodded to her. Then she turned away, yelling to the children.

'Come on! Run! Run for your lives!'

The children turned and began running. Inevitably, the oldest led the way, pulling away from the smaller children. Only one turned back. It was the small boy on Bumper's back, in front of Rob. He seized the reins and held Bumper still for a moment.

'Can I stay and watch Will Treaty kill the Stealer?' he asked.

'No! Now get going!' Maddie yelled at him. 'Run, Bumper! Run!'

Reluctantly, the boy released the reins and Bumper turned, trotting along the road, overtaking the children who had begun running already.

'At least someone's got faith in me,' Will said, with the ghost of a smile. He looked back to see Ruhl's men beginning to spread out in a long line, either side of the road. He nodded to himself. Maddie had been right. With open ground on either side, they would try to outflank him, and there was little he could do about it.

He counted them. There were eleven men in the line. Most of them were now waist-deep in the long grass. Two remained on the road itself. That would be Jory Ruhl and the tracker, he thought, wondering idly where the tracker had come from. Those two were still fully exposed on the road and for a moment he was tempted to try a long shot at Ruhl. After all, the slaver had no idea who he was facing and he wouldn't be expecting the sort of uncanny accuracy with which a Ranger could launch his arrows.

Then, reluctantly, he discarded the notion. His first order of business was to get rid of the tracker, to give Maddie and the children a better chance of escaping. His own personal revenge would have to wait — although not too long.

Calmly, unhurriedly, he drew an arrow from the quiver. He inspected it for flaws, although he knew there would be none, and nocked it to the string.

He turned side on, the massive longbow ready, but as yet undrawn, as he watched the small figures approaching on the road. The men on either side were making heavier weather of it, pushing through the waist-high grass, and Ruhl and his tracker had unintentionally got ahead of them. They were within long bowshot now, but Will waited a little longer. He rarely missed but he wanted to make sure of this shot. Mentally, he reviewed his actions. Draw, sight, release. Then, when he knew the shot was going to hit its target — and he could usually tell within the first few seconds — he would loose a second arrow at Ruhl.

'Come on,' he muttered. 'Just a few more metres.'

And then he was ready. The bow came up to the shooting position. He saw the sighting picture, which included the bow's elevation, the line of the arrow and the tiny target, hundreds of metres away. He felt his forefinger touch against the corner of his mouth as he drew back against the eighty-five-pound pull of the yew wood, felt the intense pressure of the thick string against the reinforced tips of his gloved fingers.

With a separate part of his mind, he saw the figure on the road stop, as if he sensed imminent danger. Too late.

He released and the arrow shot away from the bow. In the moment after releasing, he knew it was a good shot. His hand automatically found another arrow, nocked it. The bow came up and he switched his aim to Jory Ruhl, sighted and released again.

Ruhl became aware that he was ahead of the line of advancing men. He hesitated, calling to Enrico to stop. As he did, he heard a hissing sound, then an ugly thud.

Enrico cried out in surprise and pain and threw out both arms, staggering back under the impact of the speeding shaft. Then he crashed over on his back, his sightless eyes staring up at the sky.

In that split second, Ruhl realised that only one kind of archer could have pulled off that shot and he recognised the significance of the dark, cowled cloak the archer wore.

'A Ranger!' he yelled. And simultaneously, he realised that he would be the next target. He threw himself flat on the road, feeling and hearing the hiss of the arrow that passed just overhead to slam into the hard-packed surface behind him.

Clutching the crossbow to his body, he rolled down the camber of the road, into the long grass.

Will saw Ruhl drop flat to the road a split second before the arrow cleaved the air where he had been standing. He cursed bitterly. Ruhl had rolled off the road into the grass. There was no sign of him. But Will knew the shot had missed.

He looked out to the right. The men at the far end of the line were working their way out to get behind him, moving in a long arc that kept them at extreme bowshot range. On the left, the same thing was happening.

He pursed his lips thoughtfully. If he could put an arrow into one of them, that would lower the odds. Even if he missed and the arrow went close, it would slow the man down.

He drew, sighted and shot. The arrow arced away. A few seconds later, the slaver dropped into the waist-high grass and disappeared. Will had no idea whether or not he had hit him. He thought not. But now the man had to move on hands and knees, and he was unsighted. That should slow him down.

He swung smoothly to the left, drawing and nocking an arrow as he did so.

His target there was running, hoping that his speed and the distance between them would put Will's aim off. Will's lip curled slightly. He drew and shot. The two actions were almost casual, as if he had hardly taken aim. But as the arrow sped on its way, he knew it would hit its mark.

He lost sight of it eventually, then heard a brief cry and saw the slaver on the left of the line clutch both hands to his throat, then fall.

'That's two gone,' he said to himself. Then he saw movement on the right in his peripheral vision. The slaver there was up and running. But by the time Will had nocked another arrow, he had dropped prone in the grass again, disappearing from view.

Will frowned. The long grass was making shooting difficult. If they had been on clear ground, with the slaver hidden behind a log or a boulder, he could have tried a clout shot — aiming high into the sky to let the arrow plunge down almost vertically onto the target. But the featureless grass made it difficult to judge distance. And he'd never see the eventual spot that the arrow hit.

Some sixth sense warned him of danger and he turned back to the centre of the line, where three men were advancing at a run.

He snapped off an arrow, missed as the man he had targeted sidestepped unexpectedly. Almost immediately, he had another shaft on the way. This time there was a cry and the man stumbled back as the heavy arrow hit him. But then he rose again and came on. The shot had wounded him, no more.

There was no time to try again. The man out on the right was up and running and already he had bypassed Will's position. Will hesitated, glanced left and saw another had taken the left flanker's place. He too was running, then he dropped into the grass and was lost to sight.

'Time I wasn't here,' Will muttered. He looked north. Maddie and the children were disappearing over the distant skyline. They were several kilometres away, which gave him a little room to move.

He turned and ran full speed down the road, stopping after a hundred and fifty metres to play the game out again. He had a sinking feeling that it was a losing game, but he planned to spin it out as long as he could. And if he could infuriate Ruhl sufficiently, perhaps the slaver might forget about recapturing the children. His thirst for vengeance over Will might let them escape.

He stopped and turned to face the enemy. Three shots. One left, one right, one slightly left of middle.

The first two did no more than scare the out-flankers, sending them diving for cover once more. The third hit Ruhl's dark-cloaked henchman squarely in the neck. He stared wide eyed at the feathered shaft that protruded below his chin, looked at Ruhl, cowering in the long grass, and tried to speak.

The only sound he could make was a choking gurgle. Then his legs collapsed under him and he crashed to the earth.

Will saw him fall.

I'm improving the odds, he thought. But I'm not doing it fast enough.

They were running left and right now, but before he could react, they had gone to ground in the long grass again. The men in the middle of the line were advancing more slowly, staying low and under cover. But things were getting out of hand as the men on either end of the extended line moved past Will's position. He had to pin them down. His hand brushed the feathered ends of the arrows in his quiver as he assessed how many he had left. There were about a dozen, maybe one or two more.

He decided it might be time to sacrifice accuracy for volume. The left flankers were up again and he loosed three arrows at them in rapid succession. Then he spun on his heel and let another three go in the general direction of the men on the right flank. By chance, one of them came to his feet just as the first arrow thudded into the ground, several metres from him. He promptly dropped back into cover, shouting a warning to his companions. Will checked the left flank again. The sudden rapid volley had had the desired effect. The men there were nervous about committing themselves again too soon.

He nodded, satisfied. 'Time to move,' he said and took off running down the road again.

Cowering in the long grass at the side of the road, Jory Ruhl looked at the still body of his henchman. They had been together for two years now, and if Ruhl could be said to have a friend, this man had been one. Looking at the grey-shafted arrow lodged in his throat, Ruhl tried to remember how many the Ranger had shot so far. He had been shooting at a prodigious rate. Sooner or later, he must run out of arrows.

Staying down and out of sight, he yelled to those around him.

'I want that man alive! Don't kill him. Take him alive!'

Fifty-two

The sun had sunk below the western horizon and dusk was rolling across the landscape.

Maddie plodded on, herding the children ahead of her. She had long ago given up the attempt to keep them running. They couldn't manage it. She laughed sardonically as she had the thought. *She* couldn't manage it, let alone them.

She looked up, counting them. She had developed a morbid fear that one of them would drop out, falling onto the long grass beside the road, and she would not notice. They were all here, she thought. Then she hesitated. Had she counted ten, or nine?

Her mind was playing tricks on her, she realised. She was too exhausted to think straight. And if she was in such a bad way, how were the children managing? She recalled Will's words: *If you're still ahead of them at sunset, look for a good hiding place off the road.*

Easier said than done, she thought. Where could they

hide in this open country? She turned and looked down the road behind them. There was no sign of any pursuit. Neither was there any sign of Will. Her eyes filled with tears as she remembered how she had left him to face Ruhl and his men alone.

'I should have stayed with you,' she said softly, even though she knew he would never have allowed her to do so. In her mind's eye, she could see the slavers spreading out in a long line to encircle Will, possibly waiting till his supply of arrows was exhausted then moving in and killing him.

Or would it be as simple as that, she wondered. From what the children had told her, Jory Ruhl was capable of savage acts of vengeance against those he thought had thwarted him. And Will had certainly done that.

Possibly they had tortured him before killing him. Maybe they were still doing so.

She looked to her left and saw the low line of cliffs she had noticed when they had first passed this way. She stopped, trying to force her mind to think clearly. She had noticed something about those cliffs, but what was it? It had to do with Will's instruction to her — something about hiding. She realised she was swaying with exhaustion. The children had stopped too. Several of them sank to the road and fell instantly asleep on the hard-packed earth and fine gravel. Tug and Bumper halted in place, looking at her curiously for instructions.

The cliffs. Hiding after sunset. What was it? Then she remembered. She had seen what looked like caves at the base of the cliffs. Caves and tumbled rocks where they could hide and find shelter and rest for the night. In the dark, they'd be invisible from the road if Ruhl and his men passed by.

Suddenly, she was re-energised and she strode among the children, shaking and prodding those who had lain down.

'Get up! Wake up! We've got to get off the road!' she shouted at them. Predictably, Julia had been one of those to collapse and fall asleep. She whined now as Maddie poked her behind with the tip of her bow.

'Stop it! That hurts! Leave me alone!'

'It'll hurt more if I use an arrow,' Maddie told her grimly. 'Now get up!' She emphasised the order by kicking Julia lightly in the side of the knee — not enough to injure her, just enough to cause pain. Julia howled in protest. But she clambered to her feet, as did the others.

Maddie pointed to the line of cliffs. 'There are caves over there and we can spend the night in them,' she said. 'You can sleep all you want once we get there. But for now you have to make one last effort. Now come on!'

She started off the road and they shambled after her. Suddenly mindful that Ruhl's tracker might still be alive, she stopped them. Ten of them walking one behind the other would leave an unmistakable trail through the grass, visible even in the dark.

'Spread out,' she told them. 'Don't all walk behind me. Spread out to the sides.'

They obeyed numbly. The promise that they could soon rest lifted them for one last effort and they pushed their way through the grass towards the dark line of cliffs, stumbling, occasionally falling full length, but managing somehow to keep going.

At last, they reached the shelter of the tumbled rocks at the foot of the cliffs. Maddie had picked out one opening in the cliff face — a large hole that promised to open into a sizeable cave. But it turned out to be nothing more than a shallow depression, no more than two metres deep. She had a moment of panic. What if all the cave entrances proved to be like this one? She tried another and was equally disappointed. The cave was barely four metres deep and very narrow. There wasn't enough room for ten children, two horses and an exhausted apprentice Ranger.

She inspected another three with similar results. Oddly enough, it was one of the smaller holes that proved to be the right choice. It was little more than a narrow slit in the cliff face, just over two metres high. But inside, it opened into a wide, high space. The floor was covered in soft sand and there was room for all of them. Bumper and Tug had a difficult time squeezing through the entrance, but they made it. Maddie looked around, satisfied. There was even a chance that pursuers, if there were any, having checked the larger caves, would ignore this insignificant opening altogether.

'I'm sorry we've got nothing to eat,' she said. Then she realised she was talking to herself. Her companions weren't interested in food. They had each picked a spot and they were lying sprawled on the sand, sleeping the sleep of the totally exhausted.

'I suppose I should set a watch,' she said, knowing there was nobody to keep it but herself. Bumper snorted at her. *Sleep. We'll warn you if anyone's coming.*

'I suppose you will,' she said. She took off her cloak, folded it and used it as a pillow. She lay back on the sand

and sighed contentedly. Before the sigh had died away, she was asleep.

There were no more arrows.

Will watched as the men who encircled him began to move closer, gradually becoming bolder as they realised that he wasn't shooting — that he had nothing left to shoot.

He shook his head hopelessly. He'd played the game out as long as he could, hoping to give Maddie enough time to get away. Now it was over, ending the way he had known it would. They had outflanked him, then begun to close in from all sides. He'd kept them at bay as long as he could, snapping off shots at them whenever he saw a chance to do so. And now there were eight men surrounding him, slowly moving in. Two of them had arrow wounds, but they were still capable of fighting. All he had left were his saxe and his throwing knife.

He slipped his bow into the leather loop at the back of his boot and bent forward, using his body and back muscles to unstring it. He'd crafted the bow himself and it was one of the best he had ever made. Somehow, he didn't want such a fine weapon to fall into the slavers' hands. He tossed it away, into the long grass.

Ruhl was facing him, barely fifteen metres away. He could make out the man's features in the gathering dusk, could see the anger there, and the hatred.

Come a little closer, Jory, he thought. His hand hovered over the throwing knife in its scabbard. The men around him all carried spears and one of them had a crossbow trained on him. Ruhl, aware of his own limitations as a marksman, had passed it over to him. His own favoured long-distance weapon was the javelin, and he had three of the light spears in a leather tube on his back. A sword was in his hand as he moved closer.

Just another step, Will thought. His muscles tensed as he prepared to draw the throwing knife and send it spinning into Ruhl's heart.

He heard a slight noise behind him. Something flicked past his eyes and suddenly a noose of rope tightened round his arms, pinning them at the elbows. He turned, furious that he had waited too long and the chance to kill Ruhl was gone.

The Stealer laughed, guessing what was going through Will's mind.

'Good work, Anselmo,' he said.

The Iberian quickly dropped more loops of the rope around Will's arms, pulling them tight. 'You killed my friend,' he snarled, as he moved around in front of Will, thrusting his bearded face close to the Ranger's.

Will raised one eyebrow sardonically. 'Glad to hear it,' he said. 'Pity I missed you.'

Without warning, Anselmo jerked his head forward and butted Will in the face. Will staggered, unable to regain balance with his arms pinioned, and fell awkwardly. Ruhl stepped forward quickly, aiming a kick at him as he lay helpless. Then he reached down, grabbed the front of his jerkin and hauled him roughly to his feet. They confronted each other for several seconds.

'And I'm doubly sorry I missed you,' Will said.

Ruhl's face contorted in anger and he drew back his fist

to hit Will. The Ranger faced him calmly, waiting for the blow. But Ruhl hesitated, frowning as he stared at the bearded face before him.

'I know you,' he said. He searched his memory, trying to recall where he had seen that face before. A recollection came to him. He'd been on a boat — a punt — slipping away from a river bank. And this man had been facing him, barely five metres away.

'You're Treaty,' he said softly. Then, with mounting anger, he continued. 'You're the one who killed or captured my men. You hounded us across the country and destroyed my business. Now you're trying to do it again. What have I ever done to you, for pity's sake?'

'You killed my wife,' Will told him. His voice was emotionless, but his eyes were cold as stone.

Ruhl nodded his head, remembering, understanding.

'Yes. The Courier, wasn't she? Well, actually, as I recall, she did it to herself. Ran back into that burning inn and got herself trapped, silly girl. I didn't do it. She did.'

'You were responsible,' Will said.

Ruhl tilted his head, considering the accusation. 'Well, I suppose some people might put it that way. But it's all water under the bridge now, isn't it? Or should I say, smoke over the inn?'

He laughed. He studied Will carefully, looking for signs of an explosion of rage. Instead, he saw only icy hatred in those brown eyes.

'I'm going to kill you, Ruhl. I thought you should know.'

Ruhl smiled at him, shaking his head. 'It's good of you to warn me, but I don't think you are.' He gestured at the rope wound around Will's arms and body. 'After all, you're a little helpless, aren't you?'

'I'll manage. Believe me,' Will told him. But again, the Stealer shook his head mockingly.

'I believe you want to. I believe you would if I gave you the chance. But I'm not going to do that. I'm going to do something else entirely.'

He gestured to the Iberian who had secured Will. 'Tie him up properly, Anselmo. Make sure he can't get away. Then bring him back to camp.'

He waited as the sailor expertly trussed Will, securing his arms and wrists, and tying his ankles together, leaving a short length of rope between them so that the Ranger could only hobble awkwardly. Will tried the knots, testing the strength of his arms and wrists against them. But the rope was new and the Iberian sailor knew his business. Will couldn't budge them a centimetre.

Ruhl stood back, watching the process with a satisfied smile. Then, as Will stood silently, he moved closer again.

'Don't you want to know what I plan to do to you?' he asked.

Will shrugged. 'Not really.'

'Well, I'll tell you anyway. In memory of your lovely wife, I think I'll burn you to death.'

Fifty-three

Bumper's low rumble brought Maddie awake.

She had slept for two hours — a deep, satisfying sleep — and she felt refreshed and revitalised. But the warning sound from Bumper reached through the veils of sleep and alerted her conscious mind. She came awake with a start, feeling a sudden rush of alarm.

Bumper and Tug were both facing towards the narrow entrance to the cave. Their ears were pricked and Bumper's chest and shoulder muscles were trembling in warning spasms. They had heard or sensed something.

She rose, patted them both and whispered to them to relax. Then she moved to the entrance and peered carefully round the edge. She could see or hear nobody nearby. Emboldened, she slipped outside and moved towards a large rock, dropping behind it as she surveyed the surrounding terrain.

There were two men on the road. They were a little past the spot where she had led the children off the highway and towards the caves, so they had obviously seen no sign that she had done so. She blessed her sudden instinct to have the children spread out. Even a non-tracker would have seen the deep swathe they would have cut through the grass if they'd moved in a tight-knit group.

She had no doubt who the men might be and her heart sank. If they had come this far, it meant that Will had been taken. He never would have let them pass otherwise. He was probably lying dead somewhere back along the road. Her eyes filled with tears but she shook them away, angrily. If that were the case, she wanted to know. She wanted to be sure. And if he were dead, she would take her revenge on Ruhl and his gang — starting with the two on the road.

They had paused uncertainly, looking up the road to the north, seeing no sign of the fugitives. She could just hear the dim mutter of their voices. They looked around the surrounding area and she forced herself to remain still. Movement could give away her position. As it was, she was just another dark mound among the rocks.

The men's voices were raised as they began to argue. She still couldn't make out the words but the gestures and body language were unmistakable. One of them kept gesturing to the north. Obviously, he thought they should continue. The other threw up his arms in disgust and turned back to the south, beginning to retrace his steps.

His companion shouted angrily at him. Then, with a shrug of resignation, he followed suit. They were still arguing as they headed back towards Hawkshead Bay.

Maddie waited until they were out of sight, then hurried back inside the cave. She hesitated, weighing her choices. All her instincts were telling her to go after Will, to see if he was alive and if he needed help. But if she did, she would be deserting the children.

She paced the sand floor of the cave for several minutes, torn by indecision. She knew Will would tell her that her responsibility lay with the children. But she couldn't bring herself to agree. This was Will, her godfather, her mentor. She thought about the hours they had spent together in the woods around Redmont, the hours of calm, patient instruction and his quiet pleasure when she succeeded in a task he had set her. And she knew she couldn't desert him. Even if he were dead, she had to know what had become of him — and if she abandoned him now, she might never find out.

Her decision made, she looked around for Tim Stoker and saw him sleeping soundly by the wall of the cave. She moved to him, dropped to one knee and shook his shoulder gently. His eyes flew wide open and she could see the instant alarm in them.

'It's all right,' she said. 'It's Maddie.'

The panic in him died down and he knuckled his eyes drowsily.

'What time is it?' he asked.

Maddie shrugged. She had no idea of the exact time.

'It's still night,' she said. 'I want you to take charge here. I'm going back to find Will.'

'What's happened to him?' he asked. The tension was back in his body and it was evident in his voice.

She shook her head. 'I don't know. He may have been taken by the Stealer.' She didn't say *he may have been killed*. She feared that saying it might make it real.

Tim looked around at the sleeping children. The cave was dim and quiet, with only the occasional murmuring of one of the former captives as they tossed in their sleep.

'Should I wake them up?' he asked but again she shook her head.

'Let them sleep. Go back to sleep yourself. You're safe here. I'll be back for you tomorrow, when I've found Will.'

He nodded uncertainly. He felt safe and protected while she was around. Without her, he knew they were all vulnerable.

She patted his shoulder encouragingly. 'Just relax. You'll be fine.'

'If you say so,' he replied. But his voice told her that he didn't really believe it.

She donned her cloak and checked her weapons, then led both horses out through the narrow opening. She left them unsaddled. It was easier for them to negotiate the narrow split in the rock face that way. Once in the open, she saddled them both.

She knotted Tug's reins around his neck so they wouldn't hang down to trip him, then swung up into Bumper's saddle.

'Follow, Tug,' she ordered and the little grey tossed his head obediently. She touched Bumper with her heels and cantered slowly across the open ground to the road. She rode up onto the raised surface and looked to the south. There was no sign of the two men but she didn't want to come upon them unexpectedly so she held Bumper down to a walk, moving along in their tracks.

They had been moving for twenty minutes when she caught sight of moonlight glinting on something in the long grass by the side of the road. She dismounted and walked down the camber to check. It was Will's bow. The stray beam had caught the waxed surface of the wood or she never would have seen it. Her spirits fell. Ruhl and his men had obviously caught up with him here. Probably, as she had surmised earlier, he had exhausted his supply of arrows and tossed the bow to one side so that they wouldn't have it. She picked it up, turning it over in her hands, sadly running her finger along the smooth surface of the wood. She looked around but there was no sign of his body and she began to feel a ray of hope.

Perhaps they had taken him prisoner. Perhaps he was still alive.

She ran back to the horses, cramming Will's bow into the arrow case behind Tug's saddle, and mounted Bumper. She unslung her own bow and made sure the flap in her cloak that covered her arrows was open. She didn't care now if she caught up to the two kidnappers on the road ahead of her. In fact, she found she was hoping that she would.

She nudged Bumper forward and he responded instantly, striding out in a full gallop so that he fairly flew along the road, his hooves barely seeming to make contact with the hard-packed surface. Tug, with no rider to burden him, kept pace easily, a couple of metres behind and to the side.

Overhead, the moon beamed its light down on them, so that the road seemed like a pale ribbon running through the grass. The two little horses pounded on, striding in perfect unison so that they sounded like one horse running, not two.

Five minutes later, she crested a small hill and saw the two slavers ahead of them.

The hill had masked the drumming hoofbeats but now the men heard them and turned in panic to face her. They were two hundred metres away and she urged Bumper to greater speed, dropping the reins on his neck and guiding him with her knees, reaching behind her for an arrow.

The man on the right had a crossbow. He raised it, aiming at her. She waited a second or two, letting his aim steady, then nudged Bumper, urging him left, then a second later, right again.

The double shift of direction did the trick. The man panicked, overcorrected and jerked at the trigger lever too quickly as he tried to keep her in his sights. She heard the quarrel buzz past on the left like an angry hornet. Then she rose in her stirrups, drawing back the arrow. She touched Bumper lightly with her right knee and he crabbed a little to the right, as he had been trained, leaving her with a clear shot straight ahead.

At eighty metres, she released, waiting for the split second when Bumper's four feet were all clear of the ground. The bow thrummed and she saw the arrow speed away to its mark. The crossbowman was straining to re-cock his weapon when the arrow struck him. He dropped the crossbow and staggered a few paces, before falling face down on the road.

His companion looked at him in horror. Then he began to run towards her, his arm drawing back the throwing spear that he carried.

Calmly, without haste, she reloaded and shot again. Her bow was lighter than Will's and didn't have the same staggering hitting power. But the man dropped the spear and stopped in his tracks, staring in horror at the arrow in his side. He clutched the wound and fell to his knees, doubled over. He was sobbing in pain as Maddie swept past him at full gallop, leaving him behind in a swirl of dust.

She didn't draw rein until she was three hundred metres from the clifftops at Hawkshead Bay. Then she eased the horses down to a trot, edging off the road so their hoofbeats were muffled by the thick grass. At a hundred metres' distance, she swung down from the saddle while Bumper was still moving. Signalling to the two horses to stand fast, she crouched low and ran to the edge of the cliff, dropping to hands and knees in the last few metres, creeping forward, fearful of what she might see.

Fifty-four

Will was tied to a thick stake, set firmly in the coarse sand of the beach.

The stake had been one of the supports for the mess tent, but Ruhl had his men uproot it, then replant it deep in the sand, inland from the tents. Will's hands had been dragged behind the stake and tied securely there. His feet had been tied together at the ankles, then secured to the bottom of the pole. Finally, a third rope had been looped round his throat and the pole, keeping him standing upright.

Around his feet, and reaching as high as his knees, the slavers had placed a vast stack of brushwood. It was already tinder dry, but Ruhl had soaked it in oil to make sure it would burn instantly, and fiercely. The throat-closing smell of the oil reached Will's nostrils, making him want to cough. He resisted the urge, not wishing to give Ruhl any satisfaction.

He had been tied here for several hours and his hands and feet were numb. Again and again, Will had tried to force the ropes apart, trying to stretch the fibres, or find some give in the knots themselves. But it was a futile effort. He tried once again, but he couldn't feel his hands any more. If the ropes weren't loosened soon and the circulation restored to his hands and feet, he thought, he'd lose fingers and toes, or even the hands themselves.

Then he shrugged. Losing fingers was going to be the least of his worries.

Further down the beach, about twenty metres away, Ruhl and his remaining men were seated round the camp fire, passing a flagon of Iberian brandy from hand to hand. As Will watched, the Stealer took a long swig, then placed the flagon to one side.

He rose, a little unsteadily, then stooped and took a flaming brand from the fire.

Weaving slightly, Ruhl made his way up the beach to where Will stood, trapped against the stake, unable to move. Will felt his stomach clench. This would be the third time Ruhl carried out the charade of pretending to light the fire around him.

On the previous two occasions, he had taunted Will, placing the flaming torch a few centimetres from the stacked firewood, then pulling it back again at the last minute. Then he would repeat the action, so that Will never knew when his last moments were about to come.

Would this be the time he would go ahead with his threat?

Now Ruhl stood before his captive, unsteady on his feet, his face flushed with the effect of the alcohol. He leaned forward, peering at the bearded face before him, trying to see some sign of fear, some plea for mercy.

'Well, Treaty, is this the time? Are you about to go to meet your lovely wife once more? What do you say?'

He dipped the flaming end of the brand close to the piled oil-soaked wood. Will stared straight ahead, resisting the almost overwhelming temptation to watch as the flames wavered, inches away from the stacked branches.

'How about it, Treaty? Are you going to ask me for mercy? If you do, I might give you an easy end. Just a quick sword thrust and you won't have to worry about these flames.'

The burning brand waved in front of Will's face, so close that he could feel its heat against his eyes, feel his beard and eyebrows beginning to singe.

'Nothing to say? You'll make plenty of noise in a minute, when I drop this torch in the fire . . . whoops!'

He let the torch drop, clumsily catching it again just before it fell into the stacked firewood. Will felt his stomach heave with fear. But he showed no sign of it.

'That was a near-run thing, wasn't it, Treaty?' Ruhl sneered. He rolled his eyes and waved the torch above the firewood once more, making a mocking sing-song noise.

'Get on with it, Jory. Kill him and make an end of it. Stop taunting the man.'

One of the slavers had turned from the camp fire to watch Ruhl's performance. He had seen him tormenting the Ranger twice before, and seen that the bearded man showed no sign of fear. He felt a grudging respect for him and, in inverse proportion, a diminishing regard for his leader. Ruhl was enjoying himself too much, he thought.

Killing an enemy was one thing, but continuing to taunt and sneer and pretend, then pulling back at the last minute, showed a level of malice that even a hardened criminal couldn't stomach.

But Ruhl now turned on his underling in a fury.

'You don't tell me what to do, Anders!' he shouted, his voice rising to a high-pitched level just short of hysteria. He strode angrily back down the beach to the camp fire, tossing the flaming branch to one side as he went, and confronting the man who had challenged him. He stood over the man, shouting abuse at him. Will heaved a sigh of relief and sagged a little against the cruel bonds that held him.

'He's my prisoner!' Ruhl shouted. 'I want to hear him beg! I want him to plead for mercy! And I will hear him do it and you will shut up. Or you will join him. Do . . . you . . . understand?'

The man shifted back. He was at a disadvantage, sitting while Ruhl stood over him. He knew Ruhl was more than capable of carrying out the threat he had just made. But he'd worked for the Stealer for some months now, and he also knew that if he showed weakness, it could prove fatal. Ruhl preyed on weakness. Besides, he doubted that his companions would back Ruhl up and tie him to the stake with the Ranger.

'It's not going to happen, Jory, that's all. As I say, kill him and be done with it.'

'I'll kill him when I am ready to kill him,' Ruhl said, speaking with exaggerated precision and care. 'And not when some third-rate cutpurse like you tells me to. Understand?'

Anders nodded. He'd shown enough defiance, he thought. 'Whatever you say, Jory,' he muttered. Ruhl reached past him for the flagon and sat down heavily, his back to the prisoner tied to the stake. He didn't see Will sag with relief as his death was postponed yet again.

And he didn't notice that one of the shapeless rock outcrops that studded the beach behind Will had moved several metres closer to the Ranger while he was berating his henchman.

Maddie's heart thumped against her ribs. She could hear it pounding and she wondered how it was not audible to those on the beach.

She'd taken in the situation in the camp, then crept silently down the cliff path to the beach, close by the cave entrance. From there, she had moved stealthily from one large rock to another, dropping into cover as she reached each one. It was a blessing that the beach was so littered with large rocks, and that Ruhl had elected to place the stake and the fire so far up the beach, and not further down, in the clearer ground past the camp fire. She'd watched the Stealer as he taunted Will and she realised that the man was insane — dangerously insane.

Sooner or later, he would carry out his threat and set fire to the piled brushwood around Will's knees. And she sensed that it would be sooner. If he moved towards Will again, she believed that the time for threats would be over. Will would never give in and beg, she knew. And she sensed that Ruhl knew it as well by now. Next time he left the fire, Will would die. She was huddled on the beach now, a shapeless mass under her cloak, and only a few metres behind Will. Cautiously, she raised a corner of her cowl. The gang — what remained of them — were sitting round the fire drinking again. They were staring into the flames, which she knew would ruin their night vision. Emboldened by the realisation, she crept forward, a few centimetres at a time to avoid making noise, until she was directly behind Will. Crouched low, hidden by the pile of firewood, she drew her saxe and sliced quickly through the rope around his legs.

She felt him tense as the rope fell away and she stood slowly, staying concealed behind him.

'It's me. Maddie,' she breathed. 'Hold on a moment and I'll have you free.'

Will groaned softly, trying to suppress the noise. His arms and legs had been constricted by the tight bonds for hours. As the blood rushed back to his numb legs and feet, it was sheer agony. Then the saxe sliced through the rope binding his hands, and the rope around his throat.

His hands and forearms also felt the unbearable stabbing pain of returning circulation and he sagged against the stake, unable to maintain his balance and letting out a louder groan of agony. This time, the men around the fire heard him. One of them stood up.

'What was that?'

He saw Will lurch a pace away from the stake, then clutch his arms around it as he desperately tried to regain his balance.

'It's the Ranger! He's loose!'

Pandemonium broke out as they grabbed for their weapons and scrambled to their feet. Maddie dropped the saxe to one side and hastily unwound her sling from her waist, loading a shot into the pouch.

Initially, blinded by the bright flames they'd been staring into, none of Ruhl's men noticed the dark shape behind Will. But as Maddie stepped clear to one side, her loaded sling swinging gently behind her, they saw her and hesitated.

'Who's that?'

'There's someone with him!'

Only Ruhl reacted immediately. He pointed to the two figures beside the stake.

'Get them! Kill them!'

But as he said the words, Maddie's first shot smashed into one of his men.

Studying the tableau from the top of the cliff, she had noticed that two of them wore boiled-leather breastplates and she doubted that her bow would have the power to punch through them. Accordingly, she had elected to use the sling, leaving the bow and quiver behind for the awkward climb down the cliff. Now, she realised she had made the right choice.

The lead ball, travelling with tremendous force, smashed into the leather breastplate just below the man's heart, bending and deforming the leather, driving a huge dent into it. The ball didn't penetrate, but the shock of the impact did. It was transmitted directly and virtually undiminished to the slaver's body. Two ribs caved in and a huge bruise began to form immediately. His heart faltered, picked up again. The man gave a strangled cry and fell to the ground, knees drawn up, trying to breathe, and feeling knives of pain slice into his ribs as he did.

The slaver beside him barely had time to look at his comrade in horror before Maddie's second shot hit him on the right shoulder, shattering the large bones there, smashing the joint beyond any possibility of repair and sending him reeling. Faint with pain, he sank to his knees, doubled over, then toppled onto his side, keening softly.

The other three kidnappers looked in shock at their companions, seeing them struck down by some terrible, unseen force out of the darkness. They exchanged a glance, then turned and ran, dropping their weapons behind them.

Maddie let them go, searching for Jory Ruhl. She'd taken the others first, as they were armed and, so far, Ruhl had done nothing but scream orders. Now she saw him, stooping to retrieve something close by the fire. He stood upright and she realised he was holding a short javelin. But he wasn't looking at her. His gaze was fixed on Will, as he slumped against the stake, arms and legs cramping terribly, unable to move.

Ruhl's right arm went back, then started to come forward. Maddie leapt to Will's side and shoved him out of the path of the weapon. He fell with a startled cry across the stack of firewood. Maddie's hand went to her shot pouch, moving with the smooth, automatic precision that came from constant practice. She was loading a ball into the sling when she felt a terrible impact against her right hip — an impact that drove her back several paces, and was followed by a searing burst of agony down her upper leg.

She looked down and saw that Ruhl's short javelin had transfixed her thigh, just below the hip. She felt a moment of disbelief.

'I've been hit,' she said incredulously. She had never expected such a thing to happen. But it had.

The evil, barbed head was buried deep in her thigh and she felt the leg give way under her, unable to bear her weight. Blood was coursing down her leg and she fell, causing more agony as the shaft of the javelin jarred against the ground. Grinding her teeth against the pain, she fought the waves of nausea that threatened to overcome her. Tears streamed from her eyes with the pain and shock and she felt herself slipping away. She couldn't breathe. The awful trauma of the terrible wound seemed to have paralysed her lungs.

Her vision began to fail, until it seemed she was watching events through a long, narrow tunnel, with darkness on all sides. She saw Ruhl stooping to pick up another flaming brand from the fire. Then he started up the beach towards Will. She tried to call to her mentor, but no sound came. Tried to reach out to him, even though he was metres away and beyond her reach.

And then the world turned red, then black.

And there was nothing any more.

Fifty-five

Will lay awkwardly on the stacked firewood. He tried to rise, but the branches shifted and gave way beneath his hand and he floundered awkwardly.

He could see Ruhl approaching. The flaming branch in his hand lit his face with a demonic glow and Will could see the contorted expression, where hate and revenge were mixed in equal proportions. In another minute, he would hurl that flaming branch into the fire and Will would be enveloped in the flames.

He cursed the savage, crippling cramps in his arms and legs that restricted his movement so badly. He tried to rise again and failed once more. But he managed to crawl away a little, so that he was on the edge of the stacked timber. His right hand clawed at the sand as he scrabbled to drag himself clear and it closed over a familiar shape.

It was the hilt of Maddie's saxe, lying on the sand where she had dropped it minutes before. Clumsily, he reversed the knife so he was holding it by the blade. Ruhl was only metres away, the flames on the brand licking angrily, ready to incinerate Will.

Awkwardly, gritting his teeth against the cramping pain, Will threw the saxe.

As it left his hand, he knew it was the worst throw he had ever made. Impeded by the cramping of his stiff muscles, he flicked it clumsily, without the precise control that he normally would put into such a throw. It struck Ruhl – he was too close for the throw to miss – but it struck him hilt first, hitting him on the forehead above his right eye.

The blow was painful, but in no way lethal. The heavy brass pommel cut his eyebrow and blood trickled down into his eye. Instinctively, Ruhl flinched away, and trod on a branch that had rolled clear of the stacked firewood.

It was an uneven branch, bent and twisted halfway along its length, so that it turned and rolled awkwardly under his foot. He stumbled backwards, then tried to recover, throwing his weight forward.

But, distracted by the blood in his eye, he overcompensated and lost his footing. He found himself falling forward, towards the pile of oil-drenched firewood stacked around the stake. The loosely stacked branches gave way under him as he hit them and at that instant, he realised that he still had the flaming branch in his hand, and that it was underneath him.

There was a second's pause as he scrabbled for a handhold in the shifting branches. Then the firewood ignited with an explosive *WHOOF!*

Ruhl screamed as the flames shot up, enveloping him instantly, catching his clothes and hair. He struggled to rise again but the stacked branches collapsed further, defeating his efforts. He tried to scream again but the burning air and flames scorched his throat and lungs and he made a terrible, inhuman grunting noise.

Will, on the far side of the fire, felt the flames licking eagerly towards him. Instinctively, he avoided Ruhl's mistake of trying to find purchase among the shifting, moving branches. Desperately, he rolled sideways, clear of the flames. As he felt the sand underneath him, he continued to roll, moving farther and farther away. His face was burnt. His eyebrows were singed away and his beard and hair were badly frizzled. But he was clear. And feeling was returning to his arms and legs. Painfully, he dragged himself further away from the fire, his horrified gaze fixed on the twisting, jerking, blackened form in the middle of the flames. He tried to shut out the awful grunting, gagging sounds that were coming from it.

Then, at last, they stopped.

Will pushed himself up to a sitting position, his pain-spasming legs stretched out in front of him. Gradually, the cramps were becoming less and less severe. But he still could only move clumsily. Now that he had time to think, he wondered dully where Maddie had gone. He remembered that she had shoved him aside, out of the path of Ruhl's javelin. But he hadn't seen what had become of her. Odd, he thought, that she hadn't tried to help him escape the fire. He twisted his head, looking around for her.

'Maddie?' he said, his voice no more than a croak. Then he saw the dark figure crumpled on the beach a few metres away.

He shoved himself to his feet, fighting against the suddenly recurring cramps that stabbed his muscles as he moved too quickly, and lurched towards her, a huge, inarticulate cry of pain and rage and sorrow coming from his throat and echoing off the cliff face.

He dropped to his knees and felt his heart stop as he saw the cruel javelin buried in her thigh. Sheets of blood had soaked her clothes, looking black under the moonlight. Her face was deathly white and she had lost an inordinate amount of blood. He knew there was a major artery in the thigh, but he thought it was on the inside, and the blood was seeping out, not pumping and spraying as it would with a severed artery. He shuffled forward on his knees and put his fingers to her throat, feeling for a pulse.

There was none.

Again, he let out that terrible, heart-torn cry of pain and sorrow.

He felt a slight flutter under his questing fingers. Then the pulse began to beat. Faintly, weakly. But there. Maddie was alive and his heart surged with relief.

Then it lurched again, this time from fear. She was alive. But she was badly injured and she had lost a lot of blood. She was still losing it, and he had no medical supplies, no bandages, no way of staunching the flow. He had to remove the javelin from the wound. But he knew that as soon as he did, she would lose blood twice as fast as she was now.

He thought of the medical pack that he carried among his saddle bags and looked up at the cliffs above him.

'I hope you brought the horses, girl,' he said. He let out a piercing whistle.

Ten seconds passed, then he heard an anxious whinny. Looking up, he saw Bumper and Tug peering over the crest of the cliff at him. He lurched to his feet, holding up a hand to stop them coming further.

'Stay,' he ordered. He knew they would never manage that rough, rock-strewn path down. He would have to carry Maddie up to them. His brain began working, planning coherently now. Ruhl had taken his saxe and throwing knife when he was captured and he remembered seeing the slaver toss them down beside the camp fire. He was going to need them. He turned, wincing as cramp hit him again. It seemed that if he moved incautiously, stretched a muscle or turned the wrong way, the cramps would strike without warning. But they were becoming less and less savage the more he kept moving and kept the blood supply flowing back to his muscles. He limped down the beach to the camp fire, trying to ignore the terrible stench of burning flesh that came from the fire round the stake. It was dying down now, and he could see the blackened, deformed shape in the pile of embers. He shook his head and turned away, searching for his knives. He found them and buckled on the belt and scabbard, then limped painfully back up the beach to Maddie.

He drew his saxe and cut a metre-long strip from the hem of her cloak. He tied it round and round her thigh, above and below the head of the javelin, pulling it as tight as possible, then tying it off firmly to staunch the steady flow of blood.

He sat back on his heels, frowning at the metre-and-a-half-long shaft of the javelin. He couldn't move her with that still in place. But he didn't want to pull it free from the wound until he had his medical kit to hand. He'd have to break it off short, he realised, even though doing so would undoubtedly cause Maddie intense pain. He took several deep breaths, then seized the shaft in both hands, jerking his left hand down quickly and powerfully, holding the short end as steady as he could with his right.

The shaft broke with a loud snap. Maddie screamed once, then fell silent again. He studied her face. Pale as a ghost. But her eyelids fluttered. She was still alive.

He knelt on one knee and pulled her up to a sitting position. Then he bent forward and, grabbing her belt, heaved her up over his right shoulder, her head hanging down his back, her feet in front of him. He took a long, deep breath, knowing what was coming, then surged to his feet, using the big muscles in his thighs and calves to lift her.

Searing cramps hit him immediately, his thigh muscles knotting in agony as they took the strain. He bellowed in pain, his cry echoed by Maddie's involuntary scream as he moved her. He stood with her over his shoulder, swaying uncertainly. Then he took a step towards the base of the cliffs, waiting to see if the pain would surge through his tortured muscle again. It didn't, so he took another step. This time, one thigh muscle cramped and he gasped in agony, then forced himself to take another step. Then another.

He found it helped if he gave vent to the pain, so he screamed as he staggered across the beach and up the uncertain footing of the path. He stumbled and slipped and slid but somehow he remained on his feet. And with every third step, he yelled as loud as he could.

He made it past the two switchbacks, knowing that if he looked up and saw how far he had to go, he would never make it. So he kept his eyes down on the treacherous rocks and shale that threatened to trip him and send him sprawling. One foot in front of the other, yelling to dispel the pain in his thigh muscles. Another foot. Slip and recover. Then go on. Another step. Another stumble. Keep going. *Keep going!* Now he was yelling the two words instead of just bellowing with pain. He heard Tug's encouraging whinny and it sounded much closer than he expected it to be.

Then his lowered eyes saw the top of the path, and the long grass that grew along the clifftop, and he realised he had made it. Instantly Tug was alongside him, whinnying and neighing softly. He gripped the saddle to support himself and guided the little horse to a clear spot, where he laid Maddie down. He removed her cloak and rolled it under her head as a pillow. Then he hunted around the area, chopping dry branches from a stunted bush, finding other dry branches that had blown on the wind, and built a small fire.

His movements were much freer now, although an incautious action could still trigger cramping again and his muscles ached from the aftereffect of the cramp. It was similar to a severe bruise, he thought. He found the medical pack and unrolled it, preparing a long bandage roll and the small pot of the special wound salve that all Rangers carried. He threaded a needle with silk thread and laid it down on the spread-out canvas roll. Once he started, he would have to move quickly, removing the javelin head from the wound, anointing it with the healing salve, then sewing the lips of the wound together. Finally, he would wind the bandage round and round her upper leg, keeping it tight enough to stem the flow of blood from the wound, but not so tight that it would restrict the healing flow of blood through the injured limb. Recent events had taught him only too well of the disastrous consequences if he shut off the blood flow entirely.

Once he was ready to begin, he moved quickly and positively. He cut the blood-soaked leggings away with his saxe, exposing the bare skin around the wound.

His throwing knife was resting tip first in the hot coals of the fire. Years ago, the healer named Malcolm had told him that this would destroy the tiny malignant organisms that could penetrate the wound and cause infection. He waited till it glowed red hot, then removed it, waving it in the air to let it cool. With his left hand, he loosened the makeshift bandage around Maddie's thigh, unwinding it gently and watching as the blood began to seep out once more. He seized the shortened shaft of the javelin and tugged gently, hoping against hope that it might slide clear. But the barb caught in the flesh inside the wound and held it. Maddie stirred, crying out in pain. He gritted his teeth and slid the throwing knife into the wound, keeping it in contact with the javelin's head, sliding it down until he could feel where the barb was caught, then carefully working it around to free the barb.

The javelin moved several centimetres. Maddie cried out in pain once more. He stopped, wiped the perspiration from his brow with his left hand, then went back to work, using the knife blade to shield the barb and stop it catching again. Slowly the javelin head slid clear of the wound, although, inevitably, it caused damage on the way out. As it came out, a gush of red blood followed it. Will hurled the javelin to one side, then mopped at the wound with a clean cloth. He smeared the salve onto a pad of cotton and thrust it into the wound, working it around to spread the healing ointment in all directions. Then he pinched the lips of the wound together and went to work with the needle and silk thread. Maddie flinched and cried out each time he punched the needle through her skin. He shook his head helplessly.

'Sorry, my girl. But it has to be done,' he muttered.

He drew the last stitch tight, then quickly bound round and round the upper leg with the bandage he had prepared. The blood was still seeping slowly from the wound and it stained the first few layers of bandage red, then pink. But the flow had slowed considerably, till it was little more than a trickle. The stitches and the bandage contained it, and the wound salve was inside the injury, ready to work its healing way.

Just as long as Maddie could survive the shock of the wound, and his subsequent ministrations.

She was barely breathing. Her pulse was light, like the heartbeat of a tiny bird. He knelt beside her, holding her hand, head bowed. The horses stood over the pair of them, watching with concern in their big, compassionate eyes. Tug could feel Will's worry. Bumper could feel Maddie's pain.

'Don't die, Maddie. Don't die. Please don't die. I can't lose you too. Please don't die.'

He repeated the words over and over like a manic litany as he kept watch over the stricken girl.

She saved my life, he thought. How can I face Horace and Evanlyn if I let her die? Then he went back to his mumbled plea, over and over again.

'Don't die, Maddie. Don't die, Maddie. Please don't die.'

But there was nothing more he could do for her, he knew. He could only wait, and repeat that exhortation over and over again. He looked at that pale face — far too pale, he thought — and in his exhaustion it turned into Alyss's face, lying still and lifeless. Then his vision cleared and he knew it was Maddie and he felt she was slipping away and his heart was a giant pit of sorrow inside his chest. He couldn't bear the idea of losing her, not after she'd healed the black pain of his losing the love of his life.

'Don't die, Maddie. Don't die, Maddie. Please don't die, Maddie.'

The words ran together and tumbled over one another until they became a meaningless blur. But still she lay there, white faced. Will had seen death many times before, on a dozen different battlefields, and he knew that this was how it looked.

Dawn began to streak the eastern sky over the sea. He could hear birds moving and calling, fluttering through the low bushes and long grass, rustling the branches and leaves as they hunted unwary insects. The day was a normal day, just like the day before. But it would always be different because he would remember this day as the day he lost Maddie.

'I'm hungry. What's for breakfast?' she said.

His head jerked up and he looked at her. Her eyes were open and she was smiling at him. It was a weak smile, but a smile nonetheless. He felt his heart lurch wildly inside his chest, with hope and relief and joy.

'What's for breakfast?' he repeated numbly. 'After all that you've put me through, that's all you can say?'

She shrugged, then winced as the movement caused her pain.

'What can I tell you? I'm my father's daughter.'

He began to laugh. And somewhere, the laughter turned to tears and he was sobbing uncontrollably — immense sobs that racked his entire body and floods of tears that coursed down his cheeks. And he knew the tears were the ones he had never been able to shed for Alyss. They were for her. And they were for Maddie. And they were for him.

Most of all for him.

And as the sun rose behind him, he remained bent over Maddie, sobbing, the tears falling onto her cheeks below him until she patted his hand awkwardly and comforted him.

'It's all right, Will. It's all right now.'

It was full daylight when Tim Stoker found them. He had left the cave to come in search of them. He had found the bodies of the two men Maddie had overtaken the night before and equipped himself with the spear that one of them had dropped.

He stood before them, armed with the oversized weapon that was way too large for him.

'Will Treaty,' he said, 'is Ranger Maddie all right?' He was doubtful because, if she was, he had no idea why the bearded Ranger would be leaning over her, weeping softly.

Will looked up at the worried young face and smiled. It occurred to him that he hadn't smiled — really smiled — in a long, long time.

'She's fine. Who are you?'

'I'm Tim. So can you take us home now?'

Epilogue

Six months later

Gilan folded the parchment and placed it back in a leather folder. He looked up at the assembled faces, the sea of grey and green cloaks that surrounded him. There was an eagerness about them all, he could see. The Gathering was nearly over for this year and it was almost time for the feasting and tale telling and singing that would mark the end of the assembly.

'That's just about all the appointments and promotions for this year,' he said, and an expectant buzz ran through the assembled Rangers.

'But before we get to the feasting —' he indicated the long table set out under the trees, laden with food and drink '— there is one more item of business.'

Another buzz ran through the group, this one not quite so expectant. It had more of a sense of *what now?* about it. He held up his hands apologetically.

'It's only going to take a few minutes,' he said, 'then you can all get busy stuffing yourself with too much food.'

A small ripple of amusement ran through them and they settled back. They knew Gilan wasn't one of those speakers who would say, 'I'll keep this short,' and then drone on for an hour or more.

'And it has to do with the reason why our two honoured guests are here with us today,' he added, nodding in the direction of Cassandra and Horace, seated at the front of the group.

That caused a stir of interest. The assembled Rangers had wondered why the crown princess and the champion knight of the realm had arrived earlier that morning for the final day of the Gathering. It was highly unusual for outsiders to be included — even royal outsiders. Heads turned to study the couple. Cassandra smiled graciously. Horace flushed and lowered his head. He still wasn't at home with public appearances.

'As you know,' Gilan went on, 'when the Corps takes on an apprentice, that title is given as a courtesy until the satisfactory completion of the first twelve months of training. At that point, the bronze oakleaf is awarded and the title Ranger's apprentice becomes official.'

They nodded. They all knew that.

'But today, we have among us a first-year apprentice who, after only nine months of training, has already proved worthy of the official title and the award of the bronze oakleaf. She is also, coincidentally, our first female recruit and has proved that the right girl is more than capable of serving in our Corps and carrying out all the duties expected of a Ranger.'

Now, *that* got a reaction. Most of them had heard rumours that a girl had been recruited, although they had no idea who had been appointed as her mentor. Gilan and Halt had decided that it might be best not to let out information about Maddie, in case the experiment didn't work out.

Some of the Rangers seated at the rear of the audience stood and peered around, hoping to get a view of the first female Ranger. But of course Maddie was sitting with her cowl up and was indistinguishable from all the other cowled figures around her.

'In the course of the last nine months, she has passed every test set by her mentor — an extremely hard judge, if I might say — and has introduced a new weapon to the Corps. I suggest you might ask her to demonstrate this when the official side of things is over.'

'Which will be when?' a lugubrious voice called from the middle of the crowd and everyone laughed.

Gilan nodded good-naturedly in the direction of the speaker. 'Not long to go. But to continue. Not only has this recruit shown her ability in training, she has proved her worth and her courage in the field as well. Six months ago, she undertook a mission with Will Treaty — whose name you may be familiar with — to break up a slaving ring on the east coast and return ten kidnapped children to their homes.'

Now more and more heads were turning, seeking the whereabouts of the new Ranger.

'And in the process,' Gilan continued, 'she saved Will's life. Something that has been done by very few people in the past.' He nodded towards a silver-haired figure in the third row. 'Halt is one of those, of course. And the other two are the girl's parents . . .'

He paused dramatically. There was a lot of the ham about Gilan. 'And they are . . . Princess Cassandra and Sir Horace, the Oakleaf Knight, the Sunrise Warrior and champion knight of the realm.'

Now the Rangers were all on their feet, understanding why Cassandra and Horace were present, wanting to see this girl who had done so much in such a short time. Someone in the rear ranks began to clap, then they were all applauding, and shouting out to Gilan.

'Let's see her!'

'Where is she?'

Gilan smiled and beckoned to Maddie. She rose, throwing back the cowl of her cloak, and made her way to the podium where he stood. She was still limping slightly, he noticed. She would probably have that limp for the rest of her life.

As she turned to face the members of the Corps, the clapping changed to cheering and whistling. She looked around the sea of faces, picking out some she knew. Will, of course, had both fingers in his mouth and was emitting a piercing whistle, and contriving to grin hugely at the same time. Halt was standing, nodding slightly and smiling. For Halt, that was the equivalent of bugles and drums. Lady Pauline was also present, a concession to Halt's prestige and position as a senior figure in the Corps. She was whistling as well, Maddie saw with surprise.

As for her mother and father, they were beaming with pride. Maddie waved coyly to them and was shocked when her mother suddenly leapt to her feet and pumped her fist in the air, emitting a cry that sounded something like:

'Wooph! Wooph! Wooph!'

Horace stared at his wife, somewhat nonplussed. She grinned at him and pumped her fist even harder.

'Wooph! Wooph! Wooph!'

'Congratulations, Maddie. How does it feel to be a pioneer?' Gilan said softly in her ear.

She felt him placing the chain over her head. She reached up and took the bronze oaklcaf pendant between finger and thumb, holding it out so she could see it. Her eyes misted with tears of pride.

'And now let's eat!' Gilan shouted, and the cheering redoubled.

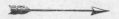

They had feasted. They had laughed. They had drunk toasts to fallen members of the Corps — Liam among those named. They had sung, concluding with the traditional Ranger song that ended every gathering — *Cabin in the Trees*. Maddie joined in on the song, thinking how appropriate it was to the Ranger life, thinking of the little cabin she had shared with Will for the past nine months.

Now she stood in a small circle of those closest to her: Cassandra and Horace, Halt and Pauline, Gilan and, of course, Will. She kept reaching up and touching the tiny bronze oakleaf around her neck. Gilan and Will understood how she felt. They had shared that sense of disbelief and joy when they had been awarded their oakleaves, bronze and silver.

Horace enveloped his daughter in a bear hug. 'I'm proud of you,' he said. 'So proud.'

There was a catch in his voice and, when he released her, he turned away so that the others wouldn't see him wiping away a tear. She patted his shoulder.

Then her mother hugged her as well. But when she released her, Cassandra produced a rolled parchment from within her sleeve. 'This is for you,' she said and handed it to Maddie.

The new Ranger's apprentice looked at it curiously. It looked very official, she thought.

'What is it?'

Cassandra smiled at her. 'It's your reinstatement. Officially, you are once again a royal princess of Araluen. You've earned it,' she added.

Maddie hesitated, looking quickly at Will. He looked away. This was her decision and he wasn't going to influence her.

'Well, that's wonderful, and I'm very grateful. Very grateful indeed . . . but . . . could it wait a while?' she said.

Her mother looked at her, confused. 'Wait a while? What for? You've proved you're worthy of it. You don't have to do any more. It's time for you to come home.'

'But . . . I'd rather finish my training as a Ranger,' Maddie blurted out.

Halt and Gilan turned away to hide their grins. Cassandra glared accusingly at Will.

'This is your fault!' she shouted at him. 'I might have known it!' She turned back to Maddie. 'But that'll be another four years!' she said, her voice rising in disbelief and anguish.

Maddie nodded, chewing her lip nervously. 'It'll be over before you know it,' she said. 'And I'll visit you often.'

Cassandra, for one of the rare times in her life, was speechless. She looked around the faces of the group. Suddenly, she had a sense of *déjà vu* as her memory took her back to a day many years ago. She was a young girl, standing on a balcony at Castle Araluen, Horace beside her, as they watched Will riding away with Halt. He had just chosen life as a Ranger over life at the Araluen royal court. Now it was happening again.

'I've been here before,' she finally managed to say.

Horace nodded, knowing what she was thinking. 'And I told you then, Rangers are different from the rest of us. I was right then. And I'm right now.'

Cassandra opened her mouth and shut it again several times. Finally, she appealed to Horace, whose strength and common sense had supported her on so many occasions through their life.

'What should I say?' she asked.

He smiled at her, then at Maddie.

'Say yes,' he told her.

Also available from

JOHN FLANAGAN:

ARE YOU READY TO GO INTO BATTLE?

THE OUTCASTS

Turn over for a preview of book one —
Brotherband: The Outcasts . . .

CHAPTER ONE

Twelve years prior

*W*olfwind emerged from the pre-dawn sea mist like a wraith slowly taking physical form.

With her sail furled and the yardarm lowered to the deck, and propelled by only four of her oars, the wolfship glided slowly towards the beach. The four rowers wielded their oars carefully, raising them only a few centimetres from the water at the end of each stroke so that the noise of drops splashing back into the sea was kept to a minimum. They were Erak's most experienced oarsmen and they were used to the task of approaching an enemy coast stealthily.

And during raiding season, all coasts were enemy coasts.

Such was their skill that the loudest sound was the lap-lap-lap of small ripples along the wooden hull. In the bow, Svengal and two other crew members crouched fully armed, peering ahead to catch sight of the dim line where the water met the beach.

The lack of surf might make their approach easier but a little extra noise would have been welcome, Svengal thought. Plus white water would have made the line of the beach easier to spot in the dimness. Then he saw the beach and held up his hand, fist clenched.

Far astern, at the steering oar, Erak watched his second in command as he revealed five fingers, then four, then three as he measured off the distance to the sand.

'In oars.'

Erak spoke the words in a conversational tone, unlike the bellow he usually employed to pass orders. In the centre section of the wolfship, his bosun, Mikkel, relayed the orders. The four oars lifted out of the water as one, rising quickly to the vertical so that any excess water would fall into the ship and not into the sea, where it would make more noise. A few seconds later, the prow of the ship grated softly against the sand. Erak felt the vibrations of the gentle contact with the shore through the deck beneath his feet.

Svengal and his two companions vaulted over the bow, landing cat-like on the wet sand. Two of them moved up the beach, fanning out to scan the country on either side, ready to give warning of any possible ambush. Svengal took the small beach anchor that another sailor lowered to him. He stepped twenty paces up the beach, strained against the anchor rope to bring it tight and drove the shovel-shaped fluke into the firm sand.

Wolfwind, secured by the bow, slewed a little to one side under the pressure of the gentle breeze.

'Clear left!'

'Clear right!'

The two men who had gone onshore called their reports now. There was no need for further stealth. Svengal checked his own area of responsibility, then added his report to theirs.

'Clear ahead.'

On board, Erak nodded with satisfaction. He hadn't expected any sort of armed reception on the beach but it always paid to make sure. That was why he had been such a successful raider over the years — and why he had lost so few of his crewmen.

'All right,' he said, lifting his shield from the bulwark and hefting it onto his left arm. 'Let's go.'

He quickly strode the length of the wolfship to the bow, where a boarding ladder had been placed over the side. Shoving his heavy battleaxe through the leather sling on his belt, he climbed easily over the bulwark and down to the beach. His crewmen followed, forming up behind him. There was no need for orders. They had all done this before, many times.

Svengal joined him. 'No sign of anyone here, chief,' he reported.

Erak grunted. 'Neither should there be. They should all be busy at Alty Bosky.'

He pronounced the name in his usual way — careless of the finer points of Iberian pronunciation. The town in question was actually Alto Bosque, a relatively unimportant market town some ten kilometres to the south, built on the high, wooded hill from which it derived its name.

The previous day, seven of his crew had taken the skiff and landed there, carrying out a lightning raid on the market before they retreated to the coast. Alto Bosque had no garrison and a rider from the town had been sent to Santa Sebilla, where a small force of militia was maintained. Erak's plan was to draw the garrison away to Alto Bosque while he and his men plundered Santa Sebilla unhindered.

Santa Sebilla was a small town, too. Probably smaller than Alto Bosque. But, over the years, it had gained an enviable reputation for the quality of the jewellery that was designed and crafted here. As time went on, more and more artisans and designers were drawn to Santa Sebilla and it became a centre for fine design and craftsmanship in gold and precious stones.

Erak, like most Skandians, cared little for fine design and craftsmanship. But he cared a lot about gold and he knew there was a disproportionate amount of it in Santa Sebilla — far more than would normally be found in a small town such as this. The community of artists and designers needed generous supplies of the raw materials in which they worked — gold and silver and gemstones. Erak was a fervent believer in the principle of redistribution of wealth, as long as a great amount of it was redistributed in his direction, so he had planned this raid in detail for some weeks.

He checked behind him. The anchor watch of four men were standing by the bow of *Wolfwind*, guarding it while the main party went inland. He nodded, satisfied that everything was ready.

'Send your scouts ahead,' he told Svengal. The second in command gestured to the two men to go ahead of the main raiding party.

The beach rose gradually to a low line of scrubby bushes and trees. The scouts ran to this line, surveyed the country beyond, then beckoned the main party forward. The ground was flat here but, some kilometres inland, a range of low hills rose from the plain. The first rose-coloured rays of the sun were beginning to show about the peaks. They were behind schedule, Erak thought. He had wanted to reach the town before sun-up, while people were still drowsy and longing for their beds, as yet reluctant to accept the challenges of a new day.

'Let's pace it up,' he said tersely and the group settled into a steady jog behind him, moving in two columns. The scouts continued to range some fifty metres in advance of the raiding party. Erak could already see that there was nowhere a substantial party of armed men could remain hidden. Still, it did no harm to be sure.

Waved forward by the scouts, they crested a low rise and there, before them, stood Santa Sebilla.

The buildings were made of clay bricks, finished in whitewash. Later in the day, under the hot Iberian sun, they would glisten and gleam an almost blinding white. In the pre-dawn light they looked dull and grey and mundane. The town had been built with no particular plan in mind, instead growing over the years so that houses and warehouses were placed wherever their owners chose to build them. The result was a chaotic mass of winding alleys, outlying buildings and twisting, formless streets. But Erak ignored the jumble of houses and shops. He was looking for the repository — a large building set to one side of the town, where the gold and jewels were stored.

And there it was. Larger than the other buildings, with a substantial brass-bound wooden door. Normally, Erak knew, there would be a guard in place. But it seemed his diversion had achieved the result he wanted and the local militia were absent. The only possible resistance could come from a small castle set on a cliff a kilometre away from the town itself. There would possibly be armed men there. But the castle was the home of a minor Iberian nobleman and its location here was a mere coincidence. Knowing the snobbish and superior nature of the Iberian nobility, Erak guessed that the castle lord and his people had as little to do with the common tradesmen of Santa Sebilla as possible. They might buy from them, but they wouldn't mix with them or be eager to protect them in an emergency.

They headed for the repository. As they passed a side street, a sleepy townsman emerged, leading a donkey loaded with what seemed to be an impossibly heavy stack of firewood. For a few seconds, head down and still half asleep, the man failed to notice the force of grim-faced, armed sea wolves. Then his eyes snapped open, his jaw followed suit and he froze in place, staring at them. From the corner of his eye, Erak saw two of his men start to detach from the main body. But the firewood seller could do them little harm.

'Leave him,' he ordered and the men dropped back into line.

Galvanised by the sound of Erak's voice, the man dropped the donkey's halter and took off back into the narrow alleyway from which he had emerged. They heard the soft sound of his bare feet flapping on the hard earth as he put as much distance between himself and the raiders as he could.

'Get that door open,' Erak ordered.

Mikkel and Thorn stepped forward. Mikkel, whose preferred weapon was a sword, borrowed an axe from one of the other sea wolves and together, he and Thorn attacked the heavy door. They were Erak's two most reliable warriors, and he nodded appreciatively at the economy of effort with which they reduced the door to matchwood, placing alternate axe strokes precisely where they would do the most good, each building on the damage the other had caused.

The two men were best friends. They always fought together in the shield wall, each trusting the other to protect his back and sides. Yet they were a contrast in body shapes. Mikkel was taller and leaner than the average Skandian. But he was powerful and hard muscled. And he had the reflexes of a cat.

Thorn was slightly shorter than his friend, but much wider in the shoulders and chest. He was one of the most skilled and dangerous warriors Erak had ever seen. Erak often thought that he would hate to come up against Thorn in battle. He'd never seen an opponent who had survived such an encounter. Belying his heavy build, Thorn could also move with blinding speed when he chose.

Erak roused himself from his musing as the door fell in two shattered halves.

'Get the gold,' he ordered and his men surged forward.

It took them half an hour to load the gold and silver into sacks. They took only as much as they could carry and they left easily the same amount behind.

ABOUT THE AUTHOR

John Flanagan's bestselling *Ranger's Apprentice* adventure series originally comprised twenty short stories, which John wrote to encourage his twelve-year-old son, Michael, to enjoy reading. The series has come a long way since then. Now sold to more than twenty countries, the series has sold over four million copies, regularly appears on the *New York Times* Bestseller List and has been shortlisted for children's book awards in Australia and overseas. John, a former television and advertising writer, lives with his wife, Leonie, in the Sydney beachside suburb of Manly. He is currently writing further titles in the *Ranger's Apprentice* and *Brotherband* series.